Peach Blossom Pavilion

Peach Blossom Pavilion

Mingmei Yip

A V O N

AVON

A division of HarperCollins*Publishers*
77–85 Fulham Palace Road,
London W6 8JB

www.harpercollins.co.uk

This paperback edition 2014

1

First published in the U.S.A by Kensington Publishing Corp, New York, NY, 2008

Copyright © Mingmei Yip 2008

Mingmei Yip asserts the moral right to
be identified as the author of this work

A catalogue record for this book is
available from the British Library

ISBN-13: 9780007570126

Set in Simoncini Garamond

Printed and bound in Great Britain by
Clays Ltd, St Ives plc

MIX
Paper from
responsible sources
FSC
www.fsc.org **FSC® C007454**

Find out more about HarperCollins and the environment at
www.harpercollins.co.uk/green

For Geoffrey,
Who gives me both the fish and the bear's paw.

When there is action above and compliance below,
this is called the natural order of things.

When the man thrusts from above
and the woman receives from below,
this is called the balance between heaven and earth.

– Dong Xuanzi (Tang dynasty, AD 618–907)

ACKNOWLEDGEMENTS

As everyone knows – or doesn't know – writing and polishing a novel is long and difficult. Most difficult of all is to make your book known to the world. I could not have achieved this without the generous help and kindness of many people.

I am forever grateful for my husband Geoffrey Redmond, endocrinologist and expert on women's hormone problems, who is also an excellent writer. He endures his writer wife's eccentricities with good humour and has given her the constant support and help most other writers could only dream of. Geoffrey's compassion, wisdom, love, and amazing *qi* have turned this treacherous red dust into a journey filled with pleasure, excitement, wonder, and trust.

Susan Crawford, my cheerful, positive-thinking agent, who not only found for me an ideal publishing house – Kensington – but also a dream editor, Audrey LaFehr.

Others to whom I must express gratitude include:

Tsar The-yun, who taught me the *qin* as it was played in ancient China. Without her inspiration, the protagonist in this novel could not have been conceived.

The late Huang Tzeng-yu, my Tai Chi teacher, a man with strong *qi* and moral character, from whom I learned the 'strength of steel wrapped in cotton' – the balance of *yin* and *yang*, resilience and flexibility.

Hannelore Hahn, founder and executive director of IWWG (International Women's Writing Guild) and her daughter Elizabeth

Julia Stoumen, whose inspiration and support to authors are like flowers for butterflies.

Teryle Ciaccia, my good friend and fellow Tai Chi enthusiast, whose good *qi*, concern, and kindness provide great strength in my life.

Kitty Griffin, gifted children's book writer and extraordinary teacher, for her generous help, inspiration, and friendship.

Ellen Scordato, my instructor at New School University and virtuoso grammarian, who generously answers my numerous questions with patience and kindness.

My writer friends, Sheila Weinstein and Esta Fischer, to whom I am indebted for their helpful readings and suggestions.

Elizabeth Buzzelli, writing instructor and colleague at IWWG, who gave me one suggestion of extreme importance.

Neal Chandler, director of the Cleveland Writer's Workshop, for his untiring work in teaching writing.

Claudia Clemente, a fellow writer who welcomed me when I was a lonely International Institute of Asian Studies fellow in Amsterdam.

Elsbeth Reimann, whose kindness and smiling face always makes me happy.

Eugenia Oi Yan Yau, distinguished vocalist, professor of music, my former student and best friend to whom I am thankful in more ways than I can express. And her husband Jose Santos, for his computer expertise.

Last but not least are my beloved singer-father and teacher-mother who arranged for me to take music and art lessons at a very young age. Sadly, they are no longer in this life. If they are reading these words in their new incarnations, I want to express my indebtedness for their faith in the transformative power of art.

Prologue

Precious Orchid

The California sun slowly streams in through my apartment window, then gropes its way past a bamboo plant, a Chinese vase spilling with plum blossoms, a small incense burner, then finally lands on Bao Lan – Precious Orchid – the woman lying opposite me without a stitch on.

Envy stabs my heart. I stare at her body as it curves in and out like a snake ready for mischief. She lies on a red silk sheet embroidered with flowers in gold thread. 'Flower of the evil sea' – this was what people in old Shanghai would whisper through cupped mouths. While now, in San Francisco, I murmur her name, 'Bao Lan,' sweetly as if savouring a candy in my mouth. I imagine inhaling the decadent fragrance from her sun-warmed nudity.

Bao Lan's eyes shine big and her lips – full, sensuous, and painted a dark crimson – evoke in my mind the colour of rose petals in a fading dream. Petals that, when curled into a seductive smile, also whisper words of flattery. These, together with her smooth arm, raised and bent behind her head in a graceful curve, remind me of the Chinese saying 'A pair of jade arms used as pillows to sleep on by a thousand guests; two slices of crimson lips tasted by ten thousand men.'

Now the rosy lips seem to say, 'Please come to me.'

I nod, reaching my hand to touch the nimbus of black hair tumbling down her small, round breasts. Breasts the texture of silk and the colour of white jade. Breasts that were touched by many – soldiers, merchants, officials, scholars, artists, policemen, gangsters, a Catholic priest, a Taoist monk.

Feeling guilty of sacrilege, I withdraw my nearly century-old spotty and wrinkled hand. I keep rocking on my chair and watching Bao Lan as she continues to eye me silently. '*Hai*, how time flies like an arrow, and the sun and moon move back and forth like a shuttle!' I recite the old saying, then carefully sip my ginseng tea.

'*Ahpo*, it's best-quality ginseng to keep your longevity and health,' my great-granddaughter told me the other day when she brought the herb.

Last week, I celebrated my ninety-eighth birthday, and although they never say it out loud, I know they want my memoir to be finished before I board the immortal's journey. When I say 'they,' I mean my great-granddaughter Jade Treasure and her American fiancé Leo Stanley. In a while, they will be coming to see me and begin recording my oral history.

Oral history! Do they forget that I can read and write? They treat me as if I were a dusty museum piece. They act like they're doing me a great favour by digging me out from deep underground and bringing me to light. How can they forget that I am not only literate, but also well versed in all the arts – literature, music, painting, calligraphy, and poetry – and that's exactly the reason they want to write about me?

Now Bao Lan seems to say, 'Old woman, please go away! Why do you always have to remind me how old you are and how accomplished you were?! Can't you leave me alone to enjoy myself at the height of my youth and beauty?'

'Sure,' I mutter to the air, feeling the wrinkles weighing around the corners of my mouth.

But she keeps staring silently at me with eyes which resemble two graceful dots of ink on rice paper. She's strange, this woman who shares the same house with me but only communicates with the brightness of her eyes and the sensuousness of her body.

I am used to her eccentricity, because she's my other – much wilder and younger – self! The delicate beauty opposite me is but a faded oil painting done seventy-five years ago when I was twenty-three.

And the last poet-musician courtesan in Shanghai.

That's why they keep pushing me to tell, or sell, my story – I am the carrier of a mysterious cultural phenomenon – *ming ji*.

The prestigious prostitute. *Prestigious* prostitute? Yes, that was what we were called in old China. A species as extinct as the Chinese emperors, after China became a republic. Some say it's a tragic loss; others argue: how can the disappearance of prostitutes be tragic?

The cordless phone trills on the coffee table; I pick it up with my stiff, arthritic hand. Jane and Leo are already downstairs. Jane is Jade Treasure's English name, of which I disapprove because it sounds so much like the word 'pan fry' in Chinese. When I call her 'Jane, Jane,' I can almost smell fish cooking in sizzling oil – Sizzz! Sizzz! It sounds as if I'd cook my own flesh and blood!

Now the two young people burst into my nursing home apartment with their laughter and overflowing energy, their embarrassingly long limbs flailing in all directions. Jade Treasure flounces up to peck my cheek, swinging a basket of fruit in front of me, making me dizzy.

'Hi, Grandmama, you look good today! The ginseng gives you good *qi*?'

'Jade, can you show some respect to an old woman who has witnessed, literally, the ups and downs of a century?' I say, pushing away the basket of fruit.

'Grandmama!' Jade mock protests, then dumps the basket on the table with a clank and plops down on the sofa next to me.

It is now Leo's turn to peck my cheek, then he says in his smooth Mandarin, 'How are you today, *Popo*?'

This American boy calls me *Popo*, the respectful way of addressing an elderly lady in Chinese, while my Jade Treasure prefers the more Westernised Grandmama (she adds another 'ma' for 'great' grandmother). Although I am always suspicious of *laofan*, old barbarians, I kind of like Leo. He's a nice boy, good-looking with a big body and soft blonde hair, a graduate of journalism at a very good university called Ge-lin-bi-ya? (so I was told by Jade), speaks very good Mandarin, now works as an editor for a very famous publisher called Ah-ba Call-lings? (so I was also told by Jade). And madly in love with my Jade Treasure.

Jade is already clanking bowls and plates in my small kitchen, preparing snacks. Her bare legs play hide and seek behind the half-opened door, while her excessive energy thrusts her to and fro between the refrigerator, the cupboard, the sink, the stove.

A half hour later, after we've finished our snacks and the trays are put away and the table cleaned, Leo and Jade sit down beside me on the sofa, carefully taking out their recorder, pads, pens. Faces glowing with excitement, they look like Chinese students eager to please their teacher. It touches me to see their expressions turn serious as if they were burdened by the sacred responsibility of saving a precious heritage from sinking into quicksand.

'Grandmama,' Jade says after she's discussed it in English with her fiancé, 'Leo and I agreed that it's best for you to start your story from the beginning. That is, when you were sold to the turquoise pavilion after Great-great-grandpapa was executed.'

I'm glad she is discreet enough not to say *jiyuan*, prostitution house, or worse, *jixiang*, whorehouse, but instead uses the much more refined and poetic *qinglou* – turquoise pavilion.

'Jade, if you're so interested in Chinese culture, do you know there are more than forty words for prostitution house . . . fire pit; tender village; brocade gate; wind and moon domain—'

Jade interrupts. 'Grandmama, so which were you in?'

'You know, we had our own hierarchy. The prestigious book chamber ladies,' I tilt my head, 'like myself, condescended to the second-rate long gown ladies, and they in turn snubbed those who worked in the second hall. And of course, everyone would spit on the homeless wild chickens as if they were nonhuman.'

'Wow! Cool stuff!' Jade exclaims, then exchanges whispers with Leo. She turns back to stare at me, her elongated eyes sparkling with enthusiasm. 'Grandmama, we think that it's better if you can use the "talk story" style. Besides, can you add even more juicy stuff?'

'No.' I wave them a dismissive hand. 'Do you think my life is not miserable enough to be saleable? This is my story, and I'll do it my way!'

'Yes, of course!' The two heads nod like basketballs under thumping hands.

'All right, my big prince and princess, what else?'

'That's all, Grandmama. Let's start!' The two young faces gleam as if they were about to watch a Hollywood soap opera – forgetting that I have told them a hundred times that my life is even a thousand times soapier.

PART ONE

1

The Turquoise Pavilion

To be a prostitute was my fate.

After all, no murderer's daughter would be accepted into a decent household to be a wife whose children would be smeared with crime even before they were born. The only other choice was my mother's – to take refuge as a nun, for the only other society which would accept a criminal's relatives lay within the empty gate.

I had just turned thirteen when I exchanged the quiet life of a family for the tumult of a prostitution house. But not like the others, whose parents had been too poor to feed them, or who had been kidnapped and sold by bandits.

It all happened because my father was convicted of a crime – one he'd never committed.

'That was the mistake your father should never have made,' my mother told me over and over, 'trying to be righteous, and,' she added bitterly, 'meddling in rich men's business.'

True. For that 'business' cost him his own life, and fatefully changed the life of his wife and daughter.

Baba had been a Peking opera performer and a musician. Trained as a martial arts actor, he played acrobats and warriors. During one performance, while fighting with four pennants strapped to his thirty-pound suit of armour, he jumped down from four stacked chairs in his high-soled boots and broke his leg. Unable to perform on stage anymore, he played the two-stringed fiddle in the troupe's orchestra. After several years, he became even more famous for his fiddle playing, and an amateur Peking opera group led by the wife of a Shanghai warlord hired him as its accompanist. Every month the wife would hold a big party in the house's lavish garden. It was an incident in that garden that completely changed our family's destiny.

One moonlit evening amid the cheerful tunes of the fiddle and the falsetto voices of the silk-clad and heavily jewelled *tai tai* – society ladies – the drunken warlord raped his own teenage daughter.

The girl grabbed her father's gun and fled to the garden where the guests were gathered. The warlord ran behind her, puffing and pants falling. Suddenly his daughter stopped and turned to him. Tears streaming down her cheeks, she slowly pointed the gun to her head. 'Beast! If you dare come an inch closer, I'll shoot myself!'

Baba threw down his precious fiddle and ran to the source of the tumult. He pushed away the gaping guests, leaped forward, and tried to seize the gun. But it went off. The hapless girl fell dead to the ground in a pool of blood surrounded by the stunned guests and servants.

The warlord turned to grab Baba's throat till his tongue protruded. Eyes blurred and face as red as his daughter's splattered blood, he spat on Baba. 'Animal! You raped my daughter and killed her!'

Although all the members in the household knew it was a false accusation, nobody was willing to right the wrong. The servants were scared and powerless. The rich guests couldn't have cared less.

One general meditatively stroked his beard, sneering, 'Big deal, it's just a fiddle player.' And that ended the whole event.

Indeed, it was a big deal for us. For Baba was executed. Mother took refuge as a Buddhist nun in a temple in Peking. I was taken away to a prostitution house.

This all happened in 1918.

Thereafter, during the tender years of my youth, while my mother was strenuously cultivating desirelessness in the Pure Lotus Nunnery in Peking, I was busy stirring up desire within the Peach Blossom Pavilion.

That was the mistake your father should never have made – trying to be righteous and meddling in rich men's business.

Mother's saying kept knocking around in my head until one day I swore, kneeling before Guan Yin – the Goddess of Mercy – that I would never be merciful in this life. But not meddle in rich men's business? It was precisely the rich and powerful at whom I aimed my arts of pleasing. Like Guan Yin with a thousand arms holding a thousand amulets to charm, I was determined to cultivate myself to be a woman with a thousand scheming hearts to lure a thousand men into my arms.

But, of course, this kind of cultivation started later, when I had become aware of the realm of the wind and moon. When I'd first entered the prostitution house, I was but a little girl with a heart split into two: one half light with innocence, the other heavy with sorrow.

In the prostitution house, I was given the name Precious Orchid. It was only my professional name; my real name was Xiang Xiang, given for two reasons. I was born with a natural *xiang* – body fragrance (a mingling of fresh milk, honey, and jasmine), something which rarely happens except in legends where the protagonist lives on nothing but flowers and herbs. Second, I was named after the Xiang River of Hunan Province. My parents, who had given me this name, had cherished the hope that my life would be as nurturing as the waterway of my ancestors, while never expecting that it was my overflowing tears which would nurture the river as it flows its never-ending course. They had also hoped that my life would sing with happiness like the cheerful river, never imagining that what flowed in my voice was nothing but the bittersweet melodies of Karma.

* * *

Despite our abject poverty after Baba's death, it was never my mother's intent to sell me into Peach Blossom Pavilion. This bit of chicanery was the work of one of her distant relatives, a woman by the name of Fang Rong – Beautiful Countenance. Mother had met her only once, during a Chinese New Year's gathering at a distant uncle's house. Not long after Baba had been executed, Fang Rong appeared one day out of nowhere and told my mother that she could take good care of me. When I first laid eyes on her, I was surprised that she didn't look at all like what her name implied. Instead, she had the body of a stuffed rice bag, the face of a basin, and the eyes of a rat, above which a big mole moved menacingly.

Fang Rong claimed that she worked as a housekeeper for a rich family. The master, a merchant of foreign trade, was looking for a young girl with a quick mind and swift hands to help in the household. The matter was decided without hesitation. Mother, completely forgetting her vow never to be involved in rich men's business, was relieved that I'd have a roof over my head. So, with her departure for Peking looming, she agreed to let Fang Rong take me away.

Both Mother and Fang Rong looked happy chatting under the sparkling sun. Toward the end of their conversation, after Fang Rong had given Mother the address of the 'rich businessman,' she shoved me into a waiting rickshaw. 'Quick! Don't make the master wait!'

When the vehicle was about to take off, Mother put her face close to me and whispered, 'From now on, listen to Aunty Fang and your new master and behave. Will you promise me that?'

I nodded, noticing the tears welling in her eyes. She gently laid the cloth sack containing my meagre possessions (a small amount of cash and a few rice balls sprinkled with bits of salted fish) on my lap, then put her hand on my head. 'Xiang Xiang, I'll be leaving in a month. If I can, I'll visit you. But if I don't, I'll write as soon as I've arrived in Peking.' She paused, a faint smile breaking on her withered face. 'You're lucky . . .'

I touched her hand. 'Ma . . .'

Just as I was struggling to say something, Fang Rong's voice jolted us apart. 'All right, let's go, better not be late.' With that, the rickshaw puller lifted the poles and we started to move.

I turned back and waved to Mother until she became a small dot and finally vanished like the last morning dew.

Fang Rong rode beside me in silence. Houses floated by as the rickshaw puller grunted along. After twists and turns through endless avenues and back alleys, the rickshaw entered a tree-lined boulevard.

Fang Rong turned to me and smiled. 'Xiang Xiang, we'll soon be there.'

Though the air was nippy, the coolie was sweating profusely. We bumped along a crowded street past a tailor, an embroidery shop, a hair salon, and a shoe store before the coolie finally grunted to a stop.

Fang Rong paid and we got out in front of the most beautiful mansion I'd ever seen. With walls painted a pale pink, the building rose tall and imposing, with a tightly closed red iron gate fiercely guarded by two stone lions. At the entrance, a solitary red lantern swayed gently in the breeze. An ornate wooden sign above the lintel glinted in the afternoon sun. I shaded my eyes and saw a shiny signboard, black with three large gold characters: PEACH BLOSSOM PAVILION. On either side, vertical boards flanking the gate read:

Guests flocking to the pavilion like birds,
Beauties blooming in the garden like flowers.

'Aunty Fang,' I pointed to the sign, 'what is this Peach—'

'Come on,' Fang Rong cast me an annoyed look, 'don't let your father wait,' and pulled me along.

My father? Didn't she know that he was already dead? Just as I was wondering what this was all about, the gate creaked open, revealing a man of about forty; underneath shiny hair parted in the middle shone a smooth, handsome face. An embroidered silk jacket was draped elegantly over a lean, sinewy body.

He scrutinised me for long moments, then his face broke into a pleasant grin. 'Ah, so the rumour is true. What a lovely girl!' His slender fingers with their long, immaculate nails reached to pat my head. I felt an instant liking for this man my father's age. I also wondered, how could the ugly-to-death Fang Rong catch such a nice-looking man?

'Wu Qiang,' Fang Rong drew away his hand, 'haven't you ever seen a pretty girl in your life?' Then she turned to me. 'This is my husband Wu Qiang and your father.'

'But Aunty—'

Now Fang Rong put on an ear-reaching grin. 'Xiang Xiang, your father is dead, so from now on Wu Qiang is your father. Call him De.'

Despite my liking for this man, in my heart no one could take the place of my father. 'But he's not my de!'

Fang Rong shot me a smile with the skin, but not the flesh. 'I've told you that now he is, and I'm your mother, so call me Mama.'

Before I could protest again, she'd already half-pushed me along through a narrow entranceway. Then I forgot to complain because as we passed into the courtyard, my eyes beheld another world. Enclosed within the red fence was a garden where lush flowerbeds gave off a pleasing aroma. On the walls were painted lovely maidens cavorting among exotic flowers. A fountain murmured, spurting in willowy arcs. In a pond, golden carps swished their tails and gurgled trails of bubbles. A stone bridge led across the pond to a pavilion with gracefully upturned eaves. Patches of soothing shade were cast by artfully placed bamboo groves.

While hurrying after Fang Rong and Wu Qiang, I spotted a small face peeking out at me from behind the bamboo grove. What struck me was not her face but the sad, watery eyes which gazed into mine, as if desperate to tell a tale.

When I was on the verge of asking about her, Fang Rong cast me a tentative glance. 'Xiang Xiang, aren't you happy that this is now your new home? Isn't it much better than your old one?'

I nodded emphatically, while feeling stung by those sad eyes.

'I'm sure you'll like it even better when you taste the wonderful food cooked by our chef,' Wu Qiang chimed in enthusiastically.

Soon we arrived at a small room decorated with polished furniture and embroidered pink curtains. Against the back wall stood an altar with a statue of a white-browed, red-eyed general mounted on a horse and wielding a sword. Arrayed in front of him were offerings of rice, meat, and wine.

In the centre of the room was a table set with chopsticks, bowls, and dishes of snacks. Fang Rong told me to sit between her and Wu Qiang. With no other etiquette, she announced that dinner would begin. A middle-aged woman brought out plates of food, then laid them down one by one on the table. After filling the bowls with rice and soup, she left without a word.

During the whole meal, Fang Rong kept piling food into my bowl. 'Eat more, soon you'll be a very healthy and charming young lady.'

I'd never before tasted food so delicious. I gulped down chunks of fish, shrimp, pork, chicken, and beef, washing them down with cup after cup of fragrant tea.

When dinner was finished, I asked, 'Aunty Fang—'

'Did you forget that I'm now your mama?'

Her stare was so fierce that I finally muttered a weak, 'Mama.' I swallowed hard. 'After dinner, are we going to see the master and the mistress of the mansion?'

Barely had I finished my question when she burst into laughter. Then she took a sip of her tea and replied meaningfully. 'Ha, silly girl! Don't you know that we *are* your new master and mistress?'

'What do you mean?'

'That's what I mean – I am the mistress and my husband is the master of this Peach Blossom Pavilion.'

'What is Peach Blossom Pavilion?'

'A book chamber.'

I looked around but didn't see any books, not even bookshelves.

Fang Rong cast me a mysterious look. 'A cloud and rain pavilion.'

Now Wu Qiang added soothingly, 'This is . . . ah . . . a turquoise pavilion.'

'What—'

Fang Rong spat, 'A whorehouse!'

Wu Qiang looked on with a mysterious smile while his wife

burst out in a loud laugh. Then she chided me affectionately. 'Why do people always have to have the entrails drawn?'

She was referring to the Chinese saying that when one paints a portrait, he even includes the intestines – an act redundant and stupid.

Shocked, it took several beats before I could utter, 'But didn't you tell us that the master is a merchant of foreign trade?'

Fang Rong laughed, her huge breasts and bulging belly shivering. 'Ha! Ha! It's true. From time to time we do entertain British, French, and American soldiers here. Don't you know you've just arrived at the night district of *Si Malu*? This is the most high-class *shangren* lane, where all the book chambers are found!'

I felt a queasiness simmering in my stomach. 'You mean . . . I was sold into—' Fang Rong's harsh voice pierced my ears. 'No, you were not sold, silly girl! You were given to us as a gift—'

Using his long-nailed pinky to pick some meat from between his teeth while stealing a glance at me, Wu Qiang added, 'We didn't even have to pay your mother.'

'That's why we never forget to make offerings to the Buddha, Guan Yin the Goddess of Mercy, and,' her sausage finger pointing to the sword-wielding, horse-riding general, 'the righteous, money-bringing White-Browed God.' Fang Rong winked, then pinched my cheek. 'So, little pretty, see how they look after us!'

Now, as if he were my real father, Wu Qiang looked down at me tenderly, his voice unctuous. 'Xiang Xiang, don't worry. From now on, you'll have plenty of good food to eat and pretty clothes to wear. You'll see we'll take care of you like you're our own daughter.'

But they were not my mother and father. That night, alone, helpless, and abandoned, I cried a long time before I fell asleep in the small, bare room to which I'd been led.

My only hope was that my mother would write to me and soon come to visit.

2

The North Station

In the following days, it surprised me that my anger at being tricked into the prostitution house had gradually waned. I had to admit, with embarrassment, that life here didn't seem to be so bad after all. Fang Rong kept her promise to my mother – I was well clothed and fed. Moreover, I felt relieved to be spared, not only from accompanying clients but also from the menial chores like washing clothes, scrubbing floors, cleaning spittoons, emptying chamber pots. Those jobs were given to maids – girls too plain to ever serve as 'sisters.'

In comparison to their work, mine was easy: serving the sisters and their customers while they played mahjong; refilling the guests' water pipes and serving them tea and tobacco; helping the cook in the kitchen; carrying messages for the sisters; running errands for Fang Rong. Needless to say, I didn't like serving Fang Rong, but I actually enjoyed the other tasks. Especially the mahjong playing – when the game was finished, the customers always tipped me generously by secretly pushing money into my hand.

Moreover, when the game finished and dinner was served in the banquet room, a puppy would always materialise to gobble bits of food thrown down by the guests and sisters. He was so cute that whenever I saw him, I'd pick him up, squeeze him in my arms, and bury my face into his fluffy yellow fur. Strangely, he was never given a name, but was just called 'Puppy.' One time when I'd asked a sister why didn't the puppy have a name, she laughed, 'Because we don't want to bother. Why don't you give him one?' And I did. So he became *Guigui* – good baby. Guigui began to recognise me and follow me almost everywhere. His favourite place was beside me in the kitchen while I helped the chef, Ah Ping.

Ah Ping, a fortyish, mute, and half-witted woman, always secretly fed me and Guigui with goodies. For a chef, she was unusually thin. I always stared at her hollow cheeks and wondered why she never seemed to have any appetite. Or why she only spoke with jumbled sounds which no one could understand.

I carried out my chores mostly during my spare time. My main duty in the pavilion was to learn the arts – singing parts from Peking and Kun operas; playing the *pipa* – a four-stringed lute resembling a pear; painting; and practising calligraphy.

The painting and calligraphy teacher was Mr. Wu, an old man in his forties. I felt very fond of him not only because he painted well, but, also because he was a very kind teacher – never scolding but gently redirecting my brush to show me how to form the strokes more elegantly. The opera teacher, Mr. Ma, was younger than Mr. Wu, but also pretty old – thirty-eight. I didn't like him, for he looked at me strangely and would accidentally brush his hand against my face, my belly, sometimes even my breast (when he demonstrated how to lead my breath from my chest down to my *dantian* – cinnabar field).

A young woman named Pearl was assigned to teach me to play the *pipa*. Beautiful with shiny black hair and sparkling white teeth, Pearl was the most popular sister in the pavilion. Although I was extremely fond of her, somehow she also made me feel uneasy. I found it hard to tell what kind of a person she really was – sometimes sweet and lively like a rabbit, at other times arrogant and difficult like a cat. Though usually bright and bubbly, at moments she would become sad, as if burdened with forbidden secrets.

Besides Pearl's unpredictable temper, I had another source of unease in the turquoise pavilion – the pair of sad eyes peeking out from the bamboo grove and staring at me whenever I passed the courtyard.

However, I felt happy and content with my art lessons and fine food; Fang Rong and her husband seemed almost parental to me, so I had little inclination to complain.

Life in this turquoise pavilion was really not so horrible as it was described by people outside.

Yet one thing made me sad. I'd been here nearly four weeks now, but Mother had never written to me nor come to visit as she'd promised. Counting on my fingers, I suddenly realised that she would be leaving for Peking tomorrow. So I went to Fang Rong and asked for her permission to let me leave the pavilion to see my mother off.

Although she smiled, the big mole between her brows looked as if it were about to leap toward me in full force. 'Ah, you foolish girl. Don't you know the rule in Peach Blossom? You can only be allowed to go outside the main gate on the following occasions: when you get an invitation from some very important guests, that's only after you've become very popular and much sought after; when I take you out for business like fixing your hair or having clothes sewn for you; when the pavilion organises an outing to entertain important parties.'

'What do you mean?' I stared at her mole to avoid her eyes.

'Don't ask too many questions; it never does a little girl any good.' Her voice grew very sharp and harsh. 'Anyway, you're not going out, not tonight, not anytime, not until I tell you to, you understand? Now go and help Ah Ping in the kitchen. Tonight we'll have a police chief, a banker, a cotton merchant, and many other important people to entertain.'

In the corridor on my way to the kitchen, I heard an assortment of noises – singing, chatting, *pipa* plucking, mahjong playing, Fang Rong's yelling – drift from the different chambers. The sisters were putting on make-up, dressing, practising their singing, or tuning their instruments one last time before the guests arrived. Today was a Saturday and business seemed unusually good. I peered down the street from a latticed window and saw shiny black cars pull up at the entrance, disgorging important-looking men – some clad in elegantly tailored silk gowns, others in perfectly pressed Western suits.

As I was watching the ebb and flow of cars, I felt a pool of sadness. Did my mother have any inkling that I was now living in a prostitution house and not a rich man's residence? Why didn't she come to see me?

I blinked back tears and hurried to the kitchen. Seeing me, Ah Ping's pale face brightened. She gave me an affectionately chiding look, then pretended to hold a plate in one hand, while her other hand made a pouring motion. After that, she shrugged as if to warn, *Ah, Xiang Xiang, if you're late again next time, all the choice morsels will be gone!*

She went to close the door, then returned to ladle bits of abalone, shark fin, and fish from the various cauldrons. She set the delicacies on a plate and pushed it across the table toward me. I was not hungry, but in order to please her, I picked up a piece of abalone and popped it into my mouth. As I was savouring the rubbery taste, I heard the grating of paws on wood.

'Aunty Ah Ping,' I threw down my chopsticks, 'it's Guigui!'

I dashed to open the door and let the puppy in. He yapped, then furiously licked my feet and wagged his tail. I scooped him up and began to feed him with the food from my plate. He lapped and gobbled happily.

Some strange sound emitted from Ah Ping's throat. She was protesting that I shouldn't feed the puppy with the delicacies reserved for important guests. I stuck out my tongue. She smiled back, then signalled me to continue eating.

But the only thing I wanted now was to see my mother. Tears swelled in my eyes as I buried my face into Guigui's.

Ah Ping gestured with her hands. *Something wrong?*

'Aunty Ah Ping, I have . . . a stomach ache, so can I—'

She waved toward the door. *Go.*

'Are you sure?'

She nodded.

'Then thank you very much.' I put Guigui down on the floor. He protested by pulling the hem of my trouser leg with his teeth. 'But Aunty Ah Ping—'

Again, she waved frantically, then leant her cheek on her hands. *Go, go take a nap.*

I hurried down to the courtyard, and after making sure that no one was hiding within the bamboo groves, treaded cautiously along the hidden path until I reached the main gate. Heart pounding, I hid behind the bamboo foliage for the right moment to escape. I waited until the denizens of the establishment – Fang Rong, Wu Qiang, the sisters, the maids, the amahs, the male servants, the guards – appeared for the ritual of greeting the arriving guests. While they were kowtowing and pouring flattery to the important visitors, I slipped out.

Once clear of the gate, I ran all the way to the main street and hailed a rickshaw.

'Hurry, hurry!' I kept shouting to the coolie's scrawny back.

He turned and scrutinised me, his dull eyes menacing under the street light. 'Little miss, this is a long way, so I have to save my energy. You don't want me to fall down in the middle of the road; do you?'

So I kept my mouth shut and listened to his tortured grunts until he finally entered a long, dark passage and pulled to a stop in front of a dilapidated house. I thrust a few coins into his calloused hand, then ran toward the low building. Dim light seeped out from underneath our cracked door. I knocked on the thin wooden plank, my heart pounding and my mouth sucking in big gulps of air.

The door creaked open and light flooded from behind Mother's back. Eyes widened, she dropped open her mouth. 'Xiang Xiang, what a surprise! I've been worried to death about you!'

Choked with emotions, I could only utter a loud 'Ma!' then thrust myself into her arms.

Mother led me inside and took me to sit down on the floor. The room was practically empty except for two suitcases and a few odds and ends.

She was dressed in a threadbare black smock and trousers. Her hungry eyes scrutinised me for long moments. 'Xiang Xiang, you look so different!' she exclaimed, stroking my face. 'Now your body is much stronger and your face rounder. I'm so glad that you're well fed.' She touched my floral cotton top and trousers. 'Look at you in this pretty outfit!' Before I could respond, she plunged on excitedly, 'Xiang Xiang, I'm so glad that we finally have a piece of good luck!'

'But Ma—'

'Xiang Xiang, try not to complain too much; learn to be grateful.'

So how could I have the heart to tell her the truth – that I'd been tricked into a prostitution house? Besides, I was indeed well clothed and fed and not too badly treated. Although Peach Blossom Pavilion was a prostitution house, it was indeed also a mansion for rich men and I did work there as a maid. So why distress Mother with the rest of the truth? Therefore, when she went on to ask me this and that about my new life, I simply told her not to worry.

When I asked Mother why hadn't she come to see me, she sighed, '*Hai*, Xiang Xiang, I've been very busy going from house to house to borrow money to pay off our debts before I leave this dusty world.' She paused to put one strand of my hair in place. 'I did try to go to your place, but the address Aunty Fang gave me was wrong. I've been asking around anyone who might know her, but,' Mother stopped in midsentence to look at me tenderly, 'anyway, you're here now.'

I scribbled my address and gave it to her. 'Ma, this is the right address, so you can write me after you've arrived in Peking.'

She carefully folded the paper as if it were a hundred silver-dollar bill and put it into her purse.

My heart slowly shattered inside.

Autumn was fading into winter. The weather had already turned chilly and most of the leaves on the white parasol trees had fallen, and were strewn along the Huangpu River bank.

After a rickshaw ride and an interminable walk, my mother and I dragged our numbed bodies toward the North Train Station, dreading the moment of departure. Only one thought occupied our minds: We never knew when we would see each other again.

Staring at the parasol leaves scattered in intriguing patterns along the asphalt ground, Mother said, her voice smeared with melancholy, 'Xiang Xiang, we Chinese say "falling leaves returning to their roots." You understand what this means?'

I looked up and caught her eyes beaming with tears. 'Yes, Ma, it means that no matter what happens, we should always find our way home.'

A wry smile broke out on her bloodless face. 'Will you remember this?'

I nodded, too choked with sadness to say anything. Also because I was thinking: But Ma, where's our home? I don't think we have one to go back to any more! The turquoise pavilion, although it also had a 'mama,' was definitely not my home, nor was the nunnery my mother's. But I swallowed my words as well as my tears.

We arrived at the station and stepped inside the crowded lobby. Mother hurried to join the queue to buy tickets. I watched rich *tai tai* chatting languidly while waiting for their servants to buy them first-class passage.

After a while, Mother rushed back to me, waving the ticket in her hand. We hurried to the train. In the past, I had always felt excited by trains. I'd liked listening to their 'Wu! Wu!' sound and watching the white smoke puffing out from their noses like steamed snow, while imagining the exotic places they would take me to. But now I dreaded this black monster. Soon it would grab my mother and take her away from me to a walled temple filled with bald-headed women reciting unintelligible sutras as if they were talking to ghosts!

'Xiang Xiang,' Mother said, while tenderly putting a Guan Yin pendant around my neck, 'now hurry back to Aunty Fang and behave. Always obey her as if she were your real mother and never cause any trouble; you understand?'

I felt tears stinging my eyes. 'But Ma, that fat, ugly pig is not my mother!'

Thwack! Mother slapped my face.

I started to cry. 'Ma, why don't you take me with you?'

'You think I've never thought of that?' She sighed, pulling out a handkerchief to wipe my tears. Her voice came out soft and low.

'Sorry that I hit you, Xiang Xiang. But do you have any idea what kind of a life it is to be a nun? It's fine with me since my prime has passed and now I'm but a worthless old woman. But you're young and beautiful and have a bright future waiting before you, so I won't let you squander it in a nunnery. Besides,' she sighed again, 'one of the novice nuns told me that the Mother Abbess said . . .' She stopped in midsentence.

'Said what?'

'That you're too beautiful to be a nun, and she fears your beauty will bring bad luck to her temple.'

Usually my heart would leap to heaven when people said that I was pretty, but now it sank to the bottom of the sea. 'How do they know that I'm pretty?'

'I told them, because I'm so proud of you.' Mother patted my head. 'Xiang Xiang, I know a servant girl's life isn't easy. But it's only temporary. We'll find a way out sooner or later. Now listen to me. After you've seen me off, go right back to your master. And don't forget it's very important that you obey him and his wives, and try your best to get along with everyone, otherwise you won't have a roof to live under nor even thin rice gruel to warm your stomach. Remember, not only that you must put up with any hardship, you have to endure it with a smile, so no one will see a trace of bitterness.' She paused to search my face. 'Xiang Xiang, instead of complaining, you should thank heaven for all this, you understand?'

I nodded, licking and tasting the salt of my tears. 'Ma, when will we see each other again?'

'Not for a while, but we will.' Mother squeezed out a smile. 'We can always write to each other. Or maybe I can even try to come back here to see you.' She paused, 'There are many temples on the western side of the Taiyi Mountain south-west of Peking. I think I'll settle there, but I'm still not sure in which one. I'll write you as soon as I arrive.'

She sighed, looking at me with her tear-misted eyes. '*Hai*, Xiang Xiang, I know no matter how decently they treat you in your new house, you're still a maid after all.' She considered for a moment, then spoke again thoughtfully, 'Just remember one thing: We can't beat fate, but we can play along and make the most out of it. Try to be happy.' Mother went on, 'Also, be careful what you tell about yourself in the new house. Don't say anything about how your baba died. Be cautious.'

I nodded.

Mother gave me a quick hug. 'Xiang Xiang, I'm afraid our paths must part now. May Guan Yin be with you till we meet again.'

With that, she hurried toward the train, tripped, pulled herself up, then, without turning back, mounted the black monster. With her back to me, she frantically waved her one-way ticket until her familiar slender figure vanished among the crowd.

I stared hard at the tracks that would take her away to the nunnery in Peking but would never bring her back.

3

The Dark Room

With the 'Wu! Wu!' sound of the train still ringing in my ears, I hired a rickshaw to go back to Peach Blossom. When I got off the vehicle and started to walk, I felt both the bitter cold wind and my own tears stinging my cheeks.

To my surprise, as I sneaked up to the main gate, I saw Fang Rong standing there, thrusting forward her fat, wrinkled neck. Once she spotted me, she hollered, 'Catch this little bitch!'

Immediately, a huge lump of a man appeared out of nowhere and grabbed me. His hold was so tight that his fingers pinched deeply into my flesh. Before I could scream, I felt blows on my head and slaps on my face.

Then Fang Rong's voice screeched next to my ear like an out-of-tune fiddle. 'I told you that you can't go out by yourself! Where have you been?!'

'To . . . see my mother off to Peking.'

'See your mother off? Are you blind? Don't you see your mama is right here in front of you?' More slaps on my face, then, 'To the dark room!'

I was immediately blindfolded, lifted up, and carried away. Although the man walked fast, it still seemed a long time before he dropped me down and removed my blindfold. I was thrown into a dim, airless cubicle, and immediately I knew that people didn't have to die to go to hell. It was right here on earth.

The stench of the damp, rotten floor pierced my nostrils. Although I could hardly see anything in the dark, I could hear squealing, which made me aware that I was not alone.

I banged on the iron door. 'Mama, let me out! Please let me out!'

Fang Rong's voice sneered, 'Mama? Haven't you just told me that your mama has already left for Peking?' A deafening pause, then, 'Now see whether you dare to run away again!' followed by a peal of chilling laughter and footsteps marching triumphantly away.

I didn't know how long I'd been banging on the door before I felt so exhausted that I groped around and slumped on a wobbly cot.

It was then that I noticed the squealing again.

My heart flipped. Was there another person here? Or were there ghosts?

I quickly pulled the filthy blanket over my head. Then I felt something cool and hairy brushing against my hand. I screamed and jumped off the bed.

Rats.

They were everywhere – to keep me company!

I vomited though I hadn't had food in my stomach for hours. Suddenly a frenzied squealing almost froze my heart – the rats were swarming to vie for my vomit!

Another wave of nausea sloshed in my stomach, but this time nothing came out of my mouth. My throat felt scorched. I wrapped the blanket tightly around myself and tried to forget my fear in sleep, but the coldness of the room made my teeth chatter, freezing me awake. Finally thirst became so unbearable that I got off the bed, stomped my feet to scare away the rats, then slipped off my trousers and tried to pee. Maybe I could ease my thirst by drinking my own . . .

But nothing came, not even one drop, then suddenly I felt something slimy scurry up my leg.

I screamed. But that didn't stop the rat from climbing inside my trousers. He was now squirming around my crotch. Cold sweat broke out all over my body. I screamed more. The filthy creature kept bumping until I realised that he must have been as scared as I. Crying hysterically, I snatched off my trousers and flung him off.

Overcome with disgust, I banged my head on the door and hollered, 'Let me out! Let me out!' But there was no response except more screeching – this time my own – echoing eerily in the ghostly room. I kept banging and hollering. When nothing happened, I used my whole force to hit my head on the door.

'Let me die!' My scream bounced in myriad directions. Suddenly, I felt something damp and sticky flow down from my scalp, then a salty, metallic tang seeped into my mouth . . .

I peed and lost consciousness.

When I woke up, I found myself still surrounded by filth and darkness, but luckily the squealing was gone – the rats were now probably easing their full bellies by taking a nap. But my stomach was like a drum frantically beating and my throat was scorched as if I'd just swallowed burning coals. I tried to scream but my voice only came out in a whisper.

As I fidgeted on the bed, I felt something strange – slimy and sticky – underneath my backside. I felt around with my hand, then put my fingers below my nose.

'Blood! Blood!' I heard my scream bouncing off the walls.

Instinctively I reached for my head, but the blood there had already dried. Again I touched the spot where I'd lain and felt the wet, warm bed. Strange, I didn't see how I could have hurt my bottom so badly that it bled. As I was brooding, a gradual pain rose in my stomach, followed by a warm surge of fluid oozing from between my thighs. It was then that I realised it was my *yin* part that had been bleeding.

Panicked, I shot up from the bed, dashed toward the gate, and thrust my fists on the cold iron. 'Mama! Mama! Please let me out! I'm going to die! I'm dying!'

I didn't know how long I'd been banging until a state of lethargy and semi-consciousness took over my whole being. And the screeching began again . . .

* * *

I lost count of time. But I thought it must be the second or even the third day when a loud clang of the door jolted me awake. In burst Fang Rong and Wu Qiang. When I tried to shield my face from the blinding harsh light, Fang Rong slapped off my hand.

'Oh, Mama!' I was stunned; I couldn't believe I'd just called her Mama! Was I so desperate to have a mother's comfort?

I suddenly realised that instead of comforting me like my mother, she might hit me. Again I swung up my hand to shield my face.

But to my utter surprise, Fang Rong squeezed a big grin and cooed, 'Ah, my dear daughter, how you've suffered!' She laid her damp, fleshy palm on my forehead. 'Thank heaven you don't have a fever.' Then, 'Are you hungry?'

I nodded my head like a pounding jackhammer.

'Now do you want to go back to the pavilion and have something to eat?'

Again I nodded until I felt my head almost dislodge from my neck.

As I was struggling to get up, Mama's eyes widened, her finger pointing to the bed. 'Oh heaven, what happened?' Then she twisted her fat neck to face me. 'Xiang Xiang, what did you do to yourself?'

It was then that I remembered the blood. 'I'm bleeding.' I paused, then uttered weakly, 'But I didn't do anything.'

Mama snatched up my hand to examine my wrists. Not able to find any cuts, she reached to touch the stains on the bed, then spun me around and yanked down my trousers.

'Mama!' My cheeks burned with humiliation. My hands tried to pull my trousers back up only to be slapped off by Fang Rong's bear-like paws.

Then, to my utter shock, she burst out laughing while her husband looked down modestly at his nails.

Mama spun me back to face her. 'Don't you realise that your great-aunt has just come to visit?'

Neither of my parents had ever mentioned a great-aunt. 'But I don't have one,' I said, pulling up my trousers.

'Hasn't your mother ever told you about your great-aunt?'

I shook my head. 'Where is she now?'

The two exchanged meaningful glances. Then Fang Rong laughed so hard that her fleshy face looked like a fat, melting candle.

Mama stopped to catch her breath, then, 'Hmmm . . . your mother must have felt too embarrassed to tell you. But why should she? Since she'd already been *fucked* by your father to have you.'

'What is *fuck*?' I imitated her tone.

'Xiang Xiang,' Wu Qiang stared into my eyes, 'fuck means when a man puts his—'

Mama cut him off sharply. 'Wu Qiang, stop being overeager. You can leave that to me.'

Some silence, then Fang Rong spoke again. 'Xiang Xiang, you're not a little girl any more.' She winked. 'You've just turned into a woman.'

I had no idea what she was talking about.

Mama went on, 'Xiang Xiang, since your so-called mother was too lazy and too proper to explain about affairs of the wind and the moon,' she tapped her chest, 'you're lucky to have a real mama to enlighten you.'

Although I still didn't understand what she meant, I felt too exhausted to ask, let alone to defend my mother's 'laziness.'

Seeing that I was on the verge of collapse, Mama said, her tone turning very tender, 'My dear daughter, you must be starving, so why don't we all go to eat?'

My feet were so weak and wobbly that Fang Rong and Wu Qiang had to half carry me back to the pavilion.

Fang Rong asked her maid Little Red to bathe me. While I was being washed, neither of us mentioned anything about the dark room. Eyes closed, I enjoyed the sensation of the hot water sloshing against my bare flesh. I tilted my head to let the steam, like a spring breeze, massage my face. Little Red's sponge rubbed and swished on my neck, back, and shoulders, synchronising with my contented sighs.

When she finished, Little Red poured out the red-tinted water, then took out a thick, folded cloth.

When she tried to position it between my legs, I yanked away her hands. 'Little Red, I'm not going to wear this ridiculous thing!'

She chuckled. 'Xiang Xiang, then would you rather let everybody in the pavilion know that *that thing* of yours has come?'

'Why are you people all talking in riddles today? What is *that thing* of mine, do you mean my great-aunt? But I don't have one!'

Little Red giggled more.

'What's so funny?'

'Xiang Xiang, every girl has a great-aunt,' she leaned close to me and lowered her voice even though there were only the two of us in the room, 'that means her monthly red classic.'

Before I could respond, she went on, 'When a girl grows up, every month she'll begin to bleed. But the blood oozing out from her lower hole is not ordinary blood. It's blood from inside her stomach. If a girl has not been with a man . . .' Little Red paused to whisper into my ears, 'That means fuck – then her eggs will not mix with his seed but flow out from her *yin* part with the blood. But if the girl has been fucked by a man and gets pregnant, she'll stop bleeding – until the baby is born. So now your great-aunt has begun her visit, that means you can have a baby.'

Her last sentence sent a tremor across my chest. 'Oh heaven, does it mean that I'm going to have a baby?'

She answered my question with another one, 'Xiang Xiang, have you already been *fucked*?'

I had no chance to respond before she plunged on, 'If you have, you'll be in *big, big* trouble, for I'm sure Mama and De are waiting to sell your virginity for a high price.'

Waiting until she finished, I spat out, 'What's *fuck*?'

Little Red looked surprised. 'That's what all the sisters are doing here, and you don't know? How long have you been here?'

'A month.'

'Hmmm, if Mama doesn't have time to teach you yet, then let me tell you what fuck is.' Little Red paused, then continued, 'It means when a man puts *that thing of his* inside a woman.'

In order not to appear too ignorant, I put up a knowing smile.

She threw me a suspicious glance. 'Xiang Xiang, are you sure you're still a virgin?'

'A virgin?'

'That means someone who has never been fucked.' Little Red's voice rose higher and higher. 'Xiang Xiang, how come you have no idea about all this? What did your mother teach you at home?'

'Poetry, literature—'

'All right, I know you're well learned in the five classics. But how come she never told you about the monthly red classic?'

I remained silent.

She said, 'Xiang Xiang, I just told you, "fuck" means when a man puts *that thing of his*,' she cast me a mysterious look, 'I mean his *yang* instrument – into the woman's *yin* hole.'

'But why would a man want to do that?'

'Why? Because he enjoys doing it, that's why! Besides, then he can make her have a baby.' Another pause before she went on excitedly, 'Your father also fucked your mother to have you!'

'Oh no!' I protested vehemently. 'My father was a scholar gentleman, he wouldn't have done such a sickening thing to my mother!' No matter how hard I tried or how far I stretched my imagination, I just couldn't picture my refined father putting *that thing of his* into my elegant mother's hole.

'Yes, of course, he did.' Little Red's voice jumped high like a frog. 'If not, then where do you think you came from, picked up from a rubbish bin, or burst from a stone?!'

I was struck speechless both by the bin and the stone.

Little Red plunged on, 'Xiang Xiang, believe me. Your parents fucked to have you. I bet they must have fucked hard and also tried out all kinds of beneficial positions and enjoyed them tremendously. Otherwise, it's impossible that you'd be born so beautiful!'

'What does that have to do with being beautiful?'

'Because if a couple enjoys fucking, the *qi* they thrust into each other is unusually good, and that will always generate beautiful babies.'

I stared hard at Little Red's potato face, frog eyes, pug nose, then almost blurted out, 'Then your parents must have hated each other bitterly,' but stopped myself just in time.

Right then we heard Fang Rong's voice shooting up from downstairs. 'What are you two doing upstairs, discussing Confucius' classics? Come down at once!'

And that ended our conversation. Hastily Little Red helped me put on fresh clothes, then accompanied me down to the ground floor.

In the corridor heading to the dining room, I almost fainted from the smell of food. Then I saw the dishes – steamed whole fish, garlic shrimp, crabs in ginger and scallion, braised eel in roasted garlic sauce, rabbits' legs, deers' tongues, tortoise soup – and started to drool. Fang Rong waved Little Red away, then signalled me to sit between her and Wu Qiang.

She smoothed my hair. 'See, Xiang Xiang, if you behave, you'll always have goodies like this. Now eat and drink.' She and Wu Qiang began to pile food onto my dish and pour wine into my cup.

'Thank you, Mama and De,' I said, now feeling truly grateful.

Then I gobbled and drank until I passed out again.

4

The Elegant Gathering

After that time in the dark room, I realised that at Peach Blossom Pavilion, life was not as good as it had seemed. I'd also become, however reluctantly, a woman. Nevertheless, as time passed, I was too busy occupying myself in learning the arts – and too scared – to reflect on my future. Every week I had to take lessons in singing, *pipa* playing, painting, and calligraphy, and every day I had to practise five or six hours with no rest.

One time I was so exhausted that I asked Mama for a break. A huge grin broke out on her fleshy face. '*Aii-ya*! Xiang Xiang' – she tapped her chest – 'you think I'm the one who'll be benefitting from all this practising?' Then she put her pudgy finger at my forehead and gave it a push. 'It's you, silly girl, YOU!' She paused to catch her breath. 'Wait until you get famous, maybe then you'll show some appreciation for your mama who has made you take all these lessons!'

Among all the arts, I liked playing the *pipa* – the four-stringed lute – the most. Partly because I liked the pleasant sound of the instrument, partly because I liked Pearl, my teacher. It gave me endless pleasure to watch her tilted chin, pouted lips, and slender fingers hover over the instrument like butterflies dancing from flower to flower. Also, her room was not like mine. Its silk curtains, embroidered sheets, marble-topped dressing table, gilded mirror, ornate Western clock, and paintings of pretty women fascinated me. Whenever I was there, my eyes would be busy exploring the beautiful objects while I inhaled the fragrances mingling from the flowers, the incense, and her perfumed body.

Moreover, I was intrigued by Pearl's magical power – men would turn hungry and naughty whenever they were within a fifty-yard radius. Upon spotting her, they would, like cats reaching their paws for fish, eagerly reach out for – a cheek, an arm, a leg, a hip, a breast.

Now in Peach Blossom, due to my busy schedule, I didn't have much time to think about my 'great-aunt,' nor the 'fucking' described by Little Red.

But since that day, Little Red had been so busy carrying out errands that, whenever we ran into each other in the corridor or in the courtyard, we could never finish our conversation. As to Fang Rong, although she'd promised she'd soon enlighten me about *fuck*, she was in fact either too busy scolding the sisters, kowtowing to the important guests, or gloating over her account book while flicking the fat beads of her abacus with sausage fingers.

However, I was still able to snatch tidbits of this mystery here and there in Peach Blossom.

'Good heavens, how can he possibly think he can go in me when my great-aunt is right there between us!'

'Is it true that his little brother is malnourished?'

'Do you know how it feels when a toothpick drops into a well?'

Although now I was not completely ignorant about this *fucking* business, it still seemed, in many ways, unintelligible to me. But whom to ask? Of course I'd already tried Pearl toward the end of my *pipa* lessons, but she'd either look tired or in a hurry to entertain a guest.

'Ah, Xiang Xiang,' she'd say apologetically, 'Mama has asked me to teach you but I'm just not in the mood right now.'

I had no idea whether she was really that exhausted and busy or simply reluctant to tell me, but since Mama had assigned her to be my teacher, I deemed it her duty to satisfy my *fucking* curiosity.

* * *

But there was no chance to question Pearl again because now everybody in Peach Blossom was busily preparing for the Lunar New Year. Mama had ordered the servants and maids to wash windows, scrub floors, and polish furniture. Doors were hung with colourful lanterns and pasted with red scrolls for good luck. Servants took out the red drape embroidered with one hundred fruits (for longevity) to cover the big *luohan* chair in the welcoming-guests room. The sides of the chair were tied with two poles of bamboo symbolising frequent promotions (since bamboo grows high). On New Year's Eve, we all sat and waited to see which guest would arrive first and be the one to light the red dragon and phoenix candles.

On New Year's Day, male servants lit firecrackers to send off the old year, welcome the new, and scare away evil spirits. Laughter, jokes, and words of good luck filled Peach Blossom's guest, business, and banquet rooms. After Mama and De had led us to pray in front of all the gods and goddesses, Aunty Ah Ping brought out four big silver trays filled with dim sum. In the spirit of the new year, customers indulged themselves in spending sprees – overpaying for the food, tipping everybody in sight, and gambling for high stakes.

On the tenth of January, I counted my lucky money and was elated to find almost ten silver coins – only to have it snatched away by Mama. To pay bills, she said. Feeling distressed, I went to the kitchen to find Guigui for solace. The puppy was so happy to see me that even in the middle of gobbling down the leftover food, he looked up and wagged his tail.

I picked him up and rubbed my face against his warm, fluffy fur. 'Guigui, have you been a good baby?'

He nodded, then licked my face, leaving bits of half-chewed meat on my cheeks.

A few days later, when the tumult of the New Year had finally died down, I went to Pearl's room for another *pipa* lesson. It surprised me that Pearl didn't have her *pipa* out as she usually did. Instead, she was carefully pencilling her brows in front of the mirror, while humming a tune. Why was she fretting over two thin lines instead of tuning the four strings?

I put on my best smile. 'Sister Pearl, aren't we having a lesson today?'

She lifted her brow and cast me a curious glance in her gilded, elaborately carved mirror. 'Forget the *pipa* lesson. Tonight I'll teach you some other lessons instead.'

Before I could ask, 'What about a *fucking* lesson?' she squinted at me with her elongated phoenix eyes. 'I heard that you were locked in the dark room some time ago?'

I nodded.

'So have you learned your *dark room* lesson?'

I couldn't think of anything to say, so I nodded again.

'Why did you run away?'

'To see my mother off.'

'That was a high price to pay.'

I remained silent; she asked, 'Where did she go?'

'To take refuge as a nun in a Buddhist temple in Peking.'

Pearl burst into laughter until tears rolled down her cheeks. Her hand trembled and made a wrong move, leaving her brow crooked. When she'd finally calmed down, she pulled a silk handkerchief from her jade bracelet to dab her eyes and wipe her brow.

'Sister Pearl, why is it so funny?'

She tapped a red-nailed finger at me in the mirror. 'Ha, don't you think so? Your mother's going to be a nun and you a whore, huh?'

'But I'm not—'

'Xiang Xiang, do you think you're being fed and clothed and given art lessons here for nothing? You think Peach Blossom Pavilion is a charitable organisation? Or a government-sponsored art studio?' She rapped my head. 'The earlier you are disillusioned the better, you understand?' She paused to redo her brow. 'You know, sometimes it's not too bad to be a prostitute. Especially if you become famous and meet someone who's so rich and loves you so much that he'll redeem you and take you home as his fifth or sixth concubine.' She turned to pinch my cheek with her spidery fingers. 'Is that clear, you little whore?'

As I was about to protest, suddenly I remembered my mother's saying.

> *Try your best to get along with everyone, otherwise you won't have a roof to live under nor even thin rice gruel to warm your stomach.*

Besides, when the truth is thrown like a clod of dirt on your face, how else can you respond but to swallow it?

So I swallowed hard and squeezed a smile. 'Yes, Sister Pearl.'

Pearl turned back to gaze at her powdered face in the mirror. Now beautiful and motionless, she looked like a gracefully carved statue of Guan Yin – the Goddess of Mercy – who always listens to cries of help.

I blurted out my long-held question, 'Sister Pearl, what is *fuck*?'

'Xiang Xiang!' She threw me a chiding look in the mirror. 'That word is extremely vulgar.'

'But that's what Mama and Little Red use.'

'Yes, I use that, too, but it's for adults, not a little girl like you.'

'But Sister Pearl. I'm not a little girl anymore. I'm a woman!'

'Oh, is that so?' She raised a brow. 'That means you have been fucked, haven't you?'

Her words stung like a bee. I screamed. 'No, of course not!'

She laughed, revealing a neat row of pearly teeth. 'All right, you haven't been fucked, not yet, all right?' Then she looked at me chidingly. 'Xiang Xiang, instead of saying *fuck*, why don't you say mating of heaven and earth, balancing *yin* and *yang*, or stirring up the clouds and rain?'

She cocked an eye at me. 'But why are you in such a hurry to learn all these, can't you wait to be a fucking whore?'

This time I kept my mouth shut.

She smiled flirtatiously. 'Hasn't Little Red already told you what *fuck* means?'

Before I could answer, Pearl's expression turned serious. 'Anyway, soon Mama will give you books about the secret games. You better study them thoroughly, then if you have questions, come and ask me.'

'Do you have those books?'

'I don't need them anymore,' she tapped her head, 'they're all here.' After that, she turned back to the mirror and continued to fuss over her make-up until her brows resembled two slender leaves. I understood that this signaled the *fucking* matter was to be dropped.

After Pearl had laid the finishing touch on her brow, she turned to look me in the eyes. 'Xiang Xiang, I'm going to entertain in a big party tonight, and,' she nipped my chin, 'you're coming with me, you lucky little witch.'

I was surprised to hear this. I'd never expected that I would be invited out so quickly. 'Sister Pearl, who invited me?'

Suddenly the warmth in her tone was gone. She narrowed her eyes. 'A very rich businessman. But don't think that you're already so irresistible that he invited you out. He invited *me*, you understand? You're just to tag along.'

I nodded. Tears welled in my eyes, but I wouldn't let them fall.

Seeing me on the verge of crying, Pearl's tone warmed up again. 'Ha, Xiang Xiang, you'd better start to learn about your own value. Don't you know that you're already quite famous? People have been asking around about you, "Who's that pretty girl with two enchanting dimples?" One even said, "So pretty, she'll definitely be a *ming ji* someday"!'

Ming ji – a prestigious prostitute. What would that be like?

Pearl raised her arm and rubbed perfume onto her armpits. 'It's never too early to be noticed, silly girl. Life is short here and no one has a whole eternity to flash her youth.'

She preened in front of the mirror – tilting up her chin, lowering her eyes, wetting her lips, raising her shoulder so that her bathrobe slipped to expose her smooth white flesh, caressing her breast with her red-nailed fingers. Then she started to recite a poem, 'When a flower blooms, pick it. Don't wait till there is only the bare branch left.' After that, she turned to me, her voice sentimental, 'You understand the poem, Xiang Xiang?'

I nodded, feeling too sad to say anything.

Pearl had finally finished putting on her make-up. Now she walked to the wardrobe and peeled off her bathrobe. I let out a small cry; there was not a single thread on her body!

She cocked an eye at me and chuckled. 'Never saw a naked body before, huh?'

I shook my head, while eyeing her tilted breasts, her slightly swelling belly, and the luxuriant dark area between her white thighs which looked like the rich ink my painting teacher Mr. Wu dabbed on the rice paper.

My scrutiny didn't seem to bother Pearl at all. She said, 'You'd better get used to it, Xiang Xiang. Because, trust me, you'll be seeing a lot of them very soon. But mind you,' she sneered, 'those bodies you're going to see and learn to please are very different from ours. They belong to the *chou nanren's*!'

Stinking males.

A beat passed before we burst into uncontrollable laughter. In that fleeting moment, I thought I liked her very, very much.

Pearl looked particularly attractive tonight. The red silk dress embroidered with a golden phoenix clung to her body as tightly as if the bird were painted on her skin. Her jacket's high collar wrapped around her neck like petals enveloping a bud – her coveted goose-egg-shaped face. Her long hair was pinned loosely into a bun at the nape of her neck and scented with osmanthus flower oil. She'd decorated her three-thousand-threads-of-trouble with fresh plum blossoms and a gold filigreed butterfly. Her lips, painted crimson and slightly opened in a pout, looked as if they were dying for the sweet dew of some exotic elixir. Two jade earrings – like two green eyes – twinkled enigmatically.

'Sister Pearl, you're gorgeous!' I sniffed the perfume wafting from her.

She pinched my cheek affectionately. 'Thank you, Xiang Xiang.' Then her eyes looked sad. 'Beauty is all we have,' she sighed, 'that is, besides charm.'

A long pause before her mood changed again; now she scrutinised me playfully. 'Xiang Xiang, you're a very pretty little slut yourself, too. Now get dressed.'

She picked a silk top and trousers from her wardrobe and

handed them to me. After I put them on, Pearl said, 'All right, now let me help you put on make-up.'

When we were finally ready to go out, we stared at our images in the mirror. To my surprise, I looked completely different – at least five years older. The green top and pants with pink plum blossoms, though a little loose, looked very nice on me – as if spring had blossomed all the way from my torso to my limbs. Accentuated by the pink eye shadow and black eyeliner, my eyes gave off a lustrous sparkle that I hadn't noticed before. The cinnamon pomade on my hair seemed to turn the three-thousand-threads-of-trouble into a mysterious black mirror.

'Beautiful, aren't we?' Pearl purred.

I felt both too shy and too excited to respond.

She grabbed a fur coat and a woolen shawl from her sofa. 'Now let's go and exercise our charm!' she exclaimed, then draped the shawl over my shoulders and pulled me out of the room.

Just then Fang Rong scurried toward us in the corridor. Her huge breasts undulated like tidal waves under her embroidered red jacket. 'Hurry up, Pearl, Mr. Chan is still in a meeting, but the car is already waiting downstairs. Your de and I will follow you in another car.' Like a fortune teller sizing up a new client, Mama scrutinised me for long moments, muttering, 'Ah, so beautiful; proves my old, fussy eyes are still as sharp as a cleaver!'

Outside Peach Blossom, a big, shiny, black car was waiting. Having spotted us, the uniformed and capped chauffeur came to our side and opened the door.

When I was trying to crawl in, Pearl snatched me out. 'Xiang Xiang, stop! That's extremely vulgar. Watch me.' She lowered herself onto the seat, then slowly swung in her legs. An expanse of thigh flashed through the slit of her dress.

'But Sister Pearl,' I said in a heated whisper so it wouldn't be heard by the chauffeur, 'I can see your entire thigh, even your underwear!'

After I'd gotten in, Pearl sat staring into the rearview mirror while smoothing her hair. She was still looking at her reflection when she said, 'That's the point, silly.'

The car started to move. I was so elated to be out that for the entire trip I spoke not a word, shifting my eyes to take in all the passing scenery.

After many turns, the car finally pulled to a stop in front of an ancient building with red-tiled roofs and white walls. Pearl and I got out of the car and walked toward the gate. Four big characters in walking-style calligraphy above the lintel read: WHITE CRANE IMMORTAL'S HALL.

I turned to ask Pearl, 'What is an immortal's hall?'

'A Taoist temple.'

What did prostitutes have to do with Taoists and temples?

As we stepped through the crimson gate, I finally asked, 'Sister Pearl, why would someone hold a party in a temple?'

'Ah, Xiang Xiang,' Pearl threw me a chiding look, 'the party we're now going to attend is special, a *yaji* – elegant gathering. Tonight you'll meet lots of important and famous people – artists, scholars, poets, actors, high government officials. Anyway, you're lucky to be invited, so you can start to soak in the flavour of the arts.' She paused to look at me meaningfully. 'If you want to be a *ming ji*, that is. Do you want to?'

I didn't know whether to say yes or no. Maybe both. 'Yes' because I'd like to be prestigious, 'no' because, needless to say, I hated even to *think* of myself as a prostitute. Nevertheless, I knew the two words together signified something quite different. At Peach Blossom, I'd read fine poems and seen exquisite paintings by women – including Pearl – who bore this title. Among the cultivated, rather than being despised, they were highly respected – of course, for their beauty, but even more for their many talents and detached artistic air.

As I was still wondering whether I should say yes or no, I was surprised that my head, against my will, was already nodding like a pestle hitting against a mortar.

Now Pearl whispered into my ear, 'Of course, there'll also be crude businessmen and evil people like policemen, politicians, and even *tong* members.'

Silence reigned in the air until we stepped inside the courtyard where the party was held.

I let out a small cry.

It was the most beautiful place I'd ever seen. I inhaled the aroma of food and the fragrance of sweet-smelling incense. Colourful lanterns of various shapes and sizes hung from plum trees, swaying and shimmering in the breeze. Glowing peaches had grown as big as a baby's head; a rabbit watched me wherever I moved; a carp glowed orange; a horse trotted in the wind; a fiery dragon stretched its claws and soared in the air.

Atop several tables were placed sheets of rice paper, brushes, ink stones, tea sets, wine vessels, trays of snacks, and plates of dim sum. Pearl and I floated here and there, watching some sisters paint, others rehearse poetry or sing arias of Peking and Kun operas, while yet others flirted with the guards and male servants. A few men arched their brows and smiled at us as we drifted by. Dew swayed on top of plum blossoms while in the fishpond gold carp wagged their tails.

More and more guests arrived. The men looked important and intimidating in expensive gowns or fashionable suits. The sisters were at their best – willowy bodies clad in silk, bejewelled hair shiny, make-up immaculate, as their delicate hands fussed with water pipes, clinked glasses, smoothed pomaded hair, patted fat cheeks, even delved into bulging pockets.

Then I felt a surge of guilt. In the bare fifteen minutes I'd been in this immortal's hall, I'd completely forgotten about my mother. By now she was probably in the unadorned nunnery reciting sutras and beating the wooden fish to accumulate merit for me.

'Beautiful, isn't it?' Pearl pinched my elbow, awakening me from my thoughts. 'We're still early, so let's go appreciate the lanterns before my big fish Mr. Chan arrives.' She led me past the women servants who were arranging the food and drink under the scrutinising eyes of Fang Rong and Wu Qiang.

Then she stopped in front of a big tree. Swaying down from the lanterns were slips of rice paper inscribed with calligraphy.

As I was about to read the characters, Pearl's silvery voice rose to my ear. 'Xiang Xiang, do you know that tonight is *yuanxiao*, the Lantern Festival?'

Sadness swelled inside me. Of course I knew *yuanxiao* – the festival to celebrate *tuanyuan*, family reunion. But my father was already dead and my mother a thousand miles away. Four months had gone by and I still hadn't heard a word from her as she'd promised. With no family left, how could I celebrate a family reunion? The same time last year Mother had prepared a delicious dinner, and Baba had hung up our own lanterns in my favourite shapes of a peacock and the moon goddess Chang E. After we ate the sweet, round dumplings symbolising happy reunion, my parents took me to the old city's Yu Garden. We strolled around the various famous scenic spots and appreciated lanterns, fireworks, acrobats, jugglers, lion dances. When we felt tired from all the walking and excitement, Baba took us to a street stall to enjoy the fragrant jasmine tea.

After that, we went to read the riddles. Baba, well learned in literature and all the classics, could almost always solve the difficult ones, so he'd won lots of prizes. That was why I'd also become very good at solving riddles. Last year the prize he'd won was a fan with a poem:

Last year during the *yuanxiao*, the lanterns shone as bright as daylight.
When the moon climbed on the trees' top, lovers met each other in the twilight.
This year during the *yuanxiao*, while the moon and the lanterns are still here, last year's persons are nowhere to be seen.
All that's left are tears wetting the sleeves of my spring garment.

This was a very popular poem by the Sung dynasty poet Ouyang Xiu. Baba had told me that although the poem appeared sad, its message was in fact happy. 'In the past, women and young girls were not allowed to roam outside their household by themselves. This rule was lifted during the *yuanxiao* festival, so married women would go out and have fun while young girls would meet their lovers, all under the pretext of appreciating lanterns. So the poem encourages freedom to find love.' Baba patted my head affectionately. 'Xiang Xiang, when you've grown up, I won't hire a matchmaker to choose your husband. You'll be free to look for someone you love.'

Now, remembering Baba and this poem made me extremely sad. Maybe it did convey an auspicious message as interpreted by Baba, but he'd also missed the bad omen it contained. This year, the lanterns were still there but both Baba and Mother were gone, leaving only tears to wet my winter garment.

Seeing that I was about to cry, Pearl put on the big, sweet smile which she normally reserved for her big-shot customers. 'Cheer up, Xiang Xiang! Let's look at some of the riddles.'

I dabbed the corners of my eyes and we began to read in silence. Just when I was about to give the answer, I felt a hand on my shoulder. It was Pearl, and beside her towered a thirtyish man – eyes large and hungry, forehead high, jaw square, with a long arm wrapped around Pearl's narrow waist.

He leaned his flushed face close to Pearl's made-up one and said as if he had just swallowed a fireball, 'Little Pearl, I know tonight you have to keep Mr. Chan company, but before that, can you . . .'

Pearl snatched out her fan, flipped it open, then began to fan furiously while half-nudging the young man away with her hip. '*Yor!* When does our famous gifted oil painter pay attention to a plain woman like me?'

'No, Pearl, you're the most beautiful woman I've ever seen, the lady of my dreams.'

Pearl waved him a dismissive hand. 'Then you better go to sleep now and I'll see you later in your dream.'

The man had a trapped expression. Pearl cocked an eye at me while motioning to him. 'Jiang Mou, let me introduce to you my little sister Xiang Xiang.' Then she turned to me and spoke commandingly, 'Xiang Xiang, pay respect to Mr. Jiang, the most famous oil portraitist in Shanghai. So if you're lucky and behave, maybe someday he'll be willing to paint you and make you very famous.'

'Will you, Mr. Jiang?' I asked, feeling colour rising in my cheeks.

'If your sister says so,' Jiang Mou said as his eyes kept moving all over Pearl.

Pearl continued to make small talk with Mr. Jiang while throwing him flirtatious glances and brushing his body with her smooth arms and fingers. Finally she whispered something into his ear and made a dismissive wave, at which the famous portraitist sauntered away like an obedient dog.

Pearl turned to me. 'Xiang Xiang, now why don't we start to read again?'

The lantern I'd picked was in the shape of a rooster, its riddle was written in walking-style calligraphy:

> Its body can break the bellies of evil spirits
> Its breath roars like thunder
> Its sound rips up the sky and tears off the earth
> But when you look back, it's already a heap of ashes. (an
>   object)

I yelled to Pearl, 'Firecrackers!'

She turned to look at me appreciatively, 'Good, Xiang Xiang, now read this one.' She pointed to a phoenix.

> Face as beautiful as the crescent moon and ears alert as a
>   night owl's.
> Ten thousand arms reach for ten thousand desperate
>   voices. (a personage)

Again I blurted out, 'Guan Yin, the Goddess of Mercy, who listens to the cries of the needy and goes to help!'

Pearl cocked an eye at me. 'Very good, you're really smart, eh?' Now she pointed to a lotus. 'Then what about this?'

Just then a loud explosive sound shattered the air.

'Oh, my heaven!' Pearl screamed, 'someone's got shot!'

'How do you know?'

'This is not the first time that it happened. It's too terrible. Let's go find out who's the *lucky* one.' Pearl grabbed my arm and we sped to the source of the sound.

5

Spring Moon

Pearl and I shoved through the hovering crowd and gaped.

What stared back at me was a pair of sad, flickering eyes. They were the same eyes that, from underneath the bamboo grove, had followed my every move.

Pearl sighed, yet her voice didn't sound very upset. 'I knew sooner or later something like this would happen to Spring Moon.'

I craned my neck to take a better look and saw the sad-eyed girl squirming and moaning on the ground. Blood oozed from her arm, staining the green sleeve of her dress.

I blurted out, 'Oh, heaven, we should call the police!'

A coarse voice roared. 'Who said call the police?!'

I felt my sleeve tugged. Pearl shot me a razor-sharp look to shut me up.

The evening suddenly turned icy.

Coarse Voice laughed an air-shredding laugh. 'Ha! Ha! Ha! Doesn't everyone here know that *I am* the police chief?'

I followed the voice until my gaze fell on the most evil face I'd ever seen. It belonged to a dark, solid man with a prominent jaw protruding from a wide, uncouth face. His eyes were mere slits, with the pupils darting like mice trapped in a narrow trough. His square body, stuffed into a stiff uniform the colour of chicken shit, gave the impression of a corpse.

Then, more to my surprise, nobody – none of the sisters, servants, Fang Rong, Wu Qiang, nor the guests – offered to help the poor girl. Everyone just stood there, their feet rooted to the ground and their eyes trapezing between Spring Moon and the police chief.

While his eyes scanned the onlookers like machine guns firing muted shots, everyone lowered their heads to stare at their shoes. The chief spat at Spring Moon, his saliva spraying in all directions and flickering in the lanterns' light. 'Fuck your mother, stinky slut. Has no one taught you never to say no to a police chief? Eh? You stinky stuff!'

Fang Rong shoved away the others and went up to Spring Moon, but to my utter shock and surprise, instead of offering help or comfort, she also spat on her – more vehemently than the angry corpse. 'You cheap, stupid, short-lived bitch! Don't I always tell you never say *no* to our noble guests!?' Then she turned to the police chief, her lips curling into a grin so huge I feared her teeth might be all squeezed out. 'I'm so sorry, Chief Che, but I swear to you on the honour of Buddha and Guan Yin and the righteous White-Browed God and all my ancestors that this will never happen again.'

The chief shot Fang Rong a murderous look, while swinging his gun. 'Is that how you teach your daughters? To play ladies when they're whores?'

A deafening silence. Fang Rong and Wu Qiang plopped down, engaging themselves in a succession of frantic kowtows.

Mama's voice spilled fear. 'Sorry, Chief Che, it's all our fault. Tonight I promise we'll whip this slut to death to teach her a good lesson.'

Mama kept apologising, while the police chief kept fuming. He cursed incessantly, his body shivering and his high-booted feet fidgeting. When the cold breeze blew in my direction, a strong stench of alcohol wafted into my nostrils. Everyone remained deadly quiet, intently watching what was going to happen next. It astonished me that, amid this crisis, some sisters looked entertained, as if they were watching a Peking opera comedy.

The chief's venomous words rolled out across the chill night air. 'Promise me you'll whip this slut till her skin blossoms and her flesh rots! And I mean it, you get it?!'

Now Mama and De yapped simultaneously, 'You have our word, Chief!'

The dark face snorted. His voice slashed the night air like a sword. 'Huh! If not,' he swung his gun toward the two kneeling figures, 'beware of your brains!'

The pitiful duo paraded more kowtows.

Then suddenly, hands shaking, the police chief turned to aim the gun at Spring Moon's head. A collective gasp resonated in the air. Spring Moon closed her eyes. The pool of blood slowly crept along the ground as if it had a miserable life of its own.

Eager faces, shining with curiosity, excitement, and fear, waited for the '*bang*!' to climax the evening. I felt my heart almost jump out of my chest.

Just then, to everyone's surprise, Pearl pushed through the group, stepped forward, and wriggled up to the police chief. The evil-faced stinking male turned to stare at her, now not quite sure whether to shoot or not.

Pearl wet her lips and put on her best smile. '*Aii-ya*, Chief Che,' her voice sounded as if it had been soaked for hours in a honey jar, 'why fret over a little girl? Didn't you just say that she's but a stinky stuff, a worthless slut, a whore?'

The chief kicked Spring Moon's shoulder; his boots glinted menacingly under the pale moonlight. 'Yeh! Stinky stuff! Soon-drop-dead bitch!'

Spring Moon moaned; Pearl quickly added, 'So don't you think it's not worth your bullet, Chief? Besides, why fret over a piece of dirt, just needlessly stirring your *qi* and harming your health? It's not worth it at all.' Now seeing that the police chief had calmed down a bit, she ventured to put her hand on his shoulder. 'Chief Che, you came here to get entertainment, not to get angry, right? We need you to be happy so you can take good care of our society by protecting us against all wrongs.' She turned to wink at the on-lookers. 'Right?!'

Everybody nodded and uttered a loud 'Yes!'

Slowly, Pearl moved her hand to cover the gun, then began to caress the chief's arm while slowly guiding the weapon back to its holster – like a snake returning to its hole. After that, she slipped her arm around the chief's. 'Come on, Chief Che, let's forget this piece of scum and have some fun. I'll treat you to a glass of champagne, or,' she winked, 'anything that takes your fancy.' Now she ventured to touch the chief's cheek, her red-painted nails sparkling eerily under the yellowish lantern light. 'I promise you the wine is imported from France and you'll love it just as you love justice.' Her gaze swept around the audience before she turned back to the chief, wetting her lips. 'And I'll never say "no" to a big-shot customer like you. Not that I'm stupid or smart, it's simply because I can't afford to turn down righteousness!'

'Well said!' The group clapped.

Finally, with a stunning smile, Pearl wriggled her water-snake waist and led the staggering police chief away.

Waiting until they were out of sight, people let out a collective sigh of relief. Then some stooped to examine Spring Moon. Blood continued to ooze from her arm where the bullet had grazed her. Some simply stared blankly, as if disappointed that the incident had turned out to be an anticlimax with no killing. Fang Rong ordered two of the guards to take the poor girl back to the pavilion.

I sneaked up to her and asked, 'Mama, shouldn't we get her to the hospital?'

She shot me a dirty look. 'Hospital? Ah, what big talk! But who's going to pay? You? All right, if you pay, then we'll send her to a hospital—'

'But Mama, I don't have any money!'

'Neither do I!'

Wu Qiang chimed in, 'Don't worry, Xiang Xiang. We'll ask our herbalist to treat her; it's much cheaper.'

'What about – ?'

Mama snorted. 'If she dies, she dies, that's her fate, nobody can change that, not you, not me, not Guan Yin, not Buddha, not a Western doctor nor an expensive hospital.' She waved vehemently to the guards. 'Take her back, now!' Then she spat on Spring Moon. 'Stinky stuff! Bringer of bad luck!'

After Spring Moon had been carried away, Fang Rong put on a big smile, announcing to the sisters and the guests while frantically waving her hands, 'Nothing happened; everything's all right! Now go back to the party and enjoy yourselves!'

Immediately the group dispersed – some customers went to drink; others watched Mr. Wu demonstrate calligraphy; yet others listened to the sisters sing and swing their curvy bodies to the rhythm of the music . . .

It both surprised and disgusted me that people were indeed having a good time as if nothing had happened.

Since no one was paying any attention to me, I went to sit on a bench to calm myself. Spring Moon's image kept spinning in my mind – her sad eyes, her pained face. Who was she? How did she end up in Peach Blossom? Was her family so poor that they had to sell her into the prostitution house? But she didn't look poor – she had a smooth face and nice skin. Was her father also a criminal like mine? Had she been kidnapped by a bandit?

I sat in a daze I didn't know how long until I flinched from a slap on my shoulder. I turned and saw Fang Rong's menacing face hovering above mine. And an old man's wrinkled one next to hers.

'Xiang Xiang, what's the matter with you? Don't you know that you're here to work, not to relax?'

I sprang up in no time.

Mama turned to Old Wrinkles. 'Look, Big Master Fung, this is our famous Xiang Xiang, face beautiful enough to outshine the moon and shame the flowers. Don't you think?'

Old Wrinkles scrutinised me the same way my mother had examined a choice piece of pork in the market for our *yuanxiao* dinner. 'Wonderful, wonderful! The fame has not been spread for nothing,' he mumbled, while stroking his stubble with his bony, long-nailed fingers.

Mama nipped my chin and ordered, 'Xiang Xiang, give Big Master Fung a big smile.'

'Big Master Fung, see the dimples?' She shot Old Wrinkles a flirtatious look, causing goose bumps to creep on my skin. 'Aren't they so charming that they'll suck you in and make you forget all your troubles?'

Old Wrinkles nodded appreciatively, while his eyes caressed me all over. 'Yes indeed, indeed.'

Mama went on excitedly, 'Big Master Fung, there's one more precious thing about Xiang Xiang.'

'Eh? What is it?'

Mama lowered her voice to create suspense. 'Xiang Xiang has a natural body fragrance as if her diet were nothing but flowers.'

Now, like a bulldog, Old Wrinkles leaned close to me and sniffed. 'Yes, she does smell wonderful. But I think it's just perfume.'

Mama chuckled. 'Oh, of course not, Big Master Fung. You have my word, or your money back.' She winked. 'Xiang Xiang hasn't yet received any customers, so who'd buy her perfume?'

'All right, no need to explain,' Old Wrinkles said, then he whispered something into Mama's ear to which she frantically nodded.

I could only catch tidbits of the conversation – 'fresh dewy peach,' 'mighty emperor stretches the bow,' 'golden-gun-never-drop pills' – but their manner made my skin creep and my cheeks burn. After more prurient glances directed from my head to toe and then back from toe to head, the two burst into guffaws.

When Old Wrinkles finally left, so did Mama's laughter. Now she turned to cast me a murderous look. 'Xiang Xiang, what's the matter with you? Don't stand there like a fool; come and help!'

The party went on long past midnight. After most of the guests had gone, Pearl materialised out of nowhere and joined me to go back to Peach Blossom Pavilion. When we were inside the rickshaw, I noticed that her eyes were blurry, her face flushed, and her mouth reeked of alcohol.

'Sister Pearl, are you all right?'

'Oh yes. Don't you worry about me, I'm fine. I just wonder how's Spring Moon now. *Hai,* poor girl, I hope she can pull through.'

I asked tentatively, 'Where's the police chief?'

'He was tipsy. Otherwise Spring Moon would have been shot in the head already and started her journey to the Western Paradise. Then I got him completely drunk, so his gang took him back. Hopefully by tomorrow morning he won't remember a thing. Otherwise he may still cause trouble.'

'Is he very important?'

Pearl chuckled. 'Did you see how he swung his gun? He's a local despot! Have you ever heard the saying "When a scholar argues with a soldier, even if he has reasons, he has no way to make them clear"?'

She plunged on, 'Because the soldier is armed with a gun! So he doesn't give a damn about the scholar's reasoning, he'll just shoot him!' She looked me straight in the eyes. 'And remember, Xiang Xiang, we're not even scholars, but whores.'

That night, I could not sleep at all because my mind kept spinning with the image of Spring Moon.

The next day, as soon as it became light, I went to knock at Pearl's door and heard her tell me to come in.

Wearing a high-collared gown embroidered with gold-threaded peonies, she was standing beside the large blue-and-white bowl, feeding her goldfish.

I walked up to her. 'Sister Pearl, have you heard anything about Spring Moon?'

'She's in the dark room.' Not looking at me, Pearl continued to throw morsels of bread into the bowl.

We silently watched the fish swim and wag their tails for a while before she motioned me to sit on the sofa.

It seemed strange to be resting my bottom on the soft velvet cushion while Spring Moon was down there. Creepy sensations crawled all over my body. 'But she's wounded, why did they put her there?'

'Because she offended the police chief. Nobody can afford to do that. If you do, you're asking for a bullet in your head. She's lucky that she's now only lying in the dark room, not in a grave.'

'You think she'll die?'

'You think Mama, after she's made her investment, will let her daughters die so easily? Of course not, because any living daughter is better than a dead one. Once dead, all her investment will be thrown into the chamber pot. But a living daughter . . . even if she's disfigured, Mama can still sell her to a cheap whorehouse and get some money back, even if just a few coins.' She paused, then,

'Anyway, her wound was not serious.' She sighed, 'The dark room is to teach any disobedient girl a lesson.'

Some silence passed before Pearl spoke again. 'Let's not talk about unpleasant things.' She stood up, went to the *luohan* bed, and from underneath it took out an elongated object in a brocade cover. She removed the case and carefully put the object onto the table.

I studied it for long moments before I asked, 'What is this?'

'It's a *qin* – seven-stringed zither,' she said softly, running her fingers along its length.

The wooden surface, lacquered and decorated with dots of mother-of-pearl, shone with a lovely lustre.

'So are we going to play this today?'

Pearl chuckled. 'Ah, silly girl, you think you can just learn how to play this instrument in a day? It takes years and years of hard work.'

She went on, her voice filled with emotion, 'I want to play you a piece. It's called "Remembering an Old Friend."'

I asked tentatively, 'Is it . . . Spring Moon?'

'No, but my elder sister. Spring Moon is naïve like her.'

'Where is your sister now?'

Pearl didn't answer my question. The sadness on her face suppressed my urge to further enquire. So I changed the subject. 'Sister Pearl, do you know how Spring Moon ended up here in Peach Blossom?'

Pearl smoothed the brocade cover and sighed, 'Her father was a well-off ship merchant. One time when he was shipping some precious goods from Shanghai to Hong Kong, a storm struck and destroyed everything – the goods, the ship, the sailors, and himself. So her family lost everything overnight, literally. Not only that, since they hadn't bought insurance, they had to pay for all the losses, including the goods to be delivered to Hong Kong and the compensation to the sailors' widows. After the father's costly funeral, there was nothing left. So her father's concubines sold her here to pay their debts.

'Spring Moon was thrown overnight from atop the clouds to the ground. She was used to having maids serve her, and now she is bossed around. I was told she had a really nice and handsome fiancé. So of course it revolted her to be molested by that disgusting police chief. Poor girl, that was her first day out, and she's already caused this big trouble.'

Pearl put away the *qin*, then took the pot and poured us both tea. We sipped in silence.

Then I asked, 'I don't understand why Spring Moon kept staring at me from behind the bamboo grove.'

Pearl looked me in the eyes. 'She's envious of your beauty, especially those dimples of yours.'

'She told you that?'

'No. But I can tell. I always catch her squeezing in her cheeks to have the illusion of dimples.' Pearl sighed. '*Hai*, poor girl. She still doesn't have to sleep with customers. When she does, there'll be more . . .'

'More what?'

'Nothing.'

Moments passed. Pearl once again slid the *qin* out from its brocade cover and started to tune it. The seven strings, lightly touched, emitted soft, subtle sounds as if they were whispering the secrets of heaven. When Pearl had finished tuning, she meditated for seconds, then began to play. The melodies seemed to tell a very sad tale. Mesmerised, I imagined waves of melancholy sloshing gently through the room, caressing our wounded hearts.

I also noticed something unexpected – the transformation of Pearl's face. During her *pipa* playing when she vigorously plucked the strings, she always looked animated and flirtatious. Her long hair would fall over her face and tremble like dark waves and her eyes would give out sparks like twinkling stars. But as she played the *qin*, her countenance composed itself into that of a scholar's – serious, serene, respectful. The fingers that pulled and plucked aggressively on the *pipa* now effortlessly glided and pirouetted, like dragonflies skipping over a brook, swallows touching water, or petals falling on waves.

My mind was lifted away by Pearl's elegant playing to a quiet, far-off place where I could almost see Baba sitting under a shaded bamboo grove, playing a sad tune from his fiddle and smiling wryly at me.

After she finished, we sighed simultaneously. I felt sorry that such wonderful music had to end.

'Sister Pearl.' I searched her eyes. 'The *qin* sounds so beautiful—'

She stared at me curiously. 'You find this music beautiful?'

Eagerly I nodded.

'You're very gifted, Xiang Xiang. Not many young girls have the insight to appreciate *qin* melodies—'

'Can you teach me how to play the *qin*?'

Her face darkened. 'No.'

'But . . . why not?' I felt both surprised and hurt by her refusal.

'Because I think you should concentrate on the *pipa*.' Before I could protest, she went on, 'Xiang Xiang, the *qin* won't make you famous and popular, but the *pipa* will.'

'Why? And how?'

'Because the *pipa*'s tone is short and its music tuneful. You can attract the customers' attention right away. But it'll take years of cultivation just to appreciate the *qin*, let alone to play it, and play it well. As women, we have only very limited years of youth and beauty. So by the time you've mastered the instrument, you've already lost both. Worse still, hardly any customers will be cultured enough to appreciate the *qin* – or your talent.'

'Sister Pearl,' I searched her smooth, beautiful face, 'but you've neither lost your youth nor beauty . . .'

'Because I'm exceptional.'

I wanted to say that I, too, was exceptional.

But she'd already taken a handkerchief and begun to wipe the instrument, as tenderly as if it were her lover. After that, she said 'Now I'll play "Lament Behind the Long Gate." '

'What is it about?'

'The misery of an ill-fated woman.'

6

A Lucky Day

It had been ten months since I'd arrived at Peach Blossom Pavilion yet I still hadn't received any letter from Mother. First I was angry at her – how could she have forgotten her only daughter? Then I began to worry – had anything happened to her? Those bald-headed old maids in the nunnery, what had they done to my mother? It pained me to think of Mother, her head shaved and her slender body hidden underneath a dreary grey robe, with nothing to do all day but mumble texts from yellowing sutras that no one could understand anyway.

I wanted both my mother and her hair back!

Every night after I finished work, I'd take off the Guan Yin pendant Mother had put around my neck, hold it in front of me, and ask the Goddess to protect her – wherever she was now – and remind her to write me.

Now my only comfort was Guigui. Fed with all the delicacies, not only did he grow bigger each day, he also looked cuter. I began to teach him different tricks – carrying things, kneeling, hand-shaking, kowtowing. He was so chubby with his fluffy yellow fur that sometimes he looked like a moon rolling on earth. Whenever he'd given a good show, I'd take him to the kitchen and feed him with more goodies. To repay my generosity (at the customers' expense), Guigui would tilt his fat head to stare at me curiously, then lick all over my face. He was so cute and affectionate that even when he misbehaved, I had no heart to punish him. One time he peed right under the altar where the White-Browed God was worshipped. I felt so scared that I almost flung him out of the altar room, then frantically wiped the mess clean. The White-Browed God was Peach Blossom Pavilion's most revered deity – to lure in an endless flow of money and keep the wealthy guests bewitched by the sisters. If Mama had seen the puppy pee right beneath the Money God, she'd have beaten him – and maybe me – severely.

When I was about to scold Guigui, he dropped his head and whimpered, peering at me with big, soulful eyes. So, instead of spanking him hard on his little bottom, I scooped him up and threw him in the air!

Guigui and I became inseparable. When I prayed to Guan Yin, besides my mother, I now included him when asking for the goddess's protection.

One afternoon, my heart burdened with Mother's situation, I slipped into Pearl's room. She was reclining on the sofa, reading a magazine. I watched as she picked up red-dyed watermelon seeds, splitting each between her teeth with a sensuous pop. Then her small tongue would, like a lizard snatching its prey, draw out the egg-shaped flesh into her mouth.

When I stepped across the threshold, she spat out a husk into a celadon bowl, looked up at me, and smiled. 'Xiang Xiang, shouldn't you be practising your arts in your room?'

'Sister Pearl, can you do me a favour?'

'Come sit with me.' She put down her magazine. 'What is it that you want?'

'To hear you play "Remembering an Old Friend" on the *qin*.'

'Why? You have someone to remember?'

'My mother. I miss her,' I said, feeling tears stinging my eyes.

Pearl scrutinised me for long moments, then glanced at the clock. 'All right, I still have some time before my guest arrives.'

She stood up and went to take the *qin* from underneath her bed.

Carefully she peeled off the brocade cover, laid the instrument on the table, burned incense, then tuned the seven strings. After that, she began to play. Again, I was entranced, not only by the music, but also by the movements of her fingers, as graceful as clouds drifting across the sky. Listening to the melodies pour out from her tapered fingers, all my worries seemed to vanish.

When Pearl finished, again I begged her to teach me to play the *qin*. Again, she refused.

'Please, Sister Pearl,' I could hear the urgency in my voice, 'I only want to learn "Remembering an Old Friend," so I can play it and think of my mother.'

She didn't reply, but looked down to study the floral patterns of her skirt.

'Please, Sister Pearl, just one piece.'

Now she looked up to study me.

'Just one.' I raised one finger and pleaded incessantly until her face broke into a smile like the blossoming chrysanthemums on her jacket.

'All right, you little witch. But Xiang Xiang, promise me you'll keep this a secret between us. Can you do that?'

I nodded my head like a hungry woodpecker.

'All right, now go back to your room and wash yourself thoroughly.'

'Sister Pearl, but you've just promised to teach me to play the *qin!*'

'Bathing yourself is part of the ritual of playing. After that, you have to burn incense to cleanse the air and meditate to purify your mind, before you can even touch the instrument. Never forget that when you play the *qin*, you're not just making music, but communicating with the deepest mysteries of heaven.'

I was too surprised to respond; she went on, 'I told you it's hard. Do you still want to learn?'

'Yes, Sister Pearl!'

'Good, I like your determination.' She cast me a sharp glance. 'In the past, a student had to live with her teacher and wait upon her for two years – preparing tea, cooking, cleaning the house, massaging her sore muscles – before there'd even be any mention of lessons. You're lucky that I exempt you from all these. Now go to wash!'

'Thank you, Sister Pearl,' I yelled, then dashed toward the door.

She called out at my back, 'Remember, this instrument is sacred. And don't forget your *pipa* either.'

I turned around. 'Sister Pearl, I won't.'

'Come back and I'll teach you how to tune the *qin* – as well as your mind.'

So from that day on I was secretly learning to play this venerated instrument. At the start of each lesson, I'd meticulously tune the seven silk strings, while stealing glances at Pearl and wishing I could look as beautiful and play as elegantly. I would practise until my fingers bled and grew calloused, and my shoulders felt stiff and sore. But strangely, my heart was filled with joy at the sad tunes of the *qin*.

Needless to say, I dared not forget singing, painting, nor playing my *pipa*. Pearl warned me again and again if I didn't learn the other arts well, she'd stop teaching me the *qin*. But her worry was unnecessary, for I was good at all my lessons! Mr. Wu, the painting teacher, was so pleased with my talent that he showered me with gifts – brushes of all sizes, ink stones engraved with scenes of the four seasons, rice paper sprinkled with simulated gold flakes. He also praised my poems, telling me that some were so good that they could be used as opera lyrics. He predicted that I'd be famous soon, very soon. Mr. Ma, the opera teacher, said I had a voice like a lark's, which possessed the charm to entice the sun to rise and cajole it to set. But he also flattered me by continuing to accidentally brush his hand all over my body.

Word about my talents began to spread. Some customers asked to look at my paintings. Some halted by my door to listen to my singing. Others sighed with pleasure when they had a chance to glimpse my fingers performing acrobatics on the *pipa*. My poems were passed around and discussed as if they were works by Li Bai or Du Fu.

* * *

One afternoon while I was practising 'Spring Moonlight over the River' on the *pipa*, Fang Rong burst into my room. She dropped onto the chair, breathing heavily while eyeing me happily. She studied me so hard and so long that I felt colour rise in my cheeks.

'What is it, Mama?' I asked, putting down my instrument.

She shot up from the chair and went to the mirror, motioning me to follow her.

Our reflections stared back at us from the polished surface. Mama smiled mischievously, cocking an eye at me. 'Xiang Xiang, less than a year living in Peach Blossom, see what a lovely girl I've made of you.'

I looked at my own image for long moments, and for the first time I agreed with her. But I felt embarrassed to say yes, so I remained silent.

She lifted and tousled my hair. 'But you know what? Today you'll look even prettier, for I'm taking you out to have your hair styled!'

I turned to stare at her. 'Styled?'

'Yes, most girls have never even heard of it, let alone have the money to have it done. So lucky you!'

But I had heard of it. 'You mean like . . . those stars in a movie?' Of course I'd never seen 'those stars' in a real movie, only in newspapers and magazines Baba had brought home from the warlord's house.

'Exactly! Do you want to look like a movie star?'

I turned back to look at the mirror and saw my head nodding like that of a childless woman kowtowing to Guan Yin for a baby boy.

It was a hot, sunny Friday afternoon. Besides me, Fang Rong also took two other girls to have their hair styled. One, voluptuous and very silly acting, was called Jade Vase, and the other, to my surprise, was Spring Moon. I was glad that Mama had arranged for Spring Moon to share the rickshaw with me while she shared hers with Jade Vase. Spring Moon seemed to have recovered from that horrible night and the scar on her arm turned out to be quite small. Now, I'd finally have the chance to discuss with her in detail the strong stench and scurrying rats of the dark room – and maybe even *fuck*. But we ended up gawking at the rarely glimpsed city life outside the turquoise pavilion. Our eyes couldn't detach themselves from busy Nanking Boulevard with its famous red-and-gold signboards. Our fingers kept thrusting here and there to point out remembered sights.

Spring Moon pointed at a grand building and said proudly in her high-pitched voice, 'Look, that's Xing Xing Department Store where I used to shop with my parents.'

I craned my neck and saw three Western-dressed *tai tai* studying merchandise with great intensity. Behind them shuffled amahs burdened with overflowing shopping bags.

While my eyes were appreciating the society ladies' elaborate make-up and brocade dresses, Spring Moon's finger had already shifted to an even grander building next to Xing Xing, her voice climbing higher and higher in the air. 'Look, this is Sincere Department Store. My father once bought me a gold necklace in the jewellery department on the third floor!'

She plunged on excitedly, 'My father also used to take me to the Heavenly Tune Pavilion open-air café on the top floor of the Wing On Department Store. There, I could see the whole city, including the China Peace Company, the International Hotel, and the race track!'

When the speeding rickshaw had left the two stores and the three *tai tai* behind, a silence fell between us.

To leave her to her thoughts, I turned to take in the scenes on the street.

A vendor, with two baskets in front, yelled at the top of his voice, 'Fresh and aromatic roasted chicken! Your money back if it's not aromatic!'

Next to him an elderly woman, kneeling, begged by knocking her head loudly on the ground.

A noodle seller, bare-chested and leathery-faced, was banging a brass gong to attract attention.

Under the scorching sun, a red-turbanned, black-bearded Indian policeman frantically wielded a baton to direct traffic. Sweat poured down his dark face like black bean sauce.

Then I spotted two small children followed by doting parents swarm into a candy store. When I saw the big smiles on the parents' faces, my heart was seized with grief mixed with bitterness. Since the first day I'd been taken to Peach Blossom, despite the fact that I had a mother, plus another set of 'parents' unexpectedly dropped onto my lap, I still felt orphaned. I poked my head out of the rickshaw so that Spring Moon wouldn't see the tears streaming down my cheeks.

Just then her voice rose next to my ear, startling me. 'See, Xiang Xiang, that's Mali Pig For!'

I wiped my tears while craning my neck. 'Who?'

'The famous Hollywood movie star! Over there, on the sign-board of the Peking Theatre!'

Now I saw the picture showing the huge head of a foreign woman with wavy hair and a dreamy look. Next to her were several English words that I tried but failed to read. I turned to Spring Moon. 'Can you read those chicken's intestines?'

She smiled proudly. 'Of course.' Then, her lips pouted like a chicken's ass, she began to read. '*Poor Little Rich Girl.*'

'*Wah!* Where did you learn English?'

'My father used to hire a private tutor to teach us.' A pause, then she asked regally, 'Xiang Xiang, have you ever seen a movie?'

Pathetically I shook my head.

A smile bloomed on her face. 'My father used to take me to all the movie theatres: the Peking, the Embassy, and the Lyceum. If you have a chance to go inside these places, I bet you'll be impressed. They're like palaces!'

Spring Moon's eyes turned red. I looked away into the distance across the harbour behind the hazy skyline. A ship was blowing its whistle as it passed another. Like a pair of scissors, a third ship slid soundlessly through the sapphire waves, its American flag fluttering in the breeze like a brightly coloured dress.

America! I muttered to myself. I hoped someday I'd be able to leave Shanghai to see the world, places such as America where I could meet this famous, strange woman called Mali Pig For.

Two rickshaws sped past ours; the coolies' bare feet kicked up clouds of dust.

Everything outside Peach Blossom was so real, so lively . . . and yet illusory. Life seemed a deep, confused dream.

When I was about to turn back to talk to Spring Moon, the rickshaw suddenly pulled to a stop, jolting us forward. Fang Rong paid the two heavily sweating coolies, then, with an imperious air, led us into the hairstyling establishment.

The walls of the shop were covered with mirrors, giving it a spacious, mysterious look. Pasted on the mirrors were pictures of Chinese movie stars; all had shiny, styled hair like black waves gleaming under the moon.

Upon seeing us, several men, white towels draped over their arms, hurried to greet Fang Rong. They smiled obsequiously at her but scrutinised us like wolves. After we sat down, Mama told them to fix each of us a different hairdo.

She thrust a pudgy finger at Jade Vase. 'She has an ugly mole on her forehead, so give her the weeping willow fringe to hide it.' Then she motioned to Spring Moon. 'Her face's too round and her forehead too low, so give her the one-line fringe to cover everything.' Finally she turned to me, smiling generously. 'This one's lucky; she'll get the glamorous star-studded sky.'

Wah! I almost burst into happy laughter. Star-studded sky! But I had no time to relish this honor, for the three hairstylists, smiling knowingly, had already begun to muss our hair with expertly moving fingers.

It took more than an hour for the three men to cut, wash, and style our hair. We looked at each other in the mirror and discovered that Jade Vase's forehead was covered by a narrow patch of soft hair hung low like weeping willow branches. Spring Moon's face was framed with a thick fringe and straight hair down the sides, which magically made her round face look slender. For myself, I was pleased to see my hair pulled backward to reveal my much-envied high forehead and melon-seed face. Moreover, my three-thousand-threads-of-trouble were decorated with a gold clasp blossoming with pearls! My face seemed to have changed. Suddenly it looked glamorous . . . as if I were a real movie star who'd dance with swirling dress to dreamy music in a grand ballroom hung with glittering chandeliers!

A sob woke me from my intoxication; I turned and caught Spring Moon's gaze. Her teary eyes lingered on my face like a cat pathetically pawing a fish bone.

'Spring Moon,' I took a deep breath, 'why—'

Mama's coarse voice roared in the air. 'Spring Moon, stop that! Don't envy the others. You should be grateful not only that you're still alive, but that you're alive with styled hair and a slender face, instead of one that looks like a puffed bun!'

Spring Moon shut up at once. After that, Mama quickly paid and led us out of the shop. This time she didn't hail rickshaws. To my amazement, she led us along the busiest section of Nanking Boulevard, where our rickshaws had passed earlier! More surprises came when she led us into a fabric store and announced, 'Pick what you like and I'll have them tailored into Chinese gowns and Western dresses for all three of you.'

These generous words pouring from her mouth now sounded to me as enchanting as *qin* music! Holding bolts of floral satin against my skin, I felt weak with happiness. Jade Vase oohed and aahed and *aii-ya*-ed while her fingers ran over rolls of silk that cascaded before us like rainbowed waterfalls. Even Spring Moon's sad, watery eyes now sparkled.

Half an hour later, when the shopping spree had finally come to an end, Mama asked cheerily, 'All right, it's hot, so do you girls want some ice cream to ease the heat before we go back?'

Ice cream? I couldn't believe what I'd just heard. Baba had tasted it only once – at the warlord's house – and had told me it was something soft as silk and sweet as sugar. It melted so fast in your mouth that you had to lick it hard like you did a wound.

It took the three of us a few seconds to absorb the good news before we blurted out together, 'Yes, Mama!'

Sauntering down the busy boulevard with the glittering star-studded sky on my head, visions of new dresses, and the ice cream melting tenderly in my mouth, I'd never felt luckier. The corners of my lips kept lifting despite my efforts to press them down – people on the street might think that I was crazy smiling to myself!

I delicately licked my ice cream, trying my best to prolong the enjoyment of its soothing coolness and sweetness. My eyes were taking in the colourful displays of merchandise behind shop windows. While watching, I noticed we were also being watched. Young girls stared at us with envy while suppressing giggles. Some men threw lewd glances in our direction. Workers blew whistles. Several *tai tai* pointed red-nailed fingers at us and whispered to each other, sneering.

I turned to ask Fang Rong, 'Mama, why do these people keep staring at us?'

She put on an air like the Empress Dowager's. 'Ah, my daughter, what a silly question. Why? Because they're jealous of you, that's why!' She pointed to a bony girl of ten in rags begging at the curb, 'You think people will find her pretty?' then to a middle-aged, stooped amah, 'or her?' finally to a flat-chested and plain-faced girl selling pancakes at a street stall, 'or this bamboo pole?'

Mama burst out laughing. 'Ha, ha, ha, my gorgeous little treasures,' she paused to scan the three of us before turning to pinch my cheek, 'especially you, Xiang Xiang, you'll be the queen of attention soon, very soon!'

As she said this, it seemed now that all eyes were riveted on me. Feeling dazed and dreamy, I licked hard at the ice cream, savouring its fast-melting sweetness, while assuring myself that all this good luck did not merely exist in a dream. I touched my Guan Yin pendant and secretly prayed that this day would go on forever.

Just when I was relishing the tender softness on my tongue, suddenly I felt my arm being bumped. Before I knew what had happened, commotion stirred around me like oil hissing on a hot wok.

Mama's voice clanged like a broken gong, shaking the air around her. 'Catch the little thief!'

It was then that I realised my ice cream had gone. It was now tightly held in the filthy hand of a bony, ten-year-old boy. He was desperately licking it while trying to dash across the street infested with swishing cars.

'Watch out!' I screamed to him.

Mama smacked my star-studded sky while casting me a murderous glance. 'Are you out of your mind? Don't you think this brat deserves to be hit?'

When a gap appeared in the heavy traffic, the boy sprinted, followed by a cacophony of screeching, honking, shouting, and cursing.

'Oh my heaven! He's going to get killed!' I yelled again.

Mama, after glaring at me with another killer look, hurried with the three of us to see what had happened.

To my great relief, the little boy was not killed – he was not even hit. But his feet seemed rooted to the ground, and his face was so pale that he looked like someone who had just emerged from the *yin* world, with ghosts still clinging to his legs to try to pull him back. The ice cream had spilled on the ground and was draining down the gutter like blood scared white.

The driver jumped out from the car and spat. 'Fuck your mother's cunt, you dog-fucked little bastard! Next time watch before you cross!' With that, he shoved the dazed-looking boy back onto the pavement. Before the driver got back into the car, he again hollered, 'Get out of the way! I'm driving to pick up the president of the Shanghai General Chamber of Commerce!' Then he slammed the door and sped away. After that, traffic immediately resumed.

Spring Moon clapped. 'Mama, he's fine!'

Now it was her head that was jolted by Mama's slap. 'Why do you feel so happy about this little piece of dirt? He should be smashed like ground beef!'

Then, to my surprise, she flung her big torso toward the boy and grabbed him. Mama was as strong as a bull. The boy, thrashing bony arms and legs, screamed like a chicken being slaughtered. Almost in no time, a few hooligans began to gather around us, cheering and hollering.

'Yes, strangle that little beggar!'

'*Wah*! A woman beating a man to death!'

'Hey, come and watch Peking opera, free!'

Just when they were fanning up the fire of this street drama, a fortyish man with blonde hair and a white suit appeared from nowhere. He stepped toward the two blurs of jostling flesh and, with a move of his sinewy arms, disentangled them.

Silence instantly fell among the watching crowd. Everyone's eyes were glued to the foreigner, waiting to see what direction the drama would take. To my surprise, instead of losing her temper and cursing this *yanggui zi* – foreign ghost – Mama squeezed a big grin and spoke in accented English. 'Sorli, sorli, mister. Miss understanding, miss understanding.'

Still more to my surprise, the 'barbarian' spoke, in perfect Mandarin. 'What happened?'

Mama replied in Mandarin, her grin stretching bigger and bigger, until it almost reached outside her face. '*Meishi, meishi.*' Nothing, nothing.

'Nothing?'

Right then Jade Vase chimed in, pointing to the little boy. 'He tried to rob my sister Xiang Xiang's ice cream.'

The man turned to scrutinise me. His eyes were two blue beads, strangely cool yet soothing – like my vanished ice cream. Just when I felt colour rising to my cheeks, he turned to look at the boy, who was shivering in his rags under the hot sun. 'Are you very hungry?'

The boy nodded until his head almost dislocated from his neck. 'My mother is sick and we haven't had food for three days.'

To everybody's surprise, the foreign devil took out his leather purse, pulled out several copper coins, and gave them to the boy. 'Now buy some food for the family and go home.'

The boy snatched the money, plopped down on the ground and kowtowed, then scurried like a mouse across the busy boulevard.

Abruptly Jade Vase went up to the foreigner and grinned. 'Mister, thank you for your kindness, please come and visit us in the pavilion.'

He frowned, scanning the three of us. 'What pavilion?'

Mama, now looking very excited, piped up, 'The Peach Blossom Pavilion in *Si Malu*.'

Instead of answering Mama, the foreign devil turned to look at me for long moments, his eyes sparkling with kindness, then, without saying another word, walked away. The onlookers ejected a few disappointed curses before they quickly dispersed.

To be sure to keep our new hairstyles in good condition, Mama hired a car to take us back to the pavilion. All the way, the little boy's image kept flashing across my mind – his bloodless face, his emaciated body barely covered by his rags, the way he pathetically kowtowed when given a few coins. Suddenly I thought how lucky I was – housed, fed, clothed in Peach Blossom, for free! I must be living in paradise without knowing it.

I turned to Fang Rong and tried to lift the corners of my lips as high as the Heavenly Tune rooftop café. 'Mama, thank you very much.'

'Thank me by behaving like a good girl,' she grinned, patting my arm affectionately.

Then she addressed the three of us. 'If you behave, you'll have all the nicest clothes, tastiest food, and prettiest hairdos in the world. But if you don't, you'll all end up like that little hungry ghost robbing scraps on the street, and eventually being hit by a car. Do you want to be like that little bastard soon to be smashed into ground beef?'

'No!' we roared collectively.

'Will you behave?!'

'Yes!' Our high-pitched voices slashed the air, while Mama grinned mysteriously, her face shadowed by the shade of the rickshaw.

7

The Jade Stalk and the Golden Gate

The next day when I woke up in the morning, I felt both happy and sad – happy because of my good life in Peach Blossom, sad because of my recollection of the little boy. His hollow cheeks and protruding eyes clung to my mind like snails. Then I also remembered the foreign devil, and the gaze of his pale blue eyes.

I took out my *pipa* and absent-mindedly started to play; my ears filled with the sweet murmurs of the instrument. Then in a moment, tears flooded my eyes. They ran down my cheeks and rained onto the *pipa* until it seemed to stare back at me with a tear-streaked face. I rocked it against my chest, imagining it to be my little sister who'd faithfully absorbed all my thoughts, feelings, and sadness.

'Ma and Baba,' I said to the *pipa*, 'I miss you both. Wherever you are now, don't worry about me. I promise you I'll take very good care of myself. And believe me, I'll be famous someday, very famous!'

While I was indulging in my monologue, suddenly I heard noises from outside the door. 'Guigui? Come!'

Barely had I finished my sentence when the puppy plunged into my room. I put down the *pipa* and picked him up. He began to lick my face furiously.

'All right. Enough, you bad boy. Have you been a good baby today?'

Guigui tilted his fat head, then started to kowtow and shake hands with me.

'Good,' I smoothed his fur, 'I know you're a good baby. Are you hungry? You want some goodies?'

He performed more kowtows.

Just when I was about to take him to the kitchen, the bead curtain was swept aside and this time in burst Fang Rong, balancing a big, steaming bowl on a tray between her hands. Her body, held in by her green silk gown, looked like swollen pork dumplings wrapped in greasy lotus leaves. When she moved, the rolls of fat seemed to be starting a revolution under her dress. Her bottom was just the right size for four sisters to play mahjong on. I almost chuckled at the sight.

Mama cast both me and Guigui a dirty look. 'Xiang Xiang, take that dog outside!'

'But Mama—'

'I said take him outside. Or you want me to kick him out?'

I tried to shoo Guigui out, but he protested by thrusting his body against my legs.

Mama yelled. 'Just push him out!'

Reluctantly I did.

'Now close the door and come sit down.'

After I took my seat, she glanced at my *pipa* and said, making a great effort to soften her voice, 'Xiang Xiang, stop practising for a while and have some tonic soup.'

I was surprised. It was always I who begged her to give me a break from practising the arts. She'd never spared me from labouring, let alone brought me soup.

'Why?' I asked.

'Why? To celebrate your great day, silly girl.'

Carefully, she put the tray on the table, then swiftly pulled out a chair. After her big bottom had ensconced itself comfortably, Fang Rong squeezed a huge grin. 'You'll soon find out why. Now don't ask any more questions. Drink this special soup while it's still hot. When it gets cold, it won't be nutritious any more.' She picked up the bowl and sloshed its contents under my nose. A rich aroma wafted into my nostrils. I took a tentative sip.

'It's very tasty, what kind?'

'Different herbs, lots of vinegar, and the best kind of black chicken. It took Ah Ping a whole day to cook it,' said Mama; the big grin never left her face.

She eyed me – like a mother examining her newborn to check for deformities – until I drained the last drop. Then she put the bowl back onto the tray, picked it up, and stepped out of the room. I felt warmth spreading all over my body. It must be the tonic soup taking its effect. But I knew there was a better reason – I was lucky to be living in Peach Blossom Pavilion!

Just then, to my surprise, Fang Rong burst into the room again, this time throwing several books down on the table. 'Ha,' she chuckled, 'see how absent-minded I was to have forgotten these? Now read them all to prepare yourself for your first guest.'

'What guest?' I asked, but Mama had already vanished like a whiff of smoke.

I scanned the titles – *Variegated Patterns of the Flowery War; Secret Prescriptions for the Jade Chamber; The Plain Girl's Classic; Romance of Genuine Cultivation* . . .

I picked up one of them, flipped the pages, and ran into this:

When a man and a woman are making love for the first time, their bodies touch and their lips press against each other's. The man sucks the woman's lower lip and the woman sucks the man's upper one. When sucking, they savour each other's saliva . . . Then a thousand charms will spread and a hundred sorrows resolve. Now the woman's left hand should hold the man's jade stalk. The man will use his right hand to caress the woman's jade gate. Thus the man will feel the *yin* energy and his jade stalk will be stirred. It thrusts high toward heaven, like a lonely peak towering toward the milky way. The woman feels the *yang* energy and her cinnabar crevice will become moist with the liquid flowing downward, like a river coursing from a deep valley. It is now that coupling can take place . . .

They savoured each other's saliva? *Aii-ya!* With morbid fascination, I continued to read:

> Thrusts, be they deep, shallow, slow, quick, straight, slant, east, west, are all based on different presumptions. Each has its own idiosyncrasies. The slow thrust is similar to a carp caught by a hook. A quick thrust is similar to birds flying against the wind . . .

Ha! These thrusts had certainly no comparison with those Baba had demonstrated in martial arts for defence. If someone attacked, what would happen to him if he thrust like 'a carp caught by a hook'?

Just when I was on the verge of bursting out laughing at these absurd expressions, the phrase 'nine ways of moving the jade stalk' caught my attention:

> It dives in and pulls out, like seagulls playing with waves . . .
> It plunges quickly or pokes hard, like a frightened mouse scurrying back into its burrow . . .

Then the 'six ways of penetration' forced themselves on my eyes:

> First, the jade stalk pushes down, then moves back and forth resembling a saw, like prying open an oyster to get the shiny pearl . . .

Puzzled and distressed, I slapped the book shut and let out a heavy sigh. Pearl had told me Mama would give me books to read. But I'd never imagined they would be so strange, filled with words like *jade stalk, jade gate,* yang *peak, cinnabar crevice.*

I looked at the cover: *The Art of Love,* written by someone calling himself Master Dong Xuanzi, meaning Mysterious Hole. *The Art of Love*, by Mysterious Hole, I kept savouring the strange syllables in my mouth, as if by so doing I'd be enlightened to the profoundest mystery of the wind and moon domain.

But now my mind felt like a clear sky ambushed by dark clouds.

I felt blood coursing inside me. My face was hot and my mouth dry. I grabbed the books and ran all the way to Pearl's room, only to find it empty. I hurried here and there but couldn't catch a glimpse of her shadow, nor a whiff of her perfume. In the corridor leading to the garden, I was still thinking of all the strange things I'd just read when suddenly I bumped into soft flesh. I looked up and caught Fang Rong's ominous gaze.

'Xiang Xiang!' she chided. 'Where were you? I've been looking for you all over. Come!' She led me back to my room, shoved me in, and slammed shut the door.

'Have you studied the books and the classic?' she asked in a heated whisper.

I chuckled. 'Mama, there are only five classics, the *Spring and Autumn Annals*, the *Book of Songs*, the *Book of Changes*, the—'

'All right, enough. Stop that silly bragging of yours! And wipe that complacent smile off your face! You know what? I don't care about the *Book of Changes*, I only care if my daughters can bring me lots of change! You understand?'

'But Mama, how can one bring in money by reading *The Plain Girl's Classic*?'

Now Fang Rong searched me, her eyes darting around like shooting marbles. 'Ha ha, Xiang Xiang, you are, after all, not as smart as you look!' Then she leant toward me and lowered her voice, as if to confide in me the deepest secret of the universe. 'You know what's the most precious thing about you?'

'My talent in the arts.' I wanted to add 'and my beauty' but decided to be modest.

Mama winked. 'No! Your virginity, silly girl.' She cast me a penetrating look. 'Xiang Xiang, you've never been touched by a man, have you?'

'Yes, I have.'

Now Fang Rong's small eyes suddenly rounded into two fireballs. She gripped my blouse, choking me. 'You little whore, who?'

'My baba.'

'Oh damn!' She let go of me, then wielded an accusing finger. 'You wicked slut, you fucked your own father!' Now her voice cracked like thunder. 'When you slept with him, did he touch your golden gate? Did he insert his jade stalk into your cinnabar crevice?'

'Mama, I was just about to ask you all about golden gate and cinnabar crevice and . . .'

All the tensed muscles on Mama's face seemed to relax. 'But you told me your father slept with you, so you're sure he didn't do anything to you?'

'Of course he did. He pulled the blanket for me. He told me stories—'

'Ha! That's all he did to you?'

'Yes. When I was little, I was so frightened of ghosts that I cried and cried unless Baba came and slept with me.'

'Where was your mother?'

'She went to work.'

'At night? So she was a whore like you?'

'No! It was right after Baba had broken his leg.' I blushed, stuttering, 'She had to work as a . . . a . . . night fragrance collector to pay for his hospital bills.'

Mama flung back her fat head and roared into such delirious laughter that it seemed as if all her laugh meridians had been suddenly struck open by lightning. 'Ha! Ha! Ha! Ha! Xiang Xiang, you scared the pee out of me by telling how your father slept with you while your mother collected shit!'

I felt so angry and humiliated that I couldn't utter a word.

Now she kept laughing like a lunatic chased by a drunk. Waiting until she'd finally calmed down, I changed the subject. 'Mama, you still haven't told me what is jade stalk, golden gate—'

'You have no idea what these mean? But hasn't Pearl explained all this to you a long time ago?'

'No.'

Mama widened her eyes. 'That bitch! She didn't? You stupid little whore, you'll soon have your petals opened by a man and you have no idea what a jade stalk or a golden gate is? Even if Pearl hasn't taught you, didn't the other sisters mention any of this to you? Eh?'

'But Mama, I have no time to talk with the other sisters! I have to practice my arts the whole day every day, and do errands for you!'

'All right, all right, enough of your nonsense. Anyway, you'll soon find out.'

'How?'

'When you lose your virginity. Many men will be happy to pay many pieces of gold for it. When men have sex with pretty young virgins, their jade stalks will be maddeningly stirred.' She cocked an eye at me. 'After that, they will be rejuvenated and have great longevity. Some men get rich, while others get official posts. Even their bad luck will be reversed.'

I said nothing; Mama went on, now smiling dreamily, 'Big Master Fung has already won the auction to be your *datou ke*.' She pointed to the mole between her brows. 'My third eye told me a long time ago that he'd surely win.'

'What auction and who's *datou ke* and Big Master Fung?'

She chuckled. 'Ah, Xiang Xiang, you think you're smart but you're actually pretty stupid. *Datou ke* is the first man to collect *qi* from your *yin* part. These old men are desperate to collect youthful *yin* energy. If a man can have three hundred virgins, everything comes back – teeth, black hair, vitality.'

'*Wah*, then I'd also like to collect some *yin* energy when I grow old.'

Mama laughed, shivering the flesh on her face. 'Sure, Xiang Xiang. That's why from time to time some old lesbians will come to us asking for virgins.'

'Lesbians?'

Mama winked. 'They're called mirror-rubbing girls. Because to lose their souls, two women can only rub their mirror-flat *yin* parts against each other.'

'Losing their soul! You mean they die?'

'Xiang Xiang, I'm tired of your stupidity!' Mama yelled, then paused to smile mischievously. 'But I'm sure Big Master Fung won't be tired of you.'

'Who's Big Master Fung?'

'You've seen him at the party.'

'You mean that all-wrinkled-old-and-dying?'

'Xiang Xiang, watch out for your stinky mouth!' She cast me a dirty look; her mole moved menacingly between her eyes. 'He's already paid a huge amount for your first night. So you better make him happy. Otherwise . . .' She stamped her foot on the floor.

Now all my hair stood up on end. I could almost feel hundreds of slimy creatures crawling all over me, to be followed by the all-wrinkled Big Master Fung.

Mama grinned meaningfully. 'Xiang Xiang, smart as you are, which would you prefer, a swarm of slimy rats crawling on you or only *one* Big Master Fung?'

'One Big Master Fung, of course!'

'Good girl. Behave and you'll get what you want.' She patted my head, then counted her pudgy fingers. 'Nice clothes, good food, a new hairstyle, ice cream, and now Big Master Fung and his longevity wrinkles, ha! ha! ha!'

While one minute Mama almost choked herself breathless with her lunatic laugh, the next minute she abruptly stopped, casting me a blood-curdling glance. 'Xiang Xiang, now take off all your clothes!'

'What?'

'Have you suddenly turned deaf? I said take off all your clothes! Now!' She squinted at me with her ratlike eyes. 'Just do it! Or do you want me to strip you naked?'

I began to peel off my clothes.

Fang Rong walked around me, poking and pinching my body here and there as if she were choosing a piece of pork for dinner. After more squeezing and kneading, she nodded; a satisfied smile broke out on her face. 'Ha,' she muttered as if talking to herself, 'Big Master Fung must be a clairvoyant to pay so much for a thirteen-year-old.'

Just then the door swung open and in walked Wu Qiang. Instinctively I tried to snatch up my clothes to cover my nudity.

'Leave that on the floor! Now let your de examine you.'

I felt so humiliated that tears pooled in my eyes. My clothes fell on the floor and lay there like a crumpled human form.

Mama's voice roared next to my ear. 'What do you feel so embarrassed about? It's only your de. Haven't you just told me you slept with your own father? Now stand still and let your de look at you.'

Though I looked down at my toes so I didn't have to catch Wu

Qiang's penetrating glances, I could still feel his hungry eyes ravaging all over me. My body began to tremble. I swung my arms to wrap them around my chest.

Wu Qiang pulled my arms off. His voice was smooth while his eyeballs dropped to my nipples. 'Xiang Xiang, don't worry. Sooner or later, all young girls have to become young women.' His hand was warm on my bare shoulder. 'It's no use to play lady when you're going to be a whore.'

A smile broke out on Fang Rong's face. 'Wu Qiang, be gentle, she's just a little virgin.'

Now De split his lips to reveal white, uniform teeth. 'Yes, you're right, just a little virgin.' Seconds passed before he turned to Mama and said, still smiling, 'So, what do you think?'

Mama nodded appreciatively. 'Good, everything up to par – fine bones, smooth skin, tender flesh.'

De tousled my hair and added, 'Also soft, silky black hair.' Then he reached to touch my pubic hair. 'Soft and glossy here, too.'

Mama shot him a sharp look. 'I can see that myself.'

De nodded. 'Yes, of course, of course.'

There was a dead silence; then, under Mama's icy stare, De excused himself.

After he left, Mama said, 'Put your clothes back on.'

I did. Now the same pair of eyes cast me a meaningful glance. 'Xiang Xiang, you're an extremely desirable virgin except for one thing.'

'What is it?'

'That's it, too many questions! A virgin should be docile and gentle. Before you meet Big Master Fung, you better learn how to behave. Now go to Pearl and ask her how being nice and gentle to a jade stalk will bring you lots of money, let alone endless pleasures.' She winked. 'Pearl is an expert in the secrets of the bedchamber. Ha! Ha! Ha!' After that, she picked up the books, thrust them back into my arms, and gave me a push toward the door.

Pearl was preening in front of the mirror. After I closed the door, she stared at my hair and exclaimed, 'Xiang Xiang, you look very pretty!' She patted the chair next to her. 'Come sit by me.'

A long silence passed during which she was staring at my hair in the mirror.

'Sister Pearl, don't you like my new hairstyle?'

Pearl didn't answer my question; her expression turned sad and serious. 'Did Mama also buy you ice cream, feed you with soup, then show you those strange books?'

I nodded.

'Xiang Xiang, you're going to be fucked by a man!'

'No, I'm not!'

'*Hai,* my little sister, why do you think they've been treating you like a princess?'

'I think because . . . because I'm just lucky.'

'Lucky, eh?' She sneered. 'If there's luck in this whorehouse, then we'd all be princesses, not prostitutes. But too bad, because you're going to be a *real* whore, you understand? Do you want me to draw out the entrails for you?'

Silence dropped in the room like a gutted corpse.

'And this,' she snatched the books from my arms and threw them on the table, 'is to prepare you to change from a virgin to a woman;' she paused to cast me a bitter glance, 'or from a virtuous woman to a wicked whore.'

She picked up one of the books and flipped through the pages with the illustrations. 'If you study all these positions thoroughly and master them, they'll help you to become prestigious, so prestigious that men will pay several silver coins just to sniff the fragrance wafting from your body, and lots of gold ones to taste it!'

I gasped for air, reluctant to face the ugly truth that I'd been so stubbornly avoiding.

'Xiang Xiang.' Pearl patted my head. 'It's no use to worry too much, just learn it, all right? I'm right here to help you.'

I nodded, squeezing out a bitter smile.

'Good. We'll start the lesson now.' She winked. 'There's a saying "Die under a peony grove and be a licentious ghost," meaning a woman can make a man so happy that he doesn't mind dying while having sex with her.'

I was silent, trying to absorb what she'd said.

Then she began to explain to me words like *red pearl, lute strings*, *slippery noodles*, and all the strange metaphors such as chopping open the melon and tasting its juice; the jade stalk delving into the golden gate; *yin* juices flowing like a well . . .

By the end of the lesson, I was in awe of Pearl's deep knowledge of these abstruse matters but completely exhausted.

Suddenly Pearl exclaimed, 'Oh damn! Xiang Xiang, now I have to entertain a big shot. So why don't you go study and come back to my room tomorrow?'

When I was at the door, she called to my back.

I turned and saw her sad face.

'Xiang Xiang, I like you very much.' She paused, then said, 'You better grasp your last chance to enjoy your girlhood—'

I didn't know how to respond.

'Now why don't you go and have fun with Spring Moon?'

'But if Mama knows, she will—'

'Don't worry, since I'm sure Big Master Fung has already paid a lot for you, she'll be in a good mood and won't be too harsh on you. Go and have fun in the garden near the temple.'

But I'd heard that garden was haunted by some ill-fated sisters who'd committed suicide! Of course, no one dared to ask Mama whether it was true or not. But when I turned back to ask Pearl, she'd already shut the door.

8

The Haunted Garden

I pushed open the door to Spring Moon's room and stepped in-side. She was sitting on her bed, which was strewn with several books that looked familiar to me. She shifted her body and patted the empty space next to her. 'Xiang Xiang, come sit down.'

I sat, then gestured to the books. 'You understand all of them?'

'Of course I do, Xiang Xiang.' She looked at me curiously. 'You mean you don't?'

'Only some, but then Sister Pearl explained everything to me.'

I went over in my mind the things that Pearl had told me. Clouds and rain on the Wu Mountain means coupling between a man and a woman. Rain comes from the man's *yang* part, and clouds come out of the woman's *yin* part. During coupling, a man's jade stalk (I used to call it 'little chick' but Pearl said that refers only to a child's) will insert into a woman's precious gate. After that, the man will spill out a slimy liquid (it sounded to me like a form of concen-trated pee mixed with milk, but Pearl insisted that they were com-pletely different) into the woman's body so that she'll make a baby – but that only worked for women outside the turquoise pavilion; flower girls here were not allowed to have babies. That was why Mama made me drink that tonic – or toxic as Pearl called it – soup.

But Spring Moon already knew everything. I asked, 'How did you find out about all this?'

Her expression turned sad. 'From my fiancé. Yuguan is a very handsome man and a very good lover. He would do anything to please me. Anything at all.'

'You mean like sucking your tongue, savouring your saliva, biting your ear, and letting his tall peak play around your jade gate?' I got out in one breath.

I couldn't believe that she actually nodded.

'*Aii-ya*, Spring Moon, don't you find these sickening?'

She blushed, yet her voice turned vehement. 'No, of course not! They are the most pleasurable things in the world!'

Judging from her vehemence, there might be some truth to what she'd said, but somehow I had to deny it. 'No, it's sickening,' I spat, 'and perverse!'

'Then your parents did sickening and perverse things, too.'

My ears on fire, I felt obliged to defend my parents' honour. 'No, they did not!'

'If they didn't, then what do you think you came from? Unless you didn't crawl out of your mother, but burst from a stone, or were picked up from a rubbish bin.'

This was exactly what Little Red had said.

As I was struggling to think of a clever reply, images of my parents flashed through my mind. On the Wu Mountain, my quiet, demure mother and my scholarly, elegant father were passionately sucking each other's tongue, tasting each other's saliva, and then . . . that stalk of my father's was nearing that crevice of my mother's.

While my whole body felt hot, another image forced itself into my mind – I, a baby, without a single thread on my semened and secretioned bloody body, crawling out from that valley of my mother – like a crab scurrying out from a crevice. Instantly my parents picked me up and huge grins broke out on their faces. I had never seen them look happier.

Spring Moon's voice woke me from my reverie. 'Xiang Xiang, what are you thinking about?'

Now I felt like a punctured frog. 'Maybe you're right after all.' A silence, then I asked, 'Where's your fiancé now?'

'I heard that he is engaged to someone else. He comes from a respectable scholarly family, but they're very poor. So I don't think he has the money to pay my debt to leave Peach Blossom. And even if he did, how could he disgrace his family by bringing a flower girl into its household?'

Seeing that she was on the edge of crying, I hastily said, 'It's too hot here, so let's go out!'

Spring Moon remained silent while twisting her handkerchief. Then she changed the subject. 'Xiang Xiang, has Mama told you who is going to chop open your melon?'

'I think it's the old and all-wrinkled Big Master Fung.' I made a face. 'What about you?'

'There's some rich businessman . . . anyway, I'll find out next week. Mama said he wanted me the moment he saw my feet.'

I looked down – Spring Moon did have the tiniest feet of all the sisters in the pavilion. Pearl had told me some customers liked to kiss, even suck their women's feet. And the smaller the feet, the more desirable, since these perverse *chou nanren* could stuff the whole 'three inches golden lily' into their mouth to savour its taste.

'*Aii-ya!*' I spat.

'Something wrong, Xiang Xiang?'

'Oh no.' I quickly changed the subject. 'But I thought you're not a . . . virgin anymore.'

'But I am.'

'Then what about all those things you did with your fiancé?'

Spring Moon blushed. 'His jade stalk never entered my jade gate. He mostly used his other stalk.'

I nodded knowingly, although I had no idea what 'his other stalk' was. Since I felt too intimidated to further inquire, I asked instead, 'Spring Moon, why don't we go out now?'

'But we can't leave this place without Mama's permission.'

'We can go to that old temple in the garden. Since no one goes there, no one will see us there.'

'Because it's haunted! One time they stripped a sister naked, then hung her upside down and whipped her thirty times till her bottom rotted. Then they cut her down and left her in the garden.

The next day Mama found her body, in a red dress, dangling over the altar in the temple.'

'But you told me she'd been stripped naked.'

'Mama didn't whip her to death. The sister was so humiliated that she committed suicide.' Now Spring Moon lowered her voice as if there were an invisible third party in the room. 'People said she deliberately wore a crimson outfit on her way to the Yellow Springs to see the King of Hell so she'd return as a bloodthirsty ghost!'

My heart began to pound. Spring Moon went on, 'Another time when a sister was pregnant by her secret lover, she went and jumped into the garden's well. I heard Mama felt very sorry when she died.'

'Was Mama specially fond of her?'

'No. But because right after she died, a customer came and asked for a pregnant sister.' Spring Moon lowered her voice. 'Over the years at least three sisters have ended their lives there.'

'But Sister Pearl told me that since Mama can't bear to lose her investments, she won't let the sisters die.'

'Exactly. That's why they killed themselves – to spite her.'

A long, ghostly silence fell in the room. Finally I spoke. 'I don't think there are any ghosts anyway.'

'Xiang Xiang, you must be really out of your mind!'

'Spring Moon, don't be a coward. Let's go!'

'Then what if there really are ghosts?'

'Then I'll protect you. I know kung fu.' I shot up from the bed and did a high kick.

The moon was luminous and the stars burned glittering holes in the sky. Spring Moon and I held hands as we inched cautiously along the meandering path through the bamboo groves. The night noises of the pavilion – chatting, singing, laughing, *pipa* playing – receded as we walked deeper and deeper into the heavy-foliaged alley leading to the haunted garden. After fifteen minutes, all we could hear were cries of insects, the rustling of leaves, and faint, mysterious sounds. The moon was half-veiled by bands of clouds –

like wisps of long hair streaking the face of a woman ghost. The air was hot like Mama's tonic soup; I felt Spring Moon's palm sweating in mine.

'Xiang Xiang,' her voice came out as a whisper, 'I'm scared; why don't we go back?'

'Too late now.'

'Xiang Xiang! I thought you knew your way!'

'No, I've never been here. I only heard about it from Pearl and the other sisters.'

'Xiang Xiang, take me back, right now!'

'But Spring Moon,' I lied, 'you can't turn back midway.'

'Why not?'

I racked my brain for a good reason. 'Because . . . because I was told those who'd turned back all died a mysterious death. Once you're on the way, you have to follow the *qi* leading you to the garden. You can't walk back against the *qi*.'

'Oh heaven, then what are we going to do?'

'Go to the garden first before we decide.'

We continued to walk in a silence as heavy as our hearts. Now Spring Moon held my arm so tightly that her fingernails cut into my flesh. But I didn't dare utter the slightest complaint. The path was moist, smelling of a mixture of fresh and rotting vegetation. From time to time, we had to sweep aside overgrown branches and leaves. My five senses were achingly aware of the lightest sound, smell, and movement. I could hear Spring Moon's heavy breathing punctuating the dense night air.

'Xiang Xiang,' finally Spring Moon broke the silence, 'you really don't think there are ghosts?'

'Maybe there are; I don't know.'

Her voice trembled a little. 'What about if we do run into one?'

'Since there's no turning back, we can only face it and maybe even ask, "How are you, pretty ghost, should we sit down to have a cup of tea and chat?" '

Several beats passed before we burst into nervous laughter.

'I like you, Xiang Xiang. Not only that you're so pretty, you're funny.'

Before I had a chance to reply, I noticed we'd already reached an opening. 'Spring Moon, look, we've made it.'

The underbrush opened to a level field flooded with silvery moonlight. In the distance rose a small temple with upturned eaves from which dangled two big, unlit lanterns. Swaying in the breeze, they peered through the foliage like the blinking of two sightless eyes. In front of the temple gate, leaves of ancient trees rustled like someone whispering, or crying, desperately trying to tell a woeful tale.

I felt my elbow nudged. 'Xiang Xiang, what's glittering on the ground?'

'I don't know. Let's go and take a look,' I said, pulling Spring Moon forward.

To my surprise, the glitterings were reflections of the moon in puddles.

Spring Moon danced around, chanting. 'How wonderful, moon in a puddle.' Then she screamed, startling me. 'Xiang Xiang, what's that?'

I followed her finger and saw clusters of light floating here and there. A silence, then I said, 'Don't worry; they're fireflies.' But I didn't go on to explain that I'd been told the favourite places for fireflies were cemeteries. My breath was chilled as I exhaled.

Spring Moon now looked up to gaze at the heavenly disc. Long moments passed before she asked, 'Xiang Xiang, do you remember that poem about the moon—'

I gazed at the moon and recited, 'One moon is reflected on all the waters, all waters are embraced by one moon.'

'I like that. I like you, too, Xiang Xiang; you're so smart. Oh, I'm so happy here.'

'Me, too,' I responded, 'I feel free here. No Mama, no De, no dark room, no favoured guests—'

'But also no food, no fragrant tea. Oh, I'm starving.' She put her hand on her belly. 'And I have to pee.'

'Me, too,' I said, then an idea hit me, 'Spring Moon, let's pee on the moon.'

She chuckled.

I said in a singsong tone, 'I'm Chang E, regretting swallowing the elixir I stole from my husband; I flew to the moon . . .'

'Stop that, Xiang Xiang, you're not Chang E; you can't pee on the moon!'

I walked to one of the puddles, squatted down, pulled down my pants, and peed on the reflection of the moon. When I finished, I cocked an eye at Spring Moon. 'See?'

She chased and hit me with her fist. 'You cunning fox! I should have thought of that first!'

I was running and panting. 'But you didn't!'

Finally we reached the temple.

'All right, Spring Moon,' I said, 'now tell me about you and your fiancé.'

Spring Moon pressed her finger tightly against her lips. 'Shhhh . . . Xiang Xiang, do you hear something?'

I strained my ears to listen. 'It's just the wind.'

'No, listen more carefully.'

'Some cats crying?'

'No.'

'Oh, maybe it's the ghost of that sister who hung herself after she'd been stripped naked and whipped till her bottom rotted! Listen, it's screaming like she's being slashed!'

'But Xiang Xiang, if a ghost is dead, how can it scream?'

'From a nightmare, I guess.'

'Do ghosts dream?'

'How do I know? I'm not dead yet!'

'Oh,' Spring Moon nudged me harder, while still whispering, 'Listen, Xiang Xiang, now the ghost moans, and gasps.'

'Then this one must be a hungry ghost!'

To my surprise, now Spring Moon giggled, 'I think maybe it's not a ghost, but someone's stirring up the clouds and the rain.'

'But this is not the Wu Mountain.'

Spring Moon took my hand. 'Don't be silly. Now let's go and take a look.'

'You're not afraid of ghosts anymore?'

'Shhh, be quiet. I'm sure it's not a ghost. Come, follow me.'

We walked around for a moment, then she pointed to a gap in the temple wall. Spring Moon stooped to walk in and I followed her. We felt our way along, trying very carefully not to bump into anything. After a while, it seemed we were getting closer to the source of the sound. Finally Spring Moon stopped by a doorway from which heavy sighs poured.

Feeling fear deep in my stomach, I squeezed her hand and whispered, 'Spring Moon, let's go back.'

I was both surprised and embarrassed that now she was the calm one. Again, when I was about to urge her to leave, she shot me a 'shut up' glance. Then she went up to one of the windows, licked her finger, poked a small hole through the rice paper covering the lattice, and peeked.

I whispered, 'Spring Moon, what is it?'

But she completely ignored me.

It couldn't possibly be a ghost that caused such great delight. So I also licked my finger, poked a hole in the rice paper, and looked.

To my surprise, a man and a woman, completely naked, lay together on the floor. The man was moving on top of the woman – sometimes like a fish caught on a hook, sometimes a bird flying against the wind – exactly as described in *The Art of Love* by Master Mysterious Hole. Now the woman seemed to be struggling under the man's pressure and thrusts. Although in the dark I couldn't clearly see her face, from her slaughtering-the-pig cry, I was sure she was in great pain. I had to press my hand tightly against my mouth to stop from exclaiming. Strangely enough, though frightened, I felt my heart beating faster, my ears and cheeks burning, and heat crawling up from between my legs. I nudged Spring Moon, but she kept waving a dismissive hand.

The wrestling and moaning went on and on until suddenly the man let out a sharp cry. After that, he went limp on the woman's body.

Oh, my heaven, he must have given up his soul!

I nudged Spring Moon, then placed my hand against my throat and made a slaughtering gesture. Again, she waved her hand impatiently. Now the man, as if awakening from a slumber, rolled over to lie beside the woman. The two were now facing each other, with the woman's back toward us. The man started to fondle her breasts very gently. The woman let out small moans but made no move to stop him.

Just then an insect – a butterfly I supposed – probably flew in from the window (the other one facing the courtyard), and began to hover above the couple. The woman instantly sat up and tried to catch the dancing creature. It was then that I saw her face.

I covered my mouth and tried very hard not to call out.

Pearl!

I turned to look at Spring Moon and found that she was doing the same with her mouth. Moments passed before she shoved me out of the corridor. When we'd finally groped our way out of the temple and found ourselves in the garden, we broke into a run.

When we were safely back in Spring Moon's room, she pointed to my trousers and said excitedly, 'Xiang Xiang, look, your trousers are wet.'

I turned, snatched up my trousers, and examined them. 'It's the dew.'

'Yes,' she chuckled, 'but the dew from your golden gate.'

9

The Art of Pleasing

One week later, five days before my 'big day,' Pearl invited me to go to her room for some last-minute advice on stirring the clouds and rain.

Once I sat down, she threw me a sharp glance. 'Xiang Xiang, you better be ready for your Big Master Fung when he comes to chop your melon. Don't screw up your first time, otherwise you'll be in big, big trouble. Not only will Mama and De punish you, so will Big Master Fung, since he's paid a lot.'

Pearl went on to tell me that if some customers were dissatisfied with the sister's service, they'd 'smash the cave' – wrecking the prostitution house – and the poor sister had to pay for all the losses.

Some silence, then I remembered the haunted garden and blushed deeply.

'What is it, Xiang Xiang?'

I felt as if a firefly were caught in my throat.

'Is there something you want to ask me?'

Finally I was able to manage, in a whisper, 'Sister Pearl, was . . . the man in the garden . . . Jiang Mou?'

She cocked an eye at me. 'Xiang Xiang, be careful what you say! No one can find out.'

I nodded. 'Did you let me and Spring Moon see you on purpose?'

She smiled, looking very mysterious under the yellowish light of her bejewelled lamp.

'So do you love Jiang Mou?' I took her silence as yes. 'Then why don't you marry him and leave Peach Blossom?'

'Because he's poor and he's already married.' Pearl sighed, her fingers caressing her luminous jade bracelet. 'Don't think about love, Xiang Xiang. Love never lasts; think about pleasure.'

'But that doesn't last either.'

'But unlike love, it won't bring pain afterwards.' She looked at the clock. 'We'd better start our lesson now.'

Pearl led me to sit beside her in front of the vanity table. 'Xiang Xiang,' she said, carefully studying our reflections in the mirror, 'now you know about the clouds and rain.'

I nodded.

She went on, 'The most important thing is to tease. Because if you let those *chou nanren* get there too quickly, they'll be disappointed. Remember, their wives all have the same cinnabar crevices as we do. But we have the art of coquetry to excite. You tease not only in how you look, but also in the ways you move, even when you're sleeping.'

'But Sister Pearl, sleeping has no movement!'

'But we feign sleep to seduce. Have you not heard of the phrase "crabapple sleeping in spring"? It means a beautiful woman sleeping seductively. And it's spring that makes all the difference—'

'Why?'

'Because spring is the season for lust, for the stirring of love!'

With a dreamy expression, Pearl slightly parted her lips, then the delicate tip of her tongue reached to touch her upper lip – like a rosebud emerging from a deep hole. 'We sisters are like good cooks who mix the five flavours harmoniously into a delicious soup.'

'I like soup.'

'Xiang Xiang, you don't know; do you? Before you came to Peach Blossom, all you did was study. Not much use for you now, is it?'

I said dreamily, 'My parents always wanted me to be the first woman *zhuang yuan*.' Number One Scholar.

Pearl stared at me pityingly, then spoke again, a little sharply, 'I'm also teaching you to be the Number One Scholar of charming those *chou nanren*. Have you forgotten that your "examination" is coming next week with Big Master Fung?'

She went on, 'A woman's most fascinating feature is her eyes.' Pearl lowered her eyelids and peeked down at me. Her pupils, looking glazed, slowly moved around as if she were drunk. Her eyes possessed a kind of magnetism that pulled me toward her like her lover clinging to her body. I felt colour rising to my cheeks.

'Xiang Xiang, you told me your baba taught you kung fu?'

I nodded.

'So think about your eyes as weapons for sexual kung fu. Attack like a tiger and retreat like a virgin.'

While I was trying to digest this recipe for sexual kung fu, Pearl was speaking again, 'Always look exciting. The worst is spiritless eyes they are like fish left out of water for days.'

I giggled.

She gave me a chiding look. 'Xiang Xiang, you have to gaze at your customers until they feel their bones are pickled in vinegar, until they are so numbed that they have no power left to resist you. Of course, if a customer likes modest women, then you'd pretend to be shy, breaking away your gaze from time to time. That's why in Peking opera . . . Xiang Xiang, are you paying attention?'

'Baba!' I burst into tears and ran from Pearl's room.

The next afternoon when I went to visit Pearl, she said nothing about my abrupt departure the day before. We sipped the tea she poured and sat absorbed in our own thoughts. Was she also thinking about my baba? I'd always been curious to know what was inside Pearl's head. However, although she was very nice to me, she still remained as mysterious as the halo behind Guan Yin's head.

Pearl seemed in no mood to be the teacher today. She nursed her cup for long moments before she stood up from the sofa. 'Today I better teach you how to walk. Remember, never rush, but move leisurely, like this.' She began to pace, her steps delicate and small. 'This is called "shredded steps of the golden lotus." Try to picture lotuses blossoming under your feet, or bending with the wind in the golden twilight.'

I closed my eyes and tried. But what flashed across my mind was my baba, my mother, and I rowing a boat on the West Lake covered with lotuses. Mother, looking very pretty and happy, bent her slender torso and, with her delicate fingers, reached to spread the leaves. Baba picked one of the flowers and pinned it on her hair dyed gold by the twilight . . .

Now Pearl went to rest by a wall. 'When you stand, your body should be slightly slanted – but not stooped – as if drawn to something. Moreover, it should also be in constant motion – your backside swaying, your fingers twisting a handkerchief, your fingertips stroking your teeth, your eyes darting around.'

I blurted out, 'Sister Pearl, I'm confused. My mother used to teach me just the opposite. She warned me never to sway my body, for it's very unladylike. She liked to quote the saying "A swaying tree has fallen leaves; a swaying woman has an ill fate." '

Pearl sighed heavily. 'Yes, your mother was right. But now we're no ladies, but whores.'

A long, sorrowful silence.

She stared at my feet. 'Xiang Xiang, your feet are the only flaw of your whole body; they're a little big.'

I immediately slid them under the table.

'Good, always hide your flaw. But never forget to show off your good features. So if someone has a really nice figure,' Pearl thrust out her chest, 'like me, then I always lean forward. This is called "offering the body to preach the Dharma." ' Pearl pinched my cheek. 'Xiang Xiang, sex is our only power over men. Even when you have sex with the ugliest, one-of-his-feet-already-inside-the-coffin customer, try your best to act as if he were the only man left under heaven. Remember what I teach you and you'll enjoy your *ming ji* status until the day you die.'

I nodded emphatically.

She came back to sit down by my side. 'Xiang Xiang, have you noticed in our country, nothing expresses itself directly, but always in a meandering way?'

I tried to respond, but Pearl waved me into silence. 'In China, corridors are not built in a straight line but always winding.' She glanced outside the window. 'So when we walk along, we're always in suspense about what we'll run into: a moon-shaped gate inside which are nestled clumps of bamboo, or a tiny gourd-shaped opening through which your eyes can discern a distant mountain shrouded in the mist.'

When I was reflecting on this, Pearl went to take out the *qin* and put it on the table. I went to sit opposite her, my heart instantly filled with joy.

'See, Xiang Xiang,' she said, beginning to play, '*qin* music meanders, too.'

Now Pearl glided her fingers on the instrument. 'This fingering is called "the cicada calling for autumn." When the cicada flutters its wings, it makes a lingering tone.' She stroked the strings again. 'And this lingering tone is "the monkey climbing up a tree," because a monkey climbing a tree alternates between halting and ascending.'

Finally she stopped the strings with her hand. 'Because of its meandering melodies, when the playing is over, *qin* music continues to reverberate in your heart . . . If only we could make the same impression on men's hearts.' An insinuating smile played on her lips. 'Then all the stinking males will pour the money from their fat pockets into ours. Otherwise why not just stay home and fuck their wives, which is free?'

I giggled, although I had no idea how a man would feel when fucking his wife.

Pearl cast me a chiding look. 'You know, Xiang Xiang, although we sisters are looked down upon by those *decent* women, don't you know they also envy us?'

'I can see that, Sister Pearl, because you're so much more beautiful than them and have all these pretty clothes and jewellery.'

'Xiang Xiang, what you said is true, but there's more to it. These decent women secretly admire us. For we can display our feminine beauty to our heart's content without rebuke from stodgy Confucian husbands. Besides, you know the proverb, "To be virtuous, a woman should have no talent in anything." But we're not virtuous so we can cultivate and display our accomplishments. Men need wives to give them children but they also need us to do what their yellow-faced old ladies can't – stir their hearts, tease their senses, and nourish their souls with our music, dance, and painting. Maybe we're despised, but we don't need to play stupid like those wives they leave at home.'

Now her expression turned mischievous. 'I can act horny and stir up the clouds and rain with any man I want while those women are stuck with one, even after he's dead!' When she finished, she burst into cheerful laughter as if she was truly happy to be a prostitute.

I joined her in laughing. We kept giggling until tears spilled from our eyes and we had to stop to catch our breath.

When we finally calmed down, Pearl waved her jade-bangled hand. 'Now you can take a break.'

Feeling restless, I thought I might go out into the courtyard. But it was raining, so I peered through the lattice at the raindrops hitting the leaves. After a few minutes when the rain stopped, I went out and strolled along the courtyard to appreciate its winding path. Then I sat down on a stone bench inside the small pavilion and looked through a vase-shaped opening, hoping to see a distant mountain shrouded in the mist.

Then I felt hungry and headed to the kitchen. When I stepped over the threshold, a rich aroma wafted into my nostrils. Ah Ping was not in sight. Now, my stomach suddenly ambushed by pangs of hunger, I went up to the boiling cauldron, ladled its content onto a plate, and helped myself to the delicacies.

When I was devouring noisily, Ah Ping came in.

I looked up at her. 'Aunty Ah Ping, this is delicious. Is it a new dish?'

To my surprise, her face turned white.

'Something wrong?'

She didn't reply, but kept shaking her head.

I teased her. 'It must be something really good reserved for a special guest, right? But don't worry, I only took a bite. It's really tasty, so what is it?'

Still ignoring my question, she went up to the basin and began to clean.

I continued to eat for a while before a thought entered my mind. 'Do you see Guigui? I want to share with him some of these goodies.'

Ah Ping avoided my eyes, pointing to the plate in front of me, then my stomach.

'But where's Guigui?'

She pointed again, this time more emphatically.

It took a few seconds before the bomb exploded. 'You mean . . .'

She kept nodding and wiping the pots. Then she poured from a huge pot into the basin. The kitchen was instantly filled with the sound of splashing water.

Tears streamed down my cheeks. 'You cooked Guigui?!'

She was still nodding and wiping the pots.

'Oh, how could you do that? You're disgusting!'

Now she was noisily banging the pots around.

'Oh my heaven, you cooked Guigui and I ate him!'

I dashed out of the kitchen and vomited until there was nothing left in my stomach except bile. Then I cried my heart out. 'Oh, Guigui, I'm so sorry. How could I have known she'd cooked you? I didn't know it was you!'

When I finally stopped, I took off my Guan Yin pendant and muttered a long prayer. First I asked for the puppy's forgiveness, then I pleaded with the goddess to send him to the Western Paradise, where he could soon be reborn as a human and reunite with me.

Finally calmed by my prayers, I dragged my feet back to Pearl's room. Once I sat down next to her on the sofa, I burst out crying. 'Sister Pearl . . .'

'Something wrong, Xiang Xiang?'

My grief poured out.

Pearl pulled out her handkerchief and wiped my face. 'Please tell me what's wrong.'

'Aunty Ah Ping cooked Guigui and I ate him!'

To my surprise, Pearl didn't look a bit shocked. She tousled my hair. 'I'm sorry. But why did you eat him?'

'Because I didn't know it was him!' I was mumbling between sobs.

'It's really no big deal.'

I looked up at her through my teary eyes. 'No big deal?'

'They often cook puppies here. Customers think dog makes excellent tonic soup to strengthen their jade stalk.'

'Oh heaven, it's disgusting. They're like babies!'

Pearl pulled me into her arms. 'Xiang Xiang, far worse things happen here.'

10

The Longevity Wrinkles

Four days later, when I was still feeling utterly miserable that poor little Guigui had ended up in my stomach, Little Red came and led me to Pearl's room. I knew the moment I'd been dreading was about to come. My heart sank; the soles of my slippers dragged and wailed on the floor.

Little Red half-pushed me along. 'Xiang Xiang, please hurry, today is your big day, and Mama is already getting impatient.'

'Mama.' I addressed the lump of flesh waiting for me across the threshold.

Fang Rong was all dressed up in a pink jacket with intricately knotted gold buttons the size of grapes. Upon seeing me, a huge grin broke out on her face. She motioned me to sit by Pearl's large, gilded dressing table. 'Xiang Xiang, today I'll dress you up as beautifully as a fairy,' she said, then gloated over me as if I'd suddenly transformed into a pillar of gold.

The table was covered with feminine objects: powder, rouge, lipstick, Flower Dew perfume, Snow Flower cream, tortoiseshell combs, a coral hairpin, three fresh flowers, and to my surprise, a gold bracelet and a pair of gold-mounted jade earrings.

In the mirror, Mama carefully studied me for long moments.

'You're lucky that your brows curve like crescent moons. Otherwise, I'd have to shave them, then pencil them in with ink.'

Ink? I wanted to ask but decided to keep my mouth shut.

Mama started to perform the *kai lian,* 'open the face,' for me. First she tied a red thread to her thumbs and middle fingers, then put it between her teeth. Then she started to 'saw' my face with the string, scraping off dirt and downy hair.

Fang Rong's face was so close to mine that I could count the hairs inside her wide nostrils, study the gold teeth inside her mouth, and inspect the coarse surface of her big mole. I tried to hold my breath so as not to be poisoned by hers.

'Xiang Xiang, opening your face will open you to endless good luck. You know that?'

I nodded.

'Keep your head still!'

So I froze until she finished scraping my face with the moist red thread. Next she applied powder on my face and neck – layers and layers until I couldn't help but ask, 'Mama, that's enough; why do you have to put on so much powder?'

'Because one shade of white can cover up one hundred uglinesses, and all men like it this way, that's why.' In the mirror, she cast me a chiding glance. 'You think I'd waste money on powder if men didn't like it?' Then she chuckled, shooting spittle onto my cheek. 'Fortunately, it was not me who paid for your make-up.'

'Then who did?'

'Big Master Fung, of course, who else? You little stupid!' She pointed to the dressing table. 'See this bracelet and earrings? They're all gifts from Big Master Fung. He wants you to be the prettiest little whore in Peach Blossom.' Now she cast me a threatening look. 'Big Master Fung has already spent several hundred large silver coins hosting expensive banquets and gambling parties here, so you better not let him down.'

When Mama and Little Red had finished making up my face and fixing my hair, they helped me to dress in a red silk jacket with green trousers, both embroidered with floral ribbons. Then Mama picked up the fresh orchids and pinned them in my hair.

I preened in front of the mirror. Was that girl looking curiously at the outside world from inside the glass really me? Or . . . was she just a delicate dish to be devoured?

Mama looked at my reflection and grinned till her mouth almost stretched outside her face. Even her mole looked happy. 'See what a beautiful princess you've become, Xiang Xiang. I bet no one will believe that you're but a whore, ha, ha, ha!' Then she raised her hands and stretched her pudgy fingers. 'Look, my old, arthritic hands can still work magic!' After that, she pulled me up and gave my shoulder a hard push. 'Now to the welcoming-guests hall!'

This was the first time I was properly invited into this place and for a moment I was stunned. I'd never seen a room so grand and richly decorated. The deeply polished furniture glowed like bronze mirrors. On top of a low brown chest stood a tall cloisonné vase filled with rose orchids. Their pink petals seemed to nod at me, while their branches twisted elegantly, like the cursive calligraphy demonstrated by Mr. Wu. Against one wall was a huge canopy bed, its pillars gleaming like gold bars. The red pillows were embroidered with Mandarin ducks cavorting in water. On the crimson bed sheet, the tails of a dragon and phoenix entwined intimately. Behind the bed was a long folding screen carved with scenes from the famous novel *Story of the West Chamber* – including one with the scholar playing a *qin*! Next to the bed was a gilded mirror and on the walls hung paintings, some of young beauties, others of faraway mountains. Fragrant plumes of incense wafted from a bronze burner.

In the middle of the room was an eight immortals table; on its round top precious objects had been arranged: a celadon bowl shaped like an opening lotus; a teapot and cups painted with golden peonies; black-lacquered trays spilling with candies and dried fruit. Beside the table on the floor were two many-layered boxes decorated with flowers and red ribbons.

Oh, how I wished that Baba were still alive and Mother in Shanghai so we could have all lived together happily in this beautiful room! But alas! My eyes landed on a heap of wrinkles – marring the beauty and shattering my dream. On a high table next to Old Wrinkles were a pair of red dragon and phoenix candles. Melted wax dripped like tears of blood while high, bright flames seemed to throw the heaps of wrinkles over the room like reptiles.

I instinctively drew back but Mama shoved me forward. 'Big Master Fung, here's your pretty Xiang Xiang.'

Fung's crease-buried eyes widened, searching over me like a pair of torches looking for gold. Suddenly he slapped his thigh and shouted, 'Good, very good!'

Mama chuckled flirtatiously. 'Good? Are you kidding, Big Master Fung? Xiang Xiang is the best!'

Fung caressed his stubble. 'The best? That I still have to find out, so now—'

'Yes, yes, of course, Big Master Fung, I'll leave you two alone. Enjoy your dragon and phoenix night; I guarantee you'll have your money's worth.'

'It'd better be true.' He paused to look around. 'So where's the cloth?'

I piped up. 'What cloth?'

Both the lump of flesh and the heap of wrinkles burst into laughter.

To my surprise, Mama yanked a white handkerchief from underneath the sleeve of my jacket. I had no idea when she'd hidden it there. She smiled mischievously, swinging the cloth. 'Big Master Fung, this is Xiang Xiang's *zhuang yuan* seal.'

Now I remembered that Pearl had told me about the cloth. *Zhuang yuan* was the Number One Scholar in the Imperial Examination, and the seal proving this title was red. So *zhuang yuan* seal referred to the imperial approval of the distinguished, Number One Scholar. Or in my case, my distinguished virginity.

I blinked back tears. Yes, I'd soon receive a prestigious seal! But not because I came out number one in the imperial examination, but because I would be the number one virgin *fucked* by an old man.

Now Old Wrinkles cast me a licentious glance. 'Xiang Xiang, your blood stains on the white cloth will prove that I'm the first man to chop open your melon. Otherwise you think I'd pay a fortune for a thirteen-year-old? Ha!' He pointed to the table and the two lacquer boxes. 'All the clothes, money, jewellery, food, wine are for you.'

The corners of Mama's lips lifted to her ears while her eyes threw me a sharp glance. 'Xiang Xiang, bow to Big Master Fung and thank him, quick!'

I made a deep bow and uttered a 'thank you.' Just then all of Pearl's teaching flashed across my mind. So I willed the corners of my lips to lift, while trying to aim a dazed glance to catch Fung's. But my eyes made a wrong move and landed instead on the wrinkles of his forehead.

Fung massaged his stubble. 'Come, my little beauty,' he said, reaching out his other hand to touch my face.

Mama winked to Fung, then me. 'Look at my baby Xiang Xiang, she's so beautiful that anyone would agree she's worth more than twelve hundred virgins put together, right, Big Master Fung?'

Fung burst into laughter. It surprised me that, though old and dried-up, he had a deep, resonant voice. Was it really the effect of all the virgins?

Mama chuckled, then threw a meaningful glance toward the candles on the altar. It was then that I understood the presence of the dragon and phoenix candles – a symbol of conjugal union! I felt queasiness simmering in my stomach. As well as Fung's hand practising the lingering tones on my thigh. It was then I also realised Mama had already gone, leaving me in the room with this heap of moving wrinkles.

Now all the wrinkles shifted toward me like tidal waves. 'Little Sweetie, now what are you going to do to please me?'

I shifted away from his stink of opium. 'What do you want?'

'What about a massage first?' He grabbed my hand and rubbed it against his.

Imagining that he'd soon take off his clothes and reveal more black spots and crumbling flesh, and even his jade stalk (probably looking nothing like jade but more like a rotten banana), I felt another wave of queasiness sloshing in my stomach. Oh Guan Yin, please help me get out of this room as quickly as possible!

As I was silently praying to the Goddess of Mercy hanging around my neck, a thought triggered. 'Big Master Fung.' I put up my best smile. 'What about if I entertain you first, then massage you later?'

Fung's many wrinkles seemed to be lifted. 'Entertainment? What kind?'

'What about singing?'

'If you have a good voice.' He picked up his gold-encrusted water pipe and started to inhale, making gurgling sounds. 'All right, go ahead.'

I took a deep breath, then sang an excerpt from a Peking opera aria. 'Banners are swaying outside the city gate. I lead the lion-like soldiers, swearing to protect my country!' I'd picked this one instead of something more . . . more romantic. Because, even in this beautiful room, I had no inkling of romantic feeling.

When I finished, Fung clapped enthusiastically.

I thought: Oh heaven, now what? Quick, think of something else!

Guan Yin must have again heard my prayer, for suddenly a new idea hit me. I squeezed another dimpled smile. 'Big Master Fung, I have something else to entertain you.'

'Something more? Hmmm . . . you little witch, you have a lot of tricks, eh? What is it?'

'Kung fu.'

He reached to pinch my cheek. 'Ha, kung fu? You flimsy little thing; you know kung fu?'

'Just the postures, I can't fight at all.'

He scanned me from head to toe and then back up from toe to head. 'Where did you learn it from? Not here, I don't think?'

'No, Big Master Fung, but from my father. He was a martial arts actor.'

I cast Fung a heroic glance – something which Pearl had not taught me – then performed a heaven-reaching-kick – stretching my leg as straight as a pole and as high as my head.

'Huh, not bad.' His eyes squeezed through the wrinkles to look at me incredulously.

Next I cleared off the eight immortals table, jumped on it, and did eight somersaults.

'*Hao!*' Fung yelled and clapped. 'You're really good, Xiang Xiang.'

I jumped back down from the table and held up my hands in a respectful gesture. 'Big Master Fung, you overpraise me. This skill is nothing in comparison to my father's; he could do one hundred and eight somersaults on the eight immortals table. No one can break this record, not since—' I stopped myself just in time not to reveal more about Baba.

Fung threw me a curious glance. 'Who's your father?'

'The most famous—' I quickly changed Baba's stage name from Rumbling Thunder to 'One Rumble of Thunder.'

Fung laughed. 'Ha! Of course, even though I'm not an opera fan, I've heard of your father. Only that I never thought that one day I'd collect *qi* from his precious little daughter's precious gate. Ha, what an unexpected bonus!'

Suddenly I remembered there *was* indeed an actor by the name of One Rumble of Thunder. But he'd been dead for some time. Relief washed over me.

Fung kept laughing so hard that I thought he might choke himself to death.

But he didn't. Unfortunately.

Instead, his eyes glowed like the pair of conjugal candles, and his lips sucked at the pipe like a baby's searching for a swollen nipple as he regarded me with a licentious glance.

I continued to strike out fists in all directions, then do a whirlwind of leg kicks and twists.

Now Lecherous-Old-and-Dying seemed to forget for a moment what he'd already paid for. He was busy in clapping and hollering, '*Hao! Hao!*'

Encouraged, I performed more feats. First I imitated the ferocious, head-chopping General Guan. Next I became the mischievous Monkey King, blinking and scratching incessantly. Then I turned into Na Zha, the little immortal. I ran around the room in quick, energetic steps (not those shredded golden lotus steps taught by Pearl), somersaulted, and swirled with only one leg. Finally I leaped up into the air then plopped down on the floor with my legs stretched in the shape of the Chinese character 'one.'

'*Hao! Hao!*' Big Master Fung shouted with his bell-like voice. 'All right, enough kung fu, now it's time for massage.'

Oh Merciful Guan Yin, please, don't make me touch those wrinkles, they look as if they'd crumple like soft mud under my fingers!

I put up a deeply dimpled smile, trying to delay my contact with rotting flesh as long as I possibly could. 'Big Master Fung, there's still another stunt that I haven't performed for you.'

'Still more? But Xiang Xiang,' he frowned, feigning upset, 'my muscles are aching all over!'

'Big Master Fung, just one more, you really have to see this. Please,' I grinned widely to show off my nice teeth, 'this is my consummate skill.'

'All right then, go ahead.'

I swallowed hard, took a deep breath, and jumped high, while swinging out one leg. Then, as I felt proud in hearing the air swish around me, also, to my alarm, I heard a sharp cry from Big Master Fung!

I landed on the floor with a heavy thump and looked. Alas, Big Master Fung was clutching his face, screaming like a cow being slaughtered. When he removed his hand, I saw his agonized face covered with a big red welt. As if this were not bad enough, a small trickle of blood was oozing from the corner of his mouth!

Now I was in big, big trouble. Either Big Master Fung or Mama was going to kill me, right away. But no, it would not be that easy, Mama would first throw me into the dark room to feed the rats, then, with Fung watching, she'd strip me naked, hang me upside down, and whip me till my flesh blossomed and my bones snapped apart. Before they killed me, they'd discuss which would be the best way – hanging me in the temple of the haunted garden, drowning me in the Huangpu River, chopping me into pieces, pouring petrol over my body then throwing me a lighted match . . . Or in order not to waste time, Big Master Fung would simply put a bullet through my head! Or in order not to waste the bullet, he'd just order his guard to strangle me with bare hands!

But of course he didn't do any of these. For he was now lying semi-conscious on the floor, gasping.

As I was thinking desperately of what to do, the door sprung open with a loud clang and in burst Fang Rong and Wu Qiang.

'Merciful Guan Yin!' they blurted out simultaneously. Then, in one synchronized motion, they swung their heads to face me.

'What did you do to Big Master Fung?!' Mama demanded in a murderous tone.

'I . . . I . . . didn't mean to hurt him. It was an accident . . .'

De plopped down to check on the crumpled flesh. 'Don't worry; he's still breathing evenly.'

Mama yelled at De, 'Get him some wine and medicinal oil, quick!'

De poured wine from the table and started to feed Big Master Fung with one hand, while his other hand vigorously rubbed Fung's temple.

Mama stepped close to me and asked in a heated whisper. 'Did you try to kill him?'

'No, I . . . I tried to . . . to please him.'

It surprised me that suddenly Mama's face glowed. 'You mean he liked to be tortured?' She grinned mischievously. 'Did he ask you to play the whipper and he the whipped,' she winked, 'you know, that kind of thing?'

I didn't know what she really meant, but I assumed, judging from her cheerful expression, I'd be spared from being whipped myself if I nodded. So I swung my head like a hammer on an anvil.

She pinched my face. 'Ah, you little slut. Did Pearl teach you this?'

I shook my head.

She looked at me appreciatively. 'So you've learnt all these by yourself without being taught, eh?'

I kept smiling and nodding like a lunatic.

Suddenly De yelled, 'Look!'

We turned and saw Big Master Fung opening his eyes.

De helped him to sit up.

Mama turned to stoop down beside him. A big grin broke on her face. 'Ah, Big Master Fung, you had a good time; didn't you?'

To all of our surprise, Big Master Fung lunged at her with full force. 'You . . . you . . . you should discipline your girls before you let them out to serve customers!'

Mama exclaimed, with the grin still stretching taut on her face. 'But Xiang Xiang told me you like it that way!'

'Like it that way, what are you talking about? You ugly old bitch!'

Mama cast me a murderous look.

Big Master Fung struggled to get up. After he steadied himself, he slapped Fang Rong's face, then Wu Qiang's, then did the same to mine. Before we had time to think what to do, he spat, then kicked over the table. Next he shattered the bowls, plates, vases. All the food, snacks, and wine splashed on the floor in myriad directions like scurrying mice. He picked up the phoenix candle and hurled it toward the mirror. The glass cracked and collapsed into a hundred shards glinting on the floor.

De whispered loudly to Mama, 'Oh heaven. He's smashing the cave.'

I felt a spider weaving an icy web along my spine.

Now Big Master Fung walked over to the burner. Seeing that he was about to kick it over and set the room on fire, Mama and De plopped down and frantically kowtowed. Seeing that I was still standing like a statue, Mama yanked me down and began to bounce my head on the floor as if she were pounding rice in the imperial kitchen.

'Oh merciful and generous Big Master Fung,' Mama pleaded with a voice spilling fear, 'please don't do this to us. We'll teach Xiang Xiang a good lesson. Please extinguish your angry fire!'

Without losing a bit, De added, 'She's just a child and doesn't know better. All she did was to try to please you.'

Now seizing the chance, I chimed in, 'Yes, Big Master Fung, please forgive me. I thought you liked it; you screamed that I was excellent and you acted so happy. It was just an accident.'

Mama gave out a tentative chuckle. 'Yes, so can't you just forgive the little girl and forget about the little accident?'

Seeing that Big Master Fung had calmed down a little, De pinched my hip while throwing me a meaningful glance. I immediately tugged at Big Master Fung's trousers. 'Big Master Fung, please forgive me and don't smash the cave!' I said, tears started to roll down my cheeks while I exaggerated the heaving of my shoulders.

Miraculously, those tears and heavings worked; now Fung's anger seemed to abate. He even lifted the corners of his lips to resemble a smile. 'Hmmm . . . let me think what I should do to this little naughty witch—'

De pleaded, 'Forgive her; just forgive—'

Mama chimed in, 'And forget, it's just a little girl's little mistake.'

I paraded kowtows with my head hitting loudly on the floor. 'Yes, Big Master Fung. I'm sure a generous man like you also has a generous heart, so forgive me, *please!* If not,' I took a deep breath, then blurted out in a girlish, high-pitched voice, 'my little bottom will be furiously blossomed, even right in the middle of this cool room!'

At hearing this, Big Master Fung finally burst into laughter. We all felt relieved. De swiftly stood up to pour tea for him – a gesture of respect and apology. Mama flipped open her fan and fanned him vigorously – a gesture to please and flatter. She winked to me and I immediately knelt down beside him to massage his legs.

Big Master Fung sat and smiled superciliously like an emperor being served by his fat maid, suave eunuch, and flirtatious concubine.

This went on for a long time before Fung's anger had completely dissipated.

When he finally took leave, he said, 'I'm too tired today and I need some balm for my bruises. Anyway, I'll come back.' He turned to scan us. 'And next time I'll get an imperial treatment. You understand?'

This was the first time that all three of us answered with one heart and one mind. 'Yes, Big Master Fung!'

11

Rape of the Rock

That evening I felt so relieved that I actually danced in my room. Then I bathed, changed into my pyjamas, and collapsed into the bed. But I couldn't sleep because events of the day kept spinning in my mind like a merry-go-round lantern.

Big Master Fung's face lingered. I could almost see him returning with his gang to Peach Blossom Pavilion. At first he'd ask for a massage, after that, he'd press his wrinkled, spotty body against mine and peck his stinky mouth all over my face. When I refused his demand of introducing his jade stalk inside my golden gate, he'd kick over the furniture and smash the cave!

'Heaven, help!' I jolted awake from the nightmare, the back of my pyjamas soaking wet.

While I was taking deep breaths to calm myself, I noticed a creaking sound. I flung off the bed sheet, jumped out of the bed, and went to check the windows – all tightly closed. As I was about to return to bed, I felt an arm grab me from behind. My heart knocked around like a trapped mouse. Before I could scream, a hand had already sealed my mouth. I struggled but the arm clasped me as tightly as the chain around Mama's safe.

While one hand pressed against my mouth, the other dangled

something before my eyes. A snake? Cold sweat broke out on my forehead and armpits.

Finally the person released me. 'You like this, Xiang Xiang?'

I couldn't believe it was Wu Qiang's voice!

I turned to find his face looming ominously over mine. 'De . . .' I racked my mind, trying to think of some way to placate him. 'Thank you today for helping me with Big Master Fung—'

'Your sorry doesn't mean anything. You have to do something to make amends.'

'Like what?'

Now he grinned widely, his teeth neat like watermelon seeds. 'Like,' he said, again dangling the snake.

It was not until then that I realised what it was. A whip!

Chills splashed down my spine. 'De, please don't whip me! Big Master Fung is not angry anymore!'

'Whip you?' He pinched my face with his long-nailed fingers. 'Ah, of course not, silly girl. You think I have the heart to do that to your pretty face and lovely body?' He leaned close and murmured into my ear, 'Xiang Xiang, I want *you* to whip *me*.' He winked. 'Like what you did to Big Master Fung today.'

'But I didn't—' I stopped in midsentence; how could I tell him what had actually happened?

'Don't lie to me, Xiang Xiang. We all know what you did today to make Big Master Fung a very happy man.' He paused, then, 'Anyway, now I want to be as happy as him, but this time don't overdo it, all right?' He handed me the whip, then slipped off his shirt and went to lie facedown in bed.

Aii-ya! The whip was as heavy as a drunken snake!

Wu Qiang's voice rose in the dark. 'Just whip me. The others will think it's just another customer and a sister stirring up the clouds and rain.' He hollered, 'Come on, swing the damned thing!'

I mustered up all my energy and sent it to the whip. The swinging was at first tentative, then, seeing that he actually enjoyed it, I slashed harder. And harder. Ha, now I could finally avenge myself for all I'd endured in the prostitution house! The whip fell sharper and sharper onto the squirming flesh. De moaned and cried as if he didn't know whether to feel joy or pain. Under the moonlight streaming in from the window, I saw on his back big beads of perspiration scatter like sightless pupils.

The whipping went on for ten minutes until finally he told me to stop. We both felt extremely exhausted and happy.

Then ... he pulled me down on the bed and forced his jade stalk into my precious gate.

When I was crying hysterically, Wu Qiang pulled up his trousers and cursed, 'Shit! Shit! You're a rock, a rock! Why didn't you tell me you're still a virgin?'

I kept crying.

He plunged on, 'Why are you still a virgin? Didn't Big Master Fung fuck you? Tell me the truth!'

I shook my head.

'He didn't?'

I shook my head again.

'Then what did he do?'

I was still too stunned to say anything.

De snatched up the whip and swung it menacingly in front of me. I smarted just from the smacking of leather against the cold floor.

'Are you deaf? Did you hear my question? Didn't Big Master Fung stick his stalk into you?!'

'No!'

'Oh, my heaven!' Now the whip dropped on the floor like a gutted eel. 'But you played sex games with him, you whipped him!'

'No, I didn't!'

'You didn't? Then why was he hurt?'

I told him what had actually happened.

'You kicked him in the face?'

'But just by mistake!'

Wu Qiang looked as if his only son had just jumped off the roof. Silence passed before he threw me a chilling glance. 'Don't tell your Mama anything about tonight, or I'll kill you!' Then he let out a blood-curdling laugh. 'You're smart, Xiang Xiang, which would you prefer: to be skinned alive, whipped till you become a mess of rotten flesh, or just keep your mouth shut?'

I was too stunned to reply. The handsome, scholarly-looking De had shown himself to be a wolf hidden in human skin!

Tears streaming down my cheeks, I dashed to Pearl's room, but her door was tightly closed. Sounds of her voice and the *pipa* wafted from within – she was entertaining a guest. I went to her room three more times but a male voice could be heard through the closed door, so I did not dare knock.

Waiting till next morning, I slipped into her room and told her about Big Master Fung and Wu Qiang.

Pearl spat, 'That thousand-knives-slashed bastard!' Then her eyes, instead of darting like a butterfly, now fixed on me, full of concern. 'Are you all right, Xiang Xiang? Did De hurt you?'

Of course he did, but what could I do? If I ran away and got caught, I'd end up a delicious meal for the rats in the dark room. Anyway, living in a prostitution house, sooner or later I would be 'raped.' So, what difference did it make?

So I hardened myself and lied, 'Not really. Anyway, don't worry about me, Sister Pearl. I'm fine.' I changed the conversation. 'Why was De so upset?'

'Because many people had bid for your first night and Big Master Fung won by paying the highest price. So if he comes back and finds out that you're not a virgin any more, he'll really smash the cave this time. Yesterday was nothing, he just kicked over a table and smashed the mirror and a few plates. Anyway, everyone will be in big, big trouble, Mama, you, and especially De. Since he drank the first soup of your virginity paid for by Big Master Fung, not only is it an insult to the man, but he has also lost the chance to rejuvenate himself—'

'But there are so many other virgins here—'

'But you're the prettiest one, and he's already paid a lot.'

I started to cry.

Pearl pulled me into her arms and we nestled against each other for long moments.

Finally she released me. 'Xiang Xiang, don't worry too much. Since we sisters all have a scheming heart, we can always figure a way out—'

'But how?'

'When Big Master Fung comes again, Mama will give you a small vial of chicken blood to smear on the white cloth. She always prepares the girls for that to cheat the customers. Sometimes we even smear lipstick on our lute strings to charm those *chou nanren*.'

'But I can't tell Mama this, De said he'll skin me alive!'

'All right, then I'll prepare that for you.'

'But I'll get caught by Big Master Fung!'

'You'll get him drunk first.'

'But what if he doesn't drink?'

'Ha! Don't you worry about that! If a customer doesn't drink, he doesn't whore either. They all come for the five poisons – whoring, gambling, drinking, idling, and opium.'

'Then what about if he asks me to drink with him and then I get drunk instead?'

'When a customer asks you to drink with him, get him drunk by refilling his glass, but you spit out the drink onto one of the potted plants.'

'Then what if he just won't get drunk?'

'Then feed him with opium. I'll give you some when Big Master Fung comes back. I've stored some away over the years for emergency use.'

'What about if he won't smoke opium?'

'Xiang Xiang, you're a little worrier, aren't you? But it's a good sign, proves you're cautious. I like that.' She patted my arm. 'I told you not to worry. Remember how I taught you how to seduce a man with your eyes?'

I nodded.

'I bet before Fung's lips touch any alcohol, he'll already be drunk from your gaze. Especially if you let your clothes slip down to reveal your shoulder. You understand?'

I nodded again. Moments passed before I blurted out, 'What about if he doesn't come back?'

'Ha! You mean after he's paid for everything?'

'But I kicked him in the face.'

'Xiang Xiang, you really don't know about men, do you? He won't lose interest in you until he's fucked you. Now you're still an exotic dish on top of a tall table over which the little boy in him drools. Believe me,' Pearl spat, 'he won't pull his pants up until he's tasted the delicious sauce from your golden plate!' She plunged on, 'That's why the *Whoring Classic* says, "Wives are less appealing than concubines, concubines less than prostitutes, prostitutes less than someone else's wives. And the greatest appeal of all is the woman you fail to seduce." '

Now Pearl looked at me with concern. 'But of course Fung might also come back just to smash the cave.'

All the channels in my body jolted awake. 'Then what am I going to do?'

'But it hasn't happened yet. And when it does, I'll find a way out. I always do.'

The time when Pearl had appeased the police chief and saved Spring Moon flashed across my mind. Suddenly overwhelmed by a deep emotion, I flung myself into her arms. 'Sister Pearl, thank you so much. I don't know what I would do without you.'

She rocked me gently, like a mother cooing over a sick child.

When she finally released me, I said, 'Sister Pearl, can you play the *qin* for me, please?'

She immediately took the instrument from underneath her bed. Then she lit the incense and began to tune it. 'This time I'll play you "Three Variations on the Plum Blossom." '

After Pearl had played a few notes, she stopped. 'Xiang Xiang, the plum blossom is the only flower that survives the severest winter unscathed, always standing erect and looking proud. It represents uprightness and the unconquerable spirit.' She then told me the story of the famous swordsman Nie Zheng, whose father was murdered by an evil warlord. Nie hid in the mountains and cultivated himself by playing the *qin* until he could return for justice.

Pearl sat straight and meditated, her fingers resting on the edge of the soundboard, ready to dissolve my pains and worries. Then she began to play.

Mesmerised by the purity of the *qin*'s tones and the choreography of Pearl's fingers, I could almost see Baba, hair turned white and body emaciated, marching fearlessly up a mountainside in a snowstorm. He seemed to look at me and say, 'Xiang Xiang, you can let people take away your life, but never your spirit.' Then, as his back was receding into the distance, I heard his proud voice recite, 'If there's no bitter chill to the bones, how can there be extra fragrance from the plum blossom?'

There was a chill on my life now but I would never let my spirit be taken away. I must work very hard to accumulate a lot of money so that one day I could leave Peach Blossom Pavilion and find Mother. But Baba was dead; there was no place to look for him. However, I could be like Nie and cultivate secretly – alas, not on a mountain but in a whorehouse – until I could avenge Baba's death. I'd find that thousand-knives-slashed warlord who'd destroyed our family and put a bullet in his head! But how to find this bastard?

Now all I could do was watch intently as Pearl's fingers plucked and flicked, pulled and glided zealously, like plum blossoms wrestling with the snowstorm, until tears filled my eyes. The music ended with a few soft harmonics like the fading away of thunder in a distant land.

I wiped my tears and sighed. 'Sister Pearl, can you also teach me to play this one?'

'Only if you promise me one thing. Xiang Xiang,' she said, looking deep in thought, 'remember I told you that Spring Moon reminded me of someone?'

I nodded. 'Who is it?'

'My elder sister.'

'Where is she now?'

Pearl's eyes moistened, but this time the moistness didn't make her look flirtatious, but sad. 'Gone.'

'What happened?'

'Ruby hanged herself in the temple of the haunted garden here.'

'Oh! I'm so sorry, Sister Pearl. But why?'

'I can't tell you now. Xiang Xiang, after what you've gone through, you need a good rest. Why don't you go back to your room?'

I shook my head. 'Sister Pearl, what difference does it make?'

We remained silent, staring into each other's eyes.

Finally she spoke, 'All right. But promise me to keep this a secret until the day you die. Can you do that?'

'Yes.'

She lowered her voice to a whisper. 'My father was a revolutionary trying to overthrow the Ch'ing government—'

'Oh heaven!'

Pearl cast me a sharp glance to shut me up. 'After the movement failed, he disguised himself and fled into the countryside, but the emperor's soldiers soon found him and executed him. Not only that, since he'd been extremely influential, the government also tried to eliminate all his relatives. My mother changed our names and sent me and my elder sister here where no one would look for us. Then she . . . killed herself.'

Tears rolled down Pearl's cheeks, while I remained silent, too stunned to say anything. She wiped her face with the back of her hand. 'That's why although Peach Blossom Pavilion is a whorehouse and Mama and De are nothing but monsters, I can't forget that I owe my life to coming here.

'My sister died eight years later—'

'What happened?'

'Ruby met an opera singer and fell madly in love with him. But he had no money, so she gave him her big diamond ring – a gift from her most favoured guest.

'One evening the guest saw her eating with the opera singer in a restaurant. The diamond ring was sparkling on *his* finger. Next day, when Ruby was leaving Peach Blossom to answer a call for a party, a stranger dashed up and splashed acid on her face—'

I instinctively covered my cheeks.

'Ruby never looked at her face again. She walked right back to the temple in the haunted garden and hanged herself.'

I reached to touch Pearl's hand. 'Sister Pearl, I am so sorry.'

She sighed. 'Like you, I was totally left alone in this world. So I swore I'd never let any dog-fucked stinking males break my heart and ruin my life.' Suddenly Pearl tilted her head and laughed. 'The strange thing is, the more aloof I act, the more they cling to me like babies to nipples. So I'm going to stay here for a few more years to exercise my charm.' She paused, then spoke again in a near whisper, 'I've never told anyone this but you. Actually the real reason that I stay is because of Ruby.'

'But . . . she's dead.'

'Yes. But her spirit is still alive.'

I felt my hair standing on end. 'You mean her ghost?'

Pearl didn't really answer my question. 'There's a yellow butterfly—' Again she stopped, her mind seemed to be wandering in some distant land. 'She's the reincarnation of Ruby.'

'You mean her ghost dwells in a butterfly? Why do you think that?'

'Because Ruby liked butterflies and yellow was her favourite colour. What's more, whenever I go to the haunted garden to pay respect to her, there's always a yellow butterfly hovering around me. I want to be with her as long as it lives.'

'But butterflies don't live long.'

'I believe she's already been reincarnated many times.'

'Oh,' I exclaimed, not knowing whether to believe this reincarnation business or not. But I was touched by Pearl's loyalty to her sister. If only I had a real sister like her!

Just then Pearl spoke, 'Xiang Xiang—'

'Yes?'

Now she stared at me with her eyes full of tenderness. 'Would you like to be my little sister?'

I was too overwhelmed to respond. Seconds passed before I said, 'Sister Pearl, you mean . . . but aren't we sisters already?'

'Of course I don't mean that.' She chided me affectionately. 'You know what sworn blood sisters means?'

I nodded. She went on, 'I want us to be like that. You want that, too?'

I felt too touched to say anything. That's exactly what I wanted – a beautiful, knowledgeable, and problem-solving big sister! This time my head nodded like a mallet hitting a drum in an opera battle scene.

'Good, then go back to your room now. I need to prepare for the ritual. Come to my room tomorrow after three-thirty in the morning.'

* * *

The next day I sneaked into Pearl's room as planned. To my surprise, instead of being all dressed up for the 'ritual,' she wore no make-up; her jacket and trousers, though silk, were plain white with no embroidery.

'Sister Pearl,' I sat down on the sofa next to her, 'I thought you told me we'd have a ritual—'

She nodded, arranging paraphernalia inside a basket.

My heart beat fast with excitement and fear. 'Are we going to run away?'

'No, just to the garden.'

'You mean the haunted garden where you . . .'

She picked up the basket and took my hand. 'Let's go.'

I was disappointed to see that this time the garden had no moons reflecting on puddles. It made me think of a girl, eyes shut, refusing to let people peek inside her soul. Silently I followed Pearl all the way inside the temple, my heartbeats synchronizing with her shredded golden-lotus steps.

Inside the dilapidated hall, the lantern in Pearl's hand cast its beams on a spider's web, a broken window, a dust-covered chest resembling a wounded animal. I could not keep myself from looking up at the ceiling. Thick beams radiated out from the centre. I wondered from which one Ruby's willowy body had dangled, and how many other sisters had twitched in midair, gasping futilely for one more breath on earth.

With all the lifeless bodies hanging in my mind, I was too frightened even to take deep breaths, let alone ask Pearl any questions.

Now I found myself in front of an altar, with Pearl by my side, lovely but ghostly under the lantern's ivory light. Her expression was sad, but her movements were precise. She wiped the dust from the altar with a rag, then lifted the faded altar cloth and reached underneath to take out a Guan Yin statue. Next from her basket she withdrew a small incense burner and put it beside the wooden Goddess. After that she took out a vase with fresh flowers, a plate with an assortment of fruit and another one with snacks, and a small tea set.

After she'd finished arranging these on the altar in front of Guan Yin, she turned to me and said, very softly, as if fearing she might disturb someone – although I was sure no people were around – or even ghosts. I was not sure about their presence, but I couldn't prove their absence either!

'Xiang Xiang, now we're going to light incense, pray to Guan Yin, then pledge our sisterhood in front of her as our witness. Don't ask any questions, just follow what I do.'

Pearl lit three incense sticks, then handed the last one to me. The strong aroma purified the stale hot air while tearing at my nostrils. Through the veils of smoke, Pearl's face looked unreal, like a beauty floating under water. Now she laid three tea cups in a straight line and poured tea.

At this point, I couldn't help but ask, 'Sister Pearl, there're only two of us.'

'No, three. You, Ruby, and me.'

'But she's dead!'

'Only physically.'

I shivered, then looked around to see if a long-haired, white-robed, and footless girl was floating in midair.

But nothing quivered in the air except the eerie echo of Pearl's voice. 'Xiang Xiang, offer incense and say a short prayer to Guan Yin. Just follow what I say.' She knelt down, held the incense above her forehead, and muttered, 'Bodhisattva Guan Yin, tonight please witness the pledge of me Pearl, my elder sister Ruby, and my little sister Xiang Xiang, to be sworn blood sisters.' After that, she slightly turned toward me. 'Xiang Xiang, now you say what I did.'

I knelt beside her and muttered the words nervously.

She took out a needle and a miniature cup. 'Xiang Xiang, give me your middle finger.' As I was about to ask her what was all this about, she'd already stuck the needle in my finger.

'Ahhh!' I let out a sharp cry, not quite from the pain, but from the shock.

She ignored both, while concentrating on squeezing my finger until a trickle of blood began to drip. Too stunned to say anything, I just stared at my own blood swelling into a small crimson pool against the white wall of the cup.

When my finger stopped bleeding, Pearl did the same thing to herself. Then she took out the picture of a young girl, poked the needle between her brows, and made a pretend dripping of blood into the same bowl.

After that, she laid the picture on the altar. I uttered a startled cry, 'But Sister Pearl, that's you!'

'No, that's Ruby. She was seven years older than I. But we do look alike.'

Despite the heat, I felt my spine turning into an ice pillar. I stared at the picture and then at Pearl and then back, feeling she was both alive and dead at the same time!

Pearl caught my expression and ignored it. Now she began to stir the blood in the cup. She then dipped her finger into the blood, smeared it on her forehead, then did the same on mine. After that, she swallowed the bloody liquid. She signalled me to drink the rest and I did, feeling too scared even to complain.

She muttered another prayer, 'Merciful Bodhisattva Guan Yin, from now on, no matter what will happen, Xiang Xiang and I, sisters linked by blood, will be of one heart and one mind. If either one betrays the other, she will be struck dead by lightning.'

The ominous 'struck dead by lightning' gave me a jolt, followed by a sharp glance from Pearl. Fearfully yet faithfully, I repeated the prayer after her.

Then, to my utter surprise, a yellow butterfly materialized out of nowhere, hovering above Ruby's picture.

Pearl's eyes flooded with tears. 'See, Xiang Xiang, here's Ruby. I knew she'd come. I just knew!'

I stared at the creature, trying hard to visualize a pretty young woman, but saw only a yellow butterfly.

12

Beat the Cat

The night after the ritual, I alternated between a light and a heavy heart. Light, because I felt happy that I was no longer completely alone in the world. Heavy, because I'd been dreading the day when Big Master Fung would return. But he hadn't – not yet. Mama told me he'd left Shanghai for some business – no one knew what kind, some said he smuggled gold bars, others said cigarettes – and wouldn't be back for some time. But since he'd already paid for my first night, I was not allowed to serve any other customer until he returned.

During this time, I had nothing else to do except practise my arts and wait. It was a strange feeling to be happy one moment but fearful the next. This went on until one day I realised that my great-aunt had not visited for several weeks.

I felt elated to be rid of the nuisance, if only temporarily. But when I told Pearl during one of our casual conversations, she spilled her tea. 'Damn! Xiang Xiang, you must be pregnant!'

I was so shocked that my jaw dropped. 'You mean by De?'

She nodded, wiping the stain on her dress. 'Did you drink all that soup Mama gave you?'

'Yes.'

'That's supposed to keep you from getting pregnant, so how come . . .' Her voice trailed off.

'Sister Pearl, what am I supposed to do?'

'End your pregnancy.' She stared intently into my eyes. 'Let's do it right now, Xiang Xiang, before it's too late.'

I felt my blood curdling inside. 'But how?'

She didn't answer me, but went to shuffle in one of her drawers then came back with a small package. When she opened it, a bitter aroma tore at my nostrils.

'What's that?'

'Some special herbs: safflower, angelica, rhizome, and ox-knee root. The soup will make you bleed, but it will get rid of the baby.'

Pearl left the room and in a few minutes returned with a small stove and a clay pot. She filled the pot with water, then dumped in the herbs and started the fire.

She let the contents boil for about an hour, then put out the fire and poured the concoction into a bowl. 'Here, Xiang Xiang, now drink all of it.'

I took a tentative sip and spat out the liquid. 'It's bitter to death!'

'Xiang Xiang,' she hissed, 'stop being childish! Now finish it, for heaven's sake!'

I gulped down the soup, holding my breath against the cat urine smell.

'Good,' she said, then poured the rest of the soup from the pot into the empty bowl. 'Now go back to your room and rest. Finish this second bowl of soup in an hour. I'll come to see you tonight after I've finished with my guest.' A pause, then she spoke again. 'Just to be safe, also drink raw vinegar at least twice a day and jump real hard.'

Once back in my room, I jumped like a dog trying to catch a dangling piece of duck, then, after restlessly waiting for the hour to pass, forced myself to drain the second bowl of soup. It seemed to take effect quickly, for soon I collapsed on the bed and fell into a troubled sleep.

When I woke up, it was already getting dark. I felt a terrible pain in my stomach and a splitting headache. I lit a candle, then, when I was about to get some water to soothe my parched throat, I noticed the whole bed sheet was soaked with blood. I put my hand between my thighs and felt the same warm, sticky liquid.

'I'm bleeding! I'm bleeding!' I screamed, then fainted.

When I opened my eyes, Fang Rong's face was hovering above mine. 'Good heavens! What happened?'

My voice came out weak and frightened. 'I think . . . it's my great-aunt.'

Mama was carefully examining the bed sheet. I looked around and asked, 'Where's Sister Pearl?'

'Pearl? Why do you care about her? She's out with her favoured guest.'

My heart sank. In a turquoise pavilion, no sister could afford to leave her favoured guest for any reason. That meant I didn't know when Pearl would come back for me.

Suddenly Mama sniffed the air around me, then a suspicious look fell like a shadow across her face. 'What's that smell?'

I was sure she didn't mean my period, but the herb soup.

I pretended innocence. 'What smell?'

'Get up and let me check you!'

As I was about to get up, severe cramps ambushed my stomach. I could only utter a weak, 'Mama, I can't,' before I collapsed again.

When I woke up, I found myself in a hospital. Mama was talking to a middle-aged, white-robed man while beside her fidgeted Little Red, who kept glancing at me with a worried look.

Mama asked him, 'So Doctor, how come my daughter's period is so heavy? Is she all right?'

The doctor, expressionless, said in a low, authoritative tone. 'Normally a period shouldn't be so heavy.' He paused to cast a glance toward my direction. 'How old is she?'

'Thirteen. Hmm . . . almost fourteen.'

He pushed up his glasses, looking a bit puzzled. 'Is she engaged?'

For a moment, Mama seemed unable to reply, then, 'No. Not yet.'

'Does she have an intimate friend?'

Mama cast a sharp glance at me before she turned back to the doctor, grinning. 'No. But why?'

'The reason I asked is because this heavy bleeding looks to me like a miscarriage.'

'Miscarriage?' Mama's jaw almost dropped to her chest. Her eyes looked murderous enough to kill the unwanted baby.

I'd expected a severe punishment after I'd gone back to Peach Blossom Pavilion. But to my surprise, nothing happened.

When I finally had the chance to talk to Pearl, she said, 'Big Master Fung is coming back. Believe me, Mama won't do anything to hurt you before that, because she has to present you to him in one piece.'

Pearl might be right about Big Master Fung's feeling, but not Mama's.

The next evening, before I knew what was happening, Fang Rong sneaked into my room with a servant I didn't recognise. She stripped me naked and took something from him which I realised with horror were two sharp, red hot bamboo sticks. As he held me, she stuck them through my nipples.

Tears spilled from my eyes while I screamed with pain.

She hollered, waving her long, red-painted nails, which looked like blood dripping from gashes, 'You lightning-struck-soon-drop-dead-stinky slut, is your cunt so itchy that you can't wait for Big Master Fung, eh? Who is it that you've been fucking?!'

'Nobody, it's just my period.' Better to have my nipples pierced than to be skinned alive, as De had threatened.

'Your period? Don't try to fool me; the doctor said it's a miscarriage.'

'He wasn't sure. Mama. Believe me, it's just my period!' I couldn't afford to tell the truth, nor did I dare imagine the consequences if I revealed it.

I kept screaming and pleading and insisting that it was my period until finally Fang Rong's expression softened.

'All right, Xiang Xiang, I believe you this time.' She spat, 'But if you misbehave again, I'll beat the cat. You understand?'

I nodded, swallowing both the bitterness and the pain.

Then Mama pushed up my breasts and let out a loud chuckle. 'Xiang Xiang, see how good a job I did? Now your nipples are so red and so beautifully swollen. I bet when Big Master Fung sees them, his jade stalk will thrust as high as the Himalayas!' After that, she burst into laughter and dashed out of the room with the servant.

In a state of shock and humiliation, I hastily put on my clothes, then hurried to Pearl's room, but she was not there. I wrote a note and slipped it under her door. Back into my room, I lapsed into a painful, agitated sleep. Hours passed before I was awakened by the burning sensation in my breasts. I took off my top, spat saliva on my nipples, and pressed them cautiously with my fingers.

I nursed my wounds and dozed until I heard the door creak open.

It was Pearl. She dashed toward me, blood draining from her face. 'Good heavens, Xiang Xiang! What happened?!'

I told her about the punishment.

'That wok-sizzled bitch!' Pearl pulled me into her arms and cooed, 'Xiang Xiang, you'll be all right. It could be worse.'

'Like beating up a cat?'

She nodded, eyes sparkling with tears.

'What is it?'

'A mama won't injure any sister's face or body, for that's her investment. Or starve her, for no man wants skin-wrapped bones. That's why even though the soup failed to work, Mama didn't punish Ah Ping, for she needs her to keep us looking nourished for the customers. The rule is: Hit the body but not the face. Or beat the cat but not the girl.

'Mama did it to Ruby once when she failed to bring in money. She strapped her onto the bed, put a cat in her pants, then took a bamboo pole and frantically beat the cat. You can imagine how the poor creature went wild with her scratching.' Pearl paused to stifle a sob.

'I'm so sorry, Sister Pearl.'

A silence. She carefully examined my chest. 'Now let me get something to soothe your nipples.'

Pearl left the room and came back with a small tin. She lifted the lid to reveal some white powder. 'Xiang Xiang, this is opium. I'll massage it on your nipples, and after that you'll sniff some and go to sleep. When you wake up, both the pain and the swelling will be gone.'

After the massage, I took the opium and in Pearl's arms fell into a delirious sleep.

When I woke up, the pain was still lingering on my breasts. I asked Pearl for more opium but she cast me a chiding look. 'No, Xiang Xiang. You don't want to be one of the fallen sisters.'

Three weeks later, Big Master Fung, as predicted by Pearl, came back. Mama made sure that the servants carefully cleaned and lavishly decorated the welcoming-guests room, then placed fresh flowers and sprayed perfume in it.

'Xiang Xiang, this time you'd better make Big Master Fung the happiest man under heaven.' She glowered at me with eyes murderous enough to strike me dead on the spot. 'Otherwise, beware of your skin!'

Before I was pushed into the hall, I secretly touched the pre-chicken-blood-smeared *zhuang yuan* seal tucked inside my jacket. Then I muttered a prayer to Guan Yin around my neck.

A huge grin broke out on Fung's face when I slid through the door in my shredded golden-lotus steps.

'Xiang Xiang, my little beauty, how I've missed you!' His corpse-like body was shrouded in an indigo gown embroidered with the character *shou* – longevity. His lips split to reveal two rows of long, yellowish teeth, and an expanse of gum the colour of a bruised eggplant. His hand, clawlike, reached to grab my waist.

I swallowed hard. Then, remembering Pearl's teaching and Fang Rong's warning, I immediately went to sit on his lap.

'*Aii-ya*, Big Master Fung,' I threw him a flirtatious glance, 'why didn't you come earlier? You make me wait and wait till my heart rots!' My hand, with an effort of my will, wandered to caress his cheek.

He took hold of my hand and passionately drilled his tongue into my palm, creating a wave of nausea that sloshed across my stomach.

I half-pushed him away, giggling. 'Big Master Fung, please, it tickles!'

'Tickle? Ha! Ha! Ha! You'll soon be tickled to death when my jade stalk tickles open your soft petals!'

I didn't know how to respond. Then from the eight immortals table I picked up the wine pot and poured us both full cups.

'Big Master Fung,' I handed him a cup with an orchid hand and a soul-sucking glance, 'please drink this respect wine from your humble Xiang Xiang for the celebration of our dragon and phoenix night.'

When Fung took the cup and drained the alcohol, I secretly poured mine onto the potted plant next to my chair.

Immediately I poured him another cup. 'Big Master Fung, this one is for your health and longevity.'

Obediently he finished his second cup while I again swiftly poured mine to feed the plant.

'Big Master Fung,' I poured him a third one, 'this is for the prosperity of your business.'

Now he cast me a chiding glance. 'Wait a minute, Xiang Xiang. I don't want to get drunk right away.'

'Aii-ya, Big Master Fung,' I said, pulling my dress to reveal a large part of my bare leg, 'I don't believe a veteran like you can get drunk so easily.'

Fung's hand wandered to rest on my thigh. 'All right, Xiang Xiang, but don't get me drunk. For I want to savour our wedding night.'

The last two words sent a tremor across my chest. But I put up my best smile and lifted the fine porcelain cup to his lips. He happily drained his third cup. Poor cup, to be molested by such ugly lips!

Now I poured him the fourth cup. 'Big Master Fung, this is—'

'Enough, Xiang Xiang, no more drinking. I want to strike the red—'

'But Big Master Fung,' I pulled my handkerchief and flung it at him playfully, 'this is for your offspring, so how can you turn it down?'

'Offspring?' he mumbled, face glowing and eyes glazed with alcohol. 'All right, then you have to share it with me.'

I used my sheer willpower to suppress another wave of nausea.

Suspecting nothing, he willingly took a big sip of the wine. Then, to my surprise, he leaned close to me, pried open my lips, and spat the wine from inside his mouth into mine.

The alcohol burnt all its way from my throat down to my stomach. I choked. Fung laughed, then started to caress my back affectionately. Then passionately. And I knew the most dreaded moment was to come.

This time, with mutual understanding, we went straight to where we were destined – the bed.

Before long he was on top of me, thrusting his rotten stalk inside my precious gate.

When he had finally finished his feats of thrusting and collapsing, he stuck his tongue into my mouth again, noisily sucking my saliva for one last time before he got dressed. Paradoxically, after all his vigorous stunts, he looked even younger and livelier.

Now he narrowed his eyes and looked back at the dishevelled bed sheets. Seeing that I had presented him with the bloody *zhuang yuan* seal, a look of utter satisfaction crept into his fuzzy eyes.

He hollered, '*Hao!* From today on my business will prosper and I'll have great longevity!' He took the seal from my hands, drained one more cup of wine, laughed deliriously, and staggered out the door.

PART TWO

13

Life Went On

Despite my miseries, life went on. Peach Blossom seemed to prosper more than ever, and Mama and De had never looked happier. Especially Mama. As thick ingots of silver were pressed into her hands, she would break into a huge, toothy grin and her eyes would grow as round as gold coins.

As for me, I'd become more and more accustomed to the ways of life in this gold-powdered hell. I tried to concentrate on attracting the richest guests and not dwell on the humiliation of selling my smile and my skin. I could only remind myself of Mother's advice: 'We can't beat fate, but we can play along and make the most out of it. Try to be happy.' Or Pearl's: 'If you find a customer terribly, unbearably, indescribably repulsive, just close your eyes, hold your breath, and imagine during the whole time you're but a corpse that somehow manages to squirm and moan.'

Fortunately, Peach Blossom Pavilion, though a prostitution house, was a high-class one, so we did not have to spend every minute stirring the clouds and rain. There were several services we provided to customers besides the obvious.

Ho dacha – drinking the big tea – was the best, because I entertained my customer just by playing the *pipa* and singing. I was also expected to pour his tea and wine, prepare his opium pipe, and sit by him when he was gambling, but these were easy. When the customer first arrived, a *niangyi*, woman servant, would set before him a pot of tea and a plate of roasted watermelon seeds. Then, when he was feeling more relaxed, he'd pick a sister and, as a gesture of respect, the chosen one would bring out her most refined cup and delicately pour him tea. After that, the *niangyi* would bring out snacks – tiny sweet dumplings, dried apricots, honeyed dates, dragon eye pulp.

Normally we would serve a customer to *ho dacha* for up to two hours, but if he kept us overtime, extra money would be charged. They had to get acquainted with us in this way, before we would consider agreeing to have sex. But, of course, that was the eventual outcome.

As I was glad to delay sex by serving to 'drink the big tea,' Pearl chided me, 'Xiang Xiang, don't try to fool yourself. How long can you avoid sleeping with a customer in a prostitution house? Better strive, like me, to make them beg for your favours.'

In Peach Blossom Pavilion, Pearl was the busiest sister in answering calls for parties. This was called *chutang chang* – singing outside the hall, or *chuju* – out to a party. In fact, I didn't dislike this, for we would be invited out by a customer – but only after he'd become acquainted with us – to a party, an elegant gathering, or a banquet. But first he had to send a formal invitation on red paper addressed to us with the proposed restaurant's name. Of course, we were permitted to go out not in order to have a pleasant time, but to entice the guest into asking to stay overnight at the turquoise pavilion. We called this a *zhuju*. That generally meant he'd sleep with a sister, but sometimes a customer liked the girl so much he'd even pay to spend the night without having sex, especially when she was having her period. This was called *shou yintian* – guarding the female day.

But the service best loved by all mamas was *chi huajiu*, drinking the flower wine. Instead of inviting the sister to a restaurant, the customer would sponsor a banquet in Peach Blossom. Because it lasted much longer than the *ho dacha*, the customer had to pay several times as much. Nor was the establishment shy about adding charges for extra dishes and wine to the already overpriced menu. Despite being cheated, the rich customers still seemed happy to show off their wealth to their favourite courtesans.

Sometimes we were lucky enough to make a lot of money for doing very little. Here I saw another side of Pearl. One evening, she told me that a rich silk merchant Mr. Luk would be sponsoring a banquet for us and two other sisters.

Pearl said, her expression serious, 'Xiang Xiang, since this will be your first time to serve at "drinking the flower wine," I want you to be very careful and not make any mistakes. So watch and learn from me.'

For the special occasion, Pearl put on a fish-turquoise, high-collared jacket with matching skirt, while I wore a pink silk top with elaborately knotted floral clasps over matching trousers.

Pearl had always advised me to meet customers a few minutes late, but this time she led me to the banquet hall twenty minutes early. When I asked why, she smiled mischievously. 'So we'll get the upper hand and show the others.'

When Pearl and I entered the room, Mr. Luk was sitting at the banquet table. A *niangyi* had already laid out the first course of shark's fin soup and was now offering him a towel. After wiping his face, the silk merchant stared at us with bulging eyes.

We sidled up to him in our shredded golden-lotus steps. Once seated beside him, Pearl picked up the water pipe and wiped it carefully with her silk handkerchief. 'Mr. Luk, smoking with a good meal makes you happier than an immortal. Please let me light it for you.'

Luk looked as happy as if his newest wife had just given birth to a son. 'Miss Pearl,' he put down the towel, 'your name hasn't been spread in vain.' When he began to suck his pipe, Pearl winked at me. I immediately picked up the flask and leaned close to him – Pearl had said this forced a customer to notice you – and poured him a full cup of wine.

Now he turned to look at me with admiration. Before he could say anything, Pearl was already speaking. 'Mr. Luk, I hope my little sister Xiang Xiang pleases your eyes.'

The silk merchant let out a belly laugh. 'Ha! Ha! Don't be so modest, Miss Pearl. Both of your amorous names have been sounding like thunder in my ears. That's why I'm here tonight.'

We continued to make small talk with Luk, while pouring him wine and serving him snacks. Two *niangyi* kept bringing more dishes – braised fish in broad bean sauce, spicy mustard chicken, five-fragranced duck, yoke-spilling eggs. Pearl exercised her best wit, and Luk's belly kept shivering with laughter.

In the middle of one of Pearl's jokes, two other sisters, Tiantian and Lotus Fragrance, entered the room and took their seats opposite us. By now, Pearl and I were so well acquainted with Mr. Luk that he barely noticed the entry of the two new girls. Not losing a beat, Pearl aimed a flirtatious glance at the silk merchant. 'Mr. Luk, may Xiang Xiang and I entertain you with some music?'

Luk's face glistened. '*Hao.*' Good.

Tiantian's brows creased as she whispered something to Lotus Fragrance.

Pearl ignored them. She asked a *niangyi* to bring my *pipa*. As I played, Pearl began to sing 'Romance from a Back Street.'

I held my *pipa* tenderly like a lover, then my fingers began to dance on the instrument while my body twisted back and forth so that wisps of my hair fell to half-veil my face. Pearl, a gold fan in hand, moved her arms to the rhythm, all the while swaying her waist like a water snake. Her jade bangle gleamed like waves of the West Lake.

Sweet music shivered from her cherry lips. 'You and I' – she looked into Luk's eyes at these words – 'together praise this spring morning as beautiful as the gardens of Suzhou. I'm so pleased that our arms are smooth and lips sweet, and so are our dreams . . .'

'*Hao*! *Hao!*' Mr. Luk clapped as we finished selling our music and our smiles.

Next Pearl began to play the finger-guessing game with Luk while I kept refilling his wine cup. I felt a little sorry for Tiantian and Lotus Fragrance, who could find no chance to serve the big fish customer. They could only amuse each other by talking and giggling.

A little later, when Mr. Luk was quite drunk, Tiantian finally succeeded in leaning forward to pour him tea. 'Mr. Luk, please have some tea; it'll balance off your wine.'

Lotus Fragrance chimed in, 'Yes, Mr. Luk, please, otherwise you'll get drunk. Besides, this is the best cloud-and-mist tea.'

But Luk pushed away the tea cup. He said, his eyes glazed over with alcohol and his speech slurred, 'Ha! That's what I want tonight, to get drunk! I'm having a wonderful time, and I'll become the wine immortal!' Suddenly he turned to me. 'Xiang Xiang, give me your shoe.'

As I was wondering how to respond, Pearl signaled me to do as told. Obediently I took off my embroidered red shoe and handed it to Luk. To my surprise, he held it like a jewelled box while Pearl began to pour wine into it.

Then his eyes rested on us while he made a toast. 'To your amorous names!' After that, he drained the shoe.

I almost exclaimed, *'Aii-ya!'*

Finally Luk was ready to leave. His servant came in and handed him a pouch from which he took out a fistful of coins. It must have held at least twenty or more silver coins. The whole banquet cost only ten. I laughed inside. Tonight we would make a fortune! Had Pearl not pinched my elbow, a loud *'Wah!'* would have spilled out from my mouth. Tiantian and Lotus Fragrance's eyes were as big as the egg yolks on the plate.

But to my surprise, Pearl didn't blink an eye at the silver. She turned to the *niangyi*, who was now beginning to clear up the table. 'Ah Ling, here are Mr. Luk's tips for you and all the servants here, so you should thank him.' The *niangyi* looked so upset as if, instead of being given twenty silver coins, she was robbed of forty.

Her voice trembled. 'But Miss Pearl, I don't want to be in trouble.'

Pearl cast her a sharp glance. 'Take it, Ah Ling. Otherwise it's very rude to our noble guest.'

Everyone looked startled, most of all Luk. Pearl had pulled back her hand so he had no choice but to give the silver to the servant.

Right after he'd left, before Tiantian and Lotus Fragrance could protest bitterly, Pearl waved them quiet. 'Calm down, if I don't get more money from Mr. Luk, I'll pay you double from my own pocket.' After that, she took me by the arm and led me out of the room. When we were walking in the corridor, I asked Pearl why had she let the maid have the money.

'Xiang Xiang, Luk is wrong if he thinks he can buy us so easily. This was "to stoke the arrogant fire." Remember, we're book chamber *ming ji*, not filthy, homeless whores from chicken lane. Though he thought his tip was a lot, now he knows that for me it's only enough for the servants—'

I thought what my share of the money would have been. 'But Sister Pearl . . .'

She laughed. 'Believe me, Xiang Xiang, he'll send more money tomorrow. A man like him would rather die than lose face.'

Pearl was right. The next day, Luk sent his servant to deliver fifty silver coins. Thirty specially for Pearl, ten for me, and the rest to be shared by Tiantian and Lotus Fragrance.

Despite Pearl's stratagems, the most well-off person in Peach Blossom was, needless to say, Mama. 'Easy money!' she would exclaim whenever she saw strings of cash change hands or a customer leaving my room. But not easy for me because, although I'd not been sold into Peach Blossom and didn't have to redeem myself, my debt had still rapidly accumulated – when Big Master Fung crashed the cave; my hospital bills after the miscarriage; all the expenses for my meals, lodging, clothes, art lessons. So, almost all the money I earned and the jewellery I was given would be instantly snatched away by Mama 'to pay bills.' The day that I'd pay off my debt so I could leave Peach Blossom seemed to be farther away than ever. While Pearl managed to gain a lot by working little, I tried to work extra hard just to clear my debts.

The big fish customer Big Master Fung continued to visit me since the day of his opening my petals. Both luckily and unluckily, he was now one of my regular customers. I considered this unlucky because he never got tired of sucking my tongue, tasting my saliva, and letting his flabby jade instrument play on my lute strings. The worst was, no matter how nauseated I felt inside, I still had to put on a happy smile, deploy my skilful hands, and force myself into a willing frame of mind.

Luckily though, not only was Big Master Fung very rich, he also seemed to like showing off by spending freely. Whenever he showered me with gifts and money, I found myself almost wanting to like him. At moments, I was surprised to feel some fleeting affection for him. Maybe it was out of pity, or maybe because somehow he made me think of Baba. Not that they had anything in common; only that Fung was now the man who pampered me as Baba once had.

More than once after we had visited the Wu Mountain, he said that if I continued to be nice – meaning I'd do whatever he wanted in bed – then he'd continue to indulge me like his precious daughter. But when I asked about his real daughter, he would chide me for being nosy and threaten to stop bringing me gifts.

But fortunately, whether from age or from affection for me, he never seemed to remember those threats and at the following visit usually brought me another gift. One time, it was neither jewellery nor clothes nor cash, but something so delightful and unexpected that, to my own disbelief, I voluntarily flung myself into his arms and kissed him on his lips.

A parrot!

I'd never seen such a beautiful creature. All white with a crimson beak, she conjured in my mind the image of plum blossoms blooming in the bitterest snow. Her dazzling feathers seemed to make even Pearl's most colourful outfit pale in comparison. Their silken texture was so comforting to the touch that I never tired of stroking her. Even her tail was elegant, like the fine sheep's-hair brush that I used for painting delicate beauties. Her black eyes resembled two dark marbles in a cloudless sky.

As soon as I'd laid eyes on the parrot, I decided her name must be Plum Blossom. To imbue her with the spirit of the *qin*, sometimes I'd play for the bird, especially 'Three Variations on the Plum Blossom.' I even explained to her the meaning of the piece, hoping she'd absorb the brave spirit of the flower.

Whenever I appreciated Plum Blossom's beauty, I'd also remember what Mr. Wu had said to me during one of his lessons. 'In painting, we strive for skill excelling nature, but of course, the beauty of nature is unsurpassable.'

Looking at the graceful curves of Plum Blossom's body, the subtle shadings of her white feathers, and the rich crimson of her beak, I felt I truly understood Mr. Wu's teaching. Since my poor Guigui's tragic death, besides Pearl, now the parrot had become the great comfort of my life. At quiet moments, she would perch on my shoulder while I read her poetry – Li Bai's 'Meditation on a Silent Night,' Wang Wei's 'Missing My Friend,' Meng Haoran's 'Spring Morning.' I'd chuckle with satisfaction every time her beak mimicked the sound of the phrases she'd picked up while her claws massaged my sore muscles. Sometimes when I talked my heart out to her, she'd tilt her head and listen, as if she truly understood the poems and the depth of my feelings.

To reward her attention, I'd feed her with fruits. Watermelon was her favourite, but she'd only eat the seeds while spitting out the flesh. Unfortunately, the red, sticky mess on the floor would capsize my joyful mood when it brought back to me my bloody night with De.

I'd taught Plum Blossom a few sayings, some simple greetings like: 'how are you; good morning; good evening.' Others were auspicious sayings: 'good luck; wish you good health and longevity; *gongxi facai* – wish you make a lot of money.' Some she picked up by herself: 'Feels good, eh? Want more?'

But she also learned to say, 'Kill! Kill!'

I really didn't like to hear violent words from her delicate beak, but she picked them up through my inadvertence. During Big Master Fung's last visit, after he'd finished sucking my tongue and was about to leave, I thanked him again for giving me Plum Blossom, then told him the reason for her name.

To my surprise, Fung burst into uncontrollable laughter.

I felt fire burning in my ears. 'Big Master Fung, why is it so funny?'

Fung chortled, and all the wrinkles seemed to pool around the corners of his eyes and lips. 'Ha, ha, Xiang Xiang, that's why I'm infatuated with you. You know, you'll never be a *real* whore, because at heart you're still just an innocent little girl.'

I didn't know whether this was supposed to be a criticism or a compliment. However, fearing that I might lose my big fish customer, I protested, 'But I am, Big Master Fung!'

'If you're a real prostitute, then I'm a true gentleman. Ha! Ha! Ha!' He caressed his stubble with his long-nailed fingers. 'You know why I bought you this white parrot instead of a green one? Before you met me, you were a virgin, innocent and pure like the snow.' He paused to throw me a meaningful-cum-licentious glance. 'Remember the *zhuang yuan* seal your mama prepared for us during your first night with me?'

Now I felt my whole body on fire. Had he figured out Pearl's ruse?

But he said, 'That was the reason I bought this parrot. Its white body dotted with the speck of red beak looks exactly like your blood smeared on the white cloth. So the parrot is to remind you that I was the first man who chopped open your melon and tasted your red juice.' He burst into another round of delirious laughter. 'Ha, ha, ha, ha, plum blossom flowering in the snow; what fanciful nonsense!'

Therefore, right after Fung had left my room, still humiliated by this unwelcome reminder, I chopped the empty air, exclaiming, 'Kill! Kill! Kill!'

Since that incident, I felt both happy and sad when I looked at Plum Blossom. I still loved her, only now my affection was mixed with a tinge of deep sympathy. Poor creature, unaware of all the evil of the world!

14

Mr. Anderson

Two years slid by and I found myself more and more sought after by visitors to Peach Blossom. Pearl's lessons in coquetry and the art of the bedchamber had been more valuable than I could have imagined. Yet, though I was now a little bit famous in Shanghai, I still lacked the prestigious status that Pearl enjoyed.

Spring Moon had also become popular. She was not a great beauty, but as Pearl said, she had tiny feet and sad eyes, and these qualities were extremely desirable to certain men. Although we had many things to share and I felt very fond of her, she was still preoccupied by her wealthy past and seemed to be drifting.

One time when I asked her plans about the future, her answer was, 'What's the use of having plans in a prostitution house?'

When she asked me the same question, I said, 'To be a *ming ji* like Sister Pearl.'

'Xiang Xiang, I also want to be a *ming ji*, but I'm not considered a great beauty like you.' She dabbed her eyes with a handkerchief. 'My dream is to wait for my fiancé to come here and redeem me.'

'But he's already engaged to someone else!'

Spring Moon simply turned to stare out of the window, her eyes abstract like wisps of incense smoke.

* * *

One day when I was practising the *pipa* in my room, Little Red came in and said, 'Xiang Xiang, hurry and get dressed, there're two guests waiting downstairs.' She paused, then giggled, her eyes sparkling with mischief.

'What's so funny, Little Red?'

'One has a big nose, gold hair, and round blue eyes!'

'You mean a foreigner?' My curiosity was pricked.

She nodded. 'His name is An-der-son.' She giggled again. 'Such a strange name!'

Right after I'd entered the business hall, I heard a loud 'Welcome the guests!' from one of the male servants. Next to him Mama grinned like a dog drooling in the heat. The two guests, one a plump Chinese and the other a big-boned foreign ghost, were sitting on the sofa, looking more tired than excited.

Just then, flower girls about my age hurried to stand before them. As they were being scrutinised, they started to giggle, whisper, throw glances, and elbow each other flirtatiously.

I waited a few moments, then, in a calculated rhythm, wriggled to the center in shredded-golden-lotus steps.

The two guests' eyes fell right on me, then brightened.

I smiled, catching their glances and holding them like a mother with her newborn baby. I could feel the two men's souls being sucked right into my dimples. From the corner of my eye, I could also see daggers shooting at me from other pairs of eyes. I smirked inside.

The Chinese didn't even glance toward the giggling idiots. He pointed at me and nodded. Looking disappointed, the foreign devil selected a girl called Brocade Tune.

The obsequious grin still blooming on her face, Mama ordered that tea and snacks be served. After that, she waved the other girls away. Now I was sitting next to the Chinese, and Brocade Tune was by the foreign devil. Mama addressed the plump, bespectacled Chinese. 'Ah Mr. Ho, you really have Buddha's enlightened eyes! Xiang Xiang is one of our most popular girls here.' Then her smile changed direction and bloomed before the foreigner. 'Ah, Mr. Anderson, you, too, have a good eye for the beauty of Chinese women!

Brocade Tune is guaranteed to provide first-rate service. If not, you can have your money back.'

The two guests responded by smiling politely. Mama threw each a meaningful glance, 'All right, I'll leave you two to my little beauties,' then left the room wriggling her generous bottom.

Brocade Tune and I immediately plunged ourselves into 'respectfully' pouring tea, serving fruit and snacks, and making small talk with our guests.

Mr. Ho told me he was in a shipping business located on Zhong Shan East Road and Mr. Anderson was his partner from America. America! The word sent a slight tremor through my body. I remembered how Baba used to tell me about this rich, faraway country: A film comedian by the name of Cha Li Cha Pilin. A famous president called Lin Ken who had freed the Negro slaves. A very famous torch-bearing goddess called the statue of freedom.

While Mr. Ho kept sipping his wine and telling me this and that about his business and family, I was only half-listening – busy stealing glances at the American. So strange, an American! And so hairy!

He was about my baba's age, maybe not handsome, but not bad looking either. I was most curious about his high nose and pale blue eyes. So pale that, I imagined, when he'd been born, the strange, noisy world must have scared him so much that colour had instantly drained from his soul's windows! No wonder foreigners are called ghosts. With their colourless eyes and hair, they really do look like their spirit has been snatched away by the King of Hell.

Though a barbarian, this Mr. Anderson gave me a good impression. Brocade Tune was so eager to please him that she was now almost sitting on his lap, but this American devil's hands simply refused to have any devilish intention. Then with a shock I realised – though a foreigner, he'd been speaking fluent Chinese!

However, I knew I must not neglect Mr. Ho, so I turned back to smile at him. Fortunately, my Chinese guest was now quite drunk and hadn't noticed my curiosity regarding his partner. As I continued to pour wine into Mr. Ho's glass while peeking at Mr. Anderson, I noticed he'd also been looking toward me. My heart began to bump around like a deer lost in the forest.

I'd completely lost interest in my Chinese guest but trusted his drunkenness would keep him from noticing. But, of course, not taking any chances, I kept my smile deeply dimpled, my body sensuously swaying, and my hands busy pouring wine and lighting cigarettes. Then, when there was a lull in our conversation during which Mr. Ho's glazed eyes wandered around the room, I stole another glance at the foreign devil and found that he was still staring at me.

This time, ignoring Brocade Tune's jealousy, I held his gaze long and hard. Then something clicked in my mind. Those pale, blue eyes, I'd met them somewhere! But where? My eyes lost themselves into his blue ones which seemed so soothing that they appeared to caress and melt like . . . like ice cream! Yes, he was the foreign devil who'd saved the little boy from Mama's harassment two years ago when I was out having my hair styled!

I also remembered how Jade Vase had invited him to come visit us at Peach Blossom and how he'd turned to scrutinise me, then walked away without a word.

Could he have come here today to look for me? After two long years?

Just then a *niangyi* came in and blocked our gaze. She told Mr. Ho that their two hours were up. 'Would the two gentlemen like to extend their stay?'

After Mr. Ho discussed it with his American partner, to my disappointment, they decided to leave.

'We're too tired; we've just come back from a trip,' Mr. Ho said, 'but maybe we'll come again.'

And they did.

The second time, Mr. Ho requested that he and Anderson be served separately, meaning, of course, that they wanted sex. I was afraid that I'd have to go with Mr. Ho and someone else would get the American. Ho seemed to be looking at me, but at the last minute, to my delight, he picked another sister and Mr. Anderson asked for me. A *niangyi* led us to the welcoming-guests room.

Though I'd been with many different men, I still felt nervous to serve a barbarian. Especially when his blue eyes moved curiously all over me as if I were a doll who had somehow come to life just to smile and flirt and perform the tea ceremony. Eager to please, I tried to make my hands move like an orchid dancing in the breeze and my waist sway like a willow trembling in the wind. But nervousness took over from elegance and I would have spilled a few grapes onto his lap had he not caught them in time. He was amusing, this foreign ghost.

'Mr. Anderson,' I threw him an appreciative glance, 'you want more grapes?'

He shook his head.

It was hard to know what to say to a foreigner. I thought for a while before asking, 'Have you been to other turquoise pavilions before?'

He actually blushed!

'No. Last time when Mr. Ho took me here, that was my first time.'

'You like it here?'

He didn't answer my question, but asked, 'Miss Xiang Xiang, why don't you tell me something about yourself?'

Of course I was not going to tell him how I'd ended up in Peach Blossom if that was what he wanted.

I refilled his tea as a gesture of respect. Then, staring into his blue eyes, I began to tell my tale starting from my arrival in Peach Blossom at thirteen – my chores, my training in painting, calligraphy, and music – though of course I left out the dark room, my chopped melon, the rape, the miscarriage, the hot sticks in my nipples.

When I finished, he said nothing but simply sipped his tea.

Finally I mustered up my courage and said, 'Mr. Anderson. Can I ask you something?'

He stared at me curiously. 'Yes. Of course.'

'Do you think you'd remember an incident two years ago?'

'Try me.'

'On Nanking Road, you rescued a little boy from being strangled by a woman.'

To my disappointment, instead of showing acknowledgement, he looked lost in thoughts, seemingly trying to revive his memory.

Maybe after all, this Mr. Anderson was not the man I remembered all these years, but someone else.

I went on, 'The little boy had robbed a little girl's ice cream because he was hungry. You gave him a few copper coins to buy food. Do you remember a young girl with newly styled hair decorated with a fancy pearl clasp? She was with her mama and two sisters.' I looked at him anxiously. 'Mr. Anderson, don't you remember this at all?'

A huge grin broke on his face. 'Oh yes—'

'Mr. Anderson, that girl was me!'

'Yes, now I remember.' This barbarian stared at me incredulously. 'But how you have grown!'

I proudly nodded.

He kept scrutinising me as if he'd just opened a treasure chest, then, 'Oh my! Can you really be that little girl?'

I smiled, then refilled his tea cup.

Again he looked lost in thoughts. Was it at discovering that what lay inside the treasure chest was not dazzling jewels but dark secrets?

'Mr. Anderson?'

He flashed an awkward smile. 'Yes?'

'Do you want me to sing you a song or play the *pipa*?'

'Oh yes please, whatever.'

But I had left the instrument in my room. 'Mr. Anderson, my *pipa* is upstairs, so would you like to come to my room?'

Silently he followed me up the stairs and into my room. He cast curious glances around the small place. I invited him to sit, took out my *pipa,* and started to tune it. As I began to play, Anderson pointed to one of my paintings on the wall. 'What is that instrument?'

'A *qin.*'

'Is that you playing the *qin*?'

'Hmmm . . .'

'I would like you to play the *qin* for me.'

His request surprised me.

'Have you heard the *qin* before, Mr. Anderson?'

'No, but you look different when you play it.'

I excused myself, went to take the *qin* from Pearl's room, then hurried back. Carefully I unwrapped the silk brocade, then put the four-hundred-year-old antique on the table. The thirteen *hui* – mother of pearl dots – gave out a mysterious lustre on the black surface, like stars blinking against a dark sky. The seven silk strings were stretched taut on the soundboard, ready to whisper the secrets of centuries.

When I finished tuning, I straightened my back, assumed a sober expression, and meditated. Then I let my fingers re-create the moon floating above Guan Mountain, the tipsy cavort of a drunken fisherman, the plum blossoms defying the bitter snow . . .

When my fingers left the instrument, Mr. Anderson did not utter a word. He seemed, like me, to savour the after-flavour of the tunes as they breathed their last in my room, a tiny spot on the ten-thousand-miles of red dust.

Silently, we looked at each other.

Finally he said, 'Miss Xiang Xiang—'

'Mr. Anderson, please just call me Xiang Xiang.'

'Xiang Xiang. It's such an honour to hear you play. I've never heard . . . such delicate music.'

Could a barbarian really appreciate the subtlety of the *qin*?

I decided to test him. 'Over praise, Mr. Anderson.' I paused for seconds, then, 'Do you want me to play the *pipa* now?'

He almost looked horrified. 'No, please don't. I don't want to hear any other music just now.' He cast me appreciative glances. 'And you, Xiang Xiang. You do look different when you play the *qin*.'

'How?' I tested him again.

'Your fingers are so expressive.'

I felt respect emerge from my heart. This pale-eyed, hairy man in front of me was just a barbarian but he seemed to appreciate the subtle nuances of the *qin*. How could a man from such a faraway land understand the deepest secrets of earth and the highest mysteries of heaven?

He spoke again, 'Xiang Xiang, you mind if I suggest something?'

So now, after all the compliments, he finally wanted the real thing – to balance his *yang* with my *yin*.

But his expression was serious. 'Beautiful and talented as you are, maybe you shouldn't waste your youth here.'

I couldn't believe what I'd just heard! But remembering my training, I hid my shock and kept up my pleasing smile.

He went on, 'Xiang Xiang, forgive me if I'm blunt. I just think that as refined a woman as you are, this is just not the kind of life you should lead.'

My mind clicked. Was he suggesting that he'd help me in some ways? Like paying my debts and getting me out of Peach Blossom?

Just when I was about to tell him that I didn't have the luxury to choose my destiny, he was speaking again. 'I think talented as you are, maybe you can be a teacher.'

'A teacher?' I almost chuckled. A decadent flower girl turned into a proper lady schoolteacher? What a far-fetched dream. This man's life must have been so smooth that he had no idea what went on behind dark doors in this dusty world.

'But Mr. Anderson, that's not what I'm able to do.'

He remained silent for moments before he smiled wryly. 'I'm sorry, Xiang Xiang.'

Sorry for what? I'd swallowed my question before it slipped out of my mouth. I poured a fresh cup of tea and respectfully handed it to him.

With equal deference he took it from my hand.

He'd never mentioned sex.

Mr. Anderson continued to visit Peach Blossom with Mr. Ho. While Mr. Ho liked to try out different sisters, including Pearl, Anderson always asked for me. I was sure while Mr. Ho was busy raining on the sisters' clouds, he'd think his American friend had been doing the same with me, but what had happened was nothing like that.

Each time Anderson came to my room, we simply talked and sipped tea, and I would play music. He never let go of trying to persuade me to quit prostitution. Repeatedly he'd lament that I was wasting my life and my talents – as if I didn't know. I hoped he would help by offering to pay my debts to Peach Blossom, but he never mentioned anything like this and of course I did not ask.

One time I told Pearl about Anderson and she said that Mr. Ho – now her frequent customer – told her that his American friend disapproved of prostitution.

I chuckled. 'But most foreign devils . . .'

Pearl gave me a chiding look. 'Xiang Xiang, if you think all barbarians are wild and loose, then you're wrong. Some are even more conservative than us Chinese.'

'Then why does he visit a prostitution house?'

'Mr. Ho said because he insists and Anderson goes along. And I don't think he wants to say no, since he's Ho's partner and depends on Ho to do business in China.' Pearl threw me a mischievous glance. 'Maybe Anderson likes you and wants to convert you to his religion.'

'What religion?'

'Religion of Christ.'

I'd heard about this strange religion with a creator called God and his son called Ye Hohua who tried very hard to save people's souls. One time a bearded, black-robed missionary even came up to the gate of the turquoise pavilion to stuff leaflets into the sisters' hands. There was only one word printed on the cover – LOVE.

I sighed inside. That was what I'd been waiting for, love. Not from this creator God, nor his son Ye Hohua, but a handsome, intelligent young man!

I asked Pearl, 'So you think Anderson is a member of the religion of Christ?'

'Maybe, but I'm not sure. Otherwise why does he act so virtuous in a prostitution house?'

'So you think instead of wanting to lose his soul like the other men, he's trying to save ours?'

Pearl winked. 'Do we have one?'

We burst into uncontrollable laughter.

But then Mr. Ho and his barbarian partner stopped visiting.

15

The Prestigious Prostitute

Time passed, and finally I had a new honour, of sorts.

Each day in front of Peach Blossom Pavilion, huge signboards holding flowers were sent by patrons in tribute to those special sisters who were *ming ji*. Sometimes so many were sent that they created quite a sight – billows of flowers floating on the ocean. Each sign seemed to squeeze forward to be seen. Face was gained, not only by the sister who got the most signboards, but also by the customers who'd sent them. Though the competition seemed to be among the sisters, in fact it was between their powerful backers.

Now hardly a day passed by without my name floating on this blossoming sea, often with poems of praise like this one:

> Natural as the clouds and sky, clever as the ice and snow
> Ice vase and jade bone, clarity penetrating to eternity.

This was the year I'd turned eighteen, prestigiously.

Customers now referred to me as *yanming yuanbo* – amorous name spreading far and wide. For I had become a *ming ji,* at last.

Of course I felt flattered by all this attention, but it also made me feel very sad.

I could not but remember when, each time after Baba had finished giving me reading and writing lessons, he'd look at me tenderly. 'Xiang Xiang, study hard and be prestigious someday. I hope you'll be the first woman *zhuang yuan*.'

Zhuang yuan was the title conferred on the person who'd come first in the imperial examination. Of course the imperial exam was cancelled after the Ch'ing government had been overthrown by Dr. Sun Yat-sen and his new republican government. But what Baba had hoped was that I'd become a famous scholar, bringing honour to our ancestors as well as leaving a reputation of intellectual eminence for our posterity.

Had Baba still been alive, how would he have felt about my renown – flowery and amorous – bringing nothing but shame to our family name? How would he have reacted to my prestigious status – as a prostitute?

In the middle of the night whenever I thought of Baba, I felt relieved that he hadn't lived to see my fame.

My prestigious status continued to attract all kinds of customers – scholars, poets, merchants, government officials, one time even a Catholic priest who, instead of taking me to the Wu Mountain for rain and clouds, tried to persuade me to convert to his religion of Christ so, after I died, I'd go to heaven instead of hell. These men showered me with gifts (the priest, after fondling my breasts for moments, gave me a Bible with gold edges), invited me out, and pampered me like – in one customer's word – a princess. How ridiculous. I'd much prefer he'd simply praise me with the honest *ming ji* – prestigious prostitute.

But Pearl chided me, 'Xiang Xiang, forget about honesty in a prostitution house, just be happy that those *chou nanren* are trying to please you. Would you rather they treat you like a real whore by beating you up and burning your nipples with incense?'

When Pearl said 'real whore,' I smiled to myself, for nothing could be truer than that!

One time a poor scholar told me he'd sold his most treasured Ming dynasty edition of the Five Classics in order to stir the clouds and rain with me.

When I told Pearl how sorry I felt for him, she sneered, 'Xiang Xiang, never feel sorry for those *chou nanren*, they're not worth it at all. You didn't put a knife to his throat and threaten him to sell his books and come to you, did you? Besides, how do you know he didn't lie? Maybe he stole the money to pay you or picked someone's pocket. These stinking males are all liars, all experts in farting from their mouths! If these dog-fucked assholes have consciences, then dogs don't eat shit!'

She plunged on, 'Besides, you'll continue to meet a lot of men here, and you won't have enough room in your heart to feel sorry for every single one, however miserable their stories. Xiang Xiang, listen to me, you have to harden your heart. Remember, you have only one heart but many customers. Just think of how many times these *chou nanren* can break it. So never allow it to break, not even once. Can you promise me that?'

Of course, I nodded and uttered an emphatic 'Yes!'

Along with my fame, there was another big change in my life – my name. I was no longer called Xiang Xiang, but by my art name, Bao Lan. *Bao* means precious, or treasure, and *lan* means orchid. I didn't like my new name for it was both ostentatious and common, a prostitute's name like Golden Flower, Fragrant Rose, or Silver Chrysanthemum. I'd have chosen something poetic: Snow Fairy, Cloud Immortal, Lotus Boat, Dream Lake.

But Fang Rong wouldn't give in; she widened her eyes and raised her voice. 'Xiang Xiang, can't you see that Bao Lan is the best? Can you tell me any man who likes neither treasure nor flowers?'

Of course, I knew what she meant by 'flowers.' I'd heard all the variations on this theme: the prostitution houses were *yanhua zhidi* – domains of smoke and flowers. Customers were *mianhua suliu* – sleeping on the flowers and taking refuge in the willows. The diseases they caught were named *hualiu* – plague of the flowers and willows. And like our floral namesakes, the day would come when we were only *canhua bailiu* – withered flowers and trampled willows.

Mama was right. I couldn't think of any men who liked neither treasures nor flowers. They liked them so much they even risked catching something more permanent than a night's pleasure.

She cocked me a chiding eye. 'You want a fussy name like Immortal, Fairy, or Fragrance? But there's no substance to them, that's why women with this kind of name all die young!'

Against this reasoning, what more could I say?

Mama paused to catch her breath, then, 'If you screw up your name, you screw up your business. That's why we chose Peach Blossom for our pavilion.' She plunged on, 'It's based on the famous story of the Peach Blossom Garden by . . .'

'Tao Yuanming.'

'So you know the story?'

'Of course. Some fishermen got lost while discovering a secluded world forgotten by time. In the garden, peach trees blossomed, birds sang, and the simple, innocent people enjoyed a carefree life.'

Mama shook her head. 'No, no, no. The fishermen lost their way and went through a hole into a cave which was filled with beautiful girls, tasty food, and strong wine. That's why we say *dongru mixiang* – entering the hole and bewitched by the fragrance.' She winked. 'I'm sure you know which hole and what fragrance, don't you? After they'd spent days chasing after the women, wolfing down the food, and getting drunk, they swore they would never go back to their boring life.'

Before I could protest that she'd completely messed up the story, Mama plunged on, 'That's how Peach Blossom was named.' Suddenly she slapped my shoulder, startling me. 'And that's why your name is Precious Orchid instead of nonsense like Dream Lake or Lotus Boat. Ha! Ha! Ha!'

I was well aware that my change of name signified that I was no longer a *chuji* – young prostitute – but a full-fledged one with regular customers. So now I was completely cut off from my past. This was the saddest thing, for with a different name, it would now probably be impossible for Mother to find me, notwithstanding that I'd long ago given up hope of hearing from her.

Since the first day I'd arrived in Peach Blossom Pavilion five years ago, Mother had never written to me. Was her temple life *that* busy? Or could she have simply lost my address?

One time when I'd asked Fang Rong why didn't I hear from

Mother, she said, '*Aii-ya*, why don't you ask Guan Yin?' then, 'Your mother's now a nun. And you know what nuns care about? Emptiness! Nothing!' She made a face. 'So why would she be thinking of you?'

Was it possible that Mother had risen so far above worldly concerns that she'd forgotten her only daughter? Or was she . . . dead? Whenever I imagined she might be dead, all kinds of horrible images would emerge: her bloated body floating on a river; crumpled in a rat-infested back alley; or even swinging from a beam of her temple . . .

But these thoughts came only in my blackest moments. Deep down, I still thought of her as alive. Often, in the middle of the night when I was alone, my body exhausted from my clouds being stirred by the *chou nanren's* rain but my mind achingly alert, I'd look out the window, gaze at the moon, and think of her. Would we have the chance for a family reunion? Even to sit down together and have a simple meal of noodles and buns, just like in the past?

Sometimes I missed her so much that I'd cherish the idea of running away from Peach Blossom, so I could go to Peking and find her. But, of course, I'd smother the thought right away. Because, if I were caught, I'd end up in the dark room fed to the rats; with my nipples being pierced; or a cat beaten in my pants. Even if I succeeded in escaping from the pavilion, I would have no roof above my head. And I had never forgotten that little beggar who'd grabbed my ice cream years ago. Getting to Peking would be no easy feat. Instead, since I was getting more and more popular, I imagined that someday I'd make enough money to hurl a heavy sack of gold at Fang Rong's face, then walk out of Peach Blossom. I fervently prayed to Guan Yin for that day to come.

Besides my mother, I also thought a lot about Baba and that warlord who'd wrongly accused him and had him executed. A burning desire had ignited in me – to find out this thousand-knives-slashed bastard who was the cause of my family's disintegration. If I did, I wouldn't let him go unpunished. I even relished all sorts of ways that I could torture him – slash him with a spiked whip soaked in water (which was how some mamas disciplined their daughters); fill him with water then jump on his swollen belly; force him to swallow a needle-filled bun; push him down a poisoned well; or more simply, put a bullet into his head.

Although thoughts of finding Mother and avenging Baba were never far from my mind, I still kept practising my arts to maintain my status as a *ming ji* so I could one day carry out my plan of leaving Peach Blossom.

Besides my name, I had yet another change in my life: my room, which was larger and prettier, with elegant furniture, a gilded mirror, ceramic vases, and a landscape by the famous Tang Yin. I also hung a painting of my own showing young women engaging in the four arts: painting, calligraphy, poetry, *qin*.

Not only did my customers like this painting, they thought the four beauties were actually one person – me. Naturally I agreed with them, for I *was* pretty and well versed in all of the four arts. The fact that they complimented my beauty and my talents always pleased me tremendously, even when the praises were poured from wrinkled, toothless mouths.

Now I also had my own maid, a thirteen-year-old girl called Little Rain. She was plain-looking and stupid, but I liked her because of her kind heart and loyalty. Moreover, she never failed to carry out her duties and took very good care of Plum Blossom. She'd also bring me gossip about sisters both at Peach Blossom and the other turquoise pavilions.

Since I'd become famous, Fang Rong's attitude toward me had also changed. It was more respectful, almost as if I were the first female *zhuang yuan*. Now every morning I was served with meat juice to clean my face, clear egg soup to nurture my throat, and rose petal fragrant water to wash my hair. Every night I took a bath in water steeped with expensive herbs.

Some sisters who had snubbed me now suddenly seemed unable to remember their former feelings. Sweet words poured from their lips while they begged me to reveal my secrets for captivating customers. But there were others whose envious glances betrayed a frightening hatred.

16 ✦

Red Jade

During the height of Peach Blossom Pavilion's business, only three sisters received flower signboards every day – Pearl, me, and a girl called Red Jade.

I'd never paid much notice to Red Jade. She'd been living in another quarter, working under another sister's tutelage, and had not been pretty or talented enough to attract my attention. Then, over a year, she'd miraculously transformed from a slightly plump little girl into a watery-eyed, oval-faced, fair-skinned beauty. It was generally known that she'd thoroughly mastered not only the skill of the bedchamber but also the invaluable art of flattering Fang Rong and Wu Qiang. She was the only sister who'd lived in the pavilion for four years but had never experienced any 'special treatments' – rat-infested dark room, cat in the pants, pierced nipples. Her special talent was *kou ji* – lips technique. Not the kind that imitates bird songs, cicada chirps, cats' meowing, or bubbling brooks and howling wind. Everyone in the pavilion knew that her lip technique was put to use inside the guests' rooms late at night.

Unlike Pearl, who was slender, elegant, and haughty, Red Jade was voluptuous, horny, and wild. Her big, round eyes always seemed to shine with a dazzling lustre. 'Smiling eyes' was the customers' remark. However, young as she was, when she laughed, she already had a few lines bursting from the corners of her eyes.

'An extremely licentious physiognomy,' Pearl had once told me.

I chuckled. Wasn't that a trait we prostitutes were supposed to have or, if not, strive to achieve?

Like two fat slices of ripe, juicy tomatoes, Red Jade's lips glistened all the time, even when the weather was hot and dry. When you saw them, customers said, you *had* to take a big bite. Others described them as hot red chillies. When you sucked them, not only did your tongue get burnt, but the fire would scurry all the way down to inflame your jade stalk.

However, it was neither her eyes nor her lips that were Red Jade's most prominent features, but her breasts. Big and pendulous, they always seemed to cast an enigmatic shadow wherever she went. They stuck out so far that I'd even heard a guest apologise, 'Excuse me, miss,' when he was just passing by her. I was told a lot of customers went to her just 'to have a taste of the flesh papayas.'

Although a smile always bloomed on Red Jade's face, we never knew what was on her mind. Since I hardly knew her, I neither liked nor disliked her.

But Pearl hated her bitterly. 'Xiang Xiang,' she always warned me, 'beware of this cunning fox. While she smiles, she'll stab you with a knife.'

Whenever she mentioned Red Jade's name, Pearl would grind her teeth and start her sentence with 'that whore.' This always made me want to laugh. Weren't we all whores? But Pearl thought otherwise. 'We're decent women forced or tricked into being whores, but she's a born one. This slut has indelible "whoreness" through to her marrow.' Watching how Red Jade even flirted with De, I agreed. I didn't really dislike her deep down, but because I was on Pearl's side, I had to be her enemy.

Since the three of us were now the most prestigious courtesans in Peach Blossom, even in Shanghai, customers loved to compare us – to flowers, birds, animals. Pearl, the oldest and most arrogant, became the rose, the swan, and the cat. I, the youngest and most innocent, was the daisy, the oriole, the rabbit. Red Jade, the most scheming and flirtatious, was the peony, the peacock, the fox.

One time Pearl cast me an anxious look. 'Xiang Xiang, when a girl like Red Jade can become popular, I'm afraid that's the end of our era.'

'What era?'

'Of the *ming ji*.' She sighed. 'Men are losing their taste. Red Jade's *pipa* playing is so sloppy that it makes my stomach flip. But some customers seem not to care as long as her breasts keep swinging with the music. Girls like her are taking over. We spend years perfecting our arts and to become connoisseurs of taste. But Red Jade doesn't even wait ten seconds to strip off her clothes and spread her legs!'

'But Sister Pearl, it's not true. You're still the most admired sister here, and you have many more rich and powerful customers than Red Jade.'

'Yes. But I'm also a couple of years older than she. And that makes a big difference. She has all the time in the world to catch up. I don't mean in the arts, since I don't think she cares, but in taking over my status.'

Although this had not been a worry on my mind, I didn't know how to relieve Pearl's. Finally I said, 'Sister Pearl, I don't think she can be that admired.'

'I certainly hope not.'

Now I started to read the newspapers. In keeping with my *ming ji* status, clients often contributed poems addressed to me. While the main news never interested me, I was curious to read anything about myself. Here were some that really made me happy:

Embracing the moon and playing with the wind,
Voice soaring with the clouds and resonant as the clicking
    of mala beads.

I especially liked this one, which cleverly used my name:

Lips pout like cherries breaking open.
The three-thousand-threads-of-beauty tremble over a pair
    of green jade earrings.

Precious body emanating the fragrance of Orchid,
An immortal descending on the red dust.

There were many more like these. Actually, I read them with
some trepidation because if a sister's luck changed, the poems
would shift from veneration to merciless sarcasm. I was sometimes
shocked at how the process could be reversed overnight, literally.
But fortunately, my luck seemed to hold, and so did Pearl's.

She had once said, 'Because we're Guan Yin. Not only that
we're invulnerable, we're bestowing compassion on those pitiful,
stinking males.'

So Pearl and I continued to be, without shame, the Goddesses
of Sexual Mercy.

Not all the poems were published in newspapers. Some were
executed with elegant brushstrokes on rice paper sprinkled with
gold flakes or bordered with colourful flowers. While I felt these
customers' passion blossom all the way from their fingertips to
their brush and onto the rice paper, a sadness would also surge in
my heart. I liked the poems about me but, unfortunately, none of
the men who wrote them. They were either young, awkward-
looking bookworms, middle-aged businessmen with protuberant
bellies, or arrogant, heartless dandies.

I'd ask *lao tianye* – the God of Heaven – was there someone
handsome and romantic hiding somewhere and secretly composing
a poem to win my heart? If so, why didn't he come out of hiding? If
he was there, perhaps he was too poor. I'd sigh. Please come to me;
I'll serve you free – for love.

As a child I had loved the legend of the cowherd and the spinning girl. They were so in love that they neglected their work and so
the God of Heaven placed them in the sky as constellations, separated by the Silver River of Heaven – the Milky Way. Once a year,
on the seventh evening of the seventh month, a flock of magpies,
taking pity on the lovesick couple, fly to the sky and form a bridge
so that they can meet. On this night all over China, women make
offerings to these stars, hoping for love.

So I'd written this poem:

Me, dwelling in the seventh evening of the seventh month.
You, a thousand years ago – or, a thousand years hence.
Time made us climb over history, legends and the Spring
    and Autumn Annals.
A cry from a future life, lamenting your absence in this one.
Now, passing through the tunnel of dreams, let me whisper
    to your ghost a misminted love story.
If time still rides the wrong train, then a Precious Orchid,
    hopelessly longing for you, will take her own life in the
    Silver River of Heaven.

Though the cowherd and the spinning girl meet but once a year, they would still be in each other's arms. While my arms, used as a pillow by a thousand guests, had never possessed the luck to hold the man I loved.

With a heavy heart, I'd stand by the window and recite my poem, hoping the *yuelao* – the old man under the moon – would hear my heart's prayer and tie the red thread to connect me and my future lover, whoever and wherever he was. My virginity was already lost to that human-skinned wolf Wu Qiang, but I still could hope for true love. Someone who could appreciate my talents, my feelings, sympathise with my fate, then take my hand to lead me past all the endless sufferings of this ten-thousand-miles of red dust.

Now that I was expected to entertain guests constantly, it was a rare moment when I could visit Pearl. The times I could were very precious, especially so because she'd agreed to teach me all her favourite *qin* pieces: 'Spring Morning at the Jade Pavilion'; 'Parasol Leaves Dancing in the Autumn Wind'; 'Water Immortal'; 'Dialogue Between the Fisherman and the Woodcutter'; 'Geese Descending on Sandbank.'

One time Pearl abruptly stopped in the middle of her playing and said, her voice filled with emotion, 'Xiang Xiang, the *qin* is all we have here in Peach Blossom.'

'What do you mean?'

'*Qin* music is purifying, so playing it gives me the strength to resist the evils of the world.' She paused, then went on, 'Xiang Xiang, you remember I told you to keep your *qin* playing secret? It's not what I told you that no one would appreciate your talent. Nor is it true that by the time you've mastered the instrument, you'll have lost both your youth and beauty.'

She plunged on, 'The real reason is that the *qin* is our pure land. By *not* playing it I keep something of myself that customers can't buy. When I cultivate myself by playing the *qin,* I know I'm not a complete whore. You understand?'

'I think so, Sister Pearl,' I said, digesting her saying. 'You want me to play the *qin* only for myself.'

'Exactly. So it's not a prostitute who is playing it.' She looked almost in tears. 'Xiang Xiang, you must promise me that you'll never play the *qin* to make money, or to please those stinking males.'

I nodded, then asked tentatively, 'But what about if the man is not a stinking male, but a real gentleman?'

Pearl looked at me curiously. 'Do you mean you have someone in your heart?'

I shook my head. 'I wish I had. But Sister Pearl, I . . . did play the *qin* to a customer.'

'Who?'

'Mr. Anderson, and I don't think he's a *chou nanren*.' I went on to tell Pearl how and why I'd played the *qin* for him.

She said, 'I wonder how a barbarian comes to appreciate our three-thousand-year music heritage.' Then she cocked a suspicious eye at me. 'Xiang Xiang, are you in love with Mr. Anderson?'

'Oh no, of course not! He's old enough to be my father. I only respect him for being a real gentleman.'

Pearl sighed. 'I wonder why he and Mr. Ho have stopped coming. But Xiang Xiang,' she looked at me with a serious expression, 'if he ever comes back and offers to pay your debt or even proposes marriage, accept right away even if you feel no love for him.'

I didn't know how to respond to this.

She went on, 'This kind of chance only happens here once in a lifetime. You understand?'

I hoped there could be more than one chance in life. But I nodded anyway.

'Poor girl.' Pearl reached to tousle my hair. 'I'm sure someday you'll meet someone you love.'

'But how?'

'*Hai*, there I can't help you.'

'But you told me that in a turquoise pavilion there's always a solution to any problem.'

Her eyes looked sad. 'Yes. But meeting someone you love is not a problem to be solved, it's Karma.'

'Then what am I going to do if it's not my Karma to be loved?'

'Don't worry, Xiang Xiang. Just be patient, I'm sure you will soon meet a young, handsome, talented man, leave Peach Blossom, get married, and have many sons.'

'Why sons?'

'Because sons will never have a chance to repeat our fate.'

Pearl looked down at her *qin* for long moments before she lifted her fingers and started to pluck the silk strings. Then she asked me to sing 'Beyond the Yang Pass' as she played.

Please drink one more cup of wine.
Once you've gone beyond the Yang Pass, there'll be no one
     for you.
A thousand rounds of drinking will eventually come to an
     end, but half an inch's sadness will never go away.
The Chu Sky and the Xiang River are so far apart.
You'd better ask a messenger to bring me news.
After today's farewell, we can only express our longing in
     dreams.
Maybe the geese will bring me your letters . . .

I could not sing these words without thinking of my mother. An unspeakable sadness swelled my heart to the verge of breaking. Then, remembering my promise to Pearl that I wouldn't let it break, I bit my tongue and hardened my spirit.

One afternoon as I was readying myself to answer a party call, there was a knock on my door, and a bit to my surprise, Pearl entered. These days it was rare for her to come to my room.

She perched herself elegantly on a stool next to me. 'Xiang Xiang, I hope you have been working extra hard on singing and playing the *pipa*.'

'But Sister Pearl, I never miss my practice.'

'Xiang Xiang, next week you and I are invited by the *Flower Moon News* to a dinner party at Fortune Garden Restaurant on Nanking Road. Besides us, there'll also be many sisters from other turquoise pavilions. All the sisters will be participating in the Flower Contest.'

Of course, I'd heard about the flower contests – pageants organised by customers, mainly scholars and poets, to elect the three most beautiful 'flowers.' Though only a very beautiful courtesan could win, she would also have to prove her accomplishment in the arts.

'Though they won't say so,' Pearl winked at me, 'we'll also be judged by our technique of the bedchamber.' She chuckled, 'Ha, Xiang Xiang, while these *chou nanren* would be offended by anyone even mentioning their wives, they openly discuss us and compare our sexual skills. If we were decent, married women and had sex with any man other than our husband, we'd be stripped naked and stoned to death. Yet as prostitutes, we sleep with as many men as possible. And they even honour what we do in the bedroom by publishing poems about us in the newspapers!'

Pearl kept laughing, though I didn't find this a bit funny.

She went on, 'The sisters who win will become even more prestigious, while those who fail will become laughingstocks.'

How cruel, I thought. 'Sister Pearl, do you want to be in the contest?'

'Of course. That will make me even more sought after.'

Although Pearl and I had already become prestigious, our status was informal – merely agreed upon by our customers. Not until we'd won the contest would our title become official. I understood Pearl's eagerness – she wanted both the fish and the bear's paw.

'Then why didn't you enter in the past?'

'Because after Ruby's death, I didn't feel right about it. Now seven years have passed and it's time for my mourning to end.' She considered for a moment. 'Somehow I know she wants me to participate.'

'But Sister Pearl, she's dead.' I hated to remind Pearl of her sister's death, but I regretted her morbid attachment to a ghost.

Pearl ignored my remark. 'Last week I dreamed of a yellow butterfly hovering over a newspaper printed with a winning poem about me.' A dreamy smile broke out on her face. 'I think this was extremely auspicious. Ruby was telling me that I should participate.' She paused, then, 'And I'll win.'

'But Sister Pearl, I'm not interested.'

Pearl cast me a curious glance. 'Why not? You also have a good chance, Xiang Xiang.'

That was exactly the reason I didn't want to participate. It would be fine if Pearl did become the champion – it must have been on her mind that she'd win the first place and I the second. But what would happen if I was the one who took first place? I feared that would be the end of our friendship as well as our sworn blood sisterhood.

I just couldn't afford to win the title and lose our friendship. So my only way out was not to get involved in the first place. Besides, what if neither of us won? I did think Pearl was the most beautiful and talented courtesan in Shanghai, but she was not the most flirtatious. Despite her excellence in teaching the art of pleasing, Pearl, in reality, was too proud to lower herself to flatter.

'Sister Pearl, I have no interest in this contest.'

'Xiang Xiang, I don't think you can turn down the *Flower Moon News*'s invitation. If you do, you'll be in great trouble.'

'What can they do to me?'

'People call them the "mosquito press," because they sting. They can ruin you by bad-mouthing you in their newspaper.' She threw me a meaningful glance. 'Sometimes that can be as bad as shooting you, only there'll be no bloodletting. Xiang Xiang, let's do it together, for Ruby's sake.'

When Pearl and I arrived at the Fortune Garden Restaurant, it was packed with heavily made-up and gorgeously dressed-up sisters. I spotted Spring Moon, Jade Vase, Brocade Tune, and several others from our pavilion plus a few guards and male servants. Pearl pointed out other courtesans from competing establishments: The

Silver Phoenix, Sleeping Flower Pavilion, Temple of Supreme Happiness, and Moon Dream Pavilion.

Then she nudged my elbow. 'Look, those in the far corner are from Qinghe Lane's chicken alleys. I admire their guts even to show their faces, let alone to compete with us. How ridiculous!'

I craned my neck and saw faces as round as my washing basin and lips as gross as sausages.

Now all sisters stopped what they'd been doing – chatting, sipping tea, cracking roasted watermelon seeds – to stare at us. Pearl halted by the door and swept her eyes across the room as our presence generated heated whispers and jealous glances.

She whispered into my ear, chuckling. 'We're delicate, fine porcelain, while they're all crude earthenware; don't you think?'

I slightly nodded.

'Except maybe that whore.'

I followed Pearl's eyes until I spotted Red Jade in a dazzling, gold-threaded gown. Unlike the other sisters, she seemed unflustered by our presence. While fanning herself indolently, she noisily cracked red-dyed watermelon seeds, then nonchalantly spat out the husks. Noticing our gaze, she even nodded slightly to us with her licentious smiling eyes.

'Wok-sizzled bitch!' Pearl spat. 'But I do appreciate her *sang froid* and her honest hypocrisy.'

Is there such a thing as honest hypocrisy?

Just then a fortyish man with bushy eyebrows and a flat face hurried up to us. He grinned as if he'd run into two thick sticks of walking gold. 'Miss Pearl, welcome!'

Pearl made a brief introduction for both of us. Mr. Zhu, chief editor of *Flower Moon News*, scrutinised me for long moments, then said in an excited voice, 'No need to introduce, I've heard of Miss Precious Orchid's flowery name for a long time. What a pleasure to welcome you both tonight.'

With much ceremony, he led us to seats at the front table and announced that the proceedings were to begin.

The formal session lasted for an hour during which snacks, food, tea, and water pipes were served while Mr. Zhu explained the rules of the contest.

There would be 'arts' winners and 'flower' winners. Both, of course, had to be beautiful but the former would also be based on cultivation in the arts, and the latter on cultivation in bed. The winners would be decided by vote and awarded the titles of president, vice president, and prime minister. The poems praising them would be published in the *Flower Moon News*.

'This year,' Mr. Zhu added, 'we'll introduce something new – the weeds list.'

Voices stopped and sisters perked up to listen. Zhu went on, 'Not only will we elect the most beautiful and talented sisters, we'll also elect the most detestable.'

A tense silence intervened before a gentle voice piped up, 'How detestable?' followed by laughter sprinkled here and there, some jovial, others nervous.

I turned and saw Red Jade smiling ominously.

Mr. Zhu held up his hands for silence, then looked around the room. 'The most . . . lazy, stupid, and' – he paused for a few beats before spitting out – 'ugly to death!'

Collective laughter erupted in the room.

Pearl nudged my elbow. 'Poor girls. But we don't need to worry about this, do we?'

Zhu went on, 'The detestable sisters' names will be published on the weeds list, as opposed to the flower one.'

Red Jade asked again, her voice sounding as if soaked in syrup, 'Mr. Zhu, then will there also be poems about those who're elected to the weeds list?'

'Of course, no partiality.'

Some sisters giggled, others sighed.

Pearl turned to wink at me. 'I'd like to read some of these poems, that would be fun. Don't you think?'

I remained silent, remembering Pearl's dream of the yellow butterfly hovering over the newspaper.

17

The Ways Out

The voting was supposed to go on over the next few weeks as readers sent in their ballots. Each day, the *Flower Moon News* published the latest tally. As expected, Pearl took an early lead. I tagged behind her in second place, and Red Jade was right behind me in third. Sisters from other turquoise pavilions spread the rumour that Fang Rong and Wu Qiang had bribed Mr. Zhu to fake the poll and make the three of us winners. I doubted this, for Temple of Supreme Happiness and Sleeping Flower Pavilion were equally rich, so if they competed with Peach Blossom to bribe Mr. Zhu, the price would be pushed up to an astronomical figure. I thought Mama and De would rather die than pay that much money. The reason that we were leading in the poll was simple: We *were* the most beautiful courtesans (even if Red Jade was not as talented). Especially Pearl, as the final stage of the competition was getting close, she looked even more beautiful and confident than ever, and kept telling me of her repeated, auspicious dreams of the yellow butterfly.

Then, one week before the announcement of the winners, something strange happened – Red Jade seemed to be getting more and more votes. The situation was inexplicable and alarming. Why? I kept asking myself and Pearl.

But she cast me a sharp glance. 'Stop worrying, Xiang Xiang; that whore isn't going to win. It's just not going to happen.'

Although I admired Pearl's seeming confidence, I was not so sure about her prediction. Besides, occasional frowns and sighs betrayed her inner disturbance.

Then, four days before the winners were announced, the situation had become truly appalling. Now Red Jade had ninety-eight votes, Pearl had eighty-three, and I sixty-eight. Seeing that Red Jade's tally was soaring while Pearl's was sinking, I made the drastic decision to withdraw from the contest.

I hoped by so doing all my votes would go to Pearl. I convinced all my customers – old and new alike – to vote for her.

It worked. Now two days before the announcement, Pearl's votes suddenly escalated to well over a hundred, outnumbering Red Jade's. I sighed with relief. Smiles broke out on Pearl's face again as she regained confidence that she would be announced as the winner. Her pictures and poems praising her beauty and talent would appear in many newspapers – *Flower Moon News, Flower Heaven Daily, Flower World News, Idle Emotion News, Pleasure Talk News* – in Shanghai. She would soon be crowned, officially, *the* most prestigious prostitute.

The night before the announcement, Pearl asked me to go see her right after I'd served my last customer.

When I entered her room, I saw the eight immortals table covered with plates of food, a bottle of wine, and a vase spilling with an assortment of exotic flowers. Pearl had dressed in a pink silk gown decorated with gold leaves. Flowers perched above her ears while underneath gold earrings dangled like fireflies. Her brows were shaved into two elegant brushstrokes and her lips painted the shape of a small, crimson heart. Her gold filigreed butterfly hovered elegantly on her three-thousand-threads-of-trouble, ready to take flight.

Before I could finish appreciating her, she was already speaking. 'Xiang Xiang, this morning I asked Ah Ping to prepare all these for us.' She winked, a smile blooming on her radiant face. 'You know what? You and I will have a little private celebration in advance.

Tomorrow I'll invite Mama, De, Spring Moon, other sisters, and all the maids and *niangyi* to dine out. I've already booked three tables at the Pacalo Restaurant in the French Concession.' She paused to throw me a flirtatious glance. 'Have you ever tasted French cuisine?'

I shook my head.

'Good, then you will tomorrow. Pacalo is Shanghai's most elegant and expensive Western restaurant. I promise you we'll all have a good time there.'

Of course Pearl was sure to win, but somehow her overconfidence made me ill at ease. I kept asking myself why but couldn't come up with an answer.

Her tender voice rose again. 'Xiang Xiang, don't stand there like a statue. Come, now let's first pray to the White-Browed-God and Guan Yin.'

I followed her to kneel in front of the two ceramic statues on the small altar. After she'd offered the God and Goddess incense, tea, and some of the food from the table, she began her prayer. 'The venerable White-Browed-God and the compassionate Guan Yin, please accept these offerings from me, Pearl, and my little sister Xiang Xiang. We thank you for protecting us from evil and bringing us good luck. Please continue to help us bewitch our customers and fatten our purses.'

Then she spoke to Ruby's picture placed between the two statues and whispered another prayer too softly for me to hear. After that, she asked me to sit between her and an empty seat at the table on which were placed chopsticks, a cup, a bowl, and a glass from which bloomed a napkin folded in the shape of a flower.

'Sister Pearl, is there another guest coming?'

'The guest is already here.'

I looked around the room. 'Who? There's no one here except you and me.'

She threw me a chiding glance. 'This seat is for Ruby. In my prayer, I've already invited her to join us.'

Invited a dead person to join us? I felt both a shudder and an urge to laugh. But since I didn't want to break Pearl's heart by breaking her faith, I kept my mouth shut.

Now she started to put food onto Ruby's plate and pour tea into Ruby's cup. After that, she picked up the bottle of wine and showed it to me. 'Xiang Xiang, this is the best kind of champagne. Once it's in the wine shops, all the bottles will be snapped up by the rich. So today I sent my maid to buy it on the black market.'

The bottle opened with a loud 'Pop!' Pearl smiled prettily but my heart almost jumped to my throat. The shot which had killed my father must have sounded like this, only ten times louder. The foam gushing out from the bottle's narrow neck conjured in my mind the froth dripping from Baba's mouth the moment the bullet hit his head. I bit my lip. I really shouldn't have thought of something gruesome like this during Pearl's celebration.

It was bad luck.

Now Pearl poured the three of us full glasses. After that, she clinked her glass to Ruby's and said to the empty space, her voice extremely tender, breaking my heart, 'Ruby, here's to my winning tomorrow's contest.' Then she turned to toast me. 'Xiang Xiang, to our prestige!'

'To our prestige,' I echoed.

We sipped our wine in silence, then Pearl pointed to the dishes. 'Tonight we'll eat light – steamed fish, drunken shrimp, crab meat dumplings, *dandan* noodles, fried quail, marinated duck's feet, stewed rabbits' legs, spicy deers' tails, abalone with oyster sauce, ham congee, lotus root soup – for we'll have to reserve room for the very rich French food tomorrow.'

Although the food cooked by Aunty Ah Ping was delicious as always, when I swallowed, my throat felt as if it were broken out with blisters. An invisible hand seemed to touch my face, caress my shoulder, feel the texture of my satin dress. I imagined invisible eyes from Ruby's empty place searching me with curiosity, even jealousy. I peeked at Pearl. She took a delicate bite of a crab dumpling, then chewed with her crimson-painted lips. A smile, like a butterfly, hovered on her snow-white face.

Though I'd lost my appetite, my hand, to please her, kept flicking my chopsticks into the various dishes, putting food onto her plate, then taking some for myself.

Pearl, elated, kept eating and drinking. She said dreamily, 'After

I've won the contest, I hope someone will propose so I can live the comfortable life of a rich *tai tai*.'

I was surprised to hear this. 'But Sister Pearl, I thought you didn't want to be any man's wife.'

'Silly girl,' she cocked an eye at me, 'I don't mean a housewife, but a rich *tai tai*.' Pearl sighed. 'Someday we'll be old and ugly. Mama, or whoever takes over from her, won't waste money in keeping us because no man will pay to fuck ugly old bitches. With no other way to make a living other than that of the bedchamber, what can we do but take refuge in a temple? But . . .' Pearl shook her head, 'if we don't have any money to make a large offering, we may even be turned down there.

'So the best way out is to meet someone who's so bewitched by you that he's willing to get you out of the fire pit and take you home as his *tai tai*. But this is as difficult as filtering gold from sand. Second best is to become a mama yourself. In that case not only do you make a lot of money through someone else doing the fucking, you can also get revenge by torturing the girls the same way you were tortured.' She paused for a brief moment, then, 'The hardest thing is to run away.'

When I heard the two words 'run away,' I could almost feel my blood foaming inside my arteries. I'd never told Pearl that I was resolved, someday, to do just that. I put down my chopsticks. 'Everyone watches us here, so how can someone succeed in running away?'

Pearl cast me a curious glance, then picked up a shrimp and popped it into her mouth. 'I knew one sister here in Peach Blossom who did just that. She planned carefully for a long time. First she hid her money in secret places. Then she won Mama and De's trust by being obedient and never talking back. This went on for years until Mama and De felt so relaxed that they didn't even send a guard to watch her during her outings. Then one night she got her guest dead drunk and disappeared.'

'Was she caught?'

'No, we never heard of her again. It's been ten years. She might have become a beggar, been killed by bandits, or married her secret lover; it would all depend on her Karma.' Pearl paused to sip her wine. 'Years ago another young sister by the name of Water Moon succeeded in running away from the Sleeping Flower Pavilion, then went to a temple to take refuge. But as soon as the abbess spotted her as the gate was swinging open, she quickly banged it closed.'

'Why?'

'Because the girl's beauty snatched away the old nun's breath. She insisted that the girl would bring catastrophe to her temple.'

I was shocked to hear this. Pearl's words were almost the same as my mother's years ago during our departure:

> The Mother Abbess said that you're too beautiful to be a nun.
> She fears your beauty will bring bad luck to her temple.

'Was she really that beautiful?' Actually my real question was whether she was even more beautiful than I.

'I can only tell you that after the other sisters saw her, they all went back to their room to smash their mirrors.'

'Oh . . . then . . . what happened to this girl?'

'Since she'd brought a lot of money and jewellery to donate, the abbess finally changed her mind and accepted her.'

I let out a sigh of relief, then absent-mindedly scraped rice into my mouth.

Pearl poked her chopsticks at the fish's eyes, picked them up, and put them onto my bowl. 'If you want to be smart, eat more of this.' Then she broke the fish head and started to chew, her delicate tongue sucking, licking, and spitting out bones.

Finally she accomplished the task of dismantling the head. 'But there was still more to the story. After she had her head shaved and put on a loose robe, her life was still not at peace. Her former customers just wouldn't leave her alone. They went all the way to the temple to look at her as if she were an animal in a circus. Some tried to persuade her to go back to prostitution, others thought it would be much more exciting if she was willing to entertain them as a nun prostitute, yet others were just curious to find out how she'd look with neither hair nor curves. Poor girl, she actually became a celebrity, much more prestigious than when she had lived in the turquoise pavilion—'

'Then what happened?' I asked through a mouthful of rice.

'She was so determined to be a nun that one day she pressed a red-hot iron onto her cheek—'

I dropped my chopsticks and covered my face. 'Oh my heaven!'

'Needless to say, as an ugly woman, she was finally left alone to find peace.' Pearl paused to sip more wine. 'Few sisters have her courage.'

I was too shocked to say anything.

'Xiang Xiang,' Pearl reached to unplug my hand from my cheek, 'would you please stop worrying about someone you don't even know?'

So as not to arouse her suspicion, I took an extra helping of *dan-dan* noodles and resumed eating. Then I asked, slightly changing the subject, 'What about those who got married?'

Pearl sucked on a duck's foot, then bit off a piece of webbing and chewed for a while. 'When you're used to the life here, married life may not be much better. In place of Mama, De, and the jealous sisters, you have your dictatorial husband, his ugly first wife, and a slew of spiteful concubines. After the loose ways here, it's almost impossible to put up with all the rules in a big Confucian household.

'Some ex-sisters try to behave like decent women – giving up seductive manners and gaudy clothes – forgetting that these are exactly what attracted their customers to redeem them in the first place. So their husbands soon go back to the turquoise pavilions to look for new faces. Without the husband's backing, they're just another out-of-favour concubine, spat on because of their infamous past.'

Pearl sighed. 'Once you're a whore, you always stay one. Nobody believes that you're faithful to your husband.' She spat. 'Those *chou nanren*, they want women to be both saints and sinners!' Some moments passed before she went on, 'I also knew a sister who got married, three times, but all her husbands died, so she was forced to replay the *pipa*. It's so sad.' Pearl sipped her wine while looking at me over the rim of her glass. 'We can never beat fate, can we?'

But we can play along and make the most out of it.

I remembered my mother's saying but decided to keep it to myself.

Pearl forced a smile onto her face. 'Xiang Xiang, why are we talking about all these unpleasant things when we should be celebrating my winning the contest?'

'Then why don't you tell me more about Jiang Mou?'

To my amazement, she blushed. 'I like him very much, but too bad he's both poor and married. You know, a woman like me needs a lot of money to maintain,' she said, spearing a bit of abalone, putting it into her mouth, and chewing absent-mindedly. Her eyes, now blurred by the alcohol, looked like two dreams floating on the sea. On her wrist, the jade bracelet gleamed like a green lizard flitting under moonlight.

I appreciated her for a few seconds before I tentatively asked, 'Why do you like him so much?'

Dreamily she went on, 'Jiang Mou is very good at pleasing both me and my body. He knows exactly when and what a woman does and doesn't want.'

I knew what I wanted – to find my mother and revenge for Baba. But as for my body, I had no idea what it wanted, only what it didn't – to serve any rich, stinky men who decided to visit Peach Blossom.

I blurted out, 'My body doesn't want anyone.'

Pearl smiled mischievously. 'Someday you'll meet someone you truly love; then you'll have a real soul losing.'

'What does it feel like?'

'Like strings of firecrackers popping one after another.'

A silence. Pearl poured me more wine, then picked up a quail and put it into my bowl. 'Let's eat and enjoy our life at this moment.' She paused to speak to the empty seat. 'Right, Ruby?'

I stared at the seat and felt a jolt. If Ruby's spirit was really here, then where was the yellow butterfly?

I blurted out, 'Sister Pearl, where's the butterfly?'

She looked up at me, her pupils now two seasick bugs rolling on a boat. 'Don't you worry about that.' The gold filigreed butterfly gave out a few mysterious sparks on her hair. 'There are many yellow butterflies in the haunted garden.'

That night after I'd retired into my room, I flipped and tossed in the bed like a fish sizzling in a wok, painfully alert to the slightest sound. I hoped in the morning to see Pearl's name and pictures on all the front pages of the newspapers, together with poems praising her. Yet I couldn't cast away the ominous feeling in my heart. I prayed to the Guan Yin on my neck chain, then assured myself over and over that nothing would go wrong – Pearl's and my votes combined would surely beat all the other sisters.

I kept alternately tormenting and comforting myself until I fell into a troubled sleep.

18

The Jade Stalk Refuses to Salute

I awoke to a sharp cry slashing the morning air. At first I thought it came from a bad dream, but a moment later I was snapped into reality. I jumped off the bed, flung open the door, and dashed toward Pearl's room.

Plum Blossom cried to my back, 'Kill! Kill!'

As I entered, my heart plunged at what I saw.

Pearl, stark naked, had collapsed on the floor. Sheets of newspaper, soaked with blood, lay strewn around her like red good-luck posters turned unlucky. Ah Ping was helping her to sit up.

I dashed toward Pearl but she didn't seem to notice me – her eyes were closed.

Staring at her nudity, I remembered it was a custom for sisters to pray naked in front of the White-Browed God – so he'll be aroused and grant them all their wishes. Pearl must have been praying to win the contest. The blood, I was relieved to realise, was not Pearl's, but chicken blood. Sisters all believe that drinking the crimson liquid protects them from evil spirits.

I turned to Ah Ping. 'Aunty Ah Ping, please get something to cover Pearl.'

Ah Ping dashed away, then returned to throw a blanket over Pearl.

I lowered my voice and asked the mute woman, 'What happened?'

Face streaked with tears, Ah Ping pointed to the newspaper. I picked it up and saw on the front page Red Jade's name as big as eggs and her picture as big as a chicken.

I could hear my sharp voice trembling. 'Red Jade won the contest?'

Ah Ping nodded.

I read the newspaper again and saw a poem praising her:

She possesses quality like that of the rarest jade; her
    manner is graceful as a white crane.
In her elegant room filled with precious curios and
    soothing incense,
she appreciates the moon and plays with the wind that
    seeps in through her embroidered curtains.
A born beauty with talents soaring to the highest clouds,
    she is the unique flower that captures all our hearts.

I threw down the newspaper. 'Liar! Liar!'

Ah Ping picked it up and thrust it under my eyes. I searched the whole page but couldn't find Pearl's name. I couldn't believe what I saw – and what I didn't see. Pearl hadn't won the title of vice president, nor even that of prime minister.

'What happened?' I shouted.

Just then Pearl spoke, her voice faint and ghostly, as if rising from a grave. 'Wine, give me some wine.'

Ah Ping hurried away. I knelt down and took Pearl's hand. 'Sister Pearl . . .' I tried to say something comforting but couldn't utter a word.

Pearl muttered as if talking to herself. 'Fate, this is all fate . . .'

This time I blurted out my mother's saying, 'Sister Pearl, we can't beat fate, but we can play along and make the most out of it. Try to be happy.'

Pearl jolted upright and screamed into my face. 'Try to be happy? How? Are you mocking me?'

Ah Ping was back with a bottle; she waved a hand to calm Pearl.

Pearl stared at her and then me, tears streaming from her eyes, ruining her immaculate makeup. Finally she said, her voice cracked, 'That's it; I'm done for.'

'No, Sister Pearl . . .'

Her eyes, though still glistening, seemed to have lost their power to bewitch. 'Xiang Xiang, I promise this will never happen again. Never!'

The way she spat the word 'never' almost halted my heartbeat.

A long silence. I said, 'Sister Pearl, you can participate in the contest again next time.'

She shook her head emphatically. 'There won't be any next time.'

'Sister Pearl, please don't be pessimistic—'

'You know how long I've been waiting for this? Seven years. Since seven was Ruby's lucky number, I swore to myself I would mourn her for seven years. Finally the seven long years passed and now this. Next year I'll be twenty-four and too old to have any chance. Besides . . .' Before she could finish her sentence, Pearl spat out a dollop of blood.

Ah Ping immediately snatched it up with a handkerchief. Then she made a gesture to boil water and left the room.

Now Pearl looked at me sharply. 'You didn't see my name in the newspaper, did you?'

'Sister Pearl, I'm so sorry . . .'

'Yes, you should feel sorry, because my name *did* appear in the newspaper!'

What do you mean? I wanted to ask but swallowed my words. Maybe Pearl had lost both the contest and her mind. If her name was on the newspaper then she should be the winner! Just then Pearl snatched up the newspaper, flipped it to the inside page and thrust it under my eyes.

My jaw dropped. I was so stunned by what I saw.

The name *Pearl*, as big as two fish heads, appeared right under the heading WEEDS LIST.

To find her name here was so hideous and frightening that I felt my hair stand on end. The poem 'Crushed Pearl' forced itself into my eyes:

Oh Pearl, your eyes are but two cracks and your nose a big
  chimney.
Your mouth a bloody bowl and your ears flapping clangs.
Your hands are crude and clumsy, and your breath stinks.
Even when you strip off all your clothes, our jade stalks
  refuse to salute.
So stunned by your ugliness that, alas, it can't even vomit.
You think you're a pearl hidden at the sea bottom to be
  desired, but we think you're a tarnished pearl crushed
  under the smelly feet of swine.

After I'd finished reading, I burst out crying. 'Sister Pearl, it's
lies, all lies!'

'But if it's printed in the newspaper, everybody will think it's the
truth.'

'But all your customers know it's not!'

'Then why have I lost?'

Yes, why had Pearl lost? Bewildered, I asked, my voice a mere
whisper, 'Then what are we going to do now?'

'Nothing! Xiang Xiang, that's the point, nothing. I'm doomed!'

'But Sister Pearl, you told me that in the turquoise pavilion
there's always a solution to any problem. You promised me that!' I
started to yell.

To my surprise, Pearl's expression turned calm. 'Yes,' she
sighed. 'But this happened outside Peach Blossom, not inside. So
nothing can be done.' She paused for a brief moment. 'That's why
Mama and De don't even come to me.'

It was then that I realised no one was here except me and Aunty
Ah Ping. 'Why didn't they?'

'Why?' Pearl sneered. 'Because they're now celebrating with
Red Jade in her room! Nobody here will waste sympathy on a
loser.'

'But you're not a loser, Sister Pearl, you're still the most prestigious courtesan in Shanghai!' I was screaming again.

The tears had left lines on Pearl's cheeks like prison bars. 'Yes.
But only until yesterday. From today on I'm just a tarnished prostitute . . . no more business . . . I'll be ruined.'

'Oh no, sister Pearl, it's not true. You still have many customers.'

She sneered. 'Those dog-fucked assholes? You think you can trust any of them? They'll dump me once they see my name on the weeds list! You can fool yourself, Xiang Xiang, but don't try to fool me. I'm too old for that.'

'But why will they dump you? It doesn't matter about the newspapers, the fact is you're still the most beautiful and talented sister here.'

'Maybe I was. But if you were a rich and powerful man, would you go to someone with cracked eyes, chimney nose, bloody mouth, flapping ears – who stinks? They only care about keeping face!'

'But can't your old customers also publish something nice about you in the *Flower Moon News*?'

'But, of course, Mr. Zhu was bribed. Do you think he'll publish poems complimenting me? You think he wants his wife to wake up one morning and find his corpse lying in a pool of blood in a back alley?'

A long silence. Finally I asked, 'Sister Pearl, who do you think did this to you?'

Pearl spat. 'That lightning-struck bitch!'

'You mean Red Jade?'

'Who else? Of course it's not just her, but some powerful customers of hers. No one will dare offend whoever is behind all this.'

'I wonder what magic scheme the big-papaya witch uses to manipulate all these men.' She smacked her thigh, startling me. 'I'll kill her!'

Just then Aunty Ah Ping came back with a big wooden bucket of hot water. She laid the bucket on the floor, took out a towel, and started to bathe Pearl's swollen face.

Three days later I discovered what had happened. Red Jade's now favourite guest and best customer was the Police Chief Che – the one who'd tried to shoot Spring Moon. It was Che who bought up all the votes for Red Jade.

Spring Moon had told me all this when I had run into her in the corridor.

'But I thought Police Chief Che liked Pearl!'

'He did. But Red Jade convinced Chief Che that Pearl had humiliated him during the elegant gathering . . . the one when he shot me.'

'But that happened five years ago!'

Spring Moon made a face. 'Haven't you heard the phrase "ten years is not too late for a gentleman to revenge"?'

'But Pearl didn't humiliate Chief Che. And he was drunk.'

'That's what you think. Lucky for me, I wasn't killed. But Red Jade told Chief Che that everyone had seen him let a woman tell him what to do, not only a woman, but a whore. Red Jade also told him that people still address him as Chief Che, but behind his back they call him Chief Chicken.' Spring Moon lowered her voice. 'A man like Che won't hesitate to destroy anyone who doesn't give him face.'

'But Pearl did.' I protested. 'I still remember she said to the Chief that we need him to take good care of our society by protecting us from wrongs. And also, that she'd never say no to him because of her respect for righteousness.'

'Yes. But that's exactly what Red Jade used to accuse Pearl. She told Che that Pearl made him look like a fool, for she was cooing at him and telling him what to do. Worse, Pearl also touched his *face* in public.'

A Chinese saying flashed across my mind: If you are out to condemn somebody, you can always trump up a charge.

'But doesn't the Chief realise that it's Red Jade who is manipulating him?'

'His vision is now completely blocked by her two towering peaks. He imagines that whatever troubles he has, they'll be dissolved in that deep valley between her mountains.'

I sighed, suddenly realising some truth to the saying: Men rule the world, and women rule men. But unfortunately it was not Pearl but another woman who was the ruler!

Spring Moon leant toward me and lowered her voice. 'Now Chief Che is Red Jade's favourite guest.' She paused to look around. 'I've heard that Red Jade also knows spells to bewitch men. She gets the man's picture, writes his birthday on it, and sticks seven needles into it. Then she keeps the picture pinned on the wall above her bed and calls his name every day. At night, if he falls asleep in her bed, she'll burn paper money, then fumigate his socks and shoes with the smoke. That's why the Chief is completely bewitched by her.'

Of course, I knew about these forbidden practices, but Pearl and I had never used them, for Pearl told me these were only exercised by old, ugly whores with no other ways to attract customers.

Spring Moon went on excitedly, 'I heard something else, too. Pearl's going to be dumped by her favourite guest Mr. Chan next year, because she'll turn twenty-four. He says she'll make him feel old, not to mention that twenty four – *er-si* – is bad luck because it rhymes with "easy to die." '

I felt so upset for Pearl that I couldn't utter a word. Long moments passed before I asked, 'Spring Moon, how did you know about all this?'

'Little Red told me. She'd heard Mama and De talk while she was serving them.'

For a week after the contest results were printed in the newspapers, Pearl, though devastated, still tried to lead a normal existence. However, as she'd sadly predicted, her business did decline as drastically as if she'd suddenly turned into a leper. Now Pearl usually shut herself up in her room, but sometimes would invite me in to sing while she played the *qin*. 'Lament Behind the Long Gate' was now her favourite piece. Although I'd always found the lyrics beautiful, now they sounded so sad that I could hardly bear to breathe life into them. I feared they would plunge Pearl into further depression. But she persisted and I could not deny her request.

The inner pavilion is covered with fallen petals.
In deep melancholy, Spring slips away.
Light seeps through the Western Palace where a banquet is
    being held . . .

Spring is generous, but then dreams escape.
In an instant, life has changed.

My incense is cold, and dust covers my gold-threaded
  pillow.
The flowing years have furtively passed to other hands.

Tearful eyes ask a flower, but a flower does not talk . . .
Where can I declare my sentiments?
I want to tell them to my dreams, but can I even trust my
  dreams?

While singing, I peeked at Pearl. Her hair was unkempt and her
face was pale and sunken. Her figure, instead of being outlined by
an elegantly tailored gown, was now hidden under a black top and
trousers. Maybe she'd given up trying to be attractive, unaware that
she now possessed a decadent beauty that struck me as even more
appealing. But I was a woman. What Pearl now needed was a man
– who loved her and whom she loved – to comfort her. Where was
Jiang Mou? I didn't want to ask.

I sang the refrains again as tears rolled down her cheeks.

Except for the subdued sounds of the *qin* and my voice, Pearl's
chamber was now silent while bright light and boisterous noise
streamed from Red Jade's. My heart was breaking as I looked at
Pearl's empty incense burner and the dust starting to accumulate
on her pillows and dressing table . . .

Pearl had fallen to earth after having soared to the highest
clouds.

Now I was the one who sang the lyrics while she was the one
who cried.

'Xiang Xiang.' She looked up at me and said softly, 'Promise me
that if anything happens to me, you'll take good care of the *qin*.'

Months passed and my worry about Pearl grew each day. She
now barely touched her food. Ah Ping prepared her special soup,
but she would just wave the mute woman away. Pearl's face became
drawn and she even lost her enthusiasm for talking. She would gesture or move her eyes to signal what she needed. The *ming ji* who

had once excelled in the stratagems of face and body now had no one left to please by these arts.

Worse, Pearl's opium pipe was now her most faithful companion. Whenever I approached her room, the acrid smell of the burning narcotic would tear at my nostrils. Inside, her languorous figure would be seen crouching on her bed like a crumpled statue, her lips sucking like a hungry baby's. Staring at the elaborate Bodhisattva bed made my heart sink, for now Pearl, instead of looking like the beautiful Guan Yin, had become a fallen goddess. Beside her sat her maid, patiently rolling and patting pellets of opium, then dropping them into an iron pot boiling over a charcoal stove.

It was Pearl who had warned me – after my nipples had been pierced and she'd soothed me with the narcotic – not to become addicted. But now whenever I implored her to quit, she'd just stare at me emptily with her once luminous now turned dead-fish eyes.

I tried my best to comfort her, with small gestures like putting strands of her hair in place, wiping tear streaks from her cheeks, smoothing the wrinkles from her clothes. I just wanted to let her know that she was not alone in her grief. However, her look was so distant and her spirit so far away that I could no longer fathom her real self behind the haze of smoke.

Then, two weeks later, her inconsolable grief came to an end.

One afternoon, Pearl had asked me to accompany her to the balcony. 'Xiang Xiang, the calendar says today is *li chunjie* – Establishing Spring. I think it'll be nice to appreciate spring scenes from our balcony here. Don't you think?'

'Yes, what a wonderful idea.' I was so pleased by this sign of happiness in her that I would have agreed to anything.

The distant mountains seemed completely oblivious to what had happened inside Peach Blossom. Yet, locked in by patches of mist, they had their own kind of melancholy. Among the swelling peaks rose a white tower, its upturned eaves seeming to beckon to us while asking, 'Lonely beauties, where will you find your love?'

Pearl, her face bare of make-up and her body hidden beneath a loose white robe, rested her elbow on the balustrade. Her eyes, instead of practising flirtatious glances, fixed on the shifting mist. She looked like a fairy who had just descended from the heavenly palace to this turquoise pavilion. What was she thinking? I was tempted to ask, but decided to let her be.

Suddenly her soft voice rose in the air, reciting a poem:

Here is emerald wine and red lantern.
Please my lord, come this way to my bedchamber.
Behind the shuffling, gold-embroidered curtain, tonight I
    could make you the happiest of men.
But alas, love has vanished, just like the morning dew!

How could I respond? I looked around and noticed a few branches of plum blossom reaching up from beneath the balcony. The flowers bloomed with a robust pink like that which had once adorned Pearl's lips. My heart began to pound at the auspicious sign. While the petals blushed like a young girl, the ancient branches twisted like ancient calligraphy. The new petals and old branches conjured in my mind the image of an eager young student and his wise teacher – like the relationship had once been between Pearl and me.

Tears swelled in my eyes but I blinked them back.

I remembered Pearl's explanation of the *qin* piece 'Three Variations on the Plum Blossom.' The flowers' sheer tenacity to survive within a harsh environment, she'd told me, had moved thousands of poets and painters. Over many centuries, their numerous poems and paintings extolling the plum blossom's virtue had nourished wounded hearts and strengthened lost souls.

I turned to Pearl and pointed below the balcony. 'Sister Pearl, look, plum blossoms!' That was all I dared to say, fearing if I went on she'd misunderstand and think I was trying to lecture her with what she'd taught me.

'I know,' she said without looking at the flowers or me. A pause, then her soft voice rose again, 'Xiang Xiang, have you also noticed the swallow's nest below the balcony to your right?'

I craned my neck and saw a nest half-hidden among pillars. To my delight, perching on the twigs was a swallow, now feeding her babies. Though her action of thrusting food into the eagerly opened beaks was so fast that it looked almost comical, my eyes were again in tears. I felt touched not only by the good omen of new lives and motherly love, but also by the hope that Pearl's mind, though seemingly oblivious, was once again sharp and clear!

I turned and caught her glance. To my delight, she spoke again, this time softly yet clearly, 'Once a swallow is born in her nest, though she grows up and flies away, she'll always come back. Every year. Nothing – rain, snow, thunder – can stop her homecoming. It's a ritual of respect to her life journey.'

Her remark reminded me of my conversation with my mother at the train station:

Xiang Xiang, we Chinese say falling leaves returning to their roots. You understand what this means?
Yes, Ma – no matter what happens, we should always find our way home.

But now five years had passed, and the only home I knew was Peach Blossom. And I'd never gotten a single word from Mother.

'Unless—' Pearl's voice rose, awakening me from my reminiscence.

'Unless what?'

'Her nest is destroyed.'

I turned to look at her incredulously. 'But who would have the heart to do such a thing?'

'Many things: a thunderstorm, a snowstorm, or even a strong wind. That's what nature does. Then there's destruction by men. The day will come when Peach Blossom Pavilion will be torn down.'

I felt a jolt inside, for the thought that Peach Blossom would be gone someday had never entered my mind. Not that I liked living here serving those *chou nanren*, but like the swallow's tiny nest, Peach Blossom was all I had for a home. When Peach Blossom was gone, where would we all go? Even the rats in the basement – they'd scurry onto the street, but would they be smashed by boys, cars, or falling pillars?

Pearl went on, 'Or it might also be destroyed by a little boy who happens to pass by, sees the nest, then throws a stone at it just for fun—' Suddenly she stopped.

'Sister Pearl?'

'Shhh . . .' She tilted her head, listening. 'Someone's coming.'

I heard footsteps sound closer and closer until from the corner slowly emerged a strikingly beautiful, richly attired woman – Red Jade. A strong fragrance scurried its way into my nostrils.

Her red gown was trimmed with lace in an intricate pattern like spiders' webs. I had to acknowledge that she now looked like a true *ming ji*. Under the blood-coloured mesh, the two globes looked as if they were about to burst their way to freedom. A gold and diamond spider brooch clung onto one of the full moons. On one side of her pomaded hair, a red flower precariously played hide and seek. A fan painted with flowers swayed indolently in her red-gloved hand.

Like a voluptuous goddess – or a she-vampire – walking on earth, her beauty possessed the power to halt breath and transport souls. Now wriggling toward our direction, she kept flashing the sort of overtly flirtatious smile that Pearl had warned me not to use.

Pearl stared at her with contempt. But Red Jade didn't seem to mind at all; the smile kept blossoming on her face.

We kept staring at each other for long moments before her jiggling breasts and wriggling bottom finally came to rest. 'Oh how I envy your leisure. Especially you, Sister Pearl. Now even if I want to take a break, Chief Che won't let me. How I wish I could retire early like you!'

I blurted out, 'You slut, why don't you just hold your tongue!'

Red Jade burst into laughter. 'Ha! Me a slut? What about you,' she thrust a red-gloved finger at me, then at Pearl, 'and you, aren't you all sluts? That's how we make our living here, being *sluts*. But,' she cast Pearl a meaningful glance, 'of course you're not a slut anymore, you're retired. Congratulations! Now would you two like to come to my room for a glass of champagne to celebrate Sister Pearl's early retirement as well as my winning the contest?'

Pearl spat, 'You bitch!'

Then, as Pearl was about to lunge forward, a yellow butterfly

materialised out of nowhere, and began to hover around Red Jade
– attracted to her strong perfume, I assumed.

Abruptly Pearl stopped, then tears swelled in her eyes while she
croaked a wailing 'Ruby!'

Her eyes glued to the butterfly and her expression transfixed,
Pearl now looked as if her soul were being snatched away by a
dark, unfathomable force.

'Wah!' Red Jade sneered with her shrill, saccharine voice. 'How
sentimental! You even give a worthless insect such a precious
name. You,' her high-pitched voice suddenly dropped many
notches, 'are just an ugly old bitch who crawled out from the rotten
gate of another dog-fucked bitch!'

Before we could respond to this, Red Jade lifted her fan toward
the butterfly. The insect immediately rested on it.

She snapped shut the fan. Then she opened it back up and let
the crushed yellow mess drop onto the ground.

Pearl's gold filigreed butterfly fell from her hair, hitting the floor
with a dull plop.

19

Last Journey in the Red Dust

It was Aunty Ah Ping who found Pearl's body hanging from a rafter in the temple of the haunted garden. Later it was said that a yellow butterfly hovered by the hem of her gown.

The moment Fang Rong and Wu Qiang heard of Pearl's death, they went to search her room. I offered to help. Not only was I eager to do something for my blood sister, I also wanted to find her *qin*. But to my alarm, after everything had been turned upside down, there was still no trace of the instrument.

I asked Fang Rong, 'Mama, have you seen Sister Pearl's *qin*?'

She thought for a while. 'Ah, you mean that rotten piece of wood that Pearl called an instrument? I haven't seen it for a long time. Maybe she'd finally grown tired of it and thrown it away. I heard her play it once or twice a long time ago. But you know what it sounded like? A cat's meowing!'

Mama kept babbling on while my mind went blank. Now that Pearl had boarded the immortal's journey, the *qin* would be the only thing that would link me to her. And now even this tie was severed. An overwhelming sadness rippled through my heart.

As soon as Pearl's room was empty, Wu Qiang set off several strings of firecrackers to scare away evil spirits. With the explosions ringing in my ears instead of Pearl's ghost wailing, I stared at the empty space and realised that my dearest sister was forever gone.

It didn't surprise me that Peach Blossom had decided not to carry out a full funeral for Pearl.

When I asked Mama whether she was going to hire any Buddhist or Taoist priests to recite sutras for their daughter's soul, she said, 'You think Peach Blossom is a charitable organisation that we have all this easy money to spend?' She stared at me, her eyes forlorn, even the mole between her brows looked distressed. 'Xiang Xiang, haven't you realised that every coin we earn here, if you break it open, will bleed?'

Mama was saying that all the money was hard-earned with sweat, tears, and blood. She was right. Only it was us who bled and she who got the money.

Then, to my utter disbelief, she announced that she was not going to Pearl's burial. She sighed, '*Hai*, Xiang Xiang, it's not that I'm so cold-hearted that I won't even accompany my dear daughter on her last trip in the red dust. It's because I don't have time. Look at Peach Blossom, it's packed every night. If I don't keep an eye on the minutest detail for one second, things will go wrong just like that!' Her thumb and middle fingers collided to create a small explosion. 'Do you think Pearl will forgive me for that? So, in order to appease her soul, I can't go to her burial.'

'But Mama, the burial will be held in the morning, not the evening!'

She shot me a chiding glance. 'Xiang Xiang, if I don't have enough sleep in the morning, how can I take good care of the business in the evening?' Her tone held a scolding edge. 'And don't forget I do this entirely for you and your fellow sisters, otherwise,' she paused, then blurted out, 'remember years ago that little beggar who robbed your ice cream and was almost hit by a car? If anything goes wrong in Peach Blossom, all of you will end up like him, you understand?' She smiled. 'But generous-hearted as I am, I'll pay for her coffin and costs for the burial.'

If someone kills herself, her ghost will hover near the place of suicide, harassing anyone who lives there. I wanted to tell Fang Rong that if she and Wu Qiang didn't go to pay respect at Pearl's burial nor hire monks to appease her soul, she would emerge from the *yin* world to pester Peach Blossom. But I had an idea forming in my mind and did not want to do anything to draw attention to myself.

Pearl was buried on a windy morning two days after her suicide. Mama had ordered that the incident be kept a secret. 'I don't want her former customers to come, because Peach Blossom doesn't want our rich guests to catch bad luck.'

So only Aunty Ah Ping, Spring Moon, and I went to bid Pearl farewell.

Her emaciated body had been laid in an equally emaciated coffin, then carried by two guards to the haunted garden. The three of us followed silently behind. Spring Moon was secretly wiping away tears. Aunty Ah Ping, as usual, looked as if her mind were somewhere else, while I was still too stunned by the whole thing to know what I felt.

In the daytime, the garden didn't look haunted, but sad, like a deserted woman lamenting her ill Karma behind the long, deep gate. Though it was early spring, as we made our way along the muddy earth, there was not a single patch of green to dispel the dreariness. Our black robes, fluttering in the breeze, only added another shade of gloom.

More depressing sights were yet to come. The guards, now ready to lower the coffin into the pit which lay before us like a hungry ghost's wide-open mouth, eyed us directly as if to say, 'Let's get this over with!'

Right then, Aunty Ah Ping waved them a halting hand, then tilted her bag and poured out its contents. She lit a match and began to burn the paper offerings – money, gold and silver ingots, clothes, and to my puzzlement, even a paper baby doll. She kept murmuring unintelligible prayers until the guards got so impatient that they tossed the coffin into the black hole. Then the two muscular men shovelled big spadefuls of earth onto the 'four-and-a-half pieces of wood' until it gradually vanished from sight. It was then that my tears, like water flooding from a collapsed dam, poured down my cheeks.

After the guards had tossed the last spade of mud, each pulled out a filthy rag to wipe his face and hands, then, with neither words nor a trace of emotion, strode away. The three of us stood motionless in front of the small, unmarked piece of ground where underneath lay our beloved Pearl, whose body, I imagined, was still warm. Now I was totally alone in the world. Pearl hadn't even left a note of farewell for me. How could she have abandoned me like this?

I only let my tears flow during the daytime. In the evening, I willed my lips to lift into a dimpled smile and my eyes to dance like butterflies, while my heart silently bled.

Red Jade's sudden rise to fame brought even more business and prestige to Peach Blossom. Huge signboards carved with her name and strewn with fresh flowers and colourful lanterns hung day and night above the pavilion's entrance. Every day she received piles of invitations to go out and was seen everywhere – exclusive restaurants, fashionable teahouses, night clubs, elegant gatherings, opera houses.

However, Red Jade's popularity didn't seem to affect my business. Invitations also piled high on my table and poems praising me were passed around. My faithful regulars said that I possessed something Red Jade fatally lacked – an artistic air. While I had the true manner of a refined musician and sensitive poet, Red Jade only looked like a prostitute feigning to be an artist. My painting teacher Mr. Wu had once told me she couldn't even hold a brush straight, that was why her lines were always crooked. He said, 'We painters say, "Only if the heart is sincere will the brush be straight." '

Curiously enough, Red Jade never acted antagonistic to me. When we ran into each other in the pavilion or caught each other's glance in a restaurant or at the opera, she would even nod and smile sweetly toward me. At that moment, while my heart softened, Pearl's words would ring loudly in my ears:

Beware of this cunning fox. While she smiles, she'll stab you with a knife.

How wrong, Sister Pearl. She hadn't even had to stab you with a knife and you still died.

Whenever I saw Red Jade, I'd secretly swear to myself that I would be brutal and scheming like her, so that I would be able to escape from Peach Blossom, find my mother, and discover the unknown warlord who had killed my father.

On the seventh evening of Pearl's death, after I'd served my last customer, I sneaked away from Peach Blossom and headed straight to the haunted garden. There were two things I had to do: make offerings to Pearl and pray to Guan Yin.

The moon was hidden behind clouds, leaving the sky dark and empty, as if it, too, were mourning Pearl. I stepped across the temple's threshold with a heavy heart and an equally heavy basket filled with Pearl's favourite foods, together with incense, towel, plates, cups, and chopsticks. From the lantern in my hand, a spot of yellowish light bounced around the empty floor, reminding me of a mercury lamp highlighting performers on stage. Only tonight the stage was empty, for the performer had already gone.

'Pearl,' I whispered, tears stinging my eyes.

I tilted the lantern and looked up, trying to locate the beam where Pearl had hanged herself. Had she chosen the same one that Ruby had picked seven years before? Staring at the numerous rafters, I wondered how many other sisters had willingly, or unwillingly, ended their lives dancing in midair. The image soon became so horrifying that I had to look away.

I hurried to the altar, arranged the food and tea that I'd brought, then stooped to reach for the Guan Yin statue. The Goddess looked compassionate, as usual, but also completely oblivious to the fate of Pearl, her faithful worshipper.

'Why didn't you stop Pearl from killing herself?' I asked out loud while my hands carefully wiped the goddess with a towel.

She stared back at me with inanimate eyes. I sighed, then took out Pearl's and Ruby's pictures and arranged them on the altar next to Guan Yin. Since I had no wish to stay long, I made the ritual simple. I offered incense, tea, and food to the Goddess of Mercy. Then I swore to her that I'd cultivate myself to be a woman with a thousand scheming hearts, so I could lure a thousand rich and powerful men into my arms. First, I would use their influence to get back at Red Jade, then I'd cajole enough money from them to leave Peach Blossom and find my mother. I also importuned Guan Yin to help me find the warlord, and when I did, grant me the nerve to put a bullet in his evil head.

I felt a little guilty that my prayers were full of anger, bitterness, and selfish desires. Would a Goddess of Compassion grant me all these bad-karmic, ill-intended wishes? Feeling culpable, I asked the Goddess to forgive my vengeful intentions. After that I said a short prayer to Ruby. Since I had never met her and didn't really know much about her, I could only say something like 'How are you doing? I hope you're now having a happy life with Pearl in the *yin* world.'

Finally it was Pearl's turn. I offered, with the greatest respect, her favourite Iron Bodhisattva tea, and the foods she had loved: roasted watermelon seeds, sugared ginger, steamed crab dumplings, spicy *dandan* noodles in soup.

Words poured from my lips like beans spilling from a can. 'Dear Sister Pearl, tonight is the seventh night after you set out upon the immortal's journey. I am sure now you are residing happily in the Western Paradise filled with fragrant flowers, melodious birds, auspicious animals, youthful immortals, and all the seven treasures. How is Sister Ruby? I am also sure that now you two are happily reunited. Please don't worry about me; life in the *yang* world and in Peach Blossom are all right.

'Sister Pearl, I'll never forget you, our wonderful time together, nor all the precious things you taught me, especially the *qin*. However, I have to tell you that, sadly, the day after you boarded the immortal's journey when I was helping Mama and De clean up your room, the *qin* was nowhere to be found. You told me repeatedly that I should take very good care of this sacred instrument. I'm afraid that now, having no trace of its whereabouts, I have let you down.

'Sister Pearl, even if I fail to find it in the future, I'll forever cherish the *qin* and your teaching in a secret chamber of my heart. You gave me a pure land where no one can trespass. Now without you, I don't know how long I can survive in Peach Blossom. I must escape, although I have no idea how to live outside.

'I'll keep coming here to offer you your favourite food and tea. Sister Pearl, anything you want me to do for you, please tell me in my dreams. Or anything else you need – clothes, books, car, house, silver, gold – just tell me and I'll buy paper ones and burn them for you. I hope you've finally found your peace and joy in the beautiful paradise where you are residing now.'

When I finished my prayer, my face was wet with tears and my heart bitter as a concoction brewed in an old medicine cauldron.

I began to pack. As I was about to put Guan Yin back underneath the altar, to my surprise, a small bundle slipped from the bottom of the statue. I picked it up, untied the red ribbon, and unrolled the paper.

I was stunned to see what lay in front of my eyes. It was Pearl's refined calligraphy on rice paper!

I tried very hard not to let my tears smear the ink.

Xiang Xiang:

I'm sure you'll be very upset when you know that I'll be joining Ruby and leaving you behind in the red dust. You must also be distressed that I didn't even bid you farewell. But I'm sure you'll find this letter someday, because I know you're a good, loyal sister and will come here to make offerings to Guan Yin for me. If you're not, then not only will you never see this letter, but you'll also never see the things I've left you.

Sorry that I'll leave you behind, but I have to go – without you.

My life, good or bad, happy or sad, it doesn't really matter now; the most important thing is that I've lived it, prestigiously. Although I'm thoroughly disgusted by the evil of human nature, at least I've had the chance to see through it to its very bottom. That's why I have no regret in leaving this world, for my heart is now free, and so is my vision.

After I've left, you'll not be alone in the world. You have another 'relative' – Aunty Ah Ping. Don't be upset when you've learnt the truth that I've been hiding from you.

Ah Ping is my mother.

She didn't kill herself as I've told you, only attempted suicide. She tried to jump from our apartment window but Ruby and I clung tightly to each of her feet. I was eight and Ruby thirteen. We pleaded and pleaded, begging her not to turn us into orphans. Finally we said if she jumped, we'd fall, too, by clinging to her.

Although my mother had failed to kill herself, she succeeded in drinking poison to ruin her voice – she feared that in her unsteady state of mind she might reveal who our father was and thus put our lives in danger. But sadly, after she'd lost her voice, it seemed that she had also lost even more of her mind.

She'll be sad to learn about my death, but then she'll also forget about it very quickly. That is one of the reasons I feel free to go. If she could think like a normal person, then I'd never have the heart to break hers.

Please don't blame me for leaving you behind. I have to go, Xiang Xiang. Not only can't I live with such humiliation, as I've said, but also I am thoroughly disgusted by the species called human being. Remember the oil portraitist Jiang Mou? He's never come to see me since the announcement of the contest, nor sent a word of comfort. Of course I know the reason for his absence – fear. He doesn't want our relationship to be found out, dreading that he might get in trouble. A coward. I'm sure Chief Che would never harass him, for he's not important enough to be worth the bullet!

However, just in case you run into him someday, tell him that I still love him, for he's the only man to whom I gave the best fucking years of my life.

Please take good care of Aunty Ah Ping, for me and for Ruby – your other sister you've never met. Whenever you celebrate, anything – a festival, new year, your birthday, please never forget to leave places for us. Also take good care of Plum Blossom and stroke her beautiful feathers for me.

You're a very brave and strong girl, so I'm sure you'll do well without me. Don't worry too much, for Ruby and I will accumulate merit for you in the yin world so you'll have a good life in the yang *one. I'm sure someday you'll meet someone you love, leave Peach Blossom, and live a free, happy life. Another thing I'd like you to promise me – don't try to revenge. You might not believe me, but it's true that I don't hate Red Jade any more. Having finally found my peace of mind, I don't want any trace of bitterness in my heart while I'm leaving this dusty world for paradise. There's already enough bad* qi *around us, so please don't generate more. It's very bad Karma, for it'll eventually turn on you.*

Now reach as far as you can under the altar and you'll find the qin. *Look inside the resonance box. I have something there for you. I also left other things for Mama and De so that they won't suspect my gifts to you.*

One last thing, take very good care of the qin *and yourself.*

Your sister Pearl's last writing

P.S. One more thing. I've just found out that I am pregnant but the father, I believe, is the one who would not come to see me.

I fell against the wall and cried until the wells of my tears were emptied. I felt limp with exhaustion but still I crawled over to the altar and peeked underneath. Far back, I saw the faint glimmer of brocade. Hands trembling, I reached to pull out the *qin*. Then, with utmost care and respect, I set it on the altar, turned it over, and reached my fingers inside the resonance box.

I drew out a small embroidered pouch. Again I reached in my fingers and pulled out another one. And another.

There were all together three pouches. I opened the first one and saw a small scroll:

Xiang Xiang
I hope now you have enough money to leave Peach Blossom and find your happiness.

Your sister
Pearl

I poured out the contents of the pouches and stared in disbelief at what lay in front of my eyes – banknotes, gold coins, jewellery. There was Pearl's immaculate jade bracelet that I'd so admired. And a big diamond ring that I'd never seen. This must have been her greatest treasure, which she'd prudently kept hidden from everyone at Peach Blossom. I slipped it on and watched it sparkle in the low light of the lantern.

I was overwhelmed by an unspeakable sadness. Pearl, with all this money, we could have both left Peach Blossom and found our happiness together! Why did you kill yourself over that foolish contest and that whore?

I slumped back on the floor and let my tears rain down my cheeks like pearls scattering from a broken string. When I finally regained my composure, I put the jewellery and cash back into the resonance box, then laid the *qin* on my knees and began to play 'Remembering an Old Friend' as softly as I could.

Memories of Pearl and I together kept flashing across my mind while my fingers glided sadly over the instrument's smooth surface. I played until the soundboard became so wet from tears that my fingers could no longer pluck the strings. When I set down the *qin*, the temple became so unbearably quiet that I covered my ears to ward off the silence . . .

To calm myself down, I played 'The Phoenix Hairpin' and sang. Several hundred years ago, the poetess Tang Wan had expressed her sadness when forced to separate from her husband – as I from Pearl.

As petals fall, rain bids the evening farewell.
Please don't speak to me, or I must swallow my tears and feign happiness . . .

When I was in the middle of my singing, something strange happened. A beautiful voice, soft yet crystal clear, began to join me. I halted to listen, but heard nothing. Then, as I went back to play, the singing resumed.

The voice was so pure and penetrating that I was lost in its beauty for moments. 'Pearl?'

No response, except big beads of perspiration forming on my forehead.

Of course it was not Pearl.

Heart pounding, I walked to a window and flung it open. When I looked outside, I saw nothing except the high wall, above which shone a moon resembling a huge tear.

When I finally returned to the pavilion, it was after four in the morning. In the corridor, some sisters' rooms were dark, while others' had light streaming out from underneath the doors. This *yin yang* contrast of light and darkness reminded me of the phrase *yinyang yongge* – the *yin* and the *yang* worlds forever separated, as were Pearl and I.

PART THREE

20

Chinese Soap Opera

'Grandmama, then what happened? Did you really leave Peach Blossom? And all that money and jewels, what did you do with them?'

My great-granddaughter Jade Treasure asks eagerly. Her eyes widen and sparkle like two gold coins. I chuckle at her naiveté. Then I feel touched – by her beauty, her enthusiasm, and the abundance of youth. I put on a mysterious smile while lowering my voice. 'Since I knew *qinggong* – the floating martial art – one night I just jumped out of the window, hopped onto the roof, and disappeared into darkness. As for the jewellery – since all I needed was my freedom – I tossed it all down the gutter.'

'Wow!' Jade pouts her lips, then turns to make a face at her fiancé Leo Stanley.

Leo widens his eyes into two pretty blue marbles. '*Popo*, you *did?*'

Now this American boy looks so cute that I smile. If time could fly back to eighty years ago, I would throw myself into his strong arms and kiss him on his sensuous lips! But I remind myself that I am ninety-eight. Unfortunately. Or fortunately, depending on how you look at it. And now no more a stunningly beautiful, many-talented, heavily sought-after *ming ji*, but a stunningly plain – I won't describe myself as ugly – many-wrinkled, one-foot-already-inside-the-coffin old and dying woman. Thinking of the contrast, I burst out laughing, choking myself.

However, old age can have its advantages. Like right now when the two young and beautiful creatures fuss over me – fanning my face, patting my back, stroking my hair, massaging my thigh (unfortunately it's Jade Treasure, not Leo), then bringing me ginseng tea (this time it's Leo, touchingly).

After they've finished performing their ritual of filial piety, Jade asks, 'Grandmama, why is it so funny?'

'Because I lied.'

She makes a face. 'I know. Then what really happened to you and the jewellery?' She pauses to search my eyes.

I carefully sip my ginseng tea. 'Don't worry. I've survived until today and the jewellery – at least some – has survived with me; it's now in the safe. And when I die, it'll all be yours, my little princess.'

Jade looks both pleased and embarrassed. 'Thank you, Grandmama. But you still haven't told us what happened after you'd left Peach Blossom.'

'I will. I promise I won't die until you two have my whole story. If it takes ten years to write this memoir, then I'll try my best to live till one hundred and eight.'

Jade chuckles. A full-toothed smile blooms on Leo's tanned face.

I go on, 'Although I had all the money and jewellery, I didn't leave Peach Blossom right away. First, I thought that once I left, I'd never go back. But because Pearl was buried in Peach Blossom, I just didn't feel right leaving when her remains were still "warm." If she'd mourned for Ruby for seven years, I thought I had to mourn for her at least half that, which was three-and-a-half years. Besides Pearl,' I pause, then, 'there was another reason I didn't leave Peach Blossom right away.'

'What is it?' Jade asks, her face glowing with curiosity.

Now Leo stares at me with his long-lashed eyes. 'Yes, what is it, *Popo*?'

I take a long, meditative sip of the ginseng. 'It's because of Big Master Fung.'

Jade exclaims, 'You mean that old-wrinkled-and-dying?'

'Jade, show some respect for elderly people, if not for what they are, at least for what they've experienced. Besides, he's dead, and it's very bad manners for Chinese to bad-mouth a *yin* person. Worse, it's bad luck.'

My great-granddaughter chuckles. 'Grandmama, which is it? Bad manners or bad luck?'

If Jade thinks she can outsmart me, she's wrong. She forgets that at ninety-eight, I've consumed more salt than she has rice and crossed more bridges than she's wriggled her yellowish-white butt on roads.

Of course the reason I scolded Jade was not that I cared to defend Big Master Fung – old-wrinkled-and-dying – since that was exactly what I used to call him behind his back. Rather it was for my own dignity, because now I'm exactly like my bitterest enemy – wrinkled, old, and dying. That's why people say 'life comes full circle.' But how come the circle never goes back to the point where we were all young and beautiful?

Now Jade says, her voice shrill, her expression horrified, 'Grandmama, don't tell me that you fell in love with Fung!'

What an imagination. 'Oh, no!' I laugh out loud. 'Of course not, my dear Jade.' I stare at her. 'Don't worry, your great-grandmother has never lost her taste. But . . . I did feel attached to him in some ways.'

'You're kidding, Grandmama? Attached to an old . . . oops—' She hides her mouth and giggles.

I continue, 'Although I knew Fung was an evil person, he was truly nice to me, pampering me like a real daughter.'

Jade asks, 'Really, why?'

But I'm not going to tell them everything right away. I never forgot, even eighty years later, how Pearl taught me the technique of delay.

'Never offer your body right away to those *chou nanren,*' she'd told me. 'Retreat and advance, lean forward and step back, only then do you finally yield. The customer knows you'll always give in because you want the money. However, with no pretense, there's no enjoyment.'

So I down the last drop of my ginseng tea and hand Jade my cup. 'I want some more tea, please.'

I can't believe she just hands the cup to her fiancé. 'Leo, get Grandmama more ginseng tea.'

After Leo has gone to the kitchen, I chide her, 'Jade, I don't think you should boss Leo around like this.'

'But he likes to serve you, Grandmama.'

'Maybe, but that doesn't mean he likes you to tell him what to do. He's a good man, so don't ever let him slip from your grasp. Treat him well.' I cast her a meaningful look. 'Jade, true love only happens once in a lifetime.'

My great-granddaughter's face glows and her eyes sparkle. 'Then what about you, Grandmama? Who is your true love?'

Just then Leo comes back with the hot tea. Carefully and respectfully and with both hands (imitating the Chinese way), he hands the cup to me. 'It's very hot, *Popo*, be careful.'

'Thank you, Leo,' I smile.

After Leo has sat down, Jade kisses his cheek, lays her head on his shoulder, and puts her hand on his thigh, while squinting triumphantly at me.

I shake my head. I only told her to be nice to her fiancé, not blatantly show off her affection in front of her great-grandmother!

'Grandmama, who is your true love?' she says, then kisses Leo again.

Now Leo looks at me with curiosity, his eyes resembling two dreams painted blue. 'Yes, *Popo*, please tell us your love story.'

I feel so touched by this young couple's eagerness to learn about an old woman's love that my eyes swell with tears. Some silence passes before I go on, 'But I thought that you two wanted to hear about Big Master Fung.'

'That, too, of course!' Jade exclaims.

'But I'm hungry now. I have to eat first, otherwise I won't have enough energy to tell you about *both* Big Master Fung's affection and my true love.'

Jade creases her pretty brows. 'Oh Grandmama, please don't tease us like this. Tell us now.'

But I decide again to try my skill of teasing, which has grown rusty over the years.

'No, not until I've eaten. I need the *qi*. Don't you want me to live till one-hundred-and-eight?'

When we enter the Chinese restaurant situated at a corner of Polk Street, several people turn to stare at us. Of course I'm not so naïve or vain to think that they're staring at me – although it would have been true eighty years ago – but at my beautiful great-granddaughter and her tall fiancé.

This restaurant has an artistic name – Mirroring Green Pavilion. I almost chuckle. In the past this name would have been perfect for a prostitution house! Jade said she picked this one especially for me because they're promoting a special dish of a special kind of Chinese black fungus, which is supposed to be very good for women's skin and hormones. But what does she know about true Chinese cuisine? Let alone any effect on women's hormones? Besides, I'm already ninety-eight, what do I need those hormones for – to seduce a one-hundred-year-old soon-to-be-corpse?

I am very tempted to tell my experience of tasting the most prestigious Chinese cuisine – *manhan quanxi,* the Imperial Manchurian-Han Banquet, which takes three months to gather the ingredients, three weeks to cook, and three days to eat. But I suppress my urge to boast, as well as my contempt for this kind of fake, pretentious, Americanized Chinese restaurant.

Now a black-suited captain hurries to us, aims an ear-reaching grin at Jade, then shows us to a table by the window. With a slick movement of his white-cuffed hand, he lights a candle on the white-clothed table, then turns to ask me, 'Old lady, what would you like to drink?'

Jade blurts out, 'Stop calling her old lady, she's my grandmama and the last most famous *ming ji* in China!'

Heads turn and eyes rivet on me.

If this had happened eighty years ago, I'd have straightened my shoulders and thrown out my chest, then my tongue would have run along my lips while my eyes shot the onlookers soul-losing bullets. But now I only wish that I had really learned the floating martial art so I could jump out of the window, fly up on the roof, and disappear into darkness.

Back home, I'm still hungry. For I'd already lost my appetite the moment my prestigious status was exposed in that fake restaurant. How ironic. Americans would die to become prestigious! Just look at how they worship celebrities!

Knowing that I'm upset, now Jade puts on a very sweet smile and says very gently, as if she were talking to her antique, cracked porcelain doll, 'Grandmama, you want me to fix you something, Coke, cookies?'

'Do you really consider it fixing something to open a Coke and put cookies on a plate?'

But she doesn't answer my question, she is still busy smiling. 'All right, all right, Grandmama, I'm sorry. Then why don't you tell us now about Big Master Fung and your love?'

'Yes, Grandmama, please.' Leo immediately joins his beautiful, utterly spoiled princess in pleading.

'All right, then listen very carefully,' I say, my ninety-eight-year-old heart secretly melting when my glance catches Leo's.

21

Melting the Ice

Needless to say, Fang Rong and Wu Qiang were insanely happy about the jewellery and cash that Pearl had left for them.

Mama laughed, the gold and diamond glittering in her pupils. 'That was a really good, filial daughter, still thought of her parents even when she was going to die. Now I forgive her committing suicide. Ha! Ha! Ha!'

De chimed in, his hands sexually harassing a gold brooch (I was sure in his mind, he was now fondling it on Red Jade's breast). 'She also chose the right moment to die – at her prime. Otherwise, in a few years she'd be too old to be a *ming ji*.'

Mama interrupted. 'Yes, how could we afford to keep her here if she couldn't bring in you-know-what? Who could blame us if no one is willing to pay for someone who's crack-eyed, chimney-nosed, clang-eared, and stinks like a swine?'

The evil duo burst into laughter, their hands clutching Pearl's hard-earned jewellery, which, if broken open, would surely spill her blood and tears. I felt an impulse to grab her long gold necklace from Fang Rong's and Wu Qiang's evil fingers and strangle them with it.

It was obvious that Mama and De did not suspect that their filial daughter had also left part of her jewellery and money to me. I was grateful for Pearl's ingenuity. I now kept Pearl's *qin* in my own room and played it almost every day. Since my practice did not interfere with my bringing rich customers to Peach Blossom, Fang Rong and Wu Qiang never said anything to me about it. All the jewellery and money stayed safely inside the *qin*'s resonance box.

People seemed to get over the shock of Pearl's death very quickly. Of course they still gossiped about her – why she'd killed herself; how she'd lost out in her rivalry with Red Jade; how she'd gained her prestigious status by mastering both the technique of the *pipa* and the bedchamber; her rumoured esoteric recipes for shrinking vaginas and enlarging jade stalks. But rarely did I hear laments that her life had been cut short by the evil of the human heart.

Now people's attention turned to Red Jade. Her pictures, together with poems praising her beauty and her talent in the erotic arts of pleasing, appeared frequently in the mosquito press and gossip magazines. One rumour went that one of the movie companies was seriously considering getting her out of Peach Blossom and making her into a star.

One time I overheard one customer say to another, 'With those smiling eyes and swinging papayas, she'll be perfect to play the slut!'

The other burst into roaring laughter. 'And I bet she'll become famous pretty quickly. For what star has the experience to play a whore as realistically as she!'

Every night music, laughter, and light spilled from Peach Blossom like water spurting from fountains. Long, shiny cars snaked to line up in front of the pavilion's crimson gate. Even the corners of the stone lions' lips seemed to be lifting higher and higher each day, welcoming the pilgrims' offerings pouring into their masters' safe.

Like Pearl, now I completely understood the cruelty of the human heart. But I had no intention to leave this *jinfen diyu* – Gold-Powdered Hell. Not yet. Not until I'd entirely won Fang Rong's and Wu Qiang's trust so they'd feel completely relaxed with me. I had to accord with the Tao – wait for the propitious moment – to carry out my plan.

I wouldn't survive failure.

* * *

A few weeks after Pearl's death, I dreamt that she, all dressed up in a red, gold-threaded gown, appeared in the distance whispering my name. Between us was suspended a bridge so entwined with thorns that neither of us could cross. Underneath the bridge a gravestone lay submerged in water with the inscription:

Pearl 1900–1923
Here lies a woman of prestige – poet, painter, prostitute

Clusters of plum blossoms floated around the grave, and from among the patches of pink, one white flower rose tall and high, nodding to me in the cold, bitter wind. I tried to approach Pearl, but she kept receding, while tenderly calling my name. Desperate, I leaped forward into the air, only to plunge toward her grave . . .

I woke up soaking wet. The dream was so vivid that for a moment I believed I was really plunging down toward the lake with a worried-looking Pearl calling my name. I blinked several times to make sure I *was* in Peach Blossom, in my room with its solid wood furniture, gilded mirror, ceramic vases, and scrolls of paintings and calligraphy . . .

As my mind was swaying between dream and reality, I heard a cheerful 'good morning.' I looked up and saw Plum Blossom. Soaked in rays of the morning sun, her beak looked so red and her feathers so white that I was reminded of '*Nuer Hong – Daughter's Blush*,' a story I had heard from my mother.

A young father, after the birth of his first daughter, buried a big jar of wine in his garden. Nobody was allowed to even touch the jar – not until the baby had grown into a young girl and was betrothed. Sixteen years passed like a horse leaping across a ravine. On the daughter's wedding night, the father, now a middle-aged man, dug out the jar, broke the seal, and poured the velvety liquid for his guests. Seeing that the wine reflected the rouge on his beautiful daughter's face, the father named it Daughter's Blush.

My baba, right after I'd been born, had also stored a jar of wine for my wedding – one that had never happened.

Now I looked at Plum Blossom through my watery eyes and

returned her greeting. 'Good morning.' Then I got off the bed and went up to stroke her feathers, this time for Pearl.

Plum Blossom pecked my hand affectionately. Scurrying back and forth on the stand, I imagined she was practising the *qin*'s lingering tones with her feet, or even the shredded-golden-lotus steps demonstrated by Pearl. For a moment I smiled, then my sadness returned. I sat down at the table and started to grind ink, slowly and meditatively. Watching the shallow of the stone slab gradually fill with a widening pool of black, fragrant liquid, my heart was appeased. Next I spread out a sheet of rice paper printed with pale plum blossoms. I picked up my brush, dabbed it into the ink until the white tip was soaked black, then watched a poem bloom on the paper.

> Wordlessly you left,
> hovering in midair,
> like the plum blossom above the snow.
>
> Now you look down on us who still float in the ancient sea
>   of suffering.
> Will someone pick up that luminous Pearl from the sea
>   bottom and place it on the altar before Guan Yin?
>
> Will you reach down, with your long pink nails, to pick up
>   this Precious Orchid planted in the sea of mud?

I read and reread the poem silently to imprint it upon my mind. Then I recited it to Plum Blossom.

She nodded in approval, screeching, 'Good luck, wish you make a lot of money!'

I smiled back, put the rice paper on a plate, and carried it to the window. I meditated, then looked up and whispered to the sky. 'Sister Pearl, since your departure, my sole solace has been to immerse myself in the *qin*. Whenever I pluck the seven silk strings, their bittersweet tunes bring you close to me. Only their lingering tones can lift my heart above this evil world.

'I also like to play the *qin* to Plum Blossom. After you've left, she is my only friend and the only creature in the whole world whom I can trust. She likes *qin* music, too, for every time I finish playing, she'll say, "Feels good, eh?" '

'I've just composed this poem for you and hope you like it. I'll write you more. Without you in Peach Blossom now, I live in a different world. I miss you.'

After my monologue, I burned the poem and scattered the ashes outside the window. The confetti dancing in the air made me think of the phrase *tiannu sanhua* – heavenly maiden showering flowers. Only the flowers were all black – to match my mood.

Plum Blossom rounded off my ritual by squealing, 'Feels good, eh? Want more?'

Almost two years went by. From time to time I'd think of the cause of Pearl's death – Red Jade. And the notion of revenge would flicker in my mind. But how, since she was gone from Peach Blossom? Shortly after Pearl's death, Red Jade had been spotted by a film director and since then lived a new life under the mercury-vapour lamps. In less than a year, she'd made herself famous playing spoiled rich girls, dissolute concubines, and shameless prostitutes. The whole thing struck me as extremely amusing – a real prostitute got popular by pretending to be a prostitute!

To my bitterness, the fame she acquired now possessed a quality even more dazzling than a *ming ji*'s. Pictures of her in gorgeous dresses and seductive poses were seen almost everywhere; huge signboards of her hung above the Peking and Lyceum Theatres. Among her fans were not just men, but also women, even decent housewives who relieved the tedium of their lives through fantasies of Red Jade's more glamorous one. Red Jade – once a near-prisoner in a whorehouse – was now the goddess of sexual freedom and a symbol of the emancipated woman.

As for me, I'd been working extra hard to improve my painting, calligraphy, and music. But I had to spend far more time with favoured guests than with the *qin*. I knew I needed to look cheerful and not hold back in the arts of the bedchamber. Yet some customers could still sense – despite my passionate act – the chill inside my squirming body and my wandering mind. One described me as having the body of an attacking tigress, but a heart like a sealed vase. Another quoted the Chinese saying 'As beautiful as plum and peach, as cold as ice and frost' to describe me.

However, my 'icy' nature, instead of turning customers away, ironically attracted more. Some customers even set up a club, its members competing to see who could become the champion of ice-melting. But as time went on, the ice did not melt. It only proved once again the truth of Pearl's teaching when she'd talked about Big Master Fung:

Believe me, he won't pull his pants up until he's tasted the delicious sauce from your golden plate!

How true, Sister Pearl. A man will always wait for a beautiful woman whom he has failed to seduce!

I still thought of Pearl every day though now her name was rarely mentioned in Peach Blossom. That she could be happily celebrating with champagne one evening, plunged into despair the next, and hanging from a rafter two weeks later made me realise how short our time was. The Chinese saying ran over and over through my mind:

Hongyan baomeng – all beauty has a tragic end.

To escape the sadness and loneliness that pervaded my life, I always imagined that one day, instead of *chou nanren*, I'd meet someone intelligent, handsome, caring, and chivalric enough to melt the ice in my heart.

Though I felt a strong urge to love, and to be loved, I only met men like Zhang Zhong. No one knew where he came from nor what he did, just that one day he began to be seen in the expensive restaurants, tea houses, theatres, and turquoise pavilions in Shanghai. He seemed to have endless money to stuff in the sisters' cleavage and throw into the mamas' faces.

Shortly after Zhang Zhong had arrived in Shanghai, he invited all the *ming ji* in the Concessions to an expensive tea house. To keep him company for a Kun opera performance, the invitation said. But since none of us knew who he was, when the evening arrived, only the second-rate prostitutes appeared. That evening, Zhang vented his bitterness and humiliation by outrageously tipping the second-rate prostitutes – each received two silver coins.

The next day, his name and his legendary tipping spilled from the gossip columns of all the mosquito newspapers in Shanghai.

Zhang became famous overnight.

So, when he issued his second invitation, all the courtesans – in their most elaborate costumes, meticulous make-up, and soul-sucking smiles – descended upon Sweet Laurel Tea House.

Except me. Now that I was a *ming ji*, I was not cheap, and neither would I gain anything by acting that way. So at Sweet Laurel Tea House, the sisters' glamorous presence was paled by my haunting absence.

Just by not going somewhere, I became the talk of the town. And the obsession of Zhang Zhong.

Finally, one day he just marched into Peach Blossom and demanded to see me.

Mama, needless to say, made a big fuss over his arrival. 'Xiang Xiang! Xiang Xiang!'

Her feet pumped on the stairs and in a moment her quivering flesh plunged into my room.

She dumped her bottom on the high-backed chair. 'You know who's here? The legendary Zhang Zhong!'

I was looking at my reflection in the mirror while leisurely combing my hair. 'So?'

'So?' Mama imitated my nonchalance. 'What do you mean by "so"? He asked for you, right now!'

'But Mama, can't you tell that I'm busy right now?'

She shot up from the chair, darted to me, snatched the comb from my hand, and started to yank it down my three-thousand-threads-of-trouble. 'Please, please . . . Xiang Xiang . . .' Mama cooed. 'We can't afford to make Mr. Zhang wait.'

'Maybe you can't, but I can.' I threw Mama a contemptuous glance. 'He's just a nobody.'

Her hand tightened on my hair. 'Shhh, Xiang Xiang, watch out for your mouth!'

'If he is somebody, then who is he?'

Fang Rong's mouth dropped open, but no sound came out. She pleaded. 'Please, Xiang Xiang, for Guan Yin's sake, please see him, you have nothing to lose.'

'Nothing to lose? What about my reputation?'

'You're already the most prestigious courtesan in Shanghai.'

I considered for a moment. 'More than Red Jade?'

'But she's not a flower girl any more,' Mama flashed me a probing glance in the mirror, 'she's now a movie star.'

Ignoring her, I started to recite Du Mu's poem, 'Wandering and drinking south of the river, watching narrow waists swaying on palms, ten years' dreams of Yangzhou awakened, nothing left but a philandering fame.'

'Xiang Xiang, please, Mr. Zhang is waiting.'

'I know.'

'Then please hurry, for Guan Yin's sake!'

I chuckled. 'You mean Guan Yin approves of prostitution?'

'*Aii-ya,* Xiang Xiang, you know what I mean, plu-eez.'

'How does this legendary Mr. Zhang look?'

'A man.'

'Of course I know he's a man.'

Fang Rong squeezed an unnatural smile. 'He's rich and . . . nice looking.'

'All right, then I'll go,' I threw her a chiding look in the mirror, 'for your sake.'

Zhang Zhong turned out to be the most vulgar person I'd ever seen, more so even than Big Master Fung. I should say that he was a stinking male among the stinking males! His face and hands didn't even possess the decency of human form. But I wouldn't use the word *animal* to describe him, for no animal should be compared to such a man.

When we sat face to face at my marble-topped table, he was already drooling. His eyes kept boring into my face and body while his tongue flapped about his lips like a dog's. Perspiration, like ink, smeared the armpits of his indigo jacket.

'It's hot here, Mr. Zhang. Isn't it?' I leisurely swayed my golden fan painted with orchids.

He took out a handkerchief to vigorously wipe his face. 'Yes, it sure is.'

The diamond, jade, and gold rings on his hairy fingers flashed in the yellowish light of my room.

I called out for my maid Little Rain to bring towels and tea.

While Little Rain was arranging the table, she exclaimed, 'Mr. Zhang, what nice rings you have!'

Zhang lifted his hand. 'You like them? Then pick the one you want, it's a gift.'

Little Rain's face turned pale, her voice trembling. 'Oh no, Mr. Zhang, I can't take an expensive gift just like that.'

I cursed inside. Fool, you're all shaken up when simply offered a ring?

I turned to my maid, then deliberately said in a nonchalant tone, 'Little Rain, don't you think it's very rude to turn down an offer from our noble guest?' Then I cast her a sharp glance. 'Why don't you just pick one as you're told?'

Now both Zhang and Little Rain looked shocked.

I put on an encouraging smile. 'Go ahead, Little Rain, otherwise Mr. Zhang will really be offended.'

As expected, Little Rain pointed to the cheapest – the gold ring. She was too scared to take the diamond or the jade. She didn't want to get herself into trouble later.

Eyes riveted on me, Zhang slipped the ring off his hand and handed it to the maid.

The episode immediately became the talk of the town – with variations. The *Flower Moon News* said that it was a diamond ring; the *Flower Heaven Daily* said it was jade; the *Pleasure Talk News* said it was not Little Rain, but I, who had been given both a diamond and a jade ring.

Despite my having made a gift of his ring to my maid, Mr. Zhang continued to visit Peach Blossom and ask for me. Each time he'd bring gifts – for me, for Mama, sometimes even for Little Rain.

Of course, I was not so naïve as to believe he came only to Peach Blossom as if it were a temple where he could make offerings to me as if I were Guan Yin. I was well aware of his intention – to shower his rain onto my clouds. But now, as a *ming ji*, my clouds could shift and not be showered by customers whom I found distasteful.

Then he got desperate.

One evening, after Zhang sat down on the chair, as usual, he laid down his gift on the table with both hands. That was what he always did, as I never took anything directly from his hands. Not only did I flinch from contacting those dark lumps of flesh, I also intended him to know that despite his right to put things on my table, I had no obligation to acknowledge them.

I asked Little Rain to bring him a towel, tea, and snacks. Then, when I started to make small talk, he looked impatient and ill at ease.

I waved my fan. 'Mr. Zhang, is something on your mind?'

'Hmmm . . . not really.' He kept flicking nervous glances at me.

Not really? I could see beads of perspiration oozing from his forehead. In the past, he'd been pretty direct about matters concerning the clouds and rain: 'Should we retire to bed now, Miss Precious Orchid?' or 'It's late, I think I'd rather stay overnight here.' Not that he got anything from me in response to these little suggestions.

So this time it didn't sound like he was about to ask for sex.

'You want more snacks? Dinner perhaps?'

'Hmmm . . . no . . .'

I was getting impatient. 'Then what is it that you want?'

'Hmmm . . . Miss Precious Orchid, I think I left . . . something here during one of my previous visits.'

'Oh, really? What is it?'

'I think it's a piece of jewellery.'

'You think?' Obviously he was not a very good liar.

He swallowed hard. 'Yes, it's a piece of jewellery.'

I saw through his scheme right away. Knowing well that I would not let him thrust his rotten stalk into my precious gate, now, in this last visit, he was going to get something back for all the money he'd spent. 'Leaving a piece of jewellery here' simply meant he wanted his jewellery back.

I went and got one of my jewellery boxes, laid it on the table, and opened it.

Among my rings were two – a sapphire and a ruby – that he had given me; the rest were gifts from my other customers. I hadn't yet taken his rings to be appraised, so I didn't really know their value. But I just knew that any gifts from this crude man wouldn't be of first quality.

To my surprise, instead of taking the two rings he'd given me, he pointed to the diamond and jade ring Big Master Fung had bought me.

Though I was alarmed, I put on a calm countenance. 'You're sure this is the ring?'

'Absolutely.'

'Mr. Zhang, this is a really nice piece, so how could you be so absent-minded as to leave it here by accident?'

He didn't answer my question.

I pointed to the sapphire ring. 'You're sure it's not this one?'

He shook his head.

I pointed to the ruby. 'What about this?'

'Oh no. Mine is much more expensive.'

While he was reaching out to take the diamond and jade ring, I used my fan to halt his paw. 'Wait a minute, Mr. Zhang. I'm sure that this one is from my other admirer. Because I remember there is an inscription inside the ring. So, Mr. Zhang, if you can tell me the inscription, then my memory is wrong and this ring is yours.'

Zhang's yellowish eyes darted around. 'Of course, I asked the goldsmith to inscribe your name, Precious Orchid, on it.'

I picked up the ring and showed him the inside of the gold band, where there was no inscription.

Now he tried to pick up the sapphire ring he'd given me. 'Oh I remember now, it's this one.'

'Wait,' I again stopped him with my fan. 'Unfortunately this one I've already had it checked with a gold store; the owner told me it's fake. Mr. Zhang, rich and respectable as you are, I don't think you would have given me a fake ring to ruin your reputation, would you?' In fact, I had never taken the ring to be appraised.

He was now sweating so much that it looked as if his whole face were pouring with rain. Without a word, I picked up my jewellery box and went to put it back into the safe. When I returned, Zhang's seat was empty.

I didn't have to worry about him coming back because two days later his body was found in a back alley of the Temple of Supreme Happiness, a competing establishment.

The rumour went out that Zhang Zhong was an ex-*tong* member from Nanking. When the *tong* head had suddenly died, he took the dead boss's money and escaped to Shanghai, with the intention of joining another *tong* here. It was to arouse attention that he planned that whole incident at Sweet Laurel Tea House. Then he tried to melt the ice of the most prestigious courtesan – me – to further catapult him to fame. But it was also his 'fame' which caused his downfall. News spread back to the Nanking *tong* members and they passed the word to their Shanghai brothers to get rid of Zhang.

And that ended the whole tragic farce.

22

American Handsome

Though I had ended up ahead in my adventure with Zhang Zhong, I felt myself sinking into depression. In a few months I would turn twenty-one and would have lived in this fragranced hell for eight years. I'd served all sorts of customers – young and old, rich and poor, powerful and powerless. But not a single one had made my heart pound, my face flush, my palms sweat. Was there anyone in the world for me? If so, where was he hiding? In the seventh evening of the seventh month a thousand years past or a thousand years hence?

Every night after I had served my last customer, I'd pray: Guan Yin, Merciful Observer of Cries, if you hear me, please guide him from the edge of the world to prostrate himself before my pomegranate dress!

One evening, after the oppressive summer heat had given way to the cool of autumn, Fang Rong dashed into my room, face glowing like a cluster of fireflies. 'Ah, Xiang Xiang, your luck's up tonight!'

'How?'

'How? Don't pretend innocence. Of course because someone has asked for you!'

'Many people ask for me every night, so what's the big deal?'

Mama shot me an affectionately chiding look. 'Ah, do you really think I'm so old now that I have memory loss and forget that you're the most desired *ming ji*? But what big talk, Xiang Xiang!'

She spoke again, her entire face was seized by a smile. 'Waiting downstairs now is a very tall and handsome young man—'

'Mama, you also told me that Zhang Zhong was "nice looking," so—'

'*Aii-ya*, Xiang Xiang, then I was just trying to be polite.'

'How do I know you're not trying to be polite again?'

Mama's features tensed up. 'Xiang Xiang, trust me. Even though my old eyes are blurry, I can tell from this man's Western suit, silk tie, and shirt, as well as his gold watch, that he's very rich and has elegant taste. I bet he's a dandy who's been sent by his rich father to study abroad, probably in America. So I hope his fat wallet is well stuffed with American dollars!'

She stole a licentious glance at her own reflection in the mirror and spoke again, her voice as shrill as Plum Blossom's. 'I'd also like to go to the Wu Mountain with this American handsome if he doesn't mind my paying him, ha! ha! ha!' She reached to pinch my cheek. 'You lucky little witch.' Now even the third eye between her brows looked envious. 'Serve him well and then tell me how you liked it, all right? Now put on your best dress and makeup, quick!'

'But I'm already dressed and made-up.'

'Then my advice now is that you put on more make-up and less dress.'

The man was waiting in the welcoming-guests room, his back toward me as he appreciated a beauty portrait. Hearing my footsteps, he turned, caught my eyes, and smiled. My heart fluttered like a bird held in tight hands. He *was* indeed young, handsome, and rich! Mama had told the truth – to my surprise.

His hair, ink black, was pomaded back to reveal a slim, pale face with a high-bridged nose and big, haunting eyes. His lips sensuously balanced an ivory holder with a cigarette. The red spark at the cigarette tip hovered playfully – like a petal dancing in the autumnal air. A white suit, highlighted by a red tie and a matching kerchief, covered his almost delicate figure.

The young man extinguished his cigarette and, after sliding the holder into his pocket, approached me slowly. In a gentle voice, he invited me to sit down beside him on the sofa.

I looked up and asked, 'Sir, would you like tea or wine?'

He held my glance for several moments. 'Tea, please, Miss Precious Orchid.'

I lifted the pot, then, arranging my fingers to resemble an orchid in bloom, poured first him, and then myself, a full cup. Smiling, I raised my cup. 'Sir, to your health.' Since I thought this man must have everything he wanted in life, what else could he possibly wish for besides perpetual health?

He returned a smile and a penetrating gaze. 'To your beauty, Miss Precious Orchid.'

I couldn't believe that I blushed.

There was a long silence while we drank our tea as if engaged in sipping meditation.

'Miss Precious Orchid,' he quietly put down his cup, 'please stop addressing me as sir. My name is Teng Xiong.'

'Yes, Mr. Teng.' I blushed more.

Another silence. Then he spoke again. To my delight, instead of coarse talk about business or boasts about monetary gains, we discussed our favourite operas and opera singers – their voices, facial expressions, hand gestures, bodily movements. Then we went on to talk about painting and calligraphy: the interplay of empty and full, the power of line, the meandering quality. He seemed to feel great respect for my knowledge of the arts. When I spoke, he would listen intently, nodding or emitting a 'yes' from time to time.

I felt an instant fancy for this man; he was the first customer who'd more than pretended interest in my ideas. While talking, I cast my eyes all over Teng Xiong. His hands were fine-boned; his fingers long, tapered, and so sensitive that they almost looked like a woman's. Like an opera performer, he gestured a lot, as if his speech alone were not enough to convince. I found myself wondering: How would these hands express themselves in exploring the peaks, valleys, and crevices of my body? My heart began to beat like a battle drum and my face burn like a hot pot.

But even when our conversation had gone on for more than an hour, I still didn't see any intention in him to balance his *yang* with my *yin*. For my other customers, even scholars, the pre-Wu Mountain conversation was merely a 'civilized' act leading to the stirring of the beastly *qi*. But it seemed that this young and handsome Mr. Teng was interested only in talking. Of course, I was flattered that he respected me as an artist, but what about my face, my body, and my art of pleasing, didn't they stoke any fire in him? Determined to tempt him, I invited him to go to my own chamber – maybe he'd feel more comfortable in a private environment.

After he appreciated the decorations in my room, he pointed to my *pipa* on the wall. 'Miss Precious Orchid, I have heard of your fame on the *pipa*. Will I have the pleasure of hearing it tonight?'

I took down the instrument and began to tune it. When finished, I looked up and aimed him a flirtatious smile. 'Mr. Teng, which piece do you want to hear?'

'What about the "Thriving Spring and White Snow"?'

Determined to charm and conquer, I conjured up all the musical cells in my body and poured them into my playing. When interpreting the lyrical passages, my eyes would fix dreamily on his hands, while my mind would anticipate how they'd stir and satisfy my body's desires. When I reached an animated passage, my glances would caper like fireflies while my hair would quiver like dark waves pulled by a full moon.

After I finished, he smiled appreciatively, but only asked me to play more.

When I ended my third piece, he invited me to sit on the bed. Finally. I sighed inside. After all the *pipa* foreplay, was he now ready to thrust his jade stalk into my golden gate? But, to my consternation, he went right back to talking about the arts. This time it was I who became restless, anxious to lose my soul. Several times I hinted that he had to pay by the hour, but he seemed oblivious.

Three hours later, when he finally took leave, nothing had happened except talking and playing the *pipa*!

'Miss Precious Orchid,' he was now standing by the door, his features looked achingly desirable under the warm, yellowish light, 'it's been my wish to meet you for a long time. I'm so happy that today I finally had the chance. It's such a great pleasure and honour. I'll come again. Now good night.' After that, he was gone, leaving an emptiness knocking inside my chest like a deserted bell.

Early next morning, Fang Rong plunged into my room. She sat down across from me, then searched my face as if I'd suddenly transformed into a princess. 'Hey, Little Beauty, tell me everything about last night.'

I took a sip of my bitter tea. 'Mama, it's indescribable.'

She wet her lips, threw me a meaningful stare, and spat, *'Yor!'*

I remained silent, meditatively taking another sip.

She asked again, this time gently, 'Really, tell me; how was he? What did he do to you?'

'I told you it's indescribable.'

'But try, just try.' A long pause. Now Mama looked impatient. 'Xiang Xiang, please stop torturing me like this. I ask you; what did he do?'

'Nothing.'

'What do you mean by nothing?'

I put down my cup. 'That's what I mean, nothing.'

'You mean he didn't put his jade stalk into your golden gate?'

'Of course not. He didn't kiss my lips, nor even touch my hands.'

Mama widened her eyes. 'But he paid almost thirty silver coins for you!' She tilted her fat head, seemingly lost in thought, then suddenly, 'Oh, then his golden gun drooped! But that only means his jade stalk cannot thrust toward heaven, it doesn't mean he shouldn't use his other stalk nor demand other things from you to appease his lusty fire.' She paused, now seemingly lost in deeper thought. Then all of a sudden she yapped, startling me, 'Oh my heaven, he must be a spy!'

'Mama, what are you talking about? What would a spy do in a turquoise pavilion?'

'I don't know, maybe he's sent here from Temple of Supreme Happiness or Sleeping Flower Pavilion to look into our business.'

Since Mama's conjecture seemed ridiculous to me, I kept my mouth shut to leave her to her own nonsense.

Finally she said, 'But anyway he told me he'll definitely come again. It's fine with me if he doesn't stir your clouds – so long as he pays another thirty silver coins. Ha! Ha! Ha! That's even better – you can save your energy to serve more customers.'

A week later, as promised, Mr. Teng came back. This time he wore a black suit, black shirt, and pink tie, conjuring in my mind the image of a lotus. Once when Mr. Wu, my painting teacher, was demonstrating how to paint lotuses, he'd said, 'This beautiful flower grows out of filth. We say, "growing out of mud but not stained." Like people who live amidst evil but preserve their purity.'

Of course I knew Mr. Wu had said this to remind me that although I lived in a prostitution house, I could retain my integrity as a decent human being.

Was Mr. Teng's outfit a reminder of the same message?

This time I took him directly up to my room. We had tea and snacks and chatted. Like last time, our conversation revolved mainly around the arts. He seemed infinitely curious about such details as how long it took me to paint a landscape, a bird and flower painting, a beauty portrait. What kind of calligraphy did I like: seal script, walking style, or the drunken cursive grass style?

Then he asked me to sing him a Peking opera aria.

'Mr. Teng, which one do you want to hear?'

'Miss Precious Orchid, I'd love anything from your lips, so please pick one you like.'

'All right,' I did not omit to cast him a flirtatious glance, 'then I'll sing an excerpt from *Jita*.'

Jita – Offering Sacrifice to the Tower, is one of the most challenging arias. First, I meditated, then let my eyes float – to Guan Yin on the altar table, to Plum Blossom fidgeting in midair, to the distant hills outside the window, until they finally alighted on Mr. Teng's soul windows.

A smile broke out on his face.

I tried to attain the best way of singing this piece, once described as 'cries as sharp as the goose soaring to heaven, echoes as low as the winter cicada clinging to the pine trees.'

But alas, when singing the phrase 'Our meeting again can only happen in a dream . . .' suddenly Pearl's image flashed across my mind. Though I tried my best to hold them back, my tears splashed down my cheeks like spurting springs.

I was mortified. A courtesan should never reveal her true emotions in front of any customer! For a moment I felt so scared and humiliated that I had no idea what to do. But not Mr. Teng. He stood up from the sofa, then took out his pink handkerchief to dab my eyes. After that, he pulled me into his arms, very gently, as if I were an expensive piece of porcelain.

It felt so good. And I thought: I've fallen in love.

Now that I was feeling snug and warm, my tears burst out like water from a collapsed dam. We held each other's gaze for an eternity until my tears had dried. Then I said softly, feeling colour rising in my cheeks, 'Mr. Teng, you . . . want me to serve you now?'

To my complete disbelief, his brows knitted.

Then they quickly smoothed out, and he was now smiling handsomely. 'Miss Precious Orchid, why don't we have something to eat first? I'm starving.'

Although his hesitation lasted only a split second, it was long enough to break my heart.

He would rather taste food on a plate than taste my golden gate? I couldn't believe this! I was fucked by not being fucked! But then I thought, maybe he wanted to build up his *qi* so he could do a better job. Feeling more cheerful, I laid out the dishes prepared by Aunty Ah Ping on the eight immortals table, then poured two cups of wine. In the cosy atmosphere of my room we ate, drank, and chatted.

I was dying to find out who he was – a scholar, government official, businessman, or dandy. But whenever I tried to probe, he'd cleverly avoid my questions, steering the conversation back to art and literature.

'Miss Precious Orchid,' he looked at me deeply, 'you're very lucky to be born with such a good voice. And I know you practise very hard to achieve your skill. But do you mind if I comment on it so it can be still better?'

'Of course not, Mr. Teng.' While I didn't mind having criticism from him, it also surprised me that he was the first customer who dared do it.

He went on, 'When you change your breath, bring it all the way down to your *dantian*. Then start slow and build up. Remember *yitui weijin* – retreat in order to advance.' He looked at me intently, his face flushed an attractive pink. 'Do you agree with me, Miss Precious Orchid?'

I was so impressed that I opened my mouth but couldn't utter a word. A long pause ensued before I finally said, 'Oh, Mr. Teng, you can be my teacher. How did you learn so much about Peking opera?'

'You're overpraising me, Miss Precious Orchid.' He sipped his wine, then soundlessly put down the cup. 'I'm just a fan.'

Damn! His lips were as tightly sealed as Mama's safe.

Though I was disappointed by his reserve, his delicate evasions rendered him even more desirable.

We continued to chat. And I continued to pour him wine, serve him food, and throw him soul-sucking glances. Until I finally grew tired of all the intellectual discussions.

When he finally looked drunk and tired, I grabbed the chance and asked, 'Mr. Teng, would you like to retire to bed now?'

'Miss Precious Orchid,' he said, his eyes glazed with alcohol. 'I'm afraid I want to go home now. I'm not feeling very well.'

I was astonished to have my offer turned down a second time! What was wrong with this man? Pearl had once told me any man's eyes will bleed when he smells free sex, even if the woman is a buck-toothed and pockmarked old hag. Now this man had paid a lot for me, and I was considered, if not the most, at least *one* of the most beautiful courtesans in Shanghai. But he had no interest in exploring my cinnabar crevice with his jade stalk. Was it something wrong with him . . . or with me?

Hiding my confusion, I lifted my lips to resemble a crescent moon. 'Then, Mr. Teng, you'd better stay.'

'I'll be fine; just call me a rickshaw.'

'If that's what you wish.'

He simply nodded, while casting me a passionate glance.

When I walked him to the door, Plum Blossom suddenly piped up, 'Feels good, eh? Want more?'

Not knowing whether to laugh or cry, I looked down and stared at my feet. Pearl had once commented that they were big. Was this the reason Mr. Teng had lost his appetite for me?

After Teng left, I slumped down in a chair and sighed. If he found me undesirable, then why had he come back? Maybe he was shy, or maybe, as Mama had guessed, his gun was not loaded. I hoped not, he was such a nice-looking man! Maybe I should prepare the recipe Pearl had taught me, so next time when he came, I could not only enlarge his jade stalk but make it thrust as high as the Mountains of Heaven!

Though nothing had happened, I could not get Mr. Teng out of my thoughts. As a flower girl, the worst thing would be a customer thinking I was in love with someone else. So I was alarmed when my favoured guest Big Master Fung noticed something was amiss.

On one occasion, after we finished stirring the clouds and rain, he asked, 'Xiang Xiang, what's the matter with you? Your mind seems to be somewhere else.'

Since I couldn't afford to offend him, I apologised, then lifted the corners of my lips all the way to my ears. 'Oh no, Big Master Fung! How can my mind be somewhere else when you're right in front of me?'

Several days later, Mama told me Mr. Teng would be coming that evening. Instead of preparing the recipe for enlarging his jade stalk, I copied some verses by the famous Tang dynasty poet Wang Wei. I lit incense, meditated, then poured all my passion into the cursive calligraphy:

The red bean grows in the South
When Spring comes, how many new buds will bloom?
I wish for you to collect them till your hands are full
Because these beans are grown for love.

I remembered that whenever Baba had left home to perform with his opera troupe, he'd always carry a small pouch filled with these beans, which were only slightly bigger and rounder than grains of rice. When I'd asked him why he carried them around, he said, 'So that I can look at them and think of your mother.' He explained that these red beans are *xiangsi dou* – beans of mutual longing. *Xiangsi* also means – missing you. That's why red beans have become lovers' favourite gifts.

Mr. Teng arrived punctually at seven-thirty in the evening. As soon as we'd settled on the sofa in my room, I handed him the poem. For a long time he looked at it without speaking. Then he began to recite another poem in his clear, almost boyish voice:

By the smooth flowing waters the green willows grow
I hear the singing of my lover
The sun shines in the east but in the west it rains
Though the sky is dark, sunbeams shine through.

Listening to him, I felt both happy and sad. I knew he was using the famous Tang dynasty poet Liu Yuxi's poem to tell me that although I might think he felt no love for me, it was not true. When the sky darkens and the man's passion cannot be felt, the woman's heart is sad. However, the sun finally shines through the dark clouds, bringing her hope.

But now my heart felt like it was gnawed by hundreds of ants. What exactly did Mr. Teng mean to tell me through this poem? I wish he could have spoken his feelings more directly, instead of heading for the east while pointing toward the west.

Maybe it was time for me to take the initiative to clear up my muddled emotions. I shifted close to him, took his hand in mine, and started kissing it. He sighed with pleasure. Encouraged, I moved my lips up to his. Instantly his tongue slithered into my mouth like a snake returning to its hole. Our two snakes wrestled and caressed, entangled and released, attacked and retreated. My hands moved here and there to peel off my clothes until I wore only my stomach cover. While Mr. Teng's mouth was busy kissing mine, his hands, soft and tender like silk, rolled all over my body.

After we'd been kissing for several incarnations, I suddenly realised he was still fully clothed. How did he think his jade stalk could stir my clouds with all these encumbrances? I reached to unbutton his shirt, but to my surprise, he immediately caught my hand.

Teng said, his voice intoxicated with tenderness, 'Miss Precious Orchid, you go to bed first and turn around; I'll join you.'

It seemed a strange suggestion, but as I was being paid, I did what I was asked.

Under the silk bedcover, I slipped off even my stomach cover. Feeling sexy, exultant, but anxious, I heard Teng blow out the light, then the sound of clothes falling onto the floor, and finally, the sensuous padding of bare feet toward me . . .

My eyes closed and my heart fluttering like the wings of a newly hatched chick, I waited for him to fill my whole being with passion and love. Abruptly he slipped under the cover. He embraced me gently, his body against my bare back and bottom. I sighed with desire. But then my desire was quickly smothered by a strange sensation. When he pressed harder against me, I felt something soft and yielding. Suddenly a thought exploded inside my head – this man had breasts!

I flipped around and snatched off the cover.

But he pulled it right back.

I screamed. 'So, are you Mr. Teng or Miss Teng?!'

He lifted a finger to his mouth. 'Shhhh . . . Miss Precious Orchid, please don't act so shocked,' then he whispered next to my ear, 'anyway, what's the difference, since I love you?' After that, he sealed my lips with his – or hers.

Perhaps Teng Xiong was right; what would be the difference? After all, I was paid to do whatever pleased my customers. Enlightened to the truth, I felt a sad relief wash over me, extinguishing my body's last speck of fire. Then my hands, remembering their obligation, started to apply the erotic art of pleasing, until my customer moaned, squirmed, succumbed, and finally collapsed . . .

* * *

It took me a long time to overcome the shock caused by Teng Xiong. The blow was not so much due to the fact that she was a woman, but the dashing of my hope that Teng was to be my true love who would marry me and take me away from prostitution. Of course, I had not been so naïve that I hadn't heard that some women preferred to love other women. Pearl had told me about Hong Nainai, a *ming ji* who, after being jilted by her lover, had limited her attentions to women. She had attracted many customers as a 'mirror-rubbing girl.' For centuries, Chinese had used bronze mirrors. Because bronze would easily get dull, people specialising in polishing them would tramp along streets and alleys, calling out, 'Mirror rubbing! Mirror rubbing!' Their tool was simple: a thick 'mother' mirror and oil for lubrication. When you gave them your mirror, they would spurt oil on the 'mother' mirror, then rub your mirror against it until it shone.

Pearl had smiled meaningfully. 'So, when two women are having sex, since they don't have jade stalks, they can only rub their *yin* parts against each other like two flat mirrors.'

She went on, 'This Hong Nainai became very popular by being a lesbian sister. For she knew how to play at being a "man" while possessing all the advantages of a woman. So she was called "half-month man, half-month woman." ' Pearl winked. 'She was reputed to be extremely skillful in "spreading the slippery noodles." '

Clearly Teng Xiong was another Hong Nainai, only she paid rather than getting paid.

Now that her secret had been revealed, Teng visited me more frequently. Each time we stirred each other's clouds – since it was impossible for her to shower any rain. Although she didn't have a jade stalk, like the legendary Hong Nainai she was very skilful in rubbing my mirror. I got only a little pleasure out of this, but I still would rather have her rub my mirror than have those *chou nanren* thrust their filthy stalks into my precious gate. However, I was attracted to her as a person – handsome, elegant, unconventional. Whenever we finished making love and I was about to put on clothes, she would gently take them from me, place them at the foot of the bed and, without any clothes on herself, draw me into her arms and hold me till we fell asleep together.

Teng Xiong had a smooth, willowy body like a youth's. I liked to watch her move around my room, my eyes outlining the curves of her small breasts, slightly rounded stomach, and narrow hips. Then I'd try to imagine how she would look with long hair, or with a stomach cover, or enclosed in a tight gown, or even wearing a low-cut Western dress. Would I like her less – or more – as a 'woman'?

At another of Teng's visits, when we'd finished having sex and were sitting by the window sipping tea, she said, 'Miss Precious Orchid, I want to thank you for giving me all these good times, but if you're still disappointed that I'm a woman, please accept my apology.'

I remained silent, for I really didn't know what to say. I did enjoy being with her, but I still felt deceived. Though she treated me far more tenderly than any of the stinking males, now my dream of a happy future was shattered by the lack of what I'd so hated in the past – a jade stalk!

Although my heart felt like it was tasting the bitterest yellow lotus seed, my face put on a pretty smile. 'Please don't mention it. It's my duty to serve you.'

Her flushed face paled. 'Is that what you think? Don't you feel something more for me?'

What could be more than *that*? I thought, but said instead, 'Of course, I'm most impressed by your erudition in the arts and your elegant demeanour.'

'Overpraise.' She frowned, as if trying to search for the right words. 'Before I came here, I read poems both about you and written by you. Your name was like a thunder roaring in my ears and I desired to meet you for a long time. So you can imagine my ecstasy now that my dream has finally come true.'

I responded with another demure smile. 'Overpraise, M—' I still didn't know whether to call 'him' Mr. or Miss Teng.

'Please just call me Teng Xiong,' she said. 'Miss Precious Orchid, I must tell you,' she gulped down her tea, 'I'm in love with you.'

'You're what?'

'I love you.'

'But I can't love you back,' I blurted out. 'You're a woman, too!'

'Yes, you can.' She threw me a hard stare. 'At least you can try. Don't be offended, Miss Precious Orchid. But if you can please an all-wrinkled and spotty-skinned old man, why can't you love a handsome, gentle, and considerate woman like me? Anyway you once thought I was a man.'

Maybe she was right, why couldn't I love a woman? I thought, but asked instead, 'But . . . why do you not like men?'

'Do you like them?'

The question struck me speechless. It was true that I disliked nearly all the men in Peach Blossom. Maybe *dislike* was still too light a word, I even hated some of them.

Teng's voice rose again. 'Don't you agree that women – remember your sister Pearl – are much more refined than men? Did you prefer to spend time with a woman like her or with a man like the all-wrinkled Big Master Fung?'

Maybe Mama's conjecture was right after all. This person was a spy! Otherwise how would she know so much about me?

'How did you know about Pearl and Big Master Fung? Have you been spying on me?'

'Oh no, of course not,' she let out a chuckle, 'I wouldn't do something so distasteful. It's because you're very famous. People savour any bit of news about you. You're their goddess.'

I couldn't help but feel flattered. 'But what about Red Jade, isn't she *the* goddess?'

Teng threw her head back and laughed, looking very handsome like a real man. 'Ha, maybe Red Jade was popular among vulgar businessmen, but your admirers are scholars, poets, artists.'

'I also have vulgar businessmen as customers.'

'Yes, it's because you're haughty and condescending, that's why they want you more. There are lots of poor poet-scholars out there who're crazy about you but can't afford to pay even for ten minutes just to sniff your natural fragrance. I'm lucky that I'm rich.' She reached to take my hand. 'Precious Orchid, can you be my lover?'

I wanted to withdraw mine, but suddenly remembered that she was still paying for the hours.

'Miss Teng—'

'Please call me Teng Xiong.'

'Teng Xiong, I ... don't think so. Because I ... I don't love you.'

'Then I'll come back here until you'll love me in return.'

'How are you so sure that I will?'

'Because I'm handsome, rich, and nicer to you than all the men you've ever known. Such as Big Master Fung.'

I was shocked that she mentioned Fung's name *again*. 'Do you know him?'

Her answer dropped a bomb in the room. 'He's my husband.'

'What?'

She took another sip of tea. 'I was his fourth concubine. Because I couldn't bear him anymore, I stole his money and ran away. It happened a few weeks ago, so of course he's been looking for me.'

I covered my mouth, fearing a scream would shoot out and explode in the room. I said in a breathless hush, 'Oh my heaven, then why are you here?'

'Because I'm willing to risk my life for love.'

'Then what if he runs into you here?'

'He won't, I know his schedule. Monday is his day to accompany his first wife to the temple to make offerings, then stay overnight. Precious Orchid, I'm a very careful person. It took me two years to plan my escape. Besides, even if he does run into me here, he would never imagine that I, now a man with a different name, could possibly be his concubine.' She paused, then, 'The most dangerous-looking place is sometimes the safest.'

I noisily sipped my tea, the hot liquid burning the roof of my mouth. 'Then what are you doing now, and where have you been hiding?'

'As you know, I changed my name and disguised myself. Since I have a lot of money, I'm able to stay in hotels. My next move is to go to Peking to join a female Peking opera troupe. Of course, I'll play the male role. I was an opera singer before I married Fung.' She cast me a penetrating stare. 'That's the reason I'm here, Precious Orchid. I want you to run away with me to Peking.'

Her words sent a tremor across my chest. If I went to Peking, I could search for my mother! I slurped my tea, feeling dizzy while trying to absorb these unexpected twists and turns of life. 'Let me calm down, and please let me think.'

'Sure.' She looked at her gold pocket watch, which I now realised was once Big Master Fung's. 'I'll be back next week, but I can't wait any longer. Old Fung is looking really hard for me now.'

'But he's never mentioned anything about you.'

'Of course not. Do you think he'll go around telling everybody that his concubine stole his money and ran away? He'd rather shoot himself than lose face!'

A pause, then I asked, 'What does he do?'

'Something illegal. Sorry, Precious Orchid, I really don't want to go into this. Besides, he's a very dark person. He doesn't like to talk about his business. But,' she paused to cast me an intense look, 'he likes to talk about you.'

'Me?'

'Yes, he always boasts how beautiful and talented you are. One time when he was drunk, he even said that he was seriously considering taking you home as his fifth concubine.' Teng Xiong plunged on, 'That's what stirred my curiosity to come here. I wanted to meet my rival. But like him, I was hopelessly bewitched by you.'

I was so shocked that I remained speechless. Finally I asked, 'Teng Xiong, you're not afraid that Fung will punish or even . . . kill you?'

'Of course. But I've already stepped onto a path of no return.' She reached to take my hand. 'I'll be back one last time. Please come with me. I'll be disguised as a man, so we'll travel as husband and wife.'

She'd already planned everything as if I'd agreed! 'You're not afraid . . . that I'll . . . betray you to him?'

To my surprise, she laughed. 'Oh no, Precious Orchid, absolutely not.'

'How are you so sure?'

'I'm well versed in physiognomy. You can't even kill a rat.'

23

The Escape

Two weeks later, with only my *qin* and a few belongings, I ran away with Teng Xiong. My only regret was that I couldn't bid farewell to Aunty Ah Ping and Spring Moon.

'Will you risk everything just to say goodbye?' Teng Xiong warned. 'No one can know about our escape. Don't even trust your own shadow!'

I could only say goodbye to Plum Blossom. I put her on my shoulder and prayed that we'd be born as sisters in a future lifetime. She cocked her head and clucked, 'Wish you make a lot of money!'

I left Peach Blossom with Teng Xiong as if I was just going out to entertain a customer. Both of us were dressed up for a night on the town, she in an indigo suit with an orange silk tie, and I in a purple silk gown with red and gold flowers. She had picked a Saturday because that was the busiest night at Peach Blossom, meaning that surveillance would be relatively relaxed. An hour later, we arrived at an elegant restaurant near the Huangpu River, one in which private rooms were available. Teng slipped cash to everyone who came up to greet us – waiters, waitresses, the captain, even a servant boy and a maid. When the tipping spree had ended, we were led to the most expensive private chamber facing the river. The two guards from Peach Blossom stood right outside the room.

Through the window, I could see reflections of light blinking like peeking eyes on the black ripples. A few pleasure boats were tied beside the larger merchant ships. From these gaily painted boats drifted the sounds of women singing to the accompaniment of the *pipa*. If I were lucky, from tonight on I'd be a free woman. But could these boat-dwelling sisters ever sail away from this amorous, floating world?

Teng Xiong's pure, tender voice rose next to me, breaking up my reverie. 'Precious Orchid, anything special you want to eat tonight?'

I felt my heart beating fast in my chest. 'Order what you want. Anything will please me.'

She motioned to the captain and ordered – four bottles of the most expensive wine and a ten-course dinner.

'Teng Xiong,' I nudged her elbow and whispered, 'that's enough for a dozen people!'

She cast me a sharp glance, then ordered more – three different kinds of fragrant tea: Iron Bodhisattva, Dragon Well, Clouds and Mist, and four water pipes. The captain left, then returned with two waitresses to set down a variety of small dishes on our table.

'Mr. Teng,' he grinned obsequiously, 'these are all respect dishes from our restaurant.' After that, the three bowed deeply to us and withdrew.

Teng Xiong ignored my upset at her extravagance. She picked up the teapot and poured us both a full cup; then she clicked her cup with mine, 'Precious Orchid, to our success.'

My heart beating like a battle drum, I asked, 'Teng Xiong, do you really think we'll make it?'

'I always plan things very carefully. Just trust me.'

While we picked at the dishes in silence, the captain and the two waitresses returned with more. When finally the whole table was covered with food, Teng Xiong, to my surprise, asked the captain to invite the two guards to come in and join us. 'I'll pay the bill now. After this, we want to be completely left alone.'

I whispered into her ear, 'Teng Xiong, are you out of your mind!'

'Certainly, Mr. Teng,' the captain threw us a knowing glance, 'I understand.'

He must have thought that Teng wanted us to be left alone so we could indulge in a foursome orgy!

After the captain took the money and dragged his meatless posterior out of the room, two grinning faces flashed through the door. Teng Xiong smiled back, motioning the two guards to come sit with us. After they were seated, she poured wine into their glasses and piled food onto their plates.

'You two must be working so hard. Please accept our thanks with this wine.' She picked up her glass and made a toast, while signalling me to do the same. 'Now please relax and help yourself to the food.'

From crude faces, two pairs of bloodshot eyes glared with hunger and greed. Two pairs of chopsticks ambushed the dishes, leaving trails of sauce on the white tablecloth like the calligraphy of a drunkard. The same calloused hands that had mercilessly swung a whip or squeezed a sister's neck now wiped oily lips.

I willed my hands to stop shaking as I joined with Teng Xiong in 'wind and moon' – empty and decadent – conversation. I even let the guard next to me 'accidentally' brush his hand against my breast as he tried to reach for the biggest piece of fat pork. After some more decadent talk, I entertained the two by singing and playing finger games. With flushed faces, glazed eyes, and glistening lips, the two guards had never looked happier. At Teng's urging, but with the greatest reluctance, I took out my *qin* and began to play. As my fingers danced on the elegant instrument, the two guards washed their throats with wine and sucked hard at their water pipes between curses – 'Fuck his mother, how could that turtle egg possibly be that rich? Fuck her mother's cunt, how could she shit such *huge* breasts on her daughter?'

The room now reeked with smoke, which hung ominously in the air. I tried my best to maintain a provocative smile and high-pitched voice while my fingers – like a stripper – glided, jiggled, dived, and danced vigorously on the venerated instrument. Though tugged by a tinge of guilt that I was playing for such a vulgar audience, at least I hadn't broken my solemn promise to Pearl – I was not playing the *qin* for money.

During my 'stripping,' Teng kept piling food on the guards' plates and refilling their glasses with the gold, velvety liquid.

At last, well after midnight, the two men were besottedly sprawled on the table like two piles of slush. When it was clear that nothing would awaken them, Teng Xiong asked me to change from my gown into a loose top and trousers, pack my *qin,* and gather my few belongings. After that, making sure that no one, not even a ghost, was watching us, Teng Xiong and I quietly sneaked out through one of the back exits, hailed a rickshaw, and went straight to the North Station.

A few hours later, our train arrived in Nanking. We walked to the pier, took the ferry to Pukou, and boarded the express to Peking. Lulled by the gentle motion of the train and exhausted by the events of the evening, I slept dreamlessly. When I woke up in our first-class compartment, I found myself wrapped in Teng Xiong's arms.

She kissed me tenderly on my forehead. 'Precious Orchid, did you sleep well?'

My head felt like it was being hammered. 'Where are we? Where are the guards?'

She held me tighter. 'Precious Orchid. We're safe. In Peking.'

'You're sure?'

'Yes.'

I searched her face in the Peking morning mist, then buried mine in her chest so she couldn't see the tears swelling in my eyes.

If only Teng Xiong were a real man.

'Precious Orchid,' she smoothed my hair and cooed, 'don't sleep any more. I'm afraid we have to get off here.'

The porter picked up my *qin*, then we walked through the Peking Station and hired a car. Teng Xiong asked the driver to take us to the Grand Fortune Hotel not far from the Temple of Heaven. During the short ride I craned my neck and looked around at this strange city – pale-faced men slouching into opium dens; restaurants specialising in tortoise, snake, antelope's horn soup; a fiddler sawing his two-stringed instrument next to a contorted acrobat. As the car passed the many narrow alleys lined with single-storey houses protected by high walls, I craned my neck even higher. Inside one sturdy gate, instead of a glimpse of garden, my eyes were blocked by a tall wall.

I pointed it out to Teng Xiong. 'Why is there a wall right inside the gate?'

She smiled. 'Oh, don't you know, Precious Orchid? This is the famous ghost wall – to stop ghosts from wandering into the house. Ghosts can't meander; they can only walk in straight lines.'

But I remembered Pearl had taught me the opposite – meandering paths. Maybe because those who dwell in the *yang* world still have to go through life's twists and turns, while a ghost's world is something much simpler. In a few minutes, we arrived at the hotel, checked in, then went to our room, and headed straight to the bed – to sleep.

When we awakened, it was already afternoon. Refreshed from my sleep, I now felt extremely hungry. We bathed quickly and changed, then went out to eat in a small restaurant. I gulped down my beef noodles, pork buns, and steaming Oolong tea, but Teng Xiong picked half-heartedly at her food, her eyes watching me with the affection of a mother and the tenderness of a husband.

I held her glance for some moments. 'Teng Xiong, aren't you hungry?'

She smiled. 'Your beauty is my feast.'

After lunch, we went to buy clothes and daily necessities, then headed back to the hotel. Teng Xiong suggested we return to bed – this time to rub our mirrors. I sighed inside, thinking of the Chinese sayings: 'A full stomach leads to promiscuity,' and 'Eating and sex are human nature.'

Although I would not have chosen a woman for sex, I was grateful to Teng Xiong and thus felt obliged to please her. Besides, if I had to have sex anyway, I'd rather have it with a cultivated, handsome woman than with a *chou nanren*!

So I, again, this time voluntarily, applied my erotic arts to please.

Teng Xiong quickly succumbed to my weapons of charm – electrifying eyes, burning lips, lapping tongue, caressing hands. She moaned and squirmed, arched and wriggled until her body collapsed next to mine.

Teng Xiong enjoyed having sex with me so much that we ended up spending two whole days in the hotel without even getting dressed. It was not until my *yin* part had gotten swollen that she was willing to stop.

Since we couldn't have sex for the time being, we at last started to discuss how we might find the female Peking opera troupe and my mother. Teng Xiong was eager to join the group, but I insisted on finding my mother first. Finally she backed down, for the sake of love.

Teng Xiong told me she had more than enough money for us to relax and tour Peking before we set out, but I was in no mood for sightseeing, nor for any other form of entertainment. My sole desire now was to look for my mother, not only from love, but also from bitterness: To ask her why she had not written to me all these years. How she could be so heartless as to forget her only daughter?

The third day in Peking, Teng Xiong and I woke up at ten. We rushed to eat, dress, and pack, then immediately set out for Taiyi Mountain, situated south-west of Peking. When Mother and I had parted more than eight years ago, she'd told me she planned to enter a temple on this mountain. Since I'd never received any letters from her, I had no idea which one she'd settled in. I thought I'd start with the lowest one, then work my way up, asking any monk or nun I saw if they'd heard of her.

It was a long, arduous trip. By the time we arrived at Taiyi Mountain, it was already late afternoon. The autumn air was cool and soothing. The pale moon sitting atop a distant peak suspiciously followed our every move. Fragrant Cloud Monastery was the first temple we reached. Teng Xiong had first spotted its upturned eaves rising from amid heavy foliage. She stopped the coolies, paid them, then helped me down from the sedan chair and led me to the gate. We gently rapped the lion's head knocker, well aware that this was a sanctuary for people who didn't want to be bothered by worldly affairs.

The door sighed open to reveal a youth with a round face and shaved head. Seeing that it was a small temple – meaning that we didn't have to deal with elaborate protocol – I simply asked for the abbot.

The young monk told us to wait, then dashed away. Almost in no time he appeared again. 'Mister and Miss, our abbot invites you to the reception hall. Please follow me.'

The grey-robed abbot was about seventy, skinny, and wise-looking. He was already waiting for us at the end of the courtyard, the moonlight gleaming on his mirror-like head.

Before I could stop her, Teng Xiong had already introduced us as husband and wife.

The abbot smiled, his hand clicking a long-tasseled strand of mala beads. 'Welcome to our modest temple, Mr. and Mrs. Teng.'

'May we have the honour to know the abbot's name?'

I was pleased that Teng asked in the most polite manner.

'My Dharma name is Drifting Cloud.'

Master Drifting Cloud led us inside the hall. After we all settled on the wooden chairs, he asked the teenage monk to bring us tea and snacks.

We sipped the fragrant tea and munched nuts, fruits, and vegetarian buns while we chatted. Teng Xiong told him our background – made up, of course. Now my lesbian lover became a merchant and I the mother of his three small children. I felt a little guilty about the lie, not because I was so virtuous and honest, but because *my husband* looked so virtuous and honest lying to a respectable monk! Finally, after more lies and polite talk, I brought up the most important subject – my mother – and asked if the abbot had any clue of her whereabouts.

'I'm afraid it's rather difficult, Mrs. Teng.' He cast me a thoughtful look. 'There are more than one hundred temples scattered over this mountain—'

I was shocked to hear this. 'That many?'

He nodded. 'And you have no idea in which one your mother stays?'

'No.' I shook my head, feeling totally dejected. 'I had no idea there were so many temples here.' Moreover, there was the possibility that my mother had moved elsewhere – or even died. But I didn't mention these fears to the monk.

'Besides,' he carefully sipped his tea, 'if she's become a nun, that means she's adopted a Dharma name – Purifying Dust, Enlightening Light, Compassionate Countenance. So what's your mother's Dharma name?'

'I have no idea,' I blurted out, then blushed, feeling stupid and unfilial.

'If you don't know your mother's Dharma name, I'm afraid it will be extremely difficult to locate her. What's her lay name?'

'Su Meifang.' Beautiful Fragrance. I suddenly realised how suitable this name had been for Mother. Was she still beautiful and fragrant now being a nun?

'Then I can ask around for you about a nun who was formerly called Su Meifang.'

'Can you do that now?'

I felt my sleeve tucked. Teng Xiong whispered into my ear. 'Precious Orchid, relax, please let the abbot decide how and when to do things.'

I put up a smile, albeit not my best, for that was only for my lustful big-shot customers, not a celibate old monk. 'Please forgive my rudeness, Master Drifting Cloud.'

The monk looked out the window, stared at the moon, then turned back. 'Since it's already late, I advise you two to stay overnight here, have a nice hot meal, and rest. Tomorrow you can go to the temple called Dharma Flower and tell them that I recommend you to Abbot Master Voyage of the Heart. Since he's ninety-five and a monk who's lived forever in this mountain, he's the person who can most likely help you. Dharma Flower is only about ten miles from here. You can walk if you like, or you can hire sedan chairs.'

Teng Xiong and I put our hands together and bowed deeply.

I said, 'Thank you for your kindness, Master Drifting Cloud.'

A charming smile broke on Teng Xiong's face. 'Master, to show our gratitude, would you let us donate some fragrant oil?' It pleased me that Teng Xiong used this euphemism for offering money.

The Master smiled back, an enlightened finger pointing to the

Merit Accumulating Box. After that, he summoned the young monk to ask the cook to prepare dinner for two guests.

After the abbot had left, the young monk soon came back and took us to the Fragrant Kitchen. Rarely did I have the chance to taste something so simple yet delicious as this modest vegetarian meal. Since I'd become famous in Peach Blossom, I'd been fed with rich meat dishes of all kinds. Even when I complained about my full stomach, my customers would still pile chunks of meat onto my plate, then pour me cup after cup of wine. I couldn't even say no, because not only was it rude to turn down someone's good intention, it was also stupid. 'No' is the forbidden word in a turquoise pavilion.

Now I looked at the mushrooms, tofu, bamboo shoots, fungus, and taro and felt a tender swelling of my heart. I'd never seen food so happily offer itself to us so that, as my mother had once told me, we'd stay not only alive and healthy, but virtuous.

Mother had never really liked meat. She always said, 'I only cook a little bit of it to spice up the vegetables.' And during every first and fifteenth day of each lunar month, she'd cook vegetarian to 'cleanse our body and spirit.' Scenes of our family sitting together to enjoy my mother's simple but delicious cooking flashed in my mind. Mother had feared that if she didn't let Fang Rong take me away, I wouldn't even have cold rice gruel to fill my stomach. But instead of rice gruel, I'd been stuffed with the richest of foods. I smiled at the irony.

Teng Xiong's chopsticks suspended in midair. 'Precious Orchid, did I do something funny?'

'Oh no, it's not you.' I told her about my mother's fear, yet without revealing anything more than necessary about my life.

She reached to touch my cheek. 'I'm so sorry, Precious Orchid. But you won't feel sad any more, for I'll make you happy.' She looked as if she were about to say something more, then seemed to decide against it.

I was sure she was dying to know more about my past, but sensed this was not the right time to probe. An awkward silence fell during which we busily scraped rice into our mouths. The kitchen was quiet. The only noises, besides the clicking of chopsticks and smacking of lips, came from outside the window – insects chirping, leaves rustling, the occasional barking of a distant dog. The autumn wind blowing on the leaves made a '*Xa, Xa*' sound as if it were calling my name: 'Xiang Xiang! Xiang Xiang!'

I cocked my head and listened. I remembered as a small child, when I'd been swaying too high on a swing, anxious to have a better view of the world, or if I was out of my parents' sight skipping along stones or fascinated by some object I'd found, I'd hear them call, 'Xiang Xiang! Xiang Xiang!' Their voices, bouncing in myriad directions, would sound affectionately urgent. Instead of responding to their call right away, I'd stand still and listen, just to relish their anxiety. Wherever I was – a back street, a courtyard, the nearby market – I wanted to freeze my parents' love in eternity. Were the leaves now calling me on behalf of my long-lost mother or my long-dead baba? Tears rolled down my cheeks as a piece of bamboo shoot lay half-chewed in my mouth.

'Precious Orchid?' Teng Xiong asked, her voice tender and eyes full of concern, just like my parents.

I shook my head, then swallowed the bamboo.

Teng Xiong came over and pulled me into her arms.

This time when she pressed her lips onto mine, I responded by slipping my tongue into her mouth. I was not sure whether I felt love, but I did feel gratitude.

Moments later, the young monk reappeared. Seeing that we had finished eating, he silently beckoned us to follow him. Once we were outside, he led us along a path to a low building beside the temple. Teng swung the door open, and we saw that our modest luggage had already been placed in the unadorned room. As soon as the young monk had left and we had sat down, I felt a wave of anxiety about my mother and whether I would ever find her. To soothe my worries, I took my *qin* from its brocade cover and started to tune it. Teng Xiong remained silent, her eyes resting contentedly on me.

I finished tuning and began to play 'Parasol Leaves Dancing in the Autumn Wind.' The middle finger of my left hand rested on the edge of the soundboard while I half-closed my eyes to meditate. After that, my right hand began to pluck while the fingers of my left hand touched the silk strings as lightly as petals floating on a brook. The small, bare room instantly filled with the bittersweet murmurs of the *qin*. Soothed by the quiet sounds of my instrument, I didn't think too much about being happy or unhappy; I simply felt glad that I was alive and free. As I played, the twists and turns, flicks and sweeps of my fingers conjured in my mind the different contours – twists and turns, ups and downs – of life. The parasol leaves continued to dance in the autumn wind, in the quiet, melancholic air, before finally falling to earth . . .

Early next morning the young monk came to our room and invited us to have breakfast. Teng Xiong thanked him, then told him that, still exhausted from the trip, we would skip breakfast and sleep more. In fact, Teng Xiong wanted sex – even though we were in a temple. After we exhausted our bodies by polishing our mirrors on our visit to the Wu Mountain, we fell asleep. When we woke up, to our alarm, it was already afternoon.

'Damn! We have to get ready and leave right away!' Teng Xiong jumped out of bed and started to dress. 'I'll go and ask the young monk for some snacks.'

After a hasty meal, we were ready to leave. The young monk had already arranged two small sedan chairs to take us to the Dharma Flower Temple.

By the gate, we bade farewell to the abbot. He smiled kindly at me. 'Mrs. Teng, I wish you good luck in finding your mother. If I have a chance, I'll also ask about her for you.' Then he turned to hand a piece of paper to Teng Xiong, 'Mr. Teng, this is the way to Dharma Flower Temple. You can show it to the coolies in case they can't find their way or get lost.'

'Thank you for your kindness and generosity, Master Drifting Cloud.' We bowed to the two monks before we walked to the waiting sedan chairs.

The four coolies, though young looking, had deep wrinkles on their tanned faces. Their bodies were stout, and their calves muscular, with veins bulging like tiny green snakes. Teng Xiong told the coolies to arrange that my sedan chair be in front and hers follow right behind.

The sun was warm, the road narrow and bumpy, and the coolies silent. Eyes intent and faces alert, they concentrated on the road ahead as if they were doing slow-running meditation. An occasional tree leaning out over the road provided a moment of shade. I watched the dappled patterns flicker on the fleeting ground and felt a dizzy happiness. From time to time I'd stick my head out, turn back, and wave to Teng Xiong, calling out her name. In response, my 'husband' would put on a wide grin and cheerily wave back.

After an hour's ride, we finally reached an open field. Now we were far from everything. We could see no temple roofs, nor even smoke from a distant kitchen. Teng Xiong agreed to the coolies' request for a twenty-minute break. The four immediately went to squat down under a tree in a circle, wiped their perspiring faces with a rag, unwrapped some dried buns, and started to eat. After their meagre meal, they took out dice to gamble their paltry earnings from the trip.

Teng Xiong suggested that we explore. She called out to the coolies, 'We'll stroll around and come back in half an hour.'

The skinny one yelled back, 'Master, don't take longer than that, for we want to get you there before the sun sets.'

'Don't worry; we'll be back on time.'

Teng Xiong broke two thick branches to use for walking sticks. To test their sturdiness, she swung them in the air then hit them on the ground, making a pleasant, swishing sound.

Then, when we were ready to set out, I suddenly remembered something. 'Wait, Teng Xiong,' I said, 'I left my *qin* in the sedan chair.'

'Better just leave it there; it'll be too heavy to carry.'

Since I didn't want to tell her how 'valuable' my *qin* was, I made up an excuse. 'I want to play a nature piece for you under the trees. Besides, I don't want to take any chance that the coolies move things around and break it.'

'All right, then I'll carry it for you.'

We took the *qin* and began our journey into the woods. It was as if we'd stepped into a dream. The autumn breeze was chillingly fresh, the sun soothing like a gentle massaging hand, and the fra-

grance of the ancient trees intoxicating. Slinging my *qin* in its brocade cover over her shoulder, Teng Xiong looked like a refined,
handsome scholar who had walked out from an ancient landscape
painting. Watching her silhouette made me sad. If only she were a
real man!

We walked silently, each immersed in the moment. From time
to time, I'd stoop to pick up something – a mottled leaf, a gracefully shaped stone, a twig in the form of a calligraphic stroke. The
lyrics of the *qin* piece 'Ode to Ancient Time' poured out from my
lips:

> Sun and moon shuttle day and night.
> Clouds drift, water flows.
> Melancholy in the wind and the fragrant grass.
> Sky deserted, earth withered.
> Everything slides away.
> Now just the lament of the battle between the dragon and
>   the tiger
> So much for a life!

When I finished, Teng Xiong said, 'Precious Orchid, your
singing is beautiful, but the song is so sad.'

'But aren't most Chinese poems sad?'

'It's true. Because life *is* sad,' she murmured, seemingly lost in
thought. 'So we should enjoy life to the full while we have the
chance.' She took my hand and lifted it to her lips.

We continued to walk until we reached a small opening, in the
middle of which towered a ginkgo tree with heavy limbs, its yellow
leaves like golden rain.

Teng Xiong went up to touch the trunk and examine its bark.
'Come, Precious Orchid; take a look.'

I hurried up to look. 'It must be a hundred years old!'

'No, a thousand. This tree has witnessed the rise and fall of dy-
nasties and the lives and deaths of the great and the humble: sages
teaching, travellers losing their way, birds making their nests, lovers
pledging their vows, monks entering nirvana. Too bad it can't talk,
otherwise I'm sure it could entertain us with more stories than the

Romance of the Three Kingdoms.' She went on, her voice turning sentimental, 'I hope our love can last as long as this tree.'

I didn't respond. Although I was very fond of Teng Xiong, I didn't think I felt the kind of love for her that I'd feel for a man. But since I'd never fallen in love with a man, how would I know what that kind of love felt like?

Fearing that she'd ask me to pledge love in front of the ancient tree, I tried to distract her. 'Teng Xiong, don't you think it's a good idea to play the *qin* under this tree?'

She nodded, then carefully took down the instrument from her shoulder and peeled off its brocade cover. This time I played 'Dialogue Between the Fisherman and the Woodcutter.' I imagined Teng Xiong the woodcutter and I the fisherman who, after meeting in the forest, ate grilled fish, drank wine, and discussed philosophy.

In the midst of the forest and attuned to the spirit of the mountain, I played one *qin* piece after another: 'The Drunken Fisherman'; 'Three Variations on the Plum Blossom'; 'Lament Behind the Long Gate'; then finally 'Remembering an Old Friend.'

I sighed when my fingers finally lifted off from the instrument, then told Teng Xiong about Pearl.

After I finished, she said, 'I'm so sorry. I wish I'd had the chance to meet her.' She searched my face. 'I'm sure your sister Pearl was as lovely and talented as you are.'

'More.'

'That I cannot believe. Precious Orchid, you're just being modest.' She squinted at me. 'I'm sure you know the phrase "turquoise arises from the blue but surpasses the blue"?'

I smiled. This famous phrase was used to describe a student who surpassed his teacher. A pause, then I decided to play one more piece – 'Elegant Orchid.' Handed down from the Tang dynasty over one thousand years ago, this was perfect to play under the ancient tree.

I was still immersed in the purity of the music when suddenly Teng Xiong exclaimed, 'Oh Heaven, we've stayed here for too long!'

Quickly I slipped my *qin* back into its case. Teng Xiong snatched it from me, took my hand, and we started to run.

'You think the coolies are still waiting for us?'

'I think so, since I haven't paid them yet,' she said, the *qin* bumping against her back.

'Oh no, but Master Drifting Cloud already did! I saw him pay the coolies!'

'Oh my, then I'm pretty sure they're gone,' she pulled me along, 'and all our clothes and everything else!'

Now I noticed the weather had turned quite chilly and the sun was almost gone. 'If they've left, what are we going to do?'

'I don't know. I can't think right now, but we'll see.'

But we didn't. For an hour later, we were still groping in the forest. I realised that the worst had happened – we were lost.

Exhausted from running, walking, and worrying, we finally sat down on a rock to rest. We felt tired and hungry, but there was nothing to drink nor eat. All the food had been left in the sedan chairs.

I covered my face and cried. Teng Xiong put her arm around my shoulder.

'Teng Xiong, I'm scared!' I nestled hard against her.

'It's my fault, I should have kept track of time.' She looked around. 'I think we'll have to look for shelter and spend the night here.'

'But we might freeze to death, or be eaten alive by a tiger! And there might be snakes, I don't want to be bitten!'

She held me tighter. 'Precious Orchid, don't panic. We'll just have to be very careful. Then when morning comes, I'm sure we'll be able to figure a way out.'

24

The Bandits

Light was draining quickly from the sky and outlines of the mountains had grown dim like pale, smeared ink. We continued to stumble through the thickening mist looking for a place to rest, anything.

Then we spotted a dark object partly hidden in the shrubbery. Teng Xiong suggested, 'Precious Orchid, let's go and take a look.'

When we drew closer, we realised it was a huge bronze bell turned a deep green and covered with ancient characters.

Teng Xiong traced the inscription with her finger, 'Look, Precious Orchid, it was donated to honour a high monk who lived . . . one hundred and twenty years. So maybe it will bring us longevity, too.'

'Please, Teng Xiong, it's getting dark, and I'm scared!'

'Don't worry. The bell must mean there's a temple somewhere near here.'

I looked around but didn't see a roof or a pagoda's tip. 'Then where is the temple?'

'Be patient, it must be close by, hidden by mist or trees. Now let's—' She suddenly stopped, then spoke in a whisper. 'Listen.'

I strained my ears, then murmured back to her. 'I think I hear footsteps.'

'Me, too,' she paused, her voice tense, 'and they're getting closer.'

'That's good, should we shout to them for help?'

Teng Xiong slapped a hand tightly against my mouth. 'No! Precious Orchid. We have no idea who these people are, they may be monks . . . or they may be bandits.'

'Oh my heaven, then what are we going to do?'

Before Teng Xiong had a chance to respond, we heard laughter and loud curses drifting from behind the bushes.

Teng Xiong said in a heated whisper, 'Now I'm sure they're bandits.'

Just then I spotted shadows flickering here and there within the foliage.

Teng Xiong's suppressed whisper rose again right next to my ear. 'It's too late to run now. We'd better hide. Maybe we can get inside the bell. Here, help me try to lift it up.' She laid the *qin* on the ground, then we got our fingers around the rim of the bell and, as if suddenly aided by some supernatural power, managed to lift it above the ground.

Teng Xiong hissed, 'Get in, quick!'

I hesitated.

She crawled under the bell and reached out for me. I tried to grab the *qin* but my hand slipped. The bell fell with a loud clatter.

Inside the bell, Teng Xiong's voice sounded urgent yet muted. 'Let's lift it again, quick!'

But too late. I saw two huge heads poking out from a nearby bush.

I picked up the *qin* and started to sprint.

Trees and bushes flew past me. Instead of golden lotuses blossoming under my dainty steps, now twigs, sands, and small stones were crushed under the soles of my brutalised feet. The air slapped hard against my cheeks. Low branches tore at my arms until I felt blood trickling down my skin. The *qin* kept drumming against my back, bruising my ribs. Then, to my horror, it slipped off my shoulder and crashed onto the ground.

I let out a sharp cry and kept running. But alas, in a moment, I was grabbed from behind. Though I tried to kick and chop, two muscular arms locked around me so tightly that my martial art prowess was as lost as my *qin*. I screamed and screamed.

To my surprise, instead of pressing his hand over my mouth, the bandit burst into laughter. Meanwhile his companion moved in front of me and scrutinised me hard and long. He had a strangely evil-looking face with sharp bones sticking in all directions under taut skin. When he spoke, his voice came out high-pitched like a young girl's. I almost laughed despite my alarming situation.

'Even if you scream until your lungs burst, do you think in this no-man's-land your lover boy will hear and come to your rescue?'

Then the one grasping me from behind said, his voice harsh and mean, 'What's a pretty girl like you doing here alone in the woods, eh?' With one arm still tight around me, he grabbed my hair and wrenched my head back to stare hard at me. I could see bulging eyes as big as copper coins above a full, rumpled beard.

My mouth remained tightly shut. At least they hadn't spotted Teng Xiong.

Sharp-Bones hollered, 'Search her!'

From behind, Bulge-Eyes rubbed, squeezed, and pressed all over me, lingering on my breasts and *yin* place, 'Fuck, nothing, this bitch has nothing!'

Sharp-Bones threw me a sharp, questioning look. 'Nothing?'

'Yes. Absolutely nothing. No money, no jewellery.'

A long silence. Then Sharp-Bones piped up again, his eyes aiming licentious glances at me while his crude hand caressed his equally crude face. 'Hmmm, but she has something better than money and jewellery. Ha! Ha! Ha!'

Bulge-Eyes joined him in laughing. 'You're damn right.'

Having said that, he threw me onto the ground, tore open my top, and yanked my trousers down. As Sharp-Bones laughed, Bulge-Eyes dropped his own filthy trousers and clambered on top of me.

I screamed, this time not to fake pleasure, but from pain, anger, revulsion.

Bulge-Eyes slapped my face and banged my body onto the ground. I screamed louder, flailing my limbs under his bulky torso. He hit again, his hand thrusting as hard as his filthy stalk. I lay on the ground, paralysed, unable to stop his slime from pouring into me.

Sharp-Bones watched with knowing nods and an evil smile.

After Bulge-Eyes' stalk turned soft, he pulled up his trousers and hollered to his comrade. 'Now your turn!'

Just as Sharp-Bones was about to pull down his trousers, we heard the sound of footsteps rustling on leaves. Bulge-Eyes with one huge hand pinned me to the ground, while his other was held tightly against my mouth.

Thank heaven, it must be Teng Xiong! But how did she have the strength to lift up the bell all by herself?

The two bandits were now straining their ears and eyes, heads turning to follow the sound.

Then all of a sudden, a face thrust itself out from a bush. The evil duo let go of me, then snatched out knives and flicked them open. The sharp blades glittered like elongated eyes blinking in hell.

Although the moonlight was dimmed by the mist, I could still make out a pair of alert eyes taking in the scene. I snatched up my shredded clothes to cover my nakedness while a cry escaped from my mouth and rolled out into the darkness. I tried to stand up, but my feet wobbled and my muscles throbbed so hard that I collapsed back onto the ground. The two bandits ignored me.

Sharp-Bones hollered to the stranger in his woman's voice, 'You've just come to see your own death, you fuck-seeded bastard!'

Bulge-Eyes spat, 'Or you want to have a share of this slut, you embryo-fucked son of a bitch!'

To my disbelief, instead of turning away and running for his life, the man stepped forward. He wore a black top and trousers and his hair was hidden under a black scarf. The lantern in his hand cast an eerie, yellowish light, illuminating his face, which was unexpectedly smooth and intelligent.

When he spoke, his voice was calm and low, 'I'm afraid you two will have to let this lady go.'

Sharp-Bones burst into a shrill laugh. 'Ha! Ha! Ha! Don't tell me you feel no desire for such a beauty! What are you, a turtle egg or a eunuch?'

The young man's expression turned grave, his voice now even lower. 'As I said, you must let her go.'

'Ha! Little bastard,' Sharp-Bones spat, 'what's your rank? Don't you tell us what to do!'

The two exchanged a meaningful glance. Then Sharp-Bones said to his comrade, 'Should we teach this eunuch a lesson?'

'Sure.'

'Wait a minute.' The young man spoke again in his calm voice. 'Let me first ask you a question.'

Sharp-Bones scratched his pointed head and roared with laughter. 'A question? What's the matter with you, now trying to play scholar instead of bastard?'

Seemingly undisturbed, the young man replied, 'Can you two read?'

Bulge-Eyes looked amused. 'Ha, Ha, do we need to?' He swung the weapon in his hand. 'We have our knives!'

Sharp-Bones chimed in with a licentious sneer, shaking his hips. 'And our stalks! Ha, ha, ha!'

Suddenly the young man flipped open a scroll. I strained my eyes and saw a mystical diagram with tiger, sword, dragon, and rows of unintelligible calligraphy.

The two bandits, probably illiterate, looked puzzled.

Just then the young man snatched out a horn and started to blow, the ear-splitting sound spreading in myriad directions. With the harsh buzz still resonating in the air, he dropped the horn and took out a small bell which he started to shake vigorously, while his mouth muttered some unintelligible phrases. Next he flashed something long and soft – a dragon-headed whip! It flicked and snapped in the air like an attacking snake. Finally, as if in a magic show, he drew out a long sword, split the scroll into two, and with his lantern set it on fire. I let out a gasp.

The two bandits looked stunned; big beads of perspiration oozed from their creased foreheads. Their faces shone red in the glaring fire. Their mouths, hanging open, emitted no word.

The most extraordinary sight was yet to come. Now the fire

sprang into the shape of a huge tiger and, with full force, leaped toward the twosome.

The two bandits held their heads and screamed as if they had just been brought before the King of Hell. Instantly, they vanished into the darkness.

Instead of chasing after them, the young man started to walk toward me, then stopped when he was about ten feet away. He spoke, his voice now gentle yet cautious. 'Miss, are you all right?'

I was still too stunned to respond.

'I won't hurt you. Do you want me to help you up?'

I shook my head and he turned around – so I could pull on my clothes. I sighed inside. Did he imagine that my body had never been touched nor even seen by a man? But he must know that I'd just been raped.

Tears rolled down my cheeks. My hands clumsily buttoned up my tattered top while my eyes studied the back of this stranger who had just witnessed my unsightly nudity and saved my life.

He asked softly, 'Have you finished?'

'Yes,' I said, my voice emptied of strength.

Now he turned around and I got a closer look at his face; his eyes seemed compassionate. Approaching slowly, he said, 'I want to help you, but you have to tell me how.'

He was tall. I looked up and blurted out, 'My friend is trapped in a bell!'

'A bell, where?'

'I believe it's somewhere not far from here, but I'm not sure. I ran a long way before the bandits caught me.'

He looked at me with great concern. 'I'm so sorry; I hope they didn't—'

'But they did.' I swallowed hard. 'I mean one of them . . .' Despite my recent catastrophe, I noticed that I was the one who had been raped but he was the one who seemed more upset.

A long, awkward silence. Finally he spoke. 'I think you better look for your friend now before it's too late. I'll help.'

I told him I also needed to look for my musical instrument, which I'd discarded during my flight.

He took a good look at me. 'Do you think you can walk now?'

Again I felt pain all over. Suddenly I realised that with my torn clothes, dishevelled hair, and bruises on my face, I must look like a hag!

I lowered my head. 'Yes.'

He inched closer and held his lantern up. 'You have some bruises on your face but no cuts and no bleeding, so don't worry. It's nothing serious. The marks will go away in a few days.' After that, he took off his jacket and handed it to me. 'Please put this on.'

I blushed, suddenly noticing one of my breasts was peeking through a big tear in my top.

He looked away. 'Please hurry, I worry about your friend.'

Now I had no idea where to find the bell. So we just looked around at random. He walked in front of me, parting leaves and pushing away branches to make way. The lantern cast eerie, flickering shadows like dancing phantoms.

'Teng Xiong!' I called, straining ears and eyes.

The young man asked, 'So your friend's a man?'

'No, a woman. She just has a man's name.' Suddenly I realised that 'Teng Xiong' might not be Teng's real name. She had to use a fake name – Xiong means heroic, a common man's name – to disguise herself. The same reason I'd changed from Xiang Xiang to Precious Orchid.

So who was this young man who dressed strangely, performed magic, had seen my nudity, and now walked with me so closely in a dark forest? I hadn't even yet learned his name, let alone his background. Even if I did, how would I know that it was not just another disguise?

Although disheartened by this reflection, I gathered up my strength and continued to shout at the top of my voice, 'Teng Xiong! Teng Xiong!'

But there was no response except echoes of my own voice, the blowing wind, and the crunching of leaves under our feet.

Finally, after almost two hours' search, we gave up.

The young man said, 'It's too dark to look for anything now and I'm sure you're exhausted. So let's try again tomorrow.'

I nodded.

He looked at me with concern. 'Do you think you can walk more?'

'Yes.'

'Then we'll walk slowly.' He paused, then spoke again, measuring his words, 'Or if you don't mind, I can carry you.'

'Thank you for your kindness, but I think I can manage.' Though I ached everywhere and wanted desperately to accept his offer, I had to refuse. I wanted him to think that I was a shy, decent woman who'd rather hang herself than have any physical contact with a strange man. In ancient times, it was said, that to display their virtue, some women would even chop off their hand after it had been accidentally brushed by a man.

Hesitantly, he spoke again. 'Are you staying somewhere on the mountain?'

'I don't . . . I . . . I just arrived here.'

He said gently, 'If you don't have a place to stay, you can come to my temple.'

'Temple?' I looked up and caught his gaze.

'Yes. I'm a monk, Taoist.'

Suddenly things fit together – the scarf, the strange outfit, the lantern, the calligraphic scroll, the magic stunt. Of course, a Taoist monk! I almost cried out aloud. Then, as my initial shock had waned, I felt a sudden disappointment, as well as colour rising to my cheeks. Such a handsome man, why would he want to be a monk?

He spoke again. 'The trip back to my temple will take some time. Are you sure you can manage?'

'I'll be fine,' I said stubbornly.

In silence, I followed him and his dangling lantern until finally my legs were so wobbly and my body so pained that I collapsed on the ground.

When I regained my senses, I found myself in the monk's arms. I squirmed. 'Please let me down. I can walk.'

'You can't. Please trust me and let me help you,' he said firmly. His feet continued to plod on the ground, making small explosive sounds whenever they stepped on a fallen branch.

Too tired to argue, I closed my eyes and let him hold me tightly against his chest. His heartbeat, palpable and steady, made me feel strangely secure.

I must have fallen asleep. For when I woke up, we were already in front of a small hut. He put me down, opened the door, and led me inside. There was no decoration except an altar table, a medicine cabinet, a cauldron, and two chairs.

Before I had a chance to say something, he was already speaking. 'Please follow me.'

'Here we are,' he said, walking into a side room, where he set down his lantern and satchel. He lit another lantern near a window.

'You mean this is a temple?' I blurted out, then bit my lip. I shouldn't have said something insulting to a monk, especially not after he'd just saved my life!

He didn't answer me, but took a pot and poured us cold tea.

I sat down and sipped, then looked around more carefully. Although the room was small, it was carefully arranged. Facing the entrance was a high table holding a statue of Lao-tzu – the author of the *Tao-te ching*. A pad for sleeping was placed next to one wall, which was bare except for a painting inscribed, *The Elixir Terrace*. It depicted a scholar standing on a promontory amid tall mountains, looking at a cauldron from which vapour rose.

A bookcase filled with string-bound books and a writing table were set against another wall. Then, to my utter surprise, I spotted, on top of the table, a *qin*. I turned to scrutinise the monk's face, enigmatic in the dim light of his lanterns. Now that his topknot had loosened, wisps of hair flew here and there like cursive calligraphy.

'You play the *qin*?' I could hear the disbelief and excitement in my voice.

'Yes.'

'But you're a monk!'

He looked at me for long moments. 'Some of us have a tradition of playing the *qin*. It's a form of meditation; we hope the instrument's transcendental tones will bring us to be one with the Way.'

It seemed hardly possible that I'd been rescued at all, let alone by a Taoist monk who was also a *qin* player! 'Master, I didn't have the chance to ask your name—'

'Qing Zhen.'

Pure and True. A beautiful name. And yet I felt sad. For this was only his Taoist appellation, really only a disguise, even if a religious one. I wondered if I'd ever know his real name, the one his parents had given him.

'And your name?'

'Precious Orchid,' I said, then pointed to the *qin*. 'Can I take a look?'

'Of course, but don't you want to eat and wash first? Besides,' he pointed to my cheek, 'I think you'd better clean your face now.'

My cheeks felt hot. I must have looked horrible. My face was covered with bruises and my hair entangled with twigs and grass. My prestigious look was completely gone – in front of a handsome monk!

I blurted out, 'Do you have a mirror?'

He seemed at a loss for what to say. Then, without a word, he left the room. Soon he returned with a basin of water and a towel, and began to clean my face.

'Ouch!' I cried when the towel touched my sore cheeks.

The monk ignored my cries while his hands continued to nurse my wounds. When he finished washing my face and hands, he went to pour the water outside the room.

Coming back, he asked, 'Do you feel better now?'

I nodded. 'Can I now take a look at the *qin*, please?'

He stared at me with concern. 'Miss Precious Orchid, are you . . . all right?'

My cheeks felt hot. He must have found it strange that I, after being ravished by a bandit, could act so normal, could even have the heart to appreciate a musical instrument. *Hai!* Of course, he did not know that for eight long years, I was 'raped' every night by different stinking males!

I said softly, 'I think I'll feel better if I can look at your *qin*.'

The monk let me examine the *qin*'s surface, then its inscription at the back. *Tianfeng Xiaoxiao* – Heavenly Zephyr Whistling Deep and Clear.

'How elegant.' I ran my finger on the finely textured lacquer. 'This must be an ancient one.'

'This *qin* has witnessed at least eight hundred years of life.'

I looked up at him. 'You mean this is a Sung *qin*?'

He nodded.

'Master Qing Zhen, what a coincidence, I'm also a *qin* player!'

His face glowed. 'You are?'

I eagerly nodded.

'It would be my honour to hear you play sometime,' he said. 'But now please rest while I fix something to eat. You better have something to nourish your stomach.' After that, he left the room.

Suddenly my stomach seemed to be gnawed by a hundred rats. I realised I hadn't had anything to eat since Teng Xiong and I had left the monastery. Just then, Teng Xiong's image flashed across my mind. I covered my face and cried, 'Teng Xiong, are you all right?'

I sobbed for long moments, then finally dried my tears. Hoping that the *qin* could calm my agitated spirit, I started to tune it. As I rested my finger on the lacquered surface and was about to meditate, I thought of my *qin*. Pearl's dying gift to me was lost, together with all my money and jewellery that I'd hidden inside!

I realised I was once again completely alone in the world, and penniless as well.

'Oh, no!' I screamed.

Tears again swelled in my eyes but this time I wouldn't let them fall. I gathered up myself and began to play 'Remembering an Old Friend.' With sadness, I realised that I had not only Pearl to remember, but Teng Xiong as well. She'd been right – life is sad. Staying alive just means struggling *not* to drown in the sea of suffering.

After I finished 'Remembering an Old Friend,' I went on to play 'Lament Behind the Long Gate.' This time I sang. While I was immersed in the beauty and melancholy of the lyrics, another voice, pure, powerful, and penetrating, joined mine. I was startled. This monk, who'd been so formal and polite with me, sang in a voice which seemed to possess the sympathy to understand the deepest sorrow, the tenderness to heal all wounds, and the magic to wash away life's pains. When we finished, tears, now against my will, spilled down my cheeks. I shut my eyes, then looked up to see Qing

Zhen at the door, holding a tray atop of which lay bowls of steaming buns, soup, and rice.

I wiped the tears with my sleeve. 'I'm sorry,' I muttered. In my heart, jars of condiments toppled, spilling a mixture of taste – sweet, sour, bitter, piquant.

Qing Zhen came to put the tray on the table, then took the *qin* and hung it on the wall. He refreshed our tea and we sat down. He handed me a bowl. 'This is a special herb soup that I cooked to heal your bruises.'

I drained the bitter brew and started to eat, aware of his intent glances. But I didn't care any more about etiquette and prestige, nor even whether I looked pretty. I focused my entire attention on the food in front of me. He ate only a small amount, and when we finally finished, he took me to a small open-air enclosure where he'd already prepared a wooden tub of hot water.

'Miss Precious Orchid, take your time and don't worry. I'll be just outside standing guard.'

I peeled off my torn clothes and gingerly stepped inside the tub. The water, hot and, to my surprise, scented, felt healing against my skin. Knowing that Qing Zhen was nearby, I felt both relaxed and secure. I splashed the hot water over my face, back, and shoulders. Then, remembering the repulsive Bulge-Eyes, I splashed the water harder so the monk wouldn't hear me sobbing. I rubbed my skin so hard that it turned pink and raw. Despite the pain, it was wonderful to start feeling clean again. Looking up at the sky, I saw the bright moon and burning stars staring back at me. Pained with pleasure, I sighed.

'Miss Precious Orchid, are you all right?'

'I'm fine,' I said, suddenly feeling very conscious of my nakedness with a handsome man less than ten feet away from me. I wondered what was now on Qing Zhen's mind. As a monk, would he fancy me? Would he lust after my naked body? If he did, would his jade stalk stir? I imagined that the hot water now sloshing against my body was the warm caress of his hand. I let out a long sigh, but this time the monk didn't respond. I looked up at the sky and caught the mischievous wink of a bright, elusive star.

When I finished, Qing Zhen reached over the enclosure and handed me his Taoist robe. I quickly pulled it on, then walked back inside the hut, while he took his turn to bathe. When he came back, I was sitting on the chair next to the *qin* table. Now his body towering by the door, he looked quite different – fresh and luminous. He wore no scarf, and I could see all of his hair, long and soft, curled on top of his head like a sleeping cat.

In silence, we held each other's glance for long moments.

Then he spoke, his voice soft. 'Miss Precious Orchid—'

'Please just call me by my name.'

'Precious Orchid, let me boil some fresh tea for you.'

As he moved swiftly around to prepare tea, I could feel waves of energy radiating in the room. It pleased my eyes to see his muscular, sinewy body and his deeply concentrated expression. When he finished, he brought the tray, put it down on the table, then sat opposite me and poured us both full cups.

We sipped our tea for a few awkward moments before he asked, 'Precious Orchid, are you feeling better now?'

I nodded, my eyes exploring the enigmatic face. Although tempted to know more about him, I decided to remain silent.

He cast me a concerned look. 'Do you want to rest?'

I shook my head, then silently sipped my tea.

Finally he spoke, 'Precious Orchid,' now he looked at me as if he were a connoisseur trying to identify a piece of art, 'please tell me about your life.'

Suddenly my life seemed so complicated that I didn't know where to start. I took a deep breath. 'But I'm sure it wouldn't interest you.'

'Why do you say that?'

'Because I . . .' I was struggling as to whether I should tell him about the Peach Blossom Pavilion. 'I don't think my travails in the red dust would interest a monk.'

He looked puzzled. 'As a monk, I've seen all of this world and other ones, too.'

'I'm not so sure.'

'Why do you say that?'

'Because you're just too young.'

He laughed, then remained silent, nursing his cup.

I searched his eyes for a while before I blurted out, 'I was a sister.'

'A sister?' He looked more puzzled. 'You mean . . . a nun?'

My heart melted inside. How naïve. This handsome man in front of me had no idea what a sister meant. I changed the subject and asked instead, 'Qing Zhen, how did you end up here as a Taoist monk?'

'It was a promise to my father.'

'He didn't want you to marry and have sons?'

His eyes glowed. 'You know that while the Buddhist monks cultivate non-attachment, we Taoists, on the contrary, practice alchemy to achieve longevity?'

'I've heard about that.'

'In our family, so many people died young. My mother took the crane's flight when I was but a year old, followed by my only uncle from my father's side, then by another uncle from my mother's side. My father, frightened that he might be next, began to study the Taoist alchemy of longevity. When I'd barely turned eleven, he sent me to be a monk in the Celestial Cloud Temple. But shortly after this, he, too, died a mysterious death.'

'Oh heaven, I'm so sorry.'

He went on, his expression sad, 'I don't remember my mother. Being a monk is the only life that I know.'

'Then do you regret being a monk?'

He thought for a while. 'No. I think this is a better life for me. I like living on the mountain and I don't like to deal with all the complexities of the dusty world.' He paused to sip his tea, then, 'Last month, my master sent me to this small hut to live as a hermit to concoct a special kind of elixir for longevity. The period for the experimentation is one year, so I still have eleven months here before I go back to Celestial Cloud.'

Now I understood why this 'temple' was so small and had no other monks around. 'If you don't mind, can you tell me what you live on as a hermit?'

'I'm still connected with the main temple, so when they organise big-scale rituals, I'll go back and help.'

'Don't you feel lonely living here all by yourself?'

'I'm used to a solitary life.'

I sighed inside. Didn't he need a woman? Didn't he feel anything being with me? Instinctively my hand reached to smooth my hair and my clothes.

Qing Zhen's voice rose again. 'Precious Orchid,' he searched my face, 'I'm just a simple monk. Please tell me about your life.'

I wanted this man to think that I was a proper woman from a decent, scholarly family (this was in fact the truth!), not a decadent one losing herself in the floating world of the wind and dust, one whose arms were used as a pillow by a thousand guests, whose two slices of crimson lips were tasted by ten thousand men.

I told him everything about my life – except I changed a few details. Instead of working as a sister at Peach Blossom, I'd been a maid in a rich man's house. Then I'd run away, for two reasons: to avoid ill treatment from my master and to find my mother and the warlord. Needless to say, I also lied to him about my relationship with Teng Xiong. Now Teng was another maid who'd run away with me from the same rich man's mansion. Bringing up Teng Xiong made me feel guilty again, for her place in my heart was now completely taken by a monk.

When I finished, the monk looked long lost in thoughts. Moments passed before he spoke. 'I can't believe that your mother just left you behind and never writes. There must be something more to it. I feel some dark force has interfered.' He paused to sip more tea. 'And now, you're here to look for her. Although it'll be very hard, please don't worry too much, I'll try my best to help you. I'll also make a charm for finding her. I'm sure you two will be reunited soon.' Another silence, then, 'I'll make another one that will reach down to the *yin* world to aid your father.'

I nodded, consumed with gratitude for Qing Zhen and sadness over Baba. Then I poured out how my resolution to revenge my father had sustained me during my life as a maid amid all the tragedies, including Pearl's (another maid, my sworn blood sister) death.

Qing Zhen looked at me meaningfully. 'Precious Orchid, I understand your desire for revenge. But please don't let your young life be engulfed by all this bitter *qi*, which we Taoists consider very harmful to both your mind and body.'

'But I have to right the wrong, to carry out righteousness. Haven't you heard the proverb "One may not live beneath the same heaven as the slayer of one's parents"?'

He thought for a while. 'I know. But let me ask you a question. What if it will take you five, ten, even twenty years for you to find this warlord? Worse, what if you never find him? Will you pass your entire life tasting only bitterness? How much better to spend your time cultivating the Way.'

His questions struck me speechless. I'd never thought that I might spend twenty years in finding, or even failing to find, my father's murderer.

I blurted out, 'The *qin*, Qing Zhen, I play the *qin* to nurture my spirit.'

Now he looked at me curiously. 'Precious Orchid, how did you learn to play the *qin*?'

Damn. I bit my tongue. Once you've lied, you have to lie more to cover up your earlier ones. 'My baba taught me before I'd been sent to the rich man's house.'

Some silence, then he said, 'Precious Orchid, if your mind is filled with revenge when you play the *qin,* it shows you're still far from nurturing your spirit. I'm afraid it's only the skill that you've mastered, not the essence.'

The sharp observation of this hermit monk was unexpected.

'Precious Orchid, suppose you do have the chance to kill the warlord?'

'Then my goal in life will be fulfilled.'

'But Lao-tzu said that followers of the Tao do not seek fulfilment.'

I said stubbornly, 'My soul won't be appeased, not until I find this warlord and put a bullet in his head!'

'Whatever your plan, can you remain still until the time to act?'

I didn't respond; he went on, 'If your mind will not be appeased until you avenge your father, then I have a better solution for you.'

I studied his smooth face and his thick brows, which resembled two distant hills. 'What is it?'

'I can prepare you a *fu* and some magic water to terrify the warlord and strip him of his power.'

I failed to suppress a smile. Some moments passed. All of a sudden my energy was used up. Today's tragedies, and remembering my earlier ones, now left me drained and my eyes would not stay open.

Qing Zhen looked at me with concern. 'Precious Orchid, of course, you're exhausted, so you'd better rest now. And we'll look for your friend tomorrow.'

He let me sleep on his bed while he went to sleep on the floor in the altar room.

The next morning, I woke from a gentle pat on my shoulder. Qing Zhen's tall body was hovering over me like a mountain.

'Wake up, Precious Orchid. I've prepared breakfast. After we eat, we should go to look for your friend. It's been light for a while but I didn't have the heart to wake you.'

Before we left the hut, Qing Zhen grabbed a straw shawl and an umbrella. 'Put this on, it may rain anytime.'

Again, we were out in the woods. Black clouds gathered ominously at the distant horizon. He looked up, frowning. 'A rainstorm is coming. Let's go quickly to look for your friend.'

I described as best I could where I'd found the bell. After a long walk, we finally spotted it on the edge of an empty field.

'Teng Xiong?' I knelt down beside the bell and called out her name. My heart beat accelerated, this time less for love than for life's uncertainty. But I had no time to think. Qing Zhen had already lifted the bell and toppled it over.

I screamed. It was empty.

While I burst out crying, Qing Zhen sighed with relief. 'Your friend has escaped.'

'You're sure?'

He nodded. 'She must be nearby. I'm sure we can find her.'

'But she might have been kidnapped!' I let out a sharp cry. 'Oh my heaven, then what should we do?'

'Just keep looking. There should be a temple nearby. She might be there.'

Suddenly I felt fat raindrops pelting on my straw shawl. Qing Zhen turned to me. 'The rainstorm is starting, and we'd better return now.'

'Are you sure we can't keep looking?'

'Precious Orchid,' he cast me a chiding glance, 'I'm a mountain monk. I know how to live here. Sometimes there are mud slides; we might be buried under one.' He held the umbrella over me. 'Besides, at least we know that your friend has escaped. She should be safe somewhere.'

We quickened our pace. In a moment, the sky darkened; the wind roared like a tiger and rain poured like bats. Mud spattered relentlessly on our trousers and legs. Qing Zhen took my hand and pulled me along.

When we finally reached the hut and went inside, the monk immediately went to prepare hot soup and boil water for baths. Once I had eaten and bathed, my exhaustion returned and I went to collapse in his bed.

When I woke up, it was already quite dark outside. The wind and rain were still howling, but not as hard. I stared at the rustling trees and felt anxious but hopeful.

'Precious Orchid,' I heard Qing Zhen's voice calling gently from outside my room, 'are you awake?'

'Yes,' I said. I sat for a while in the bed, while my mind swirled with images of the hermit monk and his magical rescue of me from the bandits. Then the feeling of his muscular arms holding me against his warm chest as he carried me to the hut. I picked up his robe and rubbed my cheeks against its rough texture, inhaling the faint smell of the mountain. I hastily put it on, got off the bed, and walked into the altar room.

Qing Zhen was squatting down, stirring some kind of pleasant-smelling soup on his small stove. His back was solid like a boulder and his hair wound peacefully around on his scalp like a pagoda. I fought an urge to embrace him from behind and bury my face in his neck.

He turned around and smiled. 'I'm preparing this soup with different kinds of herbs and tree fungus to revive your *qi*.'

'Thank you, Qing Zhen.' My eyes made their nest on his. 'But I don't want it now . . .'

Qing Zhen stood up and we held each other's glance for what seemed like several incarnations. Finally he came over to me, then, as if I were his priceless Sung dynasty *qin*, picked me up, and carried me back to the bed I had just left.

With my heart beating like a lost deer bumping through a forest, I watched Qing Zhen's earnest face as he started to take off my robe, very gently, as if he were handling a newborn baby. Now I lay naked under the stare of a man, this time not a *chou nanren*, a stinking male, but one who actually made my heart beat fast and my body melt.

He blew out the lantern. In the moonlight streaming through the window, he began to disrobe, revealing a smooth, muscular body. With a vigorous swing of his hand, he pulled the ribbon off his bun and let his hair cascade to freedom.

It was a strangely touching sight – a man with long, thick, pitch-black, free-flowing hair. It seemed to say that he, unlike the Confucian scholars, was not afraid to show off his virility. Unlike Buddhist monks and nuns who shave their heads to overcome attachment, Taoists do not cut their hair to show care for their bodies.

As Qing Zhen crawled into bed next to me, I no longer thought about attachment nor non-attachment but only about his care for my body. His intent face was half hidden by his three-thousand-threads-of-trouble; his jade stalk ascended toward the Milky Way.

'Precious Orchid . . .' Qing Zhen's voice rose next to my ear. His hands and lips began to explore the nooks and crannies of my body. How could a monk so excel in the erotic art of pleasing?

He pulled me to him, burying his face in my chest. Then he cradled my breasts in his hands and began to stroke them, while from time to time brushing my nipples gently with his lips. Eyes closed, his long lashes cast flickering shadows on his face. When he spoke, his voice trembled. 'Precious Orchid, your breasts have heartbeats of their own.'

I played with his long hair and sighed with deep pleasure.

His tongue licked the inside of my ear and his teeth gently bit its outside. After that, he brushed his face over my neck, murmuring, 'I can smell fresh flowers and honey in you.' Then he slipped his hand underneath my bottom and lifted it a little. His other hand, like a waterfall, cascaded all over my body.

'Qing Zhen . . .' I wriggled, starting to lose my soul . . .

I stirred against him until finally his *yang* stalk entered my *yin* gate. The fervent thrustings emptied my mind and turned my pains into joy. We were like two animals, suddenly released after long imprisonment. Now we were beyond all attachments except to each other.

After our trip to the Wu Mountain, Qing Zhen held me gently in his arms. We both remained silent, absorbed in our own thoughts and feelings. I was savouring the after-flavour of having balanced the *yin* and *yang*. Ironically, though an expert in the art of the bedchamber, the first time I relished the gusto of a man's rain showering on my clouds was with a monk in a temple chamber.

I realised why Pearl could be so obsessed with the oil portraitist Jiang Mou – he must be adept at lovemaking.

I reached to touch Qing Zhen; he caught my hand and lifted it to his lips. Just then the wind outside seemed to call gently, 'Xiang Xiang, Xiang Xiang.'

'Precious Orchid,' he bent to kiss me, 'I love you.'

I searched his face. 'Qing Zhen, I love you, too.'

Qing Zhen silently held me tighter in his arms, as if silence was a better response and the best comfort. I nestled closer into the warmth of his chest.

'Now I have you here, I won't feel lonely any more,' he said. Moments after, he slid off the bed and lit the lantern.

'Where're you going?' I asked.

'You'll see.' He walked to the table. As I watched his naked body outlined by the moonlight, my heart was overcome by a pleasurable pain. Soon he returned with a brush and an ink stand.

'What're you going to do?'

This time he didn't answer me. He was busy grinding ink. When he finished, to my surprise, he pulled off the bedcover, gently pulled out my leg and started to write – on my thigh. The ink felt cool on my skin and its fragrance soothed my nerves.

When he finished, his face glowed and his eyes sparkled, as if he'd just emerged from a hot spring. I looked down and saw my thigh adorned with a poem in bold and vigorous strokes – like an old tree twisting its root.

> Ten fingers dance on the seven silk strings; sweet murmur-
> ings spill into the red dust.
> My soul was lost the moment your heart-shaped lips broke
> open and your jade-smooth hands began their mischie-
> vous capering.

'Oh, Qing Zhen,' I touched his face while feeling touched, 'the poem is beautiful. But how can I have the heart to bathe?'

'You can't keep it on your body, so let it stay in your mind,' he said, taking my hand. Then he looked out of the window. 'Tonight the *yuelau* – the matchmaker under the moon – ties the red thread between us. Our love will last as long as the moon.'

We lay still for a while, dozing. When I awoke, through the window the full moon shone on me. Its detached silver glow gradually wrought a change in my mood. Qing Zhen's words were our well-intended wish, but the moon, like a bright mirror, simply witnesses the endless desires of mortals and reflects them back to the world. As it watches, things arise and cease, come and go, bloom and wither. Ten years, even a year, from now, where would our love be? Would I be seeing Qing Zhen's handsome face? Would I still be beautiful in his eyes? Were we only fleeting reflections in each other's mirrors, brief instants of memory, or merely flickering shadows on the red dust?

Depressed by these uninvited reflections, I tried not to think of love, but of the pleasures of the moment. I tossed my hair, circled my tongue over my parted lips, and threw Qing Zhen a long, pene-trating glance. When his smooth body pressed against mine, I for-got the endlessness of desires, the blooming and withering. Change seemed to cease, as I felt his jade stalk harden, find its way inside me, and thrust away all my miseries . . .

25

This Woman Is Not My Husband

The next morning when I woke up, sunlight was splashing on my feet. I stretched and wriggled my toes, enjoying the warmth of the sun and the after-flavour of love. Then I saw Qing Zhen's face next to the *qin* table, watching me with a grave expression.

'Something wrong?' I sat straight up, pulling up the blanket to cover my nudity. Then I wondered: As a prostitute, why would I feel modest in front of a man? But I did, because he was not any man, but the first man I had fallen in love with.

'No.' He smiled wryly. 'I've been watching you sleep.'

I smiled back and rubbed my eyes.

'Precious Orchid, we better hurry.'

'Why?'

'Because we've already lost a lot of time – we need to look for your friend.'

I bit my lips till I felt the tangy taste of blood. I'd been so captivated by this monk that I had forgotten about Teng Xiong! How could I be so selfish and heartless?

Half an hour later, we were again searching in the woods. Despite the tugging of my conscience and my urgent calling 'Teng Xiong! Teng Xiong!' it was my poet-monk lover, not my lesbian lover, who occupied my thoughts. Although my reason told me that I should concentrate on looking for Teng Xiong, everywhere my eyes saw the image of Qing Zhen. All the passing trees were his muscular arms stretching out to embrace me, every sigh of the wind was his powerful voice calling my name, and every rustling under my feet was his moaning during the balancing of our *yin* and *yang*.

We walked for another half an hour when suddenly Qing Zhen exclaimed, 'Look, there's a Buddhist temple behind those cypress trees.' He grabbed my hand and pulled me along. 'Let's go!'

A novice monk answered the door. I explained to him about Teng Xiong and the bell.

His face lit up. 'Come in!' he said, then turned around and yelled at the top of his boyish voice, 'Miss Precious Orchid is here for Mr. Teng Xiong!'

Soon a plump, fiftyish monk hurried toward us, followed behind by an older, stooped one. Then, behind the two monks, to my great relief, the tired yet smiling Teng Xiong.

'Precious Orchid,' Qing Zhen lowered his voice, 'I thought you told me your companion was a woman.'

Before I had a chance to answer, several monks had gathered around us, excitedly explaining how, during their dawn walking meditation, they'd heard sounds from within their temple's old bell (left there after a new one had been donated by a rich patron) and rescued the semi-conscious, delirious, and parched Teng Xiong. The loud explanations exploded in the air, breaking the tranquility of the isolated temple.

Now the still weary Teng Xiong was demanding to know what had happened to me and so I explained to her and the eager monks how I'd been captured by the bandits, then finally rescued by Qing Zhen with his magical feat. Everyone's story told, silence fell during which I noticed Teng Xiong looking at Qing Zhen with suspicion and beginning hostility.

As we followed the small group of monks to the reception hall, I was well aware of Qing Zhen's silent upset and Teng Xiong's swelling jealousy. But I had no idea of what to do. Oblivious to the tension now being generated, the monks ahead were still relishing the excitement of the rescues by telling the tales over and over.

With the interruption of their monotonous routine by these exciting events, the monks' cultivation of non-attachment had instantly been thrown out of their mind's window.

After we were served tea and snacks, the plump abbot, Pure Wisdom, invited me to stay. 'Mrs. Teng, we've already prepared a room specially for you and your husband.'

'But.' I stopped short. I'd been about to say: This man is a woman and I'm not her wife! But Teng Xiong cast me a glance so sharp that my words instantly retreated back into my mouth.

She turned to smile at the monk. 'Thank you, Master Pure Wisdom. I'm sure my wife is now extremely tired after all her worries and tribulations. She needs to rest soon.'

I didn't even have the courage to direct my eyes to Qing Zhen to see his reaction. Moreover, I was glad that my sentence had been killed on the spot; otherwise, who would have believed such mumbo jumbo as 'this man is a woman and I'm not her wife'? The monks would only think that I'd become delirious after being kidnapped by the bandits.

Qing Zhen was silent. When I mustered up the courage to peek, he didn't even look angry as I'd expected – just dazed. He must have thought that I'd shamelessly lied and cruelly betrayed him. Inside, my heart slowly cracked into pieces. I could almost see the shards crash onto the floor, skittering along until they halted right under the statue of Buddha.

Now Qing Zhen was politely taking leave of the monks. Fearing he would be gone without a word to me, I walked to him and lowered my voice. 'If you must leave, at least let me accompany you as far as the courtyard.'

Once in the open space, I demanded before he had a chance to speak, 'Qing Zhen, why didn't you ask me to go back with you?'

He looked both shocked and angry. 'Precious Orchid, you're married and your husband is right here. And you want me to bring you back to the temple?'

I screamed. 'But I'm not married and Teng Xiong is not my husband. She's a woman!'

'A woman?'

'Yes! Like me! With breasts and no jade stalk!'

He didn't respond, but kept staring at me with his penetrating eyes. Finally he said, 'Precious Orchid, are you making fun of me?'

'I'm not; Teng Xiong is a woman and I am not her wife!'

'Then why does she dress like a man?'

I told him she was escaping a cruel master and this was her disguise.

Qing Zhen looked lost in thoughts. 'Then what is your relationship with her?'

Since I loved Qing Zhen, I didn't want to lie to him. But I was in a dilemma. If I told him the truth – that Teng Xiong and I were lovers yet I didn't even love her – Qing Zhen might think I was just using Teng and despise me for that.

I looked at Qing Zhen, speechless. Finally I pleaded. 'Qing Zhen, I don't want to stay here; please take me back with you.'

He still looked hurt. 'But I can't. I'm a monk and this is a temple.'

Desperate, I blurted out, 'Is that so? Then why did you seduce me?'

'I fell in love. I wasn't supposed to, but I did.'

'You love me, but you can't take me back, then what are we going to do?'

Just then Teng Xiong materialised; she marched up to stand protectively by my side, then glared at Qing Zhen. 'I think my wife has already spent too much time imposing on a celibate monk—'

Before he could respond, I said, 'Qing Zhen, believe me; I'm not his wife. He's a woman.' The statement sounded ridiculous even to my own ears.

Qing Zhen's expression turned sad and angry. 'So, Precious Orchid, do you think that I'm also a woman?'

Now Teng Xiong turned to me, eyes releasing their long-held daggers. 'So after all I've done for you, you slept with him?' She pointed an accusing finger at Qing Zhen, her tone sarcastic, 'A monk?!'

Right then a door creaked open, revealing an ancient shaved head. 'If you visit us, please keep quiet and respect the sacred tranquility of our temple.' The monk scrutinised the three of us for a few moments before pulling the door shut.

Qing Zhen cast me a bitter glance, then strode out of the temple gate.

'Qing Zhen!' I called after him, but he quickened his pace.

Teng Xiong put her hand around my shoulder and half-pulled me back to the temple.

When Teng Xiong led me back to her room, it was obvious to me that I'd better try to straighten things out with her.

Right after we sat down, I said, 'Teng Xiong, I'm very sorry, but I just couldn't help it.'

She looked at me hard and long. 'Don't fool yourself, Precious Orchid. It's just a moment's infatuation—'

'No, it's not.' I spoke through teary eyes. 'He's the first man I've ever loved—'

She threw back her head and laughed. 'Do you know what you're talking about? Didn't you tell me you could never stand any of those *chou nanren*?'

'But Qing Zhen is different, he's not like the other men.'

'Different? Precious Orchid, let me tell you. Men are all the same, they stink!' She went on bitterly, 'Maybe a jade stalk is the only thing that he has and I don't. But that doesn't mean he's better than me—'

'He *is* very good.'

'But Precious Orchid,' her tone softened; now she was pleading, 'maybe he's very good at sex, but he's still a man after all. And a man will *never* understand the real need of a woman, especially a delicate and complex woman like you. Precious Orchid, you need a woman like me to take care of you and love you, not a man, let alone a monk. How would a monk know anything about pleasing, loving, and taking care of a woman?'

'No, you're wrong. Qing Zhen is very good at all these.'

She looked both shocked and hurt.

'He saved my life and nursed my wounds after I was raped by the bandit.'

Teng Xiong pulled me into her arms and showered kisses on me. 'Precious Orchid, this is all my fault. I'm so sorry for . . . what you've gone through. I should have pushed you under the bell first, please forgive me.'

'Teng Xiong,' I delicately withdrew myself, 'it's nobody's fault. It's just bad luck. And I'm sorry. I don't mean to . . . hurt your feelings.'

She remained silent, now trying to take my hand, which I instantly withdrew. 'Teng Xiong, I love him.'

'But you love *me*, too.'

How could she be so definite? 'But it's a different kind of love,' I said, 'It's more like the way I loved . . . my sister Pearl.'

'That's fine. In fact that's better, because there's something deeper to our love since we're both women.'

I couldn't think of anything to say in response to this.

'Precious Orchid, believe me, your infatuation for him will soon pass like drifting clouds. Besides, think about it, with no money, how are you going to spend your life with him?'

This jolted me back to my unpleasant reality. I realised that since I'd lost my *qin* and all the money and jewellery, I was now but a penniless and homeless woman! And of course, as a monk, Qing Zhen wouldn't have any money either, and he didn't even offer to take me back to his temple! I started to cry, tasting the bitterness of my tears as well as that of my first love for a man.

Teng Xiong reached to wipe my face with her silk handkerchief. 'Don't cry, Precious Orchid. It's not the end of the world, just the end of a fleeting affair. Take it as a bad dream.' She looked deeply into my eyes. 'You have me and I'll take very good care of you; that's the most important thing. Besides, unlike the monk, I'm rich.' She gave her trousers' pocket an emphatic pat. 'I can buy you anything you want and treat you to any restaurant you like. Will you work in the field under the scorching sun, eat sweet potatoes and watery soup every meal, and wear a many-patched robe, all for the mere sake of a man? A refined woman like you, you are entitled to a pampered, luxurious life, not an impoverished one with a penniless monk. If a jade stalk is what you like in him,' she tilted her head and laughed, her short, silky hair glistening, 'then don't worry, I can also get one. Whatever size and texture feels the best to you.'

I didn't respond.

'Precious Orchid?'

'Yes?'
'Please stay with me.'

That evening I felt relieved that Teng Xiong was too drained to demand sex. While her body lay motionlessly beside me, I was wide awake. My body flipped and flopped on the hardwood, bug-infested bed, agonising over my unexpected desire for a man. Qing Zhen was handsome, mysterious, a monk. Somehow, he also knew how to make me feel wonderful as a woman. And I didn't even get paid. For the first time, I'd done it for love.

Just like I played the *qin* not for money, but self-cultivation. Moreover, Qing Zhen played the *qin*. Like me, he also had a purity to his heart. I loved Qing Zhen. And I'd go back to stay with him till both our brows turned white . . .

I lay listlessly till dawn came. Then, as soon as I heard the monks' chanting drifting across the courtyard, I slipped off the bed, put on my shoes and jacket, cast a farewell glance at Teng Xiong, and sneaked out of the room. After a few wrong turns, I finally saw Qing Zhen's hut in the distance, looking tranquil and welcoming. I quickened my steps. When I reached the door, I gave it a gentle push and it fell open with a sigh.

I stepped in and went straight to Qing Zhen's room. He was sound asleep, the blanket moving slightly with his breathing. With a melting heart, I slipped into bed next to him.

26

The Monk and the Prostitute

And so I lived with Qing Zhen. Needless to say, life with a Taoist monk on the mountain was totally different from Peach Blossom. There was still sex most nights, but now it was with love, and afterward I would fall into a deep, satisfied sleep in muscular, loving arms. In the morning, refreshed by the country air, I would awaken at dawn and watch Qing Zhen carry out his rituals. The small drum, bell, and clapper would smack and click in his hands, accompanied by his sonorous chanting, as he made offerings to the gods. Then it was time for a simple breakfast of congee and buns during which we'd stare into each other's eyes or look through the window at distant mountains. After that, he'd meditate, then practise the *qin* and calligraphy of *fu* – talisman.

Sometimes as it got dark, I would think: I must get ready for customers. Then I remembered that there was no all-wrinkled-old-and-dying to serve and no Mama and De to spy on me. I was free!

Yet I hadn't forgotten my resolve to find my mother. But Qing Zhen said, 'Precious Orchid, I won't let you go around the mountain asking for your mother; it's too dangerous. I'll look when I'm out by myself and we'll also look together. Be patient.'

I tried to be patient and calm, but a hidden part of my mind wouldn't let me. One night I dreamed that, after all these years of agony, I had finally found my mother. She was not a nun, but like me, a prostitute, and her clients were all monks. Her body, emaciated and scantily clad, shivered in a freezing snowstorm. Her cheeks were paper-white and her eyes, though sunken, gave out a lustre not of pleasure, but hunger. In front of her was a vegetarian dish, but whenever she'd reach for it, the plate would recede. One time she succeeded in snatching a piece of tofu, but right after she'd stuffed it into her mouth, it immediately caught fire and turned into ashes. I desperately called out, 'Ma! Ma!' but she didn't seem to hear anything. When I tried to push the food closer to her, the monks would snatch it away and gobble it down.

When I told Qing Zhen about this nightmare, he smiled meaningfully. 'I've studied the *Duke of Zhou's Book of Dreams*. Usually bad dreams are good and good dreams foretell something bad. So I think this one is favourable. It probably means that as a nun your mother has burned off her desire for food. So because of this dream you should not worry.'

So I played the *qin* and waited. Whenever Qing Zhen came back from gathering herbs, he'd tell me he had been asking about my mother but had heard nothing. So often my hopes would rise as I watched him walk back along the path to the hut, only to be disappointed by the lack of news.

Though my worries about my mother were never really gone from my mind, life on the mountain was otherwise untroubled. When the weather was especially fine and Qing Zhen had finished his daily tasks, sometimes we would go to the river, take off our clothes, and plunge into the jade green water. Once in a while he'd catch a fish, take it home, and roast it for dinner. Sometimes we'd go to the open field to fly kites. Watching a dragon, a phoenix, or a crane gliding high above my head would send pangs of joy to my heart. I'd imagine myself transformed into a giant butterfly borne by the wind, watching the glittering facets of the world below. When we were tired, we'd lie down and fall asleep in each other's arms on the grass, waking up with the sun's warmth on our faces and a hundred pleasurable sensations tingling our bodies.

* * *

But good times rarely last long. One day when I sat musing by the window, I saw ribbons of white drifting outside and knew that winter had come. In Peach Blossom, my maid Little Rain would have set out my winter garments for me to choose: fur coats, silk-cotton gowns, lamb's wool shawls. She'd also bring me snake soup sprinkled with chrysanthemum petals and the best wild ginseng root to enhance my *yang* energy. In the turquoise pavilion, winter brought warmth and luxury, but here on the mountain, all I had to ward off the cold was a padded jacket covered with stains and patches.

After a few weeks, it started to snow heavily and the mountain had turned completely white – like a wise old man. If it could talk, what advice would it give me? Then I thought of the poem:

Originally the blue sea was worry free,
It was the wind that gave him a wrinkled face.
At first the green mountain was ageless
It was the snow that turned his hair all white.

Sometimes when the knife-cutting cold had let up, Qing Zhen would take me out to stroll around the neighbourhood of the hut, or he'd go out by himself to look for tree funguses. But most of the time he stayed home. We'd play the *qin*, or I'd sing to his accompaniment. And he'd also carry out his religious activities – meditation, *fu*, alchemy. Many of these I could not share. Among all of Qing Zhen's practices, he took his inner alchemy of visual meditation and outer alchemy of concocting elixirs most seriously. The reason the master of Celestial Cloud Temple chose him over the other young adepts to work on the elixirs was because he deemed Qing Zhen the most intelligent and pure-minded. This was Qing Zhen's chance to prove himself. If he failed, he would end up as another insignificant monk, living out his remaining years ignored by the others, only to die in an obscure, cobwebbed corner of the temple. That was why he worried over the malodorous concoction in the altar room for so many hours each day. Although I didn't like the pungent smell emitting from the cauldron, my feet would frequently carry me toward it to keep myself from freezing.

One time, as Qing Zhen was stirring the ingredients in the pot, I asked what they were. He replied, 'Minerals. Cinnabar, gold, malachite, sulfur, mica, saltpetre—'

'Gold and malachite?' These seemed better employed in making jewellery than elixirs!

'I know you find this strange. But they work. Sometimes we'll also feed a young bird with red meat and cinnabar until its feathers turn red. Then we'll cook the feathers and the meat. The concoction I'm experimenting with not only prolongs life but also rejuvenates.' He smiled proudly. 'I have the *qi* of a twenty-year-old, although I'm thirty.' His grin kept stretching taut on his broad face. 'That's also why I'm never bothered by the cold.'

I saw it was hopeless to compete with this reeking cauldron. If I were his mistress, then this boiling pot would be his wife, whom he would never leave for me.

On days when Qing Zhen was reading his strange scrolls or reciting spells, I'd occupy myself by playing the *qin* – to enhance my skill and also to keep the blood circulating in my chilled fingers. Then I'd lament the loss of my own *qin* and all the money and jewellery inside. Though Qing Zhen and I had thoroughly searched around where I'd dropped it, we never found any trace. Sometimes I'd imagine its destiny – perhaps picked up by some mountain dweller to use for his cooking fire, or discovered by bandits who, after they'd taken all the valuables, would dump the *qin* to rot in the forest. But sometimes my reverie would be more optimistic – my *qin* would be found by another *qin* player who'd treasure it as he did his firstborn son.

At first I liked winter, because I could have Qing Zhen with me all the time. But as each cold day flowed into the next as inexorably as the cars snaked up to Peach Blossom every evening, I felt miserable. I didn't have warm clothes and thus could not go out. Qing Zhen would occasionally cook me special herb soups to keep the 'fire' in my body, but mostly, the meals he prepared consisted of salted and pickled vegetables with some rice. I felt my body grow-ing thinner and worried that I was becoming malnourished. But Qing Zhen kept reminding me, 'The food has to last us all winter.' When I complained about the cold, he'd admonish me, 'We have to be very careful not to use up too much charcoal because I need to keep the cauldron boiling for my alchemy.'

I'd begun to be annoyed by Qing Zhen's obsessive immersion in his alchemy. Sometimes he'd fast for several days, retire into his pu-rity chamber – a space he'd made sacred with his rituals – and med-itate. He'd take substances from the rows of drawers in his medicine cabinet – dried leaves, seeds, and brightly coloured mineral pow-ders – then pound them vigorously in the mortar. The long spells he would say over these powders could go on for hours. During these times, I was completely ignored. The tireless rituals seemed as futile to me as a loving mother's surveillance over her dead baby.

However, when night came, he would quit his other practices and concentrate on the one in which I had a part – clouds and rain. He was a good lover – gentle but also passionate and daring. He enjoyed trying out all kinds of *beneficial* positions recorded in the sex manual: the jumping white tiger; dark cicada cleaving to a tree; bamboo next to the altar; pulling silk . . .

But sex was not always enjoyable, because some days it would be so cold that we had to do it fully clothed. Worse, although Qing Zhen and I slept together every night, ours was not a marriage bed, and could never be. However much he enjoyed sex, Qing Zhen, like other Taoists, believed in the strange practice of absorbing the *yin* essence from women's jade terrace while not losing his *jing*. Qing Zhen never ejaculated inside me, but would direct his semen back to his brain. At first I liked this, for I didn't have to clean up the sticky mess afterward. But soon I began to feel differently. While Taoists do ejaculate when they consider it's time for the woman to conceive, Qing Zhen was resolved never to plant his seed in my womb. This made me unbearably sad. No matter how many times we made love or how passionately, there'd never be any little monks or little flower girls running around to keep me company, or grandchildren to cling to my knees in my old age. Though Qing Zhen talked endlessly about how sexual union represented the cosmic interaction between *yin* and *yang*, he never mentioned the results of these endeavours – babies. But even if Qing Zhen were willing to impregnate me, I was not so sure it'd work. For all the soup I'd eaten in Peach Blossom was meant to kill any burgeoning life in me. Sometimes I'd find my childlessness so unbearable that I'd let tears fall onto my flat stomach, mourning my never-to-be-born ghost baby.

As time went by, my reflections about my life grew more sombre. Not only could I not bear Qing Zhen's children, I couldn't even go out with him in public. Not that there were any parties or other social occasions on the mountain, but he always feared that if he were seen with me, he might get into trouble. So I'd gone from prostitute to kept woman, only this time my 'favoured guest' was not a rich merchant, an influential politician, nor the head of a powerful black society, but a penniless Taoist monk. I remembered Pearl had told me about prostitutes' ways out; now I'd found one she hadn't thought of: cohabit with a monk!

As the winter went on, I was possessed more and more by unwelcome thoughts. I realised I'd escaped the gold-powdered hell of the prostitution house only to plunge into the white-powdered hell of the winter mountain. But this time I couldn't even run away. For I had no money and no place to go. Qing Zhen must have sensed my frustration, for one time he held me in his arms and cooed, 'Be patient, Precious Orchid. When spring comes, everything will be fine.'

After more months of agony, the weather finally let up. Two weeks later, when there was a hint of warmth and the air smelled of new vegetation, I suggested we take the *qin* to the riverbank and play outside. At last released from such a harsh winter, I was in a very happy mood. I sat cross-legged under the rejuvenating tree, lay the eight-hundred-year-old *qin* on my lap, and played all my favourite pieces.

Qing Zhen watched my hovering fingers with admiration. 'Precious Orchid,' he said when I finished, 'your playing is so tranquil and nuanced.'

'But I like your style of vigour and passion.' I shot him a flirtatious look. 'Now your turn.'

Qing Zhen played the *Gaoshan* – High Mountain, and *Liushui* – Flowing Water. While my fingers floated on the strings like clouds drifting along the wind, his were like dragons roaring in the ocean.

After his fingers left the instrument, he said, 'The high mountain is *yang* energy and flowing water *yin* energy, so the two pieces played one after another would generate the right balance of male and female elements.'

Then, as we sat beside the rushing water of the brook, he told me the familiar story about the famous *qin* player Boya and his woodcutter friend Ziqi.

No matter what tune Boya played, Ziqi, though illiterate, would immediately grasp its meaning.

One time when Boya played the High Mountain, Ziqi exclaimed, 'Ah, how imposing, the high mountain!' Then when Boya began to play the Flowing Water, Ziqi sighed, 'The flowing water, how impressive!'

Boya was astonished, for not only was Ziqi a country bumpkin, he had never heard the pieces before, so how could he tell that one depicted the high mountain and the other the flowing water?

'How can I ever fool you with my tunes!' Boya exclaimed, praising his woodcutter friend as a *zhiyin* – one who understands sound.

Therefore, when Ziqi died, Boya, realising that no one else would understand his music as well as his friend, smashed his *qin* at Ziqi's grave and sighed, 'Why play the *qin* when there's no more *zhiyin* to understand my music!'

From then on, the term *zhiyin* had been used to describe soul mates.

'Precious Orchid,' Qing Zhen looked at me intently while a solitary bird soared behind him in the vast sky, 'you realise how lucky we are? Most people search all their life for a *zhiyin* but never find one. We're not only lovers; we're also *zhiyin*.'

Though I was used to compliments from men and usually did not take them seriously, this one from Qing Zhen touched a silk string in my heart.

*   *   *

With the arrival of spring, I expected that the misery I felt living on the mountain would melt away with the snow. But I was wrong. Because of the good weather, Qing Zhen was out almost every day collecting herbs. Occasionally he'd take me with him, but most of the time I was left behind. Stuck in the small hut by myself, I couldn't help but feel lonely. I'd practise the *qin* for hours. Now my favourite piece was 'Playing the Flute on the Phoenix Terrace,' by the Sung dynasty poetess Li Qingzhao:

The incense in the golden container grows cold
My bed sheet undulates into red waves.
Still in bed, I lazily comb my hair
Dust covers my cosmetic box.

I watch the sun rise up to the curtain hook,
Feeling the bitterness of separation.
So many things I wanted to say but never did
The parting stretches thousands of miles
At the Yang Guan Pass I failed to make you stay . . .

When I grew bored with the *qin*, I'd sing opera arias or recite poems. I also did some cleaning and cooking to pass time as well as to release Qing Zhen from these chores – though I bitterly hated them. Back in Peach Blossom Pavilion, I lifted my fingers only to pour wine, to light an opium pipe, or to play mahjong. When I was hungry, there was Aunty Ah Ping to cook me delicate meat and fish and Little Rain to bring them to me.

Remembering Peach Blossom now made me feel very nostalgic. Though I hated my slavery to Mama and De, I missed Ah Ping, Spring Moon, and my parrot Plum Blossom. Then I thought of Teng Xiong. What was happening to her now?

My mother had once told me the Buddhists believe that only after a man and a woman have cultivated for a thousand years will they generate the Karma to share the same pillow. Therefore, under the same logic, Qing Zhen and I must have cultivated in endless past lives. But what about those customers whom I hated, but was forced to share my pillow with? And what about Teng Xiong, though both women, had we also cultivated for a thousand years in our past incarnations?

One time I secretly took a scrap of Qing Zhen's paper and tried to paint her from my memory, as she liked to show herself in a Western suit and also as a long-haired woman in an elegant dress. She must have been heartbroken that morning, waking up in the simple temple room expecting to rub mirrors with me, only to find the other side of the bed cool. Would our Karma lead us to another rendezvous in this lifetime? If so, I'd try to make her the happiest lesbian under heaven.

Many days my memories would make me restless, thinking not only of Teng Xiong but also my mother. Unlike Pearl, they were still in the *yang* world, but I had no idea how to find them. When Qing Zhen was away, a few times I went out to look for temples. But no monks or nuns had ever heard of Mother. Some even suggested that she might have already left the *sangha* and become a layperson, moved to another mountain, or even entered nirvana. All these conjectures and ruminations depressed me, but when night came, as I stared at Qing Zhen's handsome, intent face above mine while feeling his vigorous movements below, all my troubles generated by this floating world would vanish into thin air. I felt love so strong as to drive away my dissatisfactions.

As the mountains and trees around us began to sparkle with a bright green, I realised I'd been living with Qing Zhen for more than nine months. I also realised that love had made me an outsider who watched from a distance as the world revolved. Perhaps Qing Zhen did sense my discontent, because he would often do things to please me – bring me bunches of wildflowers, or take me out to the woods for a picnic, or an elegant gathering of *qin* playing, though there were only the two of us. He'd even made two sets of clothes for me – monks all learned how to sew since they had no women to do it for them.

Yet, though a Taoist monk would feel satisfied to dwell on a mountain surrounded by auspicious pines and *lingzhi* funguses, I, a woman and an ex–*ming ji*, longed for friends, parties, and elaborately embroidered silk gowns. I had expected a simpler existence, but not this day-after-day monotony.

One day when the sky appeared dim like pale ink, Qing Zhen told me – since this weather was best for communicating with spirits – he was going to draft four *fu*: one for protecting me; one for finding my mother; one for aiding my father in the *yin* world; and one for stripping the warlord's power.

During Qing Zhen's deep concentration, he looked transformed, to a *xian,* an immortal. Waves of love rose to warm my body. Watching him, I felt the presence of the pure land, far from all the smoke and dust of this imperfect world. I'll love and be kind to this man for the rest of my life, I said silently to myself. Then I looked out the window and my eyes caught the gentle green of new leaves, witnessing my vow.

Much as I appreciated the care Qing Zhen put into making the *fu* for me, I was still not happy on the mountain. The legend is told that when a day passes inside the immortal's cavern, a thousand years have already gone by in the outside world. But now it turned out just the opposite: a single day on the mountain felt like a thousand years. I remembered a line from a poem by the famous Tang dynasty courtesan Yu Xuanji: It's easier to find priceless treasures than a loving man. Now my problem was, though I'd found the loving man, I still wanted the priceless treasures!

Then one day Qing Zhen told me that in a week, the Taoist festival of *Zhai Qiao* – fasting and offering – would be held at Celestial Cloud Temple. Hundreds would attend, to pray, to make offerings to the numerous Taoist gods, and to eat and be entertained. There would be operas, folk music, puppet shows, magic, and all kinds of food and games . . . .

My eyes widened and my face flushed just listening to Qing Zhen's description. I couldn't wait to go out and have fun, to be around people!

But then Qing Zhen said, 'Precious Orchid, we'll go to Celestial Cloud together, but once we've arrived, I can't stay with you.'

'Why not?'

'Because I'm a monk and everybody knows me there.'

I felt too hurt to utter a word.

'Precious Orchid,' he looked embarrassed, 'please understand . . .'

It was exactly because I understood that I felt so sad. What combination could be more sensational – and more condemnable – than a runaway prostitute and an amorous monk? Not long ago, had our relationship been found out, we would've been stripped naked, then tied together for onlookers to throw stones at. After that, if we were still 'lucky' enough to be alive, we would be taken to a lake and, with our necks and feet tied with big stones, thrown into the icy water.

I swallowed my bitterness. 'Don't worry, once we're inside the temple, I'll act just like a stranger. And I know how to entertain myself.'

I wanted very much to start a fight just to stir up the air between us. However, catching his sad glance, my words retreated inside my mouth while my heart quietly shattered.

The next day I woke up and – to my trepidation – found Qing Zhen gone. However, he'd left a message on the altar:

Precious Orchid, I'll be away for a day or two, at most three, for business. Don't worry about me, I'll bring you good news when I'm back.

Good news, what kind? That he was going to quit the temple, marry me, and have babies? But then what were we going to live on, that dead bird with its filthy feathers floating in the elixir?

As promised, Qing Zhen did come back in three days. The moment I saw his beaming face and heard his voice calling my name, my grudge vanished.

'Precious Orchid,' his eyes searched mine with tenderness, 'see what I've bought you.'

My enthusiasm was immediately cooled by what I saw – a styleless, rough-textured top and trousers plus a straw hat. Back in Peach Blossom, these were worn by maids of the lowest rank. My heart was bleeding inside, but I feigned joy. I conjured up my most prestigious, dimpled smile and directed it to Qing Zhen.

He couldn't possibly have looked happier. Like a child trying to show off by reciting poetry to his parents, Qing Zhen continued to display things he had brought back for me – pickled food, a scarf, a small purse, and a small amount of cash.

'Qing Zhen,' I searched his face suspiciously, 'where did you get the money to buy all these?'

'I earned them.'

'Did you work? Where?'

'On the street.'

'Did you sell your concoction?'

'Precious Orchid, you know I'd rather die than do that.'

'I'm sorry.' I knew I had trespassed his sacred space.

A silence, then he said, 'I've been asking for alms.'

These simple words suddenly sounded like thunderclaps bursting above my head. Qing Zhen had once told me he used to make his living by performing rituals – birthdays, blessings, funerals, casting away evil spirits. But since he was now living as a hermit monk, opportunity for this sort of work had been drastically reduced, and so was his income. Therefore, during his reclusion – especially after I'd started to live with him – finding money had been difficult.

But still, I couldn't believe that he had turned beggar!

I felt too humiliated even to look at him. Finally I said, staring at the cauldron, which now appeared like a tomb burning in hell, 'So, you've been begging?'

'Yes,' he replied, not a hint of shame in his voice.

I tried hard to keep my tone from sounding angry. 'You're not embarrassed to beg in public?'

'Taoists call this "asking for alms," "receiving donations," or "connecting the good Karma." It is nothing to be ashamed of.'

Of course, I'd seen bedraggled monks and nuns begging on the streets of Shanghai but the regular monks attached to temples looked down on them. My mother had explained to me that, since hermit monks didn't have much source of income, begging had become their main way to make a living. Sometimes I'd even given them a few coppers to bring myself good Karma. But I'd never imagined I'd be so poor as to live on alms myself.

I stared at Qing Zhen and the gifts he'd bought with the money he'd begged, while feeling a surge of anger rising within. I lost control and spat out, 'Qing Zhen, shame on you!'

He looked stunned. 'Precious Orchid, you have never talked to me like that!'

'Because I put up with you. Because I never imagined you'd turn a beggar!'

Veins throbbing in his temples, he said angrily, 'Put up with me? Don't you love me? Haven't I been nice to you?'

'Nice? When you spend all your time caring for that dead bird in your concoction?'

'But that's my vocation!'

'Yes, you only care for *your* vocation.' I tapped my chest. 'Then what about mine?' I immediately regretted that I'd said this. What if Qing Zhen told me to go back to prostitution? Then relief washed over me – I'd never told him the truth that I'd been not a maid, but a prostitute.

Now he stared at me with eyes tinted with sadness. 'You have your freedom here.'

'Freedom? I hate this mountain. It's a prison!' I screamed. 'You have your *fu,* your concoction, and your longevity exercises but what do I have? Nothing!' I started to cry.

Qing Zhen remained silent, then he gently put his arm around my shoulder. 'I'm sorry, Precious Orchid. I didn't know you were so unhappy living here with me.'

Still sobbing, I buried my head in his chest. 'It's not that. It's . . . I have no friends and no news of my mother.'

He caressed my head, cooing, 'Tomorrow you'll meet lots of people at the temple fair. And we'll also ask for your mother there.'

27

The Encounter

Celestial Cloud was situated about twelve miles away from our hut. In order to save money, Qing Zhen suggested we walk half of the way, then hire sedan chairs for the rest of the trip.

When we finally arrived at the temple at noon, its entrance was already crowded with *shanxin* – virtuous believers, also called *xiangke,* fragrant visitors, because they are constantly lighting incense as offerings to the gods. But I wondered. Did their investment produce anything more than ashes?

We had to push and squeeze our way in like eels wriggling in a crowded pond. But I didn't mind at all; in fact, I was tremendously enjoying being jostled by other people. I even stooped to pat a little boy's head and sniff the perfume wafting from an expensively dressed *tai tai.*

The temple looked impressively old. Sunlight glinted on the undulating yellow roof tiles where green dragons danced on golden clouds. Decorative banners rippled in the breeze as if waving to encourage the throng of pilgrims to make offerings in exchange for blessings. In the distance towered a white pagoda, looking like a bearded sage bestowing wisdom.

When we stepped inside the temple, we were greeted by paintings and statues showing every possible kind of god.

I nudged Qing Zhen's elbow. 'Who are all these?'

He pointed to a series of paintings depicting bearded men in elaborate robes. 'These are the highest of all the gods. They were here at the beginning of the universe.' Then he pointed to men dressed in armour and riding on ferocious beasts. 'These are the generals who command the demons to cast away evil spirits and suppress monsters.'

'There are so many!'

'That way,' he smiled mischievously, 'there are enough gods to answer all the needs of us mortals.'

I wondered: Why isn't there a goddess of romance to solve my problem with Qing Zhen?

Just then I spotted a white-robed goddess holding a baby. It was the son-sending Guan Yin. A woman, not quite young and not quite pretty, was praying in front of the statue, prostrating and knocking her head hard on the stone floor.

I pointed her out to Qing Zhen. 'Do you believe this works?'

'It depends on how sincere one's prayer is.'

I meditated hard on Qing Zhen's answer, then decided it had nothing to do with sincerity, but fate. Women are like fields; some fertile, others barren. I sighed inside. Even this Guan Yin couldn't bring me a son with Qing Zhen so long as he kept directing his semen back to his brain.

We stopped to admire a stone pillar carved with motifs of dragons and phoenixes – symbols of harmonious marriage. While my eyes outlined the graceful shapes and my hand ran along the cool texture, my heart sank. Like these birds dwelling in a soaring pillar, I was trapped and unable to fly away.

But these sombre thoughts did not last long. The temple was quickly filling up with noisy visitors. Everyone seemed to be dressed in their best. Though their clothes were hardly fashionable by Shanghai standards, watching them was a great joy after all my months of solitude. Women wriggled in colourful, embroidered jackets; their pomaded hair decorated with fresh flowers, king-fishers' feathers, or jewelled hairpins. Some men were clad in long Chinese gowns while others sported Western suits and felt hats. Although these people came from *wuhu sihai* – the five lakes and the four seas – all came for the same reasons: to cast away evil spirits, pray for good fortune, and receive blessings.

In the distance near a high platform, I saw a gathering of Taoist monks in elaborately embroidered, many-coloured robes. As they talked, they made sweeping gestures, each movement setting the robes' gold and silver threads glimmering, conjuring images of flying fish diving in and out of the ocean, their bodies shards of glittering reflections.

Once Qing Zhen spotted the other monks, he pulled me aside. 'Precious Orchid, now I have to go and join them to prepare for the ceremony.' He paused to look around, then spoke again, 'I want you to enjoy yourself. There'll be two more hours before the ceremony begins, so why don't you stroll around? This temple is huge, with many separate buildings, so there'll be more than enough to keep you diverted.' He looked at me intently, his angular face achingly handsome and mysterious in the soft light within the temple. 'Be sure to come back and watch the ceremony, but just in case you don't see me, meet me at the south gate of this building when the ritual ends. All right?'

I nodded, holding his gaze as long as I could.

He swiftly squeezed my hand, then turned to walk. After he was away a few steps, he came back. 'Precious Orchid, I'm sorry I can't keep you company. Are you sure you'll be fine by yourself?'

I nodded again, giving my pocket a discreet pat. 'I have the money you gave me.'

A smile broke on his face. 'Good, go enjoy yourself. And don't forget to meet me at the south gate.'

'I won't.'

Then he hurried forward and soon vanished into the crowd.

I walked unhurriedly, savouring the feeling of being rubbed and bumped by other human beings. The air smelled of a mixture of lush vegetation, incense, fried food, perfume, and human sweat. I inhaled deeply and sighed with satisfaction. Debris crunched and moaned under my feet; the soothing sound of distant bells trembled in the spring air. From time to time I'd even offer a smile to handsome strangers to show my good taste and appreciation.

I looked up and saw a sky as blue as the sea and as clear as a clean sheet of rice paper. The air was cool and crisp. So crisp that I could almost hear when people waved their hands and blinked their eyes.

This was the second time I'd felt a genuine sense of freedom. The first had been when I'd run away from Peach Blossom with Teng Xiong. Now her intimate yet strange name sent throbs of pain to my heart, followed by a sense of guilt. During the many months I'd been immersed in the oblivion of living with Qing Zhen, I hadn't thought much about my woman lover. Teng Xiong. While my tongue rubbed along the two words, my mind was filled with her elegant, effeminate image. I had no idea where she was now nor what she was doing. Did I dare hope she held no grudge against me for my abrupt departure? But almost a year had gone by. What if she had already fallen in love with someone else and had completely forgotten me? The thought made me sad. However, since I was the one who'd left her, I had no one to blame but myself. Rich and smart as she was, she could go wherever she pleased and do whatever she desired. That was real freedom. How I wished I were like her! If my money and jewellery had not been lost, I certainly would be better off now, much better. I could have bought a big, beautiful house, and maybe persuaded Qing Zhen to dissolve his vow as a monk and live with me. Maybe I'd also have a baby. I was sure it would be a cute little thing. Seed planted by an erudite monk in a *ming ji*! Instinctively my hand moved down to my stomach, but instead of feeling some vigorous kicking, it landed on flat, motionless flesh.

Tears pooled in my eyes as I continued to walk, passing through corridors, subtemples, courtyards. Then suddenly, through my blurred vision, I spotted a little girl. She was three or four, all dressed in red. Her round, glowing cheeks matched her dress and shoes. Her eyes were big and round like miniature mirrors reflecting two darting black marbles. As she jumped and danced around, thick plaits bounced on her shoulders like fat chopsticks.

My heart melted. I'd never seen a girl so captivating.

Now she was yanking her mother's sleeve. 'Mama, Mama,' her pudgy finger pointed to a street stall and her sugary voice chirped. 'Pudding!'

The young mother, a rich, elegantly dressed *tai tai,* stooped to pat her head. 'Is that what you want?'

She eagerly nodded.

A moment after grabbing the white-sugared pudding, the little one had already smeared it all around her lips.

I chuckled at the sight while my hand reached to pat her head. To my surprise, instead of returning my friendliness with a smile, the little round face, now drained of blood and distorted by fear, looked as pale as her pudding.

'Mama! Mama!' She dropped the pudding and yanked at the hem of her mother's dress.

The rich woman turned and our eyes met. Her glance was filled with suspicion and contempt. Then, to my utter shock and surprise, she spat as if to cast away evil spirits, then pulled her daughter away.

I watched their backs disappear into the crowd, feeling so upset that my body shivered. Suddenly I realised that it had been months since I'd looked in a mirror. With no pomade, no perfume, no make-up, but only coarse clothes and a dark-tanned face which suggested having to labour outdoors like a coolie – no wonder the *tai tai* had spat at me. They must have thought that I was a beggar girl, or a maid sent away because she'd contracted some terrible disease. Maybe the mother even thought I was a potential abductor! I felt queasiness simmering in my stomach and blood pounding in my temples. No wonder the little girl looked so scared and her mother so disgusted!

Not long ago, I had been admired as a highly cultured and refined *ming ji.* But now I even thought I could smell a stench rising from my hair and clothes. Appalled, I dashed up to the stall, threw down a few copper coins, snatched a pudding from the vendor, and frantically flicked my tongue.

'Haiii . . .' I let out a long sigh, my tortured nerves temporarily numbed by the sugary pudding.

Through my mind flashed memories of Mama taking me, Spring Moon, and Jade Vase out to have our hair styled, then buying us ice cream, then the little boy snatching it away and almost being hit by a car. Only now, I must have looked exactly like him, a beggar!

While I was feeling sorry for myself, another image rose in my mind – the blue-eyed Mr. Anderson. Nine years had passed since my eyes had first met those of the barbarian. Then we'd met again at Peach Blossom when he came with his partner Mr. Ho. But they had stopped visiting. From time to time I still wondered where he was and what he was doing. I tried hard to remember his face, but all I could see in my mind was the kindness shining through his blue eyes.

I let out another sigh, savouring the pudding and pondering the vicissitudes of life. Wandering around this huge temple complex, I felt like a stranger watching the world's twists and turns from the outside. This saddened me. When would I have the chance to belong, to grasp something permanently in my hand? While Qing Zhen had his concoction of immortality, what did I have?

Thus thinking, I stepped inside one of the temple buildings, paid for a bundle of incense, then lit it at a bronze burner. Kneeling among the other fragrant visitors, I muttered prayers for Baba, Pearl, Ruby, Mother, Qing Zhen, and Teng Xiong. After that, feeling more relaxed, I continued to stroll, losing track of the time until I heard peals of drums and gongs.

I strained my ears and hurried toward the sound. It was an open-air theatre with an ongoing performance. The area was totally packed. Those who couldn't get a seat were standing wherever they could squeeze in – along the sides, in the aisles, at the back. A few boys had even climbed up a tree to have a better view. I bought a cup of hot tea and a bun from a nearby stall, then squeezed my way to the side. Because of the many heads bobbing in front of me, I had to shift mine this way and that to glimpse the stage. The opera was *Farewell My Concubine* – a popular piece depicting the defeat of Emperor Xiang Yu during the famous battle between the Han and the Chu.

Now the Concubine Yu, all dressed up in her pearl-tasselled headgear and an embroidered, sequinned dress, was about to bid farewell to her lord Emperor Xiang. At this last moment with the man she loved and who she had faithfully followed all her life, she decided to perform a sword dance – a farewell entertainment.

The performance was excellent. The double swords glinted and flashed in the air, sometimes resembling two shimmering bolts of lightning, other times two choreographing ribbons. The fiddle's high-pitched tone wept poignantly while the drums and gongs roared like tigers.

'Hao! Hao!' Wonderful. People burst into loud applause.

I looked around. The audience seemed to be an eclectic group of city people and country folk. Immersed in the dramatic illusion, they looked happy, troubles forgotten for fleeting moments as they watched life imitated on the transient stage.

I turned back and saw Emperor Xiang, now singing:

My concubine, for years you've always stood by my side during endless battles, Today we will have to go our separate ways.

After that, Xiang asked Concubine Yu to bring wine. Yu poured two full cups, then waved a white-powdered hand and said tenderly:

Please, my lord.

Xiang's expression turning sentimental, he began to sing:

My concubine, now what I hear from all four directions is only the Chu's soldiers' song. It must be that Liu Bang has already conquered my land. My heart is dissolving and so is my qi!

Tears spilled from the concubine's eyes. With her orchid fingers, she flicked a few drops into the distance. Her silvery voice rose against the black-painted evening:

The Han soldiers have retreated, and songs of Chu floated everywhere.
If my lord's days are numbered, so will be your unworthy concubine's.

After that, Yu pulled the sword from Emperor Xiang's waist and plunged it into her own stomach.

'Oh, no!' Some audience members exclaimed with a horrified expression.

Others clapped enthusiastically. *'Hao! Hao!'*

What caught my interest was not the girl who played Concubine Yu, but the actor who impersonated Emperor Xiang. I couldn't tell whether he was handsome – his face was painted in black and white and framed by a long, artificial beard – but I was bewitched by his voice. It was the clearest, yet the most emotion-charged I'd ever heard, powerful enough to evoke roars of approval or silence the chatter of the audience. This man's voice was even more beautiful than Qing Zhen's, the only flaw being that it was not as resonant nor as wide-ranging. I stared intently at the actor, trying to imagine what his face would look like without the paint and the beard.

The audience continued to cheer and clap while the curtain slowly fell, ending the drama both on and off stage. Unwilling to detach themselves from the tragedy still burning in the air, people lingered and moved slowly. I had to squeeze and push my way through the crowd to reach the stage. Then I turned and sneaked around to the back. Inside, some actors were taking off their makeup, others chatting, yet others sipping tea and munching snacks. I craned my neck and looked but couldn't see the one who played Emperor Xiang. Tentatively I stepped inside the small area and asked a young girl, 'Little sister, who's the actor who played the emperor?'

She pointed to a corner where, to my surprise, I saw a woman's back. She was taking off her make-up in front of a small mirror.

'But little sister, that's a woman!'

'Yes, but we're all women here.' She pointed to a banner hung above the entrance. 'See? We are the all-female Golden Phoenix Opera Troupe.'

I studied for moments the four embroidered characters and the gold-threaded phoenix. Then, as I was about to enquire more about this troupe, the woman at the corner turned and our eyes met.

I was staring at the face of Teng Xiong!

A smile bloomed on her face. Then she got up and hurried toward me. Ignoring the curious eyes of the other actors and workers, we embraced.

When we finally released each other, she said, 'Come, Precious Orchid, follow me.'

Teng Xiong led me outside of the backstage area. Making sure that no one was around, she pulled me into her arms and kissed me passionately on my lips.

Long moments passed before she released me. 'Why did you leave without saying goodbye?'

I had no answer for that, so I just looked at her with my watery eyes and aimed at her my dimpled smile.

'Look at you, Precious Orchid.' She stood back to scrutinise me. 'I can't believe that several months caused such a big change. You might as well be a farm girl now. Or shave off that tangled-up hair and be a nun. Do you want that?'

I shook my head, feeling mortified. She must have guessed that I'd left her for the monk. Nevertheless, neither of us mentioned Qing Zhen.

She said, 'I'm sorry, Precious Orchid. I didn't intend to be mean. It just breaks my heart to see you . . .' Her voice trailed off.

'I must look horrible!'

'No, Precious Orchid, you're always as refreshing as spring and as beautiful as the moon. It's just . . .' She paused again, then, 'you deserve a better life than dwelling in the forest.'

Tears rolled down my cheeks.

Teng Xiong pulled a handkerchief and dabbed my eyes. 'Precious Orchid, I believe it's heaven's will for us to be together again, so please stay with me from now on.'

'But I . . . can't. I have to—'

'Yes you can. Those stinking males only know how to break a woman's heart and ruin their beauty. Let me take care of you. Please.'

And I did.

As I hadn't bade farewell to Teng Xiong when I'd left her for the monk, now I didn't say goodbye to Qing Zhen when I left him for Teng Xiong. I didn't even look for him at the temple fair after the ritual, fearing that I'd again succumb to his charm and end up going back to that mountain prison.

That evening, he must have waited and waited for me to show up and go home with him. After finishing the ritual, as it grew dark outside the south gate, he must have craned his neck to look for me. He might have even let out a sigh of relief or an exclamation of joy when he thought he'd spotted me, but alas, it was just another girl with long hair wearing a coarse top and trousers. Perspiration must have coursed down his forehead and his heart must have skipped beats while he looked and looked and still the woman he loved was nowhere to be seen. He must have wondered if I'd been kidnapped, even raped, again. Or if I'd gotten lost, or run into some horrible accident. Anything. Anything nightmarish enough to tear his heart and splatter his mind with blood.

I wondered how late had he waited in the heartbreaking darkness: two, three, four, five hours? After he'd finally gone home, though exhausted, he must not have been able to sleep even for a minute. He must have looked desperately all over for me again the next day. And the next. And the next . . . He must have been in agonies of worry. How could I do something so cruel to someone I loved so much?

I looked bitterly at my own reflection in the mirror and spat, 'Whore!'

28

Separation

As promised, Teng Xiong did take good care of me – like a newly-wed first wife. During our first night together in her hotel room, she saw how tired I was and so ran a hot bath for me. Then she bought several of my favourite dim sum. When my body finally felt clean and my stomach warmed (I had little appetite and ate only a few bites), I expected her to take my hand and we would visit the Wu Mountain together.

But she said, 'Precious Orchid, you must be exhausted, so if you want to stay up and talk, I'm happy to be your listener. But if you want to sleep,' she pointed to the spacious bed, 'that mattress is very soft and comfortable.'

I nodded, standing up from the table. She immediately came to me, tenderly caressed my face, then embraced me like an octopus. 'Do you know I've become the luckiest woman in the world?'

Not knowing how to respond, I smiled a wry smile. She took my hand, led me to bed, then flicked off the light. In each other's arms, we lay silently on the tofu-soft mattress.

Teng Xiong's voice, gentle and thin, rose in the dark like a thread of incense. 'Precious Orchid, please don't be sad.'

I remained silent. She went on, 'I promise you'll never regret coming back to me.'

'Teng Xiong, I believe you,' I said, then delicately extricated myself from her embrace and turned around so that she couldn't touch my face and feel my tears.

She gently rubbed my back for a few moments, then pulled the bed sheet to cover me. 'My Precious Orchid, fall quickly into your sweet dream village.'

The next day when I woke up, it was eleven in the morning. Teng Xiong had already ordered a simple breakfast of pork buns, scallion pancakes, and soy milk. Despite my near-starvation on the mountain, I'd had no appetite last night. But now, refreshed from a deep sleep on a soft bed and feeling secure, my stomach suddenly rumbled like a concubine's complaints. The buns tasted like lion's head meatballs, the pancakes like tender veal, and the soy milk like bird's nest soup. I gobbled down the food like a woman who has just escaped from famine.

Teng Xiong looked at me with eyes filled with tenderness. 'Precious Orchid, I can order more if you want. But I don't think you should eat too much right away.'

I ignored her remark and kept my hands pulling bits of bun and pancake up to my mouth, as if fearing they'd be snatched away.

When I finally finished, Teng Xiong said, 'Today I don't have a performance, so I'll take you out to a dressmaker and then buy you some cosmetics and whatever else you need. Then we'll come back to take a nap. And in the evening,' she smiled, 'I'll take you out to celebrate our happy reunion.'

The supper club, situated in the lively Qianmen area near our hotel, had been open for less than a month. Although I'd been invited to several supper clubs when I'd been a *ming ji* in Shanghai, those seemed but distant memories. Now I'd have my first taste of Peking nightlife – and with a woman lover! My heart started to pound when Teng Xiong helped me out of the hired car in front of a brightly painted pink building. We entered through a red gate; surrounding it were posters picturing female singers with Western clothes and hairstyles. Before I could take a closer look at the women, a guard had opened the door and gestured us in. The exotic sound of jazz and the fragrance of perfume blended with the reek of cigarettes rushed to greet us. I took a shallow breath and looked. The inside was decorated with mirrors, coloured lights, and lots of gold – columns, chairs, chandeliers. At first, it reminded me of a second-rate turquoise pavilion for Russian prostitutes. But my unpleasant recollection was quickly replaced by a cheerful mood when a captain arrived and led us to a seat by a corner.

I studied Teng Xiong across the table while she was placing orders with an attentive waiter. In her perfectly tailored black suit and red bow tie, and with the gold chain of her pocket watch dangling discreetly outside her vest, Teng Xiong looked more like a dandy than an actor. Her pomaded short hair gleamed under the club's dim light like threads of silk. Watching her elated expression and expansive, manly gestures made my heart ache with bliss mixed with tinges of gratitude. I sighed with pleasure. After a year wearing peasant clothes, I'd finally been able to put on make-up, a pretty Western dress, and be around fashionable people!

The waiter soon returned with a bottle of champagne, popped it open, then poured the pale gold liquid into our tall glasses.

After he left, a cheerful smile played on Teng Xiong's face as she clinked my glass with hers. 'Precious Orchid, to your beauty and our reunion!'

I softly echoed. 'To our reunion.'

In my mouth, the wine tasted like sweet elixir. The golden bubbles seemed to tell me that, like the setting sun, life is achingly beautiful in the moments before it vanishes. Then I remembered the poem Pearl had recited to me when I'd first entered Peach Blossom at thirteen:

> *When a flower blooms, pick it. Don't wait till there is only the bare branch left.*

I quickly took another long sip of my golden elixir – quite different from Qing Zhen's malodorous one. The dishes arrived one by one – warm bread with butter, Russian soup floating with chunks of beef, blood-streaked steak. During our sumptuous feast, Teng Xiong and I drank, ate, and chatted. Although we'd been separated for such a long time, we were women with similar fates, and so our bond renewed itself almost immediately. Bathed in the illusory, decadent atmosphere of the nightclub, she recounted her life without me – her performances with the opera troupe; the success she enjoyed; the attacks she received from the conservatives who thought it was sacrilege for women to play men's roles.

'Sacrilege, ha!' she sneered, now taking out a cigar. With sensuously moving fingers, she cut off its tip, lit it with a gold lighter, and began to puff. 'Those men,' she leant close to me and lowered her voice, 'they say that women's bodies are contaminated. So if we perform as a man, we'll offend the stage god and upset the way of Heaven.' She twiddled the obscenely plump cigar with her slender fingers. 'Absurd! Do they forget that *they* are the stinking males?' Teng Xiong laughed gallantly with a backward toss of her head, like a real man.

After she finished narrating her story, she asked me about what I'd been dreading to tell – my life after we'd separated. I feared that if I talked about Qing Zhen, I'd reveal the depth of my feelings. So I described my misery in living on the lonely mountain but left out the reason I'd endured the misery – my love for the Taoist monk. Teng Xiong, tactful as always, did not press me on the subject, which would have caused her as much unhappiness as it did me.

We continued to enjoy the lavish decor, the golden wine, the boisterous music, and the exotic food. Now the club was almost packed. Important-looking men – some gaunt with mean expressions and darting eyes, others fat with protruding bellies and greasy faces – were accompanied by heavily made-up and dressed-up women. A few couples were already undulating and scratching their feet on the dance floor. A woman in a bright green gown clung to a tan-faced man like moss to a rock. I was sure that she was now selling her smile and then later her skin.

Thinking that I no longer had to sell mine but could live an equally luxurious life, I almost smiled, then shot my handsome lover an affectionate glance. 'Teng Xiong, thanks for bringing me back to life.'

She patted my hand. 'Precious Orchid, you deserve the best. Always.' In slick movements like a rich playboy, she picked up the champagne and poured me another glass.

As I delicately sipped my wine, my eyes wandered to take in more of the scene until they landed on a crude-looking man three tables from ours. His middle finger was missing, so he held his cigarette awkwardly between his index and ring fingers. A scar slashed one bushy eyebrow into two, giving him a fierce yet miserable look, like an imperial eunuch. He seemed to have come by himself and was immersed in what he saw – us.

'Teng Xiong,' I felt my heart knocking against my ribs, 'see that man with a missing finger over there? He can't take his eyes off us; you think he's . . . one of Mama and De's men looking for me?'

Teng discreetly glanced at the man, then turned back to me and, to my surprise, smiled. 'I think it's only because he's jealous of my having such a beautiful companion.'

'How can you be sure they're not from Peach Blossom?'

'Do you think your Mama will pay for a train ticket, wine, and food in a supper club, plus a detective, to look for you here?' She paused to sip her wine, then, 'It's because he's feasting on your beauty.'

I felt flattered. 'You really think so?'

Instead of answering me, Teng Xiong cut a slice of steak and put it on my plate. 'Don't worry and eat more. This is to keep your face flushed and your *qi* abundant.'

Just then I noticed that two other equally crude men and two gaudily dressed club girls were sitting down to join the man with the missing finger.

Teng Xiong said, 'See, he's with friends. I told you not to worry. Please enjoy the moment.'

When we finished eating, Teng Xiong took my hand. 'Come, Precious Orchid, let's dance.'

'But I'm out of practice.'

'Don't worry. I'll lead you.'

Teng Xiong was as graceful on the dance floor as in bed. Her body responded naturally to the music's rhythm and her feet glided as effortlessly along the dance floor as carp in a pond. Yet as I stared at her dreamy expression, I thought only of Qing Zhen.

While my body was moving sensuously in the decadent city, what was he doing now on the lonely mountain? If he had not chosen the hermit's life, maybe now I would be dancing not with Teng Xiong, but with him. Would he move as elegantly on the dance floor as he did when performing his esoteric and erotic rituals? Would our life be perfect if he were a dandy instead of a monk?

This unpleasant thought about Qing Zhen was immediately followed by another – my mother. Why wasn't she in Taiyi Mountain as she'd told me? Maybe while now I was enjoying myself in an expensive nightclub, she was living as a hermit nun in a cold, deserted cave. Or was she already dead? If she was, then her ghost would be wandering restlessly in the *yin* world, because I hadn't been burning incense to appease it and guide it to Buddha. But if she was still alive, then her mind (if I was still on her mind) would be restless, worrying about her daughter. Guilt and then fear rose inside me. I imagined Mother, bald and emaciated, her body barely covered by a filthy, many-patched robe, pulling grass from the ground with calloused fingers. When she parted her lips to pop in a squirming worm, her mouth, toothless, was a hole as dark as hell . . .

Teng Xiong whispered into my ears. 'Precious Orchid, what are you thinking about?'

'Oh, nothing.' I put on a smile to hide the throbbing pains of my heart.

Teng held my waist and began to swing me this way and that. I remembered how as a child I'd liked to have my father push me high in the swing so I could have a better view of the world. Now that I'd finally tasted the vicissitudes of life, all I wanted was to find something unmoving to hold on to.

I clung close to Teng Xiong's slender body like a child holding on to the hem of his mother's dress.

My lover planted a kiss on my third eye. 'Are you happy now?'

'Yes,' I said. But added silently to myself, 'And no.'

The next day in the hotel room, I was awakened by Teng Xiong's kisses.

'Morning,' she murmured. Her eyes were tender and her face flushed; her hands began to search my body.

I remembered my promise: If our Karma led us to another rendezvous in this lifetime, I'd try to make her the happiest lesbian under heaven. Receiving directions from my brain, my hands, lips, and tongue began to apply their erotic art to provoke and please.

In the evening Teng Xiong had to perform, so she took me to the Double Happiness Tea House to see the Golden Phoenix Opera Troupe. The tea house was also situated in the Qianmen area. After we got out of the rickshaw, Teng Xiong ushered me through a side door that led directly backstage. Some women were chatting, others reciting their lines, yet others painting their brows with small brushes.

Before I had a chance to take in more of the scene, a girl with a goose-egg face and alert eyes dashed up to Teng Xiong and pinched her playfully on the arm. 'My master, you're late!'

Teng turned to me and smiled. 'Precious Orchid, this is Tinkling Bell, my bride on stage tonight.' Then she introduced me to the girl. 'This is Precious Orchid, my . . . friend.'

My heart sank at Teng Xiong's words. That broken bell was her 'bride,' and it seemed that I, her lover, was suddenly just a friend? I studied the girl and felt an instant suspicion. When she talked, her eyes flicked flirtatiously, her grin stretched wide on her perfect goose-egg face, and her fingers kept touching *my* lover's arm. But I didn't have much time to think more about this, for Teng was already pulling me around to introduce me to the other actresses. Although not all of them were young and pretty, they all expressed enthusiasm for promoting women's performances. Then, before I finished my conversation with the middle-aged actress who played *laodan* – old ladies – I heard Tinkling Bell's high-pitched voice announce, 'There's not much time before the show, so please get ready!'

After that, Teng Xiong came to me and said, motioning to a very young girl now standing timidly next to her, 'Precious Orchid, the performance will soon begin, so let Little Cat take you to your seat in the theatre. Hope you like my performance.' Before I left, she discreetly planted a kiss on my cheek. As I straightened up, I saw Tinkling Bell's eyes fixed upon us.

Little Cat led me out from the backstage to a seat at a front table. After I settled, the maid swiftly left and returned, to my delight, with a hot towel, food, and drink. When I reached into my purse, she smiled shyly. 'Oh no. Miss Teng already paid me.' After that, she disappeared backstage.

I blew on the cup of scalding tea, then looked around. The tea house was nearly packed. People kept streaming in while vendors moved noisily between rows hawking tea, cigarettes, and snacks – sesame cakes, sugared ginger, dried plums, roasted watermelon seeds. I noticed some richly dressed *tai tai* who came with their *amahs* – one cooing a red-faced, hysterically crying baby. A young couple talked quietly with their heads close together like a pair of kissing fish. A group of middle-aged women gossiped, sipped tea, cracked watermelon seeds, and spat the husks onto the floor. People looked happy and excited – maybe this was their first time at an all-female opera performance.

Soon the curtain rose, and the small tea house was instantly flooded with the sharp wailing of the two-stringed fiddles punctuated by frantic beatings of drums and gongs. Although Teng Xiong had told me of her days as an opera singer before she'd become Fung's concubine, this was the first time I would actually know it was her onstage – now as a young, handsome scholar.

Tonight's performance was the Peking opera version of the Kun opera *The Peony Pavilion*, a love story about a man who fell in love with a beautiful ghost, and how, due to the power of his love, finally resurrected her from the *yin* world.

Du Liniang – the young girl and female ghost – was played by Tinkling Bell. Although I didn't like her, I had to admit that her acting was gilded with magic. Her plaintive, obsessive longing for the scholar whom she'd only met in a dream melted everyone's heart. When, after a long period of suffering she finally died of lovesickness onstage, sighs were all that could be heard. The plump woman next to me kept shaking her head while wiping the corners of her eyes. A young girl two tables away sobbed audibly.

During the next scene when Tinkling Bell was being buried, my heart started to pound, for I knew Teng Xiong was soon to make her entrance. Suddenly there was a loud beating of the drums but at first only a willow branch was seen sticking out from the entrance. It was held in midair for a few agonising seconds before its master finally revealed himself – a young, white-powdered scholar. Thunderous applause exploded in the hall, drowning even the boisterous sound of the musicians.

Teng Xiong's performance was flawless – her movements were stylised but fluid and perfectly coordinated with the music. Even the ribbon swaying from her bun and the fan in her hand seemed expressive of the scholar Liu Mengmei's aroused emotions. When Liu swore his undying love for the ghost through Teng Xiong's sincere, pure voice, my eyes were filled with tears. While I wiped my eyes with the towel, my heart ached with jealousy of Tinkling Bell. How I wished I could exchange real life with that on the stage so I could be that lucky bell and Teng Xiong a real man and my real husband!

I was intrigued by the many transformations of my woman lover. Last night she'd been a dandy in a Western suit gliding on a dance floor, today she was a traditional Chinese scholar reciting poems to his ghostly lover. But all these were as a man. How would she have looked as Fung's bejewelled concubine?

Life in the city with a rich, runaway concubine-cum-famous-opera-diva was quite different from that with a penniless Taoist monk on the mountain. When Teng Xiong didn't have to perform, she'd take me to elegant restaurants to try out famous dishes – Peking duck, pig's intestines, shark's fin, sea slug. With warm, full stomachs, we'd ride in a rickshaw to appreciate the city's nightlife. Sometimes she'd stop the coolie to let us off in front of a tea house. Then we'd go in to relish scalding tea and high-pitched singing by girls with flirtatious smiles and graceful hand gestures. Yet I was always aware of something missing. I thought often of the phrase by the Tang dynasty courtesan Yu Xuanji: It's easier to find priceless treasures than a loving man. With Qing Zhen, I'd had the loving man, but not the priceless treasures. With Teng Xiong, I had the treasure and the loving, but no man. Perhaps the Buddha had it right: There is no end to desire.

So, while I lamented fate's malice, I enjoyed Teng Xiong's love and my regained luxury. Yet my life still seemed far from blissful.

Though I'd been too busy at Peach Blossom, during my time on the mountain, I'd learned that having too little to do is not much better. So now living with Teng Xiong for two months, I decided I must find ways to keep myself occupied. Teng said I could also join the opera troupe if I liked. If I didn't, she'd have enough money to support us both. I did not want to just live off her money, so I decided to join the troupe. Although I'd been taught something about performing in Peking opera, I did not have the training of a professional actor, only a semi-professional singer. Besides, the big roles were already taken by successful actresses like Tinkling Bell, and none of the others were eager to have competition for their parts. So I was only assigned to minor roles like a maid, an old woman, a page boy, sometimes even a low-class prostitute. I was paid, but one night's performance brought me less than one of my favoured guests would have tipped my maid. Worse, while playing a maid or a page boy, I had to watch Tinkling Bell flirt and lean her small, shapely body close to Teng Xiong's tall, boyish one. I could not but fear that this broken bell was trying to seduce Teng Xiong. If she succeeded, who'd take care of me, how would I survive?

Even though I wanted to hold on to Teng Xiong, I could not stop thinking about Qing Zhen. At first I thought if I joined the opera troupe and kept myself busy working, I wouldn't have time to think of him. But I was wrong. Qing Zhen's image kept slipping into my mind, not only in quiet moments when I was reading or musing, but even while performing onstage. And of course during lovemaking with Teng Xiong.

And so I'd not quite escaped from the mountain prison because Qing Zhen's ghost never left me. My body was with Teng Xiong but my mind was still with the monk. Often when Teng and I were dining quietly together, I could almost see my monk lover sitting between us, staring sadly into my eyes. Maybe he was really there, for he'd told me his alchemy could render people invisible! I would also imagine what he might be doing. Perhaps he simply continued to live the same life – meditating, playing the *qin*, experimenting with alchemy, and writing talismans – but without me. I felt sad to think that I might have spoiled the spiritual practice that was his duty to his father. But even worse was when I imagined that he might not be lonely at all because he might have already seduced another girl for his practice of balancing the *yin* and *yang*.

When I imagined all the positions he'd carry out with the other woman and the variegated ways he'd move his tongue and long fingers all over her body, a heat would gather around my chest until a moan erupted from my mouth. During these moments, I felt a strong urge to run back to him and take him from this new lover who could never give him what I had. But, of course, I'd never mustered up the courage, fearing that he might get furious at me and kick me out, or worse, his attention completely focused on the other girl – who might be even prettier than me – simply ignore me.

When my imagination had calmed down, I thought, even if Qing Zhen did forgive me and take me back, how could I spend another winter in his bare 'temple'? If I left Teng Xiong for him again and then wanted to come back, I could hardly expect her to forgive me a second time. Unable to make any decision, I continued to live with my lesbian lover while tormented by desire for a Taoist monk.

I also could not stop thinking about Mother. Though she might be near me, I had no idea where. Several times I'd travelled by car and sedan chair to the many temples on the Western Hills only to return home with a saddened heart. After several months, I finally stopped trying to look for her, though I tried not to give up hope completely.

I'd been living with Teng Xiong for a year. As time went by, somehow I knew this life could not go on forever. Though the days with Teng seemed to pass easily – we performed, discussed arts, dined in elegant restaurants, rubbed mirrors – I sensed that as a 'wind sweeping through the pavilion heralds a rising storm in the mountains,' something bad was going to happen. Recently Teng Xiong seemed less indulgent in buying me gifts. When we had sex, her performance lacked the passion she'd shown before. It was she who had used to please me in bed, but now I'd become the one who'd try to satisfy, even arouse, her. Was it Tinkling Bell? Was Teng Xiong now thinking of leaving me for her?

Whenever I would ask her if something had gone wrong, Teng

Xiong would simply say, 'Don't worry, Precious Orchid, everything is fine.'

But deep down I sensed some disaster was lurking around the corner. I could almost feel its prickly texture brushing against my arms, causing my hair to stiffen.

One night after we'd made love, I pressed Teng Xiong to reveal what she'd been keeping from me.

'All right,' she sat up and looked me in the eyes, 'Precious Orchid, but please don't get upset—'

This was the first time I sensed fear in her voice. 'Teng Xiong, after all these misfortunes, you think I can't take one more?'

Her eyes were sad, but her tone was firm. 'I'm afraid we have to go our separate ways soon.'

The statement dropped in the room like a bomb.

I sat up, startled. 'What do you mean?'

She remained silent, her fingers nervously wringing the bed sheet.

I pressed. 'Do you not . . . love me anymore? Do you now love Tinkling Bell?'

'Of course I love you. And I don't care at all about Tinkling Bell.' She paused, then, 'It's that I . . . I'm afraid I might get killed.'

'What?' While I felt a chill splash down my spine, my voice soared toward the ceiling. 'What happened?!'

'I think my husband has tracked me down.'

'Your husband? You mean my favoured guest Big Master Fung?' I pulled the bed sheet up over my chilled shoulders.

She nodded.

'Are you sure? How do you know?'

'I've been followed.'

'Teng Xiong, why didn't you tell me earlier?'

'Because I didn't want you to worry. Besides, only recently have I been quite sure of it.'

'How?'

'I've noticed in the audience a pair of eyes that follows me everywhere. At first I thought it must be some devoted opera fan. But then I noticed that instead of admiration, the eyes are full of spite. This man is not an admirer, but someone who comes with an evil purpose.' She stared at me intently. 'Remember that man with a missing finger in the supper club?'

I nodded.

'You thought he was sent by your Mama and De to follow you, and I assured you that he was not. I should have realised then that he was sent by my husband to track me down.'

'But Teng Xiong, you're disguised as a man, so how can they—'

'Precious Orchid, I work in a female opera troupe and I was an opera singer before Fung took me as his concubine.'

'Oh, my heaven! Do you think they've also noticed me as your lover?'

'I don't think so, not yet. But that's what I worry about.' Teng Xiong's fingers kept twisting the bed sheet, which was now all crumpled over her body like a mummy's wrapping. 'People in Shanghai thought you ran away with a man, and I can't see how anyone would know about our real relationship. But Fung's underlings are relentless, and sooner or later they'll find out.'

'Oh, my heaven! But how do you know it's Big Master Fung?'

'Who else?'

A long silence. Teng Xiong spoke again. 'Precious Orchid, I meant to tell you earlier, but just didn't have the heart.' She swallowed hard. 'Now I have to quit the opera troupe and leave you before it's too late.'

'Teng Xiong, I'll leave with you.'

'No.' She looked so determined that my heart sank. 'After they've verified my identity, I'll be in big, big danger. I don't want you to be involved in this. Fung is capable of anything.' She cast me a penetrating look. 'He was a warlord before he turned businessman.'

The word sent a tremor across my chest. 'A warlord? You've never told me that.'

She ignored me and went on, 'Not only had he killed innocent civilians, he even shot his own daughter.'

I blurted out, 'My father was also murdered by a warlord!'

'Your father, how?'

'The warlord didn't actually kill him, but had him executed.'

Although I'd let Teng Xiong explore my body like an adventurer setting foot on new territories, remembering my mother's farewell warning, I'd never told her about how Baba had died.

Not until now. I blurted out everything about my past.

When I finished, Teng Xiong's face was as white as the bed sheet. 'Oh, my heaven, I believe Fung was the one who had your father executed!'

It took me seconds to absorb this revelation. Then my heart began to beat like hailstones pounding on a windowpane. 'Are you sure?'

'Yes. Because I was there that night. I witnessed the whole incident.' She blinked hard, as if by so doing she might wipe the horrible images from her mind. 'It was a horrendous sight. The three were entangled, struggling to get the gun. Finally the girl succeeded in snatching it from Fung's hand. The fiddler – your father! – tried to snatch it back but she kicked him in the groin. Then Fung grabbed the gun back. His daughter seemed to go insane. She jumped on her father and started to scratch and bite. The fiddler tried to disentangle them. And that's when the gun in Fung's hand went off and it shot the girl right between her eyes . . .' Teng Xiong pointed at her third eye. Her other eyes looked as horrified as if she were the one who'd been shot.

I lifted her hand from her face and held it. 'So the girl didn't shoot herself but was shot by Fung?'

Before Teng Xiong could reply, I told her what people believed to be the 'truth' – that the warlord got drunk and raped his daughter. Humiliated, the girl grabbed her father's gun and shot herself. When she was struggling with her father for the gun and everyone stood by in horror, my father – the fiddle player – tried unsuccessfully to pull them apart and snatch away the weapon.

Teng Xiong said emphatically, 'No, the girl didn't shoot herself. Fung shot his own daughter.'

An explosion burst inside my head. I could almost see my voice leap out in the air, splashing like blood all over the wall. 'He also murdered my father!'

A long silence followed during which I was too stunned to utter a word. I couldn't comprehend that Big Master Fung, my favoured guest, who turned out to be Teng Xiong's husband, was also the warlord who'd had my father executed. I'd travelled all this way only to discover that the person whom I'd been looking for had been right in front of my eyes for all these years. I'd slept often with my father's murderer!

My throat felt dry; my hands trembled, and my mouth kept muttering, 'Oh my heaven!'

Teng Xiong reached to hold me. 'Please calm down, Precious Orchid.' Then she released me to take the pot and pour us tea.

I sipped slowly, ignoring the burning sensation in my mouth. 'I had no idea . . . he was my customer for all these years, but he never said anything about himself or his family.'

A long pause, then Teng Xiong cast me a meaningful glance. 'Was he nice to you?'

'In a way, yes. He was generous in buying me gifts.'

She searched my face. 'You know why he was nice to you?' She plunged on, 'Because you reminded him of his daughter. Like you, she had two dimples. But hers were much deeper, so deep they almost looked like two iron brackets imprisoning her. But,' Teng Xiong sighed, 'her real prison was her father's obsession. Fung loved his daughter too much for a father.'

'Then he raped her?'

'I'm sure he did. Sometimes I think he might have killed her on purpose.'

I was shocked to hear this. 'But why?'

'Because she was getting older and might reveal what he had done to her.'

Some silence, then I reached to touch her.

Teng Xiong caught my hand and kissed it. 'Since the first day I'd entered Fung's household, I thought of running away. After seeing him shoot his own daughter, I knew I *had* to. We knew he'd kill anyone who leaked a word about what had really happened.' She paused, then spoke again. 'Since his daughter's death, he's declined rapidly.'

'Why is he not in trouble?'

'Because he's still very rich. It's not easy to eliminate a person whose safes spill enough gold to blind your eyes.' Teng Xiong searched my face. 'Precious Orchid, your father was a brave man. Too brave for his own good.'

In my mind's eye, I saw Baba, blindfolded and hands and feet locked in thick chains, being escorted to the execution ground. His feet were dragging, not because of fear, but because the chains were heavy and cutting deep into his flesh. Blood and pus oozed from the ankles where I could smell rotten flesh. The King of Hell was impatiently waiting for him with sharp-nailed claws. Yet Baba's expression was calm, even proud. Because his conscience was clear. His only wrong was doing something right – refusing to be contaminated by the evils of the human heart.

The executioners lifted their rifles and aimed at Baba. To them, he was just another target for their daily practice. Another unknown victim among a half-billion Chinese. Baba's eyes flickered under the blindfold. His lips moved. But nobody knew what he was thinking or trying to say at his last moment in the red dust.

'Bang!'

The explosion ended both Baba's pride and suffering.

Blood, like crimson lizards, popped from his temple, scurried down his cheek, then leaped onto the ground.

Now the wall behind him was bare, for my baba had become a crumpled heap on the ground . . .

The scene was terrifying but then the words came back to me: One does not live under the same sky as his father's murderer. I now knew what was next for me.

'Teng Xiong, we have to separate anyway because I will go back to Shanghai, to Peach Blossom.'

She grabbed my arms. 'Precious Orchid, are you out of your mind?'

'I didn't stay alive to be a whore. Revenging my father has been my secret reason to live. I'd almost given up hope that I could find this warlord. Now it must be heaven's will that you have told me who he is.'

'Precious Orchid, please listen to me. You can't succeed in getting revenge; he's still too powerful! Even if you kill him while you're serving him in bed, imagine the consequences. It's not worth losing your life for a monster!' Now Teng Xiong was pleading. 'Precious Orchid, forget what I told you. Pretend it was a nightmare.'

'I can't.' I gulped down the scorching tea. 'I have to go back.'

'Precious Orchid, please. We've gone through all these dangers to find our freedom, so don't be a fool now. Besides, Fang Rong and Wu Qiang won't let you go unpunished for escaping!'

'The worst is they'll put me in the dark room for a few days, I can stand that. Teng Xiong, I'm sorry, but I have to go back to Shanghai.'

'Please don't! Besides, you don't have enough money to go back, do you?'

I flinched. Suddenly I realised I'd been living mainly on Teng Xiong's money – I made hardly any from the opera troupe. And her money was, in fact, Big Master Fung's money, meaning my father's murderer's blood-smeared money!

Teng Xiong spoke again. 'Before we go our separate ways, I'll give you some silver. But I'm afraid it won't last long, since we've already spent most of it.'

'How come?'

'Precious Orchid, all these expensive hotels and elegant restaurants . . .'

I was barely listening, so right after Teng Xiong finished, I said, 'Then I'll work as a prostitute again to save up money.'

She threw me a penetrating glance. 'Precious Orchid, listen to me, forget about revenge and go on with your life. I'm terribly sorry that I can't help you anymore. I am now but a clod of mud dissolving into the sea – I can hardly help myself. We must go our separate ways. I'm not going to tell the opera troupe and neither should you, but if they see you and ask about me, just tell them you have no idea where I am.'

'Where will you go?'

'I'm sorry, Precious Orchid, but I won't tell you because I don't want you to be in danger. Just forget about me and go on with your life. But don't worry too much, I'll be fine. You take good care of yourself.'

I doubted she really thought she'd be fine. Her words sounded almost like a funeral song to me. I shivered. She drew me into her arms and pulled up the bed sheet, then we cuddled against each other.

Teng Xiong gently released me, went to open a bottle of wine, and poured us both full cups. The two cups hit, giving out a tiny explosion.

'Precious Orchid, *ganbei . . .*' Unable to go on, she tilted her head and drained her cup.

I lifted my cup and poured the wine down my mouth. The bittersweet liquid inflamed my throat then, like a fiery snake, undulated down my oesophagus. I put down the cup and began to sing 'Beyond the Yang Pass' – *a capella,* since I didn't have my *qin* with me any more. Teng Xiong joined me. In the sadness of the evening, her voice sounded so pure that all my worries and fears seemed to dissolve in its romantic lingering.

Tears swelled in both of our eyes. Tears of joy. When suffering reaches its peak, there can only be total letting-go, from which exultation emerges.

Please drink one more cup of wine
Once you've gone beyond the Yang Pass, there'll be no one
for you.
After today's farewell, we can only express our longing in
dreams . . .

29

Replaying the *Pipa*

The next day, as I had dreaded, Teng Xiong was gone. She must have put something into my drink to make me oversleep. On the table, I found a leather pouch with silver coins and a letter.

> *My Dearest Precious Orchid:*
>
> *Sorry that I have to leave without saying goodbye. I wish I could have left you more money but what I took from Fung has mostly been spent – on supporting the opera troupe and the two of us. I'm not complaining; I just want you to understand.*
>
> *Pack your belongings and move on as quickly as possible. Please don't try to find me. Because not only will you put yourself in danger, it'll be of no avail.*
>
> *Only Old Heaven will decide whether our paths cross again in this or another lifetime. My only wish is that if we meet again in this floating world, you'll be able to love me. Sometimes I wish we had died under the moonlight, cuddling against each other inside that bell. That would have been a lovely ending for us, don't you think?*
>
> *I hope I can have the good Karma to be reborn as a man in my next life so you can finally love me with one mind and one heart. I pray that your Karma will be better than mine. Take*

good care of yourself so you will have a long and happy life.
Please pray to Guan Yin that my next life will be a better one.
My last thoughts will be of you.
May Heaven bless us till we meet again.

Teng Xiong.

Tears pooled in my eyes, then spilled onto the letter, smearing Teng Xiong's characters and transforming them into miniature corpses.

Slowly my eyes wandered to the window and rested on the fish-belly white of the morning sky. Then, seized by a panic, I pulled out my luggage and started frantically to pack.

Once again, I felt completely alone in the world. I dared not stay around the opera troupe and so I hid myself in a shabby inn and slept to forget my worries. The thought of going back to Qing Zhen flickered, but now that I really could do it, I realised even if I could face the man I had deserted without a goodbye, I could not face life again in that bare temple on the lonely mountain. The only person I had left now was my mother, but I still had no idea where she was. Alone in an unfamiliar city, finding her seemed beyond hope.

Days and weeks passed. Then suddenly, to my alarm, I noticed the money Teng had given me had already run low, leaving only enough for a few more frugal weeks.

My plight struck me all over again as I dropped onto my bed. 'Oh heaven, what am I going to do?' I thought out loud.

When my initial fear had waned, another idea emerged – to re-play the *pipa*.

I jolted. Was it my Karma to live out all my days as a prostitute?

Though dismayed by the idea, I couldn't think of any other way to get out of my predicament. It took me three agonising days to make up my mind. After that, as if on cue, things just fell into place.

It all happened by chance.

The owner of the inn where I stayed was a woman in her late forties, and a retired prostitute. Seeing that I was alone, depressed, and beautiful, one time she asked me if I needed help. Although the question was posed in the most courteous manner, I immediately understood she knew that I'd been a fellow sister. To my chagrin, flower girls seemed to emit a special scent which could easily be detected by their 'comrades.' But now I almost felt relieved that she had sniffed me out. It saved so much time now that we each knew who the other was.

She introduced me to Immortal Cloud – a high-class pavilion like Peach Blossom. But unlike Peach Blossom, Immortal Cloud was new and very small in scale, with only a few girls. Although I still looked young and beautiful, at twenty-three, I was considered declining from my prime in comparison to the fifteen- and eighteen-year-olds. However, the younger ones lacked my sophistication in the arts and skill at pleasing.

It did not take long for me to become quite popular.

I changed my name again. Now I was Meng Zhu – Dream Pearl. A name to commemorate Pearl.

I told the mama that I would be independent, meaning that I didn't belong to Immortal Cloud but would give them a share of what I earned. The mama said that temporary sisters keep a third while the pavilion gets the rest. The deal was harsh, but I had no choice. I also had to pay the hotel owner a commission for introducing me to Immortal Cloud. No doubt she also got one from the pavilion.

Of course I had no intention of working here long, only long enough to save up money so I could go back to Shanghai and settle with Fung. After that, if I escaped, I would devote however many years it took to finding my mother. So I deliberately kept a low profile, acting pleasing to everybody and never involving myself in any gossip or quarrels between the girls.

Besides my beauty, talent, and skill in the bedchamber, my customers also liked me because of my Shanghainese accent, which rendered me exotic and mysterious. Why would a girl come all the way from Shanghai to Peking to plunge herself into the domain of the amorous and decadent? They'd probe but all they got in response were flirtatious smiles, darting glances, and provocatively massaging hands.

I had no interest in befriending any of the three other sisters in Immortal Cloud. Not only had I become very suspicious of people, but I simply didn't feel like opening up to make new friends. None of the girls here could be compared to Pearl.

Life was not difficult here. However, though the other sisters were always pleasant to me, I could not help but fear that someday one would play Red Jade to my Pearl. The mama, though hardly as imposing as Fang Rong, still made me uneasy. I could see her brows furl when customers selected me over her own sisters. Of course with them, she kept nearly all of their earnings.

Even more disquieting, being back in a turquoise pavilion continually reminded me of my old friends. I particularly missed Spring Moon and worried about her. I was sure she'd be fine so long as things went smoothly, but if not, she'd be in trouble, for she lacked cunning and had no talent to protect herself. Now all I could do was to pray for her.

Sometimes I'd also wonder whether I should take revenge on Red Jade for Pearl's suicide. But whenever this thought arose, I'd remember Pearl's admonition in her last letter:

> *Don't try to revenge . . . I don't want any trace of bitterness in my heart while I'm leaving this dusty world for paradise . . . It's very bad Karma, for it'll eventually turn on you.*

However, if I did run into her someday, I was not sure what I would do. Spit into her face or stab her first with a smile and then with a knife? But these were merely fantasies, for now she'd never travel alone but would always be accompanied by maids and bodyguards. I cursed fate – now she'd become a rich and famous movie star while I'd lost everything and was forced to replay the *pipa*.

Nevertheless, Pearl's teaching and my talent for the work paid off. Only a few months after starting at Immortal Cloud, I'd built up my fame and accumulated a fair number of regular customers. Since I was independent, I could choose my clients. I only picked those who were rich and generous while avoiding poor scholars.

Some good Karma must have ripened because the Immortal Cloud Pavilion's most important customer, Mr. Ouyang, began to take an interest in me. He was extremely rich and powerful – the military chief of Peking. Like most men of his age, he was married with a wife, several concubines, and many children. Yet none of the women of his household were able to please and satisfy him as I could. He told me that his first wife, frigid and sombre, had been uninterested in sex for a long time. However, even during the earlier times of their marriage, he'd never succeeded in persuading her to experiment with any of the beneficial positions. One time when she'd finally agreed to try the 'banquet in the backyard,' she became so stiff and frightened that it instantly killed Ouyang's remaining appetite. And from his three concubines – one neurotic, one scheming, one simply stupid – came nothing but bickering and trouble. He had been with many *ming ji* in the past but flattered me that none could match my beauty and talent.

In fact, before I arrived, he had sometimes visited with Soaring Swallow, the prettiest of the other sisters. As he began to choose me instead of her now each time he visited, I could tell that a difficult situation was developing. Fortunately, a solution arrived. Though I wouldn't say that Ouyang couldn't live without me, he definitely didn't feel happy unless he saw me at least twice a week. And so the day came when he asked me to serve him exclusively. A rare chance that most flower girls could only dream about, so of course, I agreed. So Ouyang rented an apartment for me fifteen minutes' drive from his office. This way, not only did he not have to share me with the others, he could see me every day after work before he went home. Sometimes during lunch hour he'd even come for a brief 'rain shower.' To have only him to deal with was unexpected good fortune. So I did my best to make him feel attached to his part-time home by perfuming the apartment and decorating it with fresh flowers, then serving him nutritious homemade soup and delicate dim sum.

To show his wealth and regard for me, Ouyang hired a maid and bought antique furniture and curios to furnish our apartment. But among all these ornaments, there was only one which I deemed truly valuable – a calligraphy scroll done by Ouyang himself. Though his strokes were just average, his powerful position gave it protective powers – few would chance offending the military chief of Peking. Besides the power implicit in his signature and red seal, I also liked the poem from the *Book of Songs*:

Fair fair, the ospreys cried
On an island in the river
This noble lady, so lovely,
Befitting to be the nobleman's bride.

With the indirectness of ancient Chinese poetry, this would be read as a warning not to touch his woman – me. Not only did I feel flattered by Ouyang's appreciation, I was impressed by the subtle way he revealed his power through his calligraphy. Even though no one knew about our relationship (except a few of his guards and underlings), I felt safe with such a powerful *hufa* – protector of the Dharma – as my admirer.

Sometimes Ouyang had to go abroad for meetings and stopped coming for several weeks. At first I was happy to be left alone, but I quickly got bored. When the weather was good, I'd hire a car or a rickshaw to visit the famous scenic spots – the Forbidden City, the Temple of Heaven, the Summer Palace, Fragrant Hill Park. My favourite part of the city was Liuli Chang where an abundance of stores sold books, curios, and art supplies. The girls in the art shop began to treat me with great respect, for at each visit I'd buy the most expensive items – ink stones embellished with gods and mythical beasts; ink sticks decorated with gold leaves; the best-quality brushes and *xuan* rice paper. When tired, I'd go to a nearby tea house, order a pot of the first-rate Iron bodhisattva tea and a plate of roasted watermelon seeds. Between sips of the steaming amber liquid, I'd crack open a seed's husk, tease out the kernel with my tongue, then chew while watching life stream by outside the window. After I finished my ritual of cracking open watermelon seeds and meditating on life, I'd go home. But faced again with my lonely house, I'd wish for Ouyang to return quickly to shower me with gifts.

One time when Ouyang was back from a trip to Nanking, he said, 'Dream Pearl, since this trip was extremely successful, I decided to thank the Buddha for his blessing. So two weeks before the Lunar New Year, I'm going to sponsor a big-scale Water and Land Ceremony in the Pure Lotus Temple.' He paused to search my eyes. 'And since you've also brought me good luck, I want you to come with me.'

I was surprised and glad to hear this. 'Then what about your wives, aren't you supposed to bring them?'

'Yes, of course.'

'But they may—'

'Don't you think they know who's the boss?'

I considered that for a moment. 'Then what about the nuns—'

'Dream Pearl,' he cut me off again, 'I don't think they're interested to find out about my wives or lovers. I wonder if they can even tell. Besides,' he laughed a little, 'as Buddhists, they are supposed to be non-discriminating, aren't they?'

After hearing for weeks about the plans for the Water and Land Ceremony, I was overjoyed when the first day finally arrived. I spent two hours putting on make-up, combing, and styling my hair. Then I picked out my best dress – a purple silk cotton gown with pink and pale orange embroidery along the high collar, sleeves, and edges. Over my ear, I pinned a fresh orange peony. Although I possessed my natural body fragrance, I still generously applied the expensive French perfume Mr. Ouyang had bought me.

At six-thirty in the morning, Ouyang and I arrived at the Pure Lotus Temple in his large, black sedan. To my surprise, the temple was not atop a lofty peak but stood right at a noisy intersection in the middle of Peking, south-west to the Xuanwu city gate.

When we were walking toward the gate in the cold air, I asked my favoured guest, 'Mr. Ouyang, shouldn't a large temple be in the quiet and purity of the mountains, far from the smoke and dust of a city?'

He cocked an eye at me. 'Nowadays monks and nuns like to build their sanctuaries right in the middle of the red dust where the big donors are.'

'Is that so?' I asked, stepping across the threshold.

Veiled by the morning haze, the monastery looked languorous and sleepy. Its yellow roof tiles and saffron-coloured walls, like a maiden's shy face, peeked through the white haze. A light winter breeze wafted in pleasant odours – a mixture of vegetarian cooking and sandalwood incense. Only when I saw shaved-headed and grey-robed women hurrying in the courtyard did I feel that I was in a nunnery.

I turned to ask my big protector of the sexual Dharma, 'Mr. Ouyang, why did you pick this temple for the ceremony?'

'I didn't. It's my first wife. She comes here regularly to make offerings, so she knows the nuns well, especially the Mother Abbess – she's the most important nun in Peking, always holding big ceremonies and getting huge donations.'

Across my mind flashed not the image of the abbess, but that of a skinny, elderly, and sad-looking woman – the *yuan pei* – first wife, of Mr. Ouyang. This character type was depicted many times in novels and operas. Victims of the passage of time, they had inexorably been transformed from young, pretty, and lively girls to fat (or emaciated), wrinkled, and tiresome old hags. Some turned mean, their only remaining pleasure being venting their bitterness on their maids and daughters-in-law. Others turned taciturn and gloomy, letting their existence wane in quiet desperation. Many, having nothing left to hope for in the red dust, turned vegetarian and escaped into the world of sutras.

In my mind, I pictured the *yuan pei* withdrawing from her lavish quarters into her altar room, to seek the company of statues of Buddha and Guan Yin. Disgusted to be around humans, she'd turn a blind eye and deaf ear to gossip and strife among the concubines and daughters-in-law. The only sounds with which she felt intimate were the monotonous clanging of her wooden fish, muttered prayers, and the clicking of beads clenched in clawlike fingers. I wondered: Once in a while, would her beads' tassel brush against her thigh and awaken her sensuality, stirring memories of her happier, sexier past?

Suddenly I felt a pang of sympathy toward this woman whom I'd never met. I assumed that since she frequented a nunnery, she must belong to this gloomy type of first wife who sought escape from her sorrows behind the altar's billowing smoke. I knew I was lamenting all women's fate, including my own. If I were lucky to meet someone who'd love me and marry me, where would his love be in ten or twenty years? Even if I had the good fortune not to be deserted, I might end up just as I imagined Mr. Ouyang's *yuan pei*. Yet, however miserable her lot, a *yuan pei* was still lucky, for not only was it a great honour to be addressed as Mistress of the House, the title also bestowed privileges that a concubine could never dream to obtain.

I blurted out to Ouyang, 'How's your first wife?' then suddenly realising I was one of the causes of this woman's pain.

He cast me a curious glance. 'She never causes me any trouble as long as I pay for everything. She never had much education, but she has learned when to leave a man alone.' He went on as if talking to himself, 'I give her what she wants.'

Yes, everything except love, I wanted to say but swallowed my words.

We were now approaching the Hall of the Grand Heroic Treasures. Under the imposing yellow roof, sonorous chanting and billows of incense wafted through latticework windows. Judging from the numerous nuns and black-robed lay followers milling around, I was sure this temple's incense had been burning strong and bright. Off to the side I spotted a Buddha statue on top of which hopped a pigeon, its beak pecking at the Enlightened One's eyes.

Just then a young nun hurried to us and made a deep, respectful bow. 'Mr. Ouyang, this way, please. Your wives are already waiting inside the inner altar.'

Ouyang nodded, then signalled me to follow the novice. If his wife and concubines were here, then where would my position be? Feeling ridiculous, I turned to search Ouyang's face. 'Mr. Ouyang, I think I really shouldn't have come.'

He grinned, his brown, broad face flushed under the soft morning light. 'Don't worry. Infinite Emptiness will guide you around and take you to your place.'

While I walked behind him toward the Grand Hall, the young nun began to explain to me about the ceremony. The lavish ceremony would last seven days. In a didactic tone she recited its five purposes as she marked them off on her fingers: preaching the Buddhist Dharma; making offerings to the Buddha; giving alms to monks and nuns; showing repentance for sins; and most important, blessing all sentient beings – both alive and dead.

I studied the novice nun. Though young, she was slightly stooped and had an unmemorable face. Perhaps her parents had put her in the nunnery thinking she had no hope to marry. With a serious expression, she went on to explain that it was called the Water and Land Ceremony because the objects of the blessings included creatures of the sky: birds, butterflies, mosquitoes, flies; creatures of earth: human beings, animals, ants, spiders, cockroaches, even bacteria; creatures of the rivers and oceans: fish, shrimp, turtles, crabs, sea slugs.

I almost chuckled when she mentioned flies, cockroaches, bacteria. Why would anyone care to bless these worthless creatures while so many human beings starved and died? But then when I thought better of it, I felt deeply moved. Buddhist compassion even encompassed these lowly beings!

Infinite Emptiness went on to tell me that the ceremony was divided into the inner and outer hall, and since Mr. Ouyang was the big protector of the Dharma, we'd go to the inner one where only a select few were allowed.

The outer hall was abustle with activity. Black-robed laypeople milled around, some sneaking curious glances at me in my heavy make-up and expensive fur coat. Monks and nuns were reciting sutras accompanied by beating on wooden fish and bronze mirrors. The chanting and reciting created a sound mandala, which seemed to fill the large hall with a sacred atmosphere protecting us from all evils. Special for the occasion were many large paintings showing all the creatures of water and land as well as gods, bodhisattvas, and Buddhas. From the high ceiling cascaded colourful banners embroidered with auspicious motifs. Swaying slightly, they looked like giant hands waving welcoming gestures.

We finally arrived at the inner sanctum. Two middle-aged nuns approached us with hands put together. *'O Mito Fo.'* Hail to the Buddha of Endless Life.

Mr. Ouyang and I put our hands together and bowed in response.

One of the nuns, who had a pinched expression under two thin brows, cast me an inquisitive glance, as if asking: Who's this heavily made-up and flashily dressed woman? My cheeks felt hot. I knew that were I not standing right next to the military chief of Peking, I'd never have been allowed in here. I had no real status – less even than Ouyang's seventh or eighth concubine. My position, if any, was dependent on this powerful man's whim. I knew he'd brought me here less from affection than from his conviction that I brought him luck.

Now the nun stopped her scrutiny of me and turned to address my favoured guest respectfully, 'Mr. Ouyang, the ceremony of purification will begin right away, now please follow us to join your family.'

'Infinite Emptiness *shifu*,' Ouyang said to the young nun, who had remained deferentially silent in the presence of the older ones, 'can you please take Miss Dream Pearl to the other side?'

I knew I wouldn't be allowed to sit with Mr. Ouyang during the official ceremony, but I could not help feeling hurt when I heard this. Nevertheless, as a kept woman, I obeyed my master and followed the nun. My heels' loud tappings seemed intrusive beside the soft rubbings of the nun's cloth slippers. Then my eyes caught the hollow glance of an emaciated, fiftyish woman in a corner. Behind her sat a small group of younger women. There were three of them, all dressed in matching *haiqing* – the black robes of lay Buddhists – and sharing the same sour expression. I knew they must be Ouyang's family. Carefully I scrutinised the un-made-up faces. The two older women – probably in their late thirties – might once have been beauties. But now the contours of their figures were slack elastic bands, and their sagging faces like empty rice bags. The youngest one was pretty but not attractive. With pale face and nervously darting eyes, she looked mousy and frightened – like a bird hopping hopelessly in a small cage. Seated behind the women were Ouyang's children. There were about ten of them, from toddlers to teens, also all wrapped in black. As the littlest ones squirmed to get loose, two women, no doubt maids, were trying desperately to restrain them.

Now all the women's eyes were riveted on me – their mutual enemy. If the first wife's hands were not languorously moving a strand of prayer beads, I might have mistaken her – with her ash-coloured face and dead-fish eyes – for an abandoned statue. The youngest concubine, head lowered, cast me inquisitive, upward glances with her timorous eyes. The two older 'rice bags' scanned me from head to toe and then back from toe to head, while talking to each other in intense, suppressed whispers. From their jealous expressions, I knew they had guessed who I was. I smiled to myself. I should be the one who felt jealous – of their status as the lawful first wife and concubines, their position in society as decent women under the protection of a rich, powerful man.

But I didn't.

Who were they to feel contempt for another woman? So what if I was a prostitute? Was their situation any better? If I was enslaved to men, then we all were. The only difference being that I was paid in cash, and they with status. I aimed a flirtatious smile at all the unhappy faces, then, in shredded-golden-lotus steps, followed the nun to my place in the corner, all the while wriggling my fur-covered bottom. After I sat down, I sensuously peeled off my fur coat to reveal my garishly embroidered silk cotton gown.

A hush fell over the hall as a plump, elderly nun led five younger ones through the entrance. Each held a flask in one hand and a willow branch in the other. As they walked, each of these bald-headed, sexless creatures would dip the branch into her flask, then flick the water into the air.

Infinite Emptiness leaned close to me. 'Our s*hifu* are now purifying the room with their magical Dharma water. When they are finished, the room will become a pure land.'

Pure land. The two words gave me a jolt. Nobody here could know that I also kept a pure land in my heart – my *qin*. Though my pure land was now lost, I firmly believed that someday it would come back to me.

After the purification, Infinite Emptiness told me that the nuns were now going to invite all the unearthly beings – Buddhas, bodhisattvas, heavenly deities, ghosts from the six realms – to descend into the hall to participate in the Water and Land Ceremony.

As I watched the nuns chant and mumble mystifying incantations, I wondered whether Pearl, Ruby, and my father were among the ghosts who would cross the boundary separating their *yin* realm from the living world of *yang*. Eerie chanting began to flood the room, sending chills up and down my spine.

The older nun now raised a banner to signify that the ceremony had officially begun . . .

30

Flight to Heaven

The next morning I feigned female discomforts and begged off attending the rest of the Water and Land Ceremony. I was bored by the interminable ceremony and weary of the angry stares of Ouyang's wives and the disapproving scrutiny of the nuns. On the last day, however, Ouyang insisted that I must attend the concluding ritual so as to receive merit.

'I paid a lot for this to get good fortune for you, so please don't waste my money,' he said chidingly.

A few more tedious hours at the ceremony were far preferable to antagonising my favoured guest, so I quickly agreed to go.

To show I was not intimidated by the wives and nuns, I took extra care with my make-up and dress. Once at the ceremony, however, I was as bored as before and found myself either daydreaming or dozing off until the crowd stirred at the announcement: 'Mother Wonderful Kindness Abbess is going to perform the ritual to send the deities back to heaven and the ghosts back to the *yin* world.'

Hearing that dramatic proclamation, I sat up straight, now fully awake. My eyes strayed to the windows as I idly wondered whether any ghosts would be going through them on their way home. Turning back, I saw a lean, fortyish nun pass through the gate and walk in measured steps toward the giant Buddha facing the entrance.

Behind her trailed a small retinue of young nuns, some beating wooden fish, others reciting sutras. I couldn't see the older nun's face but her immaculate saffron robe and the elegant way she walked told me she was Wonderful Kindness, the abbess.

The bald-headed entourage bowed and prostrated to the gilded Buddha, then continued to chant and walk around the hall. As they turned to head in my direction, I could see that the abbess's face, though slightly weathered looking, was actually quite handsome. As she neared my row; I looked up and met her eyes. To my surprise, as if detecting some dirt or scars on my face, she studied me for long moments. Then her calm, emotionless face transformed. It was hard to describe the change; all I could say was she looked as if she were greatly disturbed by what she saw, but desperately trying to hide her agitation. I assumed my heavy make-up, embroidered yellow silk gown (I'd refused to put on a black robe), and hair coiled on top of my head like a snake had provoked her discomposure. Perhaps she had already surmised that I was not a decent woman, but someone who belonged to the domain of the wind and moon, now tracking licentious mud into her pure land.

But something more was happening. The abbess continued to stare hard at me until I suddenly realised – as if struck by lightning – the reason for her scrutiny. This hairless, seemingly emotionless, and depressingly slack-robed woman was my mother!

I felt tossed into a dark well of anguish and shame.

My heart beat like a whip slashing on naked flesh. When I finally gathered my scattered *qi* and was about to address her, to my utter surprise, the nun silenced me with a sharp, meaningful glance and an imperceptible shake of her head. And then, turning away, she continued to perform the ritual as if nothing had happened!

I lost track of the ceremony until at the end I found my way out with the departing crowd. I feared my confusion would prompt questions from Ouyang that I was ill-prepared to answer. Fortunately he merely nodded toward me as he accompanied his wife, concubines, and children out the door. To my relief, the car he'd arranged was waiting right near the door. I quickly climbed in and pulled the curtains over the windows.

* * *

That evening, I flipped and tossed in bed like a fish frying in a wok. All these years my mother had been alive but never cared to write! She had even refused to acknowledge me – her only flesh and blood on earth. Now the abbess of an extremely successful nunnery in Peking, yet so heartless! I wondered which was the real teaching of Buddhism: compassion? or non-attachment? Would an enlightened being have been afraid to acknowledge her prostitute daughter? All these years, I had lived in the hope of being reunited with Mother. Now I'd finally found her – only to discover that she was ashamed of me!

I was also bewildered by how different Mother looked from that evening ten years ago when she had climbed onto the train. Her eyes, lustrous then, were now two dusty beads. Her cheeks were sunken and her forehead creased. Like the other nuns, her scalp was marked by twelve scars. Had my mother really become this austere abbess, or was she just another apparition like my dream of her on the mountain?

The next morning I woke up at six and put on the coarse, home-spun clothes and the worn robe Qing Zhen had bought me – and which I'd not had the heart to throw away. My puffy face in the mirror distressed me but I paused only a moment to try to hide it with some powder. Then I hired a rickshaw and headed straight to Pure Lotus Temple.

'Hurry, hurry!' I kept shouting to the coolie's skeletal back covered only with a thin, many-patched jacket. I listened to his grunts punctuating the traffic sounds. Memories of my mother from my childhood mixed with the image of the gaunt, shaven-headed nun I had seen yesterday. Both clung to my mind like hungry ghosts.

Would my mother turn out to be like Hong Yi, the legendary high monk? At the age of thirty-nine, he cut off all worldly attachments. Shortly after he'd become a monk, his young wife brought their two small children to the temple to see him. Resolved to overcome his attachment to his family, he had them sent away.

Had my mother refused to acknowledge me for the same reason?

As I approached the temple, I feared both that I would not see my mother and that I would see her. Would she scold me severely for the life I had been living, or even just for the gaudy clothes I had worn in her temple? Yet as much as I wanted to see Mother, I hated to cause her pain. I still remembered her agonised expression when she had recognised me. Would she be better off if she never again saw her prostitute daughter?

Shrouded in the chilly morning mist, the temple was silent. No fragrant guests clamoured in the courtyard. Yesterday's boisterousness and animation were replaced by a melancholic quietude. In the distance, a few nuns were doing their cleaning meditation. Snow drifts, like jilted women, mingled with yesterday's debris, adding a deserted feeling.

As I strode rapidly toward the main building, I saw a very young nun lumbering toward me. A pail bounced from each end of a bamboo pole, which cut deeply into her thin shoulders. Water kept sloshing and spilling onto her cloth-slippered feet.

I put my hands together, smiled, and said respectfully, 'Good morning, *shifu.*'

The young nun let the bamboo pole slip off her shoulders and the pails landed on the ground with a heavy thud. More water spilled. She smoothed her robe and wiped her forehead with the back of her small hand.

'Good morning, miss.' She smiled back, revealing melon-seed-like teeth.

'*Shifu*, I'm looking for Wonderful Kindness Abbess. Would you kindly tell me where she is?'

The young nun's thin brows knitted. 'Why do you want to find her?'

For a while I weighed how to respond. How would she react if I revealed I was her abbess's daughter? So I lied. 'It was Wonderful Kindness Abbess who asked me to come visit her today.'

Now the young nun looked even more puzzled. 'She did? But that's not possible.'

I felt colour rising to my cheeks. It was like Hong Yi! Mother must have left orders not to allow me to see her. I pulled my coat around my chest to ward off the chill. 'Why . . . not?'

'Because she's already left the temple.'

My heart raced. 'When?'

'Around five-thirty, right after she finished chanting her morning lesson.'

'But why?'

'No one really knows.'

'That's strange,' I smiled amicably, 'for she *did* ask me yesterday to come to visit her. So what happened?'

The young nun cast me a curious glance. 'Last night Wonderful Kindness Abbess told us she'd seen some strange visions during the ceremony, so she needed to go right away to the mountain to meditate. We can't tell anyone where she went. She said that she'll only be back when she's gained illumination. Eternal Purity *shifu* will take over the temple's affairs until she comes back.'

I was amazed by this news. 'Did Wonderful Kindness Abbess say what kind of visions she had?'

The young nun paused to look around nervously, then plunged on, 'She didn't, but Eternal Purity *shifu* noticed that Wonderful Kindness Abbess look disturbed and acted strangely toward the end of the ceremony. Eternal Purity *shifu* said she couldn't figure out why, since our abbess is always calm.

'Fortunately we have Eternal Purity *shifu* who's been assisting her in matters big and small, but still, no important decision will be made without Wonderful Kindness Abbess's permission. We just can't imagine life here without her, even for a few weeks. There are so many things waiting for her to decide. Oh, Wonderful Kindness Abbess does so many things! Like meeting with the big *hufa* to get donations, discussing plans about the next ceremony, expanding the temple, organising charitable deeds . . .'

I was trying to understand how my mother had changed since she'd climbed on the train to Peking ten years ago. I'd been too young then to have any idea of what might have awaited her, but now I realised how precarious things must have been for her. She might have arrived at the nunnery only to be turned away. Or allowed to stay but assigned the most menial tasks. Yet now, listening to this young novice's descriptions, I suddenly realised it had not been like this at all. In ten years, the fragile, introverted housewife I'd known as my mother had somehow worked her way up to become an important, decision-making 'business nun.' A change that Baba, I was sure, would have been unable to believe.

Then the irony seized me: Both my mother and I had become prestigious, albeit her as a nun and me as a prostitute!

I asked the young nun, 'Do you know which mountain the abbess has gone to?'

'The Empty Cloud Mountain.'

'Where is this Empty Cloud Mountain?'

'West of the Temple of Heaven, about twenty miles . . .' the young nun blurted out, then slapped a hand against her mouth. 'Oh heaven, I'm not supposed to tell this!'

I put on the warmest smile I could manoeuvre. 'Don't worry, *shifu;* I won't let anyone know where the abbess is.'

The young nun didn't respond, but stared at me with suspicion. Her almond eyes widened. 'Miss, I hope you are not going to find her; are you?'

I didn't answer her question, but asked instead, 'Do you know exactly where, I mean in which temple, she is dwelling?'

She wiped the moisture from her brows. 'But Eternal Purity *shifu* said Wonderful Kindness Abbess wishes to be left alone. No one's supposed to go look for her on the mountain. Only Eternal Purity *shifu* knows exactly where she is.'

'It is on a matter of extreme urgency that I'm looking for her.'

She cast me a suspicious glance. 'Then what is it and who are you?'

I was tiring of this nun's self-importance and almost wished I'd come wearing an expensive dress with conspicuous jewellery. With some annoyance I said, 'I'm sorry. I'm afraid I can't tell you. I can only tell the abbess herself.'

'Miss, we must all wait until Wonderful Kindness Abbess knows it is the right time to come back.'

There was no point in talking to her further, so I put my hands together, bowed, and took leave.

As soon as I got home, I began to pack for my trip to Empty Cloud Mountain. When Ouyang stopped in for his lunchtime rain shower with me, I told him that I had to go back to Shanghai for a week to attend my father's funeral. I felt a bit guilty about using my long-dead baba to cover up my lie, but since I was doing this to find Mother, I was sure Baba would forgive me.

The next day, when the sky outside the window was still as dark as ink smeared on rice paper, I leapt out of bed and quickly dressed in a plain padded top and trousers. I took only a few things with me – an umbrella, another set of clothes, a quilted jacket, rice cakes, hard-boiled eggs, and a pouch filled with silver and copper coins. Then, when I was already outside the apartment, I remembered something more important and dashed back – to grab the four *fu* amulets Qing Zhen had painted for me. Since I had no idea where in the mountain Mother was staying, I decided, like last time when I'd travelled with Teng Xiong on Taiyi Mountain, to start from the base and work my way up. Whether I'd find her or not was entirely up to my Karma.

After a long, tedious ride in a hired car over bumpy roads, I finally arrived at the base of the mountain. Peddlers selling incense and other Buddhist paraphernalia accosted me but I waved them away. Finally I agreed to pay an excessive amount to two coolies to be taken up the mountain in a sedan chair. We stopped at the gate of one temple after another, as I asked about my mother. Some had already heard of Wonderful Kindness's disappearance and, sipping their tea noisily, threw out endless conjectures about this abrupt departure, never imagining that the cause was right in front of their eyes. When asked why I was looking for the abbess of Pure Lotus, I answered that I wanted to entreat her to be my Dharma teacher. Many looked at me curiously but none enquired further.

Five days had passed, and as I worked my way higher and higher up the mountain, I still hadn't any word about where my mother was. When night fell, a temple would carry out its compassion by inviting me to stay the night and to eat in their Fragrant Kitchen. To repay their kindness, I'd drop some copper coins into their Merit Accumulating Box – depending on their degree of hospitality. Though disappointed, at least I had the good luck not to be discovered by bandits. Having learned my lesson painfully, I avoided any hidden path and did not travel at night.

On the afternoon of my sixth day on the mountain, the weather suddenly turned bad. Curtains of rain swept over the path, shaking the trees, knocking down leaves and mercilessly pelting the roof of my sedan chair. The wind picked up speed, attacking like a ferocious beast. Soaking wet and battered by this invisible enemy, the coolies stumbled a few times before they finally spotted a temple. Then they demanded that I double their payment, not only for their hard work, but also because it was Chinese New Year. I'd completely forgotten the approaching holiday. Would heaven grant my New Year's wish of reuniting with Mother?

The abbot of the small monastery was an old man with a large head and a small torso. After he led me into a small reception room, he pointed to a rattan chair and invited me to sit. Though he had a kindly look, I somehow felt I should not intrude too much on his quiet life on the mountain. So, as soon as we were settled and a young monk came in to serve tea, I came straight to the point, expressing my intention to find Wonderful Kindness Abbess from Pure Lotus Temple.

The old monk looked at me intently, his eyes clear and bright. 'Miss, there are many nuns on this mountain.'

'Do you know her and where she is?'

He nodded. 'One time when Pure Lotus carried out a big ceremony for the release of hungry ghosts, she invited many temples to join, including ours.'

'But do you know where she is now?'

'Miss, I think you should go back to Peking.'

'Master, why . . . shouldn't I look for her?'

He caressed his smooth, shiny scalp. 'It's too dangerous for a young girl like you to be travelling alone on this mountain. You're lucky that you haven't run into bandits, so the Buddha must be protecting you. And if you want to learn Dharma or meditation, there are many teachers around. Besides, even if you find her, that doesn't mean she'll agree to teach you. We monks and nuns come to Empty Cloud Mountain to be left alone.' He paused to sip his tea, then said, 'She might feel disillusioned by her hectic life in a city temple. In those big temples, you have to go around begging rich people for money instead of meditating and studying sutras.

'Wonderful Kindness Abbess is very famous, but I'm sure she knows well that all worldly achievements are transient.' He looked at me sharply. 'So, miss, I think you should leave her alone. She must have exhausted herself while trying to be enlightened by the Water and Land Ceremony. Please leave her to the peace of the Dharma.'

Now the young monk began to refresh our tea. 'Master,' he said eagerly – obviously he'd been listening to our conversation – 'I heard that in the big ceremony, a flower girl got into the inner altar room . . .'

I felt a jolt inside.

The old monk cast a sharp glance at his disciple before he turned to me. 'Miss, I think that I and young *shifu* here have talked more than we should.' Now he said to the young monk, 'Bring this miss to her room and get her some dinner. But please don't bother her with any more talk.'

The next morning, although the rain hadn't stopped, I decided to go on with my search.

When I took leave of the old monk, he exclaimed, 'Miss, I hope I didn't say something to make you leave! You're most welcome to stay as long as you want.'

'*Shifu*,' I put my hands together and made a deep bow, 'I'm extremely grateful for your generosity. But I just want to go on with my trip.'

'Why not stay until the weather is completely clear? The paths are very slippery now. It's not safe.'

'There's no real safety in life anyway.'

'I agree with you.' He cast me a curious glance. 'But that doesn't mean we shouldn't be careful. Buddhism also tells us to take good care of ourselves.'

I conveyed my regret that I must take leave.

He gave in. 'Then let me give you a simple blessing before you go.'

* * *

Watching the rain streaming outside the sedan chair, I thought maybe I should have listened to the abbot and given up my search. The trip had exhausted not only me, but also my wallet. I'd stuffed too much money into too many Merit Accumulating Boxes, and tipped the coolies far more generously than I should have.

Since my mother seemed to be running away from me, why didn't I just go home and forget about her? But I knew I wouldn't die with my eyes closed if I didn't see her, at least one last time.

I must have fallen asleep, for when I opened my eyes and looked outside, everything was white. This reminded me of Baba's hair – turning white overnight after the verdict of his execution had been passed. Then a famous scene from the novel *Dream of the Red Chamber* emerged in my mind. Tricked into marrying the wrong woman after the death of his true love, the young master Baoyu decided to cut himself off from all worldly entanglements and become a monk. When he stepped out of his grand mansion and headed toward the temple, he noticed that the whole world was covered with snow. 'How white, boundless, and pure!' he exclaimed, then plunged into the snowstorm and was never heard from again.

Suddenly the sedan chair bearers stopped, jolting me awake from my reverie. Ahead of us rose a long flight of stairs.

The puller in front turned around to look at me, his face wet and his hair white from the snow. 'Miss, I think the snowstorm is getting worse.'

The stout one now came from behind. 'And we want to go home.' He pointed a gnarled finger toward the steps. 'There must be a temple up there, so why don't you pay us and get off here?'

I craned my neck and looked. The long, narrow steps seemed to soar all the way to heaven. From the mountainside, branches stretched here and there, looking like esoteric symbols struggling to show me the way to enlightenment.

I turned back to the coolies. 'How do you know there's a temple up there?'

'I heard about it,' the skinny one shrugged, 'anyway, why else would all these steps be here?'

'But it looks like nobody's been there for a long time.'

'Miss, all temples here look like this.' He paused to wipe the moisture from his face with a filthy rag. 'Now we'll either drop you off here and you go up to find the temple yourself, or if you like, we can take you back.' He cast a glance at his comrade. 'We're going home before the storm gets any worse.'

I said to the two dark faces, 'Why don't you two wait for me here for an hour. If I don't come back, you can leave. If I do, I'll pay you double.'

They jabbered loudly to each other, their eyes darting around. Then the stout one said, 'We'll wait thirty minutes and you pay us three times – or else we don't wait.'

'All right.' I took a deep breath and blurted out, 'It's a deal.'

The climb *was* never-ending. I counted the steps: ten, twenty, thirty, fifty, one hundred, one hundred twenty, two hundred, three hundred . . . until my mind became a blur. And in the deepening snow, so did the steps. Tired and short of breath, I climbed very carefully, lest I lose footing and slide back down. My throat felt dry and my lips cracked. The inconsolable rumble of my stomach sounded like an old wife's incessant complaints. I took out a bun and chewed; it tasted like a salted stone.

As if this were not bad enough, the snow was beginning to soak through my clothes. I hugged my chest but that still didn't stop my body from shivering nor my teeth from chattering. My vision was blurred from my exhaustion and the glaring whiteness. I took out and opened my umbrella, but it was immediately blown away by the wind.

'Damn!' I spat.

Although now I could not see the top of the stairs, nor where I had started from, I somehow kept going. While my leather-booted feet continued to drag me upward, the question I dreaded began to harass my mind: What if there was nothing at the end of the steps?

I panicked, turned, and mustered all my strength to scream down to the coolies. But I heard nothing except faint echoes of my own voice bouncing off the rock cliffs. To avoid the strong wind swirling down the steps, I staggered against the wall to catch my breath. I called out again to the sedan bearers, but the buffeting wind immediately knocked the breath out of my chest.

They must have left without waiting for me!

My breath froze in my chest. I started to have a feeling like floating in space. Through the blur of snow, the world seemed small yet infinite. The deep imprints of my footsteps stared back at me like enlarged eyes. Tears rolled down my cheeks. I savoured the momentary sensation of warmth prickling on my skin.

I began to feel certain that there was nothing at the end of the stairs. This thought, spinning within, synchronised with the swirling snow without. Horrible thoughts entered my mind: When the storm was cleared, someone – a monk, a nun, a pilgrim, a bandit – would discover a corpse on these steps. The battered body would look as if suspended between heaven and earth. The eyes would be wide open, as if the deceased were still resisting being dragged down to hell, since her earthly wishes had been left unfulfilled. The monks and nuns whom I'd asked about my mother would recognise my face but my identity would remain an eternal puzzle. The local gossip newspapers would desperately try to discover who I was. When they failed, they'd just fill in the puzzle with a story from their wildest imagination – a runaway girl from a rich family, lost on the mountain on her way to meet her clandestine lover, accosted by bandits, raped, then brutally murdered . . .

I shivered from the thoughts as well as the bitter snow. My breath had become harsh and laboured; my lungs felt as if they were submerged in boiling water. Delirious, I looked up at the sky and muttered a prayer, 'Heaven, let me see my mother one last time before my last moment comes. If I have to die, let me die in her arms, please!'

But heaven, looking so white and pure, seemed completely oblivious to my prayer. Though my feet felt like icy marbles, they dragged doggedly one step after another while my mind danced in the swirls of dementia . . .

To lift my spirit, I began to sing – a medley of Peking opera arias and *qin* lyrics.

The strong wind whistled and moaned to accompany my songs. After more demented singing, suddenly I felt my feet land on something unexpected – level ground. I stood still, inhaling deeply to calm and focus myself.

My eyes looked around until they lighted on a haunting sight. A woman, bald-headed, her thin body wrapped in an equally thin robe, was meditating in the full lotus position. Behind her was a small, dilapidated temple.

The scene struck me with its terrible beauty. It was completely white except for the nun's black robe under the temple's crimson roof. For a fleeting moment I wondered if I was seeing a stone statue. Or a hairless ghost.

But, of course, she was neither a statue nor a ghost, but the woman who had been Beautiful Fragrance – my mother.

My heart fluttered like snow falling on a withered lotus. Despite my recent bitterness, now I felt only sorrow seeing her emotionless face and the shivering of her frail body.

Why was she torturing herself in the freezing cold?

Overwhelmed by emotion, I had no time to think. 'Ma, I'm here!' I screamed and sprinted toward the bell-shaped figure at full speed.

To my utter surprise, the nun continued to meditate as if she were both deaf and blind – or as if my running toward her was merely an illusion. Or had time stopped forever in her world?

I kept running and screaming 'Ma! Ma!' until I slipped and fell
. . .

31

The Reunion

When I woke up, I felt cocooned in something soft and warm. I looked up and caught my mother's eyes.

'Ma . . .' I didn't know what more to say. But now that I was in her arms, what more did I need to say?

My mother said, 'Rest more, Xiang Xiang.'

Tears rolled down my cheeks. The last time I'd heard my name from her lips seemed to have been in some remote, former incarnation. How strange my name sounded now, so sweet and yet so bitter to my ears. Its mere sound brought me back to my childhood when my father had been alive and handsome, my mother a happy wife and mother, and I an indulged child.

Although her hair was gone, her crown marred with scars, her smooth face replaced by a finely wrinkled one, her name changed from Beautiful Fragrance to Wonderful Kindness – she was still my mother.

Feeling strangely comfortable, I uttered another 'Ma . . .'

'I heard you, Xiang Xiang,' my mother said in her nun's calm voice. When she touched my face, I was shocked to see a row of small scars on her wrist.

'Ma, what happened?'

'I burned them.'

'But why?'

'Same as those on my head, as offerings to the Buddha.'

I searched her face. 'It must have hurt.'

'Not if you're enlightened.'

Enlightened. What would that be like?

I sighed inside, then looked at her and blinked hard – once, twice, three times, hoping that after each blink she'd be transformed back to the mother I'd known – young, beautiful, smooth-faced, scarless.

But after endless blinks, what I saw in front of me was still the same thin, bald-headed, scarred nun that I'd encountered in Pure Lotus Temple a few days – or an entire incarnation – ago.

My eyes misty and my mind confused, I fell asleep again.

When I woke up, sounds of clanking pots drifted into my ears together with my mother's voice. 'Xiang Xiang, I've cooked some simple vegetable dishes; they'll be ready in a minute.'

I looked out the window. The sky had turned completely dark. The snow and wind were still howling like hungry ghosts searching for food. Listening to the water dripping from the eaves, I thought of life draining from an hourglass and felt an unspeakable sadness. But soon it was replaced by a small joy when I heard the wind through the trees calling my name cheerily, 'Xiang Xiang! Xiang Xiang!' Swiftly I slipped off the bed, left my room, and went into the small hall. It was practically empty except for an altar bearing a wooden Buddha statue. In front of the Enlightened One rested several miniature bowls of rice and vegetables, still steaming. Two candles burning high on the altar cast pools of warm, cosy light into the room's four corners.

This remote place must have been neglected for a long, long time. But now the floors were swept clean as a polished mirror. With my mother's silhouette flickering in the kitchen next door, the familiar sound of her setting the table, and the aroma of food, this lonely temple actually gave the illusion of a home. Home! For how few years had I a real home to go back to!

Big Master Fung's image flashed across my mind. It was this shredded-by-thousand-knives monster who had pulled our whole family from paradise and sent it plunging to hell! I felt my entire being consumed by a burning sensation. *'Sha!'* Kill. I said to myself in a heated whisper, imagining Fung's head being hit by a bullet and spurting with blood, or chopped off by a cleaver and falling on the ground, bouncing away.

But Mother was calling my name gently, 'Xiang Xiang, come sit at the table, dinner is ready.'

I sat across from my mother. As I looked at the dishes, my heart felt a happiness mixed with pain. Our reunion dinner. On Chinese New Year. Finally.

'Ma,' I asked, 'do you know it's Chinese New Year?'

'We nuns don't pay much attention to secular festivals.'

I watched Mother's serious countenance and remembered how my parents, unlike most Confucian couples, would pat and touch each other in front of me. While most men, believing their wives inferior and their bodies contaminated, would stay away from the women's quarters except to have sex, Baba had been more than happy to help Mother with her make-up and wardrobe.

The burning sensation again overcame me. I'd changed from an innocent child to a scheming-hearted *ming ji*, my mother from an attractive woman to a sexless nun, and my father from a famous actor and fiddler to a wandering ghost. All as a result of Fung.

Oblivious of my boiling emotion, Mother said, 'Eat more, Xiang Xiang, even if you find vegetarian food tasteless,' and began to pile food into my bowl.

'Ma, you're a wonderful cook. Nothing that you prepare is tasteless.' I gobbled down chunks of food and drained cup after cup of fragrant tea. My chopsticks kept flicking onto the different plates and scraping rice into my mouth. Suddenly I noticed my mother was not eating but watching me with sad eyes.

'Ma,' I said, putting down my chopsticks, 'please eat, too.'

I thought I saw tears in her eyes, but I was not sure. Without a single hair on her scalp nor a single word from her lips, she picked up some rice, put it into her mouth, and chewed, slowly, as if she were doing some kind of eating meditation.

Finally we finished our meal and I helped Mother clear away the table. After that, she brewed more tea, then, holding the steaming cups in our hands, we sat opposite each other. We both knew the time had come when we had to reach into the darkest corners of our minds, drag out our secrets, and toss them under each other's light.

Mother wanted to know at once where I'd been and what I'd done, but I insisted that she tell me about herself first.

In a neutral tone, Mother began to recount her life from the first day she had entered Pure Lotus. Every day, besides chanting and meditation, she, as a novice, had to clean and cook, and labour outdoors. Seeing that the Mother Abbess was old and frail, she also nursed her, even willingly helping her with her nature's calls and emptying her chamber pot. It was this good Karma that led to her later success. Gradually the abbess developed such fondness for her that she trusted no other nun but my mother. Therefore, before she passed away, she'd named my mother her Dharma heir. Since then Mother had worked hard to transform Pure Lotus from a modest neighbourhood temple to the most influential nunnery in the city of Peking.

When finished, Mother said, 'Though I had no choice but to be a nun, I have done my best to advance the Dharma.' She paused to sip her tea, then, 'Because I understand suffering.'

I sighed inside. I also understood suffering, but that hadn't led me to become a successful nun, but a prestigious prostitute. However, according to Buddhism's ultimate point of view, there is no difference between the beautiful and the ugly, the wise and the foolish, the good and the evil. So under the same logic, did it mean that my nun mother was ultimately also a prostitute and I, a nun?

We quietly sipped our tea and listened to the wailing of the hungry ghosts outside.

Finally I pressed Mother for more details of her life as a nun. But she insisted that a nun should not dwell too much on her past, and that it was now my turn to tell her about myself. And since she'd already guessed my occupation, she asked me to be honest with her and tell her everything which had happened since our separation in 1918.

Painfully, I unfolded my story, starting from the moment I'd been taken away in the rickshaw by Fang Rong. Finally I told Mother how I'd found out from Teng Xiong that the ex-warlord who had been my big-shot customer was also the person who had Baba executed.

I told my mother everything – almost. I left out being raped, once by Wu Qiang and the other time by one of the bandits. And I described Teng Xiong simply as a woman friend.

After I'd finished, tears rolled down Mother's sunken cheeks. 'Xiang Xiang,' she sighed, reaching to touch my hand.

I felt a jolt. This was the first time Mother, as a nun, had displayed her affection for me so directly.

Her tight, self-contained voice rose in the air. 'As a nun, I can only say all that happened to you is the result of some past, inexplicable Karma. While as a mother, I can only say I'm sorry and ask for your forgiveness.'

'But Ma, it's just bad luck on my part, you didn't do anything wrong!'

'Xiang Xiang, I understand that you're trying to be kind. But I have to face my mistakes – I shouldn't have listened to Fang Rong. I should have checked her background carefully before I put you into her hands.'

'Ma—' I was about to say that this was all in the past, but then I realised it wasn't. My favoured guest, Mr. Ouyang, was still waiting for me to come back to his luxurious apartment to warm his bed.

Mother spoke again. 'Xiang Xiang, the only thing I can blame is your Karma, something bad you did in a past life that caused your sufferings in this one.'

I found this Buddhist idea of past lives quite ridiculous. I didn't even know who I'd been in my past life, so why should I be responsible for my supposed former bad deeds?

Mother cast me a long, meaningful glance. 'But Xiang Xiang, there's a way to eliminate your bad Karma.'

'How?' I thought of Pearl's similar saying: There was always a way to solve any problem in a turquoise pavilion. But then she'd hanged herself.

'Xiang Xiang,' Mother searched me intently, 'like me, you can take refuge in the three jewels and be a nun.'

Her words exploded in my ears like gunshots. But rather than attaining sudden enlightenment, I struggled to digest this preposterous suggestion. After I willed myself to calm down, I said matter-of-factly, 'But Ma, I am a prostitute.'

'Do you like being a prostitute, and prefer to stay one?'

'Of course not, Ma, but I have no choice!'

'Now you have. From now on, let Buddha take care of you.'

'But Ma, ten years ago at the train station, I asked you to take me with you, but you said the Mother Abbess feared my beauty would bring bad luck to the temple. You remember that?'

'Yes. But the Mother Abbess hadn't said anything like that. I made it up.'

'Why?'

'So that you wouldn't come with me. Because then I didn't want you to be a nun and waste your youth.'

'But then why do you want me to be one now?'

'Things have changed, Xiang Xiang. Because although you're still very beautiful, now there's no more bright future waiting for you in the red dust.'

I felt so confused that I didn't know what to say.

She spoke again, firmly, 'Now that I am the Mother Abbess, you can certainly enter the temple. Xiang Xiang, taking refuge in the *sangha* is your only future.'

I kept staring at my beloved mother now turned a nun and a stranger. Tears pooled in my eyes. Through my blurred vision, my mother seemed to change into a pinch-faced, mean-spirited, stubborn old woman like one imprisoned in a gloomy portrait above the altar of an ancestral hall . . .

'Xiang Xiang,' her dry voice rose again, 'let me ask you again. Do you like being a prostitute?'

Did I like being a prostitute? I opened my mouth, then realised this was an extremely complicated question to answer. Obviously I hated putting on a smiling face and serving those stinking males. I hated the way their eyes threw me licentious glances while their hands wandered to squeeze my breasts and pinch my bottom. I also hated the way they thrust their jade stalk into my golden gate even when I was guarding my *yin* days. The flopping sound they made when they sucked my tongue and tasted my saliva disgusted me. Even thinking of them now made my stomach churn.

And yet, I'd gotten used to the most delicate foods and the sensuous feeling of elegant silk on my body. Hardly a day went by without a gift from one of my admirers. I slept late every morning and had food brought to me in my room while I practiced the *pipa* or wrote a poem. I was appreciated for my refinements. But of course, I knew deep down that the reason all these men adored me like a goddess was because they knew I was but a captive, whose limbs could be twisted to adopt the most obsequious posture in life as well as in bed.

Though I'd been fortunate to run into a man like Qing Zhen whom I could love, it had meant giving up all the luxuries that life as a *ming ji* had brought me. With him I was free but, ironically, only because he could not satisfy my deepest needs as a woman – for a family and children.

I had no idea what a nun's life would be like. Could a lifetime of meditation and sutra chanting really pacify my soul and heal my wounds? Yet, if Mother had obtained the ultimate goal of non-attachment, why had she looked so upset when she'd spotted me in the Water and Land Ceremony? She must have feared that her name might appear in the newspapers' gossip columns and become a laughing stock. Worse, she might even lose all her important clients – those *da hufa*, big protectors of the Dharma – who donated huge chunks of money to her temple. But it was exactly these protectors of the Buddha Dharma, so judgemental and morally superior while in the temple, who made secret visits to the turquoise pavilions to protect the sexual Dharma.

I stared hard at Mother's pale face. 'Ma, why did you stop me from acknowledging you the other day?'

'*Hai*, Xiang Xiang,' she sighed heavily, then wiped a few more tears from her eyes, 'I know you'll never forgive me for that. I'm sorry that we had to reunite under such circumstances. But of course, as a nun, I do everything for a reason.' She paused, then went on, 'Xiang Xiang, in my eyes, prostitute or not, you're my daughter and you'll always be. However, I'm sure you know that if we'd acknowledged each other during the ceremony, the whole temple would have been shocked. Those rich people in the inner hall are extremely selfish. They only sponsor the ceremony to accumulate merit for themselves. So they'd be horrified to find out not only that the abbess has a daughter, but that she works behind the dark door. Believe me, Xiang Xiang, I wouldn't mind this at all. But as a nun, I am thinking not for myself, but for the well-being of my temple. You understand?'

Of course, I knew exactly what it took to get money from these rich men; I did it myself all the time. My eyes started to fill with tears again. It seemed that, though a nun, Mother was, after all, still living in this secular world, and had not escaped its smoke and dust. After she'd climbed her way to become the abbess of the most influential nunnery in Peking, she was still flopping in the sea of suffering.

'Ma, are you happy being a nun?'

'Xiang Xiang, the first noble truth of Buddhism says: Life is suffering. We don't think of happiness, just enlightenment.'

I really did not know what to think about this.

Mother went on, 'If we accumulate merit in this incarnation, the next one will be better.' She paused to cast me a penetrating look. 'Xiang Xiang, I believe good Karma has finally arrived because now you have the chance to become a nun. So please take refuge in my temple. Then we'll be together, always, until the day we enter nirvana.'

I remembered ten years ago just as she put me into the hands of Fang Rong, she said something similar: that I was lucky to have a roof over my head. But Mother looked sad, which broke my heart. 'Xiang Xiang, although being a nun is not easy, you'll gain merit and be greatly respected. Please, Xiang Xiang, take refuge in the *sangha*.'

I wanted to tell her that, as a *ming ji*, I was also respected. My poems had been passed around and eagerly read. Peach Blossom's door had been knocked on constantly by people who'd come to beg for my paintings and calligraphy. Some even searched the rubbish pails to see if they could find any shreds of my drafts to take home to be glued back together . . .

But I said instead, 'Ma, I can't predict the future, but now is not the right time for me to consider this.'

'Xiang Xiang, *now* is the only time that you can consider anything.'

'But I have to go back to Shanghai to find Big Master Fung.'

Mother looked horrified. 'Xiang Xiang, what for?'

'Ma, it's said that one does not live under the same sky as his parent's murderer. Now that I know who he is, I'll kill him as soon as I can.'

'Xiang Xiang! It's very bad Karma even to think of killing, let alone do it. Do you want to be reborn as a snake, or a rat? If you kill the warlord, do you think you'll be happy? Please meditate with me to clear your mind of such violent thoughts.'

'Ma, you know what kept me going all these years selling my skin and smile in Peach Blossom? The hope of finding you and revenging Baba!'

'Xiang Xiang, you've found me now.' She paused, then went on, 'I know you loved your father very much, and so did I. But he's dead, so stop poisoning your mind and let go of revenge. Please take refuge as a nun and stay with me in Pure Lotus.'

My mother had become so obstinate that I saw no point in trying to explain any further. To appease her, I said that I wouldn't revenge Baba, but made no promise to become a nun.

She didn't respond. I took her silence as acceptance.

Then suddenly I remembered something and blurted out, 'Ma, why didn't you write to me all these years?'

'Xiang Xiang, but I did, almost every week! But then two months after I arrived in Peking, I received a letter from Fang Rong telling me that you'd run away and no one knew where you were. She said you'd left Shanghai.'

She reached her hand inside her robe and took out a piece of torn, stained paper. Carefully she handed it to me. 'This was your address, right?'

I nodded, tears swelling in my eyes. 'Then where have all the letters gone?'

Mother answered my question with another one. 'It doesn't matter now, does it?'

32

Back to Shanghai

Mother and I had been reunited for only a week when Karma once again thrust us on separate paths. I told her that I had promised Mr. Ouyang that I'd be back soon and could not risk offending him. Mother would continue to meditate on the mountain until she decided it was time for her to go back to Pure Lotus. Now that my first goal – finding my mother – had been fulfilled, I set about accomplishing my second – avenging Baba. Telling Mother that I'd go back temporarily to Ouyang was not a complete lie, for sooner or later I would have to go back to my favoured guest, if not to offer my breasts as his pillows and my lips as his delicacies, then at least to bid him farewell.

Instead of saying, '*We can't beat fate, but we can play along and make the most out of it. Try to be happy,*' as she had ten years ago, this time Mother's admonition was simply, 'If your Karma is not to be a nun, Xiang Xiang, then you must follow where it leads you. I hope it will be to happiness.'

Back in Peking after a tedious train ride, Ouyang didn't come to the apartment to call on me. Since I'd had a death in the family, or so he thought, it would be bad luck for him to see me, especially during Chinese New Year. I wrote him that we should see each other only after the first lunar month. This gave me ample time for making final preparations for my trip to Shanghai. Of course, I took Qing Zhen's *fu*, which had protected me on the mountain. But for Peach Blossom, I brought another kind of *fu* – Ouyang's calligraphy. I sewed a brocade case so that the scroll would travel with the dignity it deserved. To Mama and De, the name of a powerful official would be far more magical than a Taoist charm.

To be sure I would be left alone during the long train trip, I booked a private compartment. When the train finally arrived at North Station in Shanghai, I alighted, quickly hired a car, and asked the driver to take me to the Cathy Hotel in the International Settlement. This elegant and expensive hotel was a popular place for rich guests to take courtesans. It was now a perfect match for my prestige, and would impress anyone whom I might run into from Peach Blossom. Now that I had money in my pocket and an aura of elegance and wealth emanating from me, I was sure the wind would be blowing in my direction.

For the first few days after I arrived, I did nothing but eat and rest. Dressed in my expensive gowns or sexy Western dresses, I'd glide down the black marble staircase, stroll through the hotel lobby to appreciate its gleaming pillars and mahogany furniture, then ride the lift to the hyacinth-scented rooftop restaurant for high tea. After sensuously settling my bottom onto the gilded chair, I'd imagine myself a princess waiting for my prince – the tuxedoed, white-gloved, young and polished waiter – to come and take my order. While sipping tea thick with milk and sweetened with sugar, I'd stare at the glittering chandeliers, then the oil paintings on the wall. My mind, enthralled by the mysterious images, bold brush-strokes, and rich, vibrant colours, would fly to exotic places I'd seen only in my dreams.

After I finished appreciating the beautiful, my thoughts would turn to the ugly – revenge. My mind would flip and flop, considering different plans. Should I use a knife or a gun? Should I get some poison or hire a professional? Or should I rent a car to hit and run? Then I'd look around at the other diners and wonder: Would this grey-haired, distinguished foreign gentleman at the next table ever imagine within his elegant neighbour's delicate mind blood was now splashing? Would the attentive waiter guess his dainty client was about to go on a shooting spree? I almost laughed out loud, while my eyes sent mischievous glances like imaginary bullets around the elegant hall.

However, sometimes my euphoria would deflate. What if I failed to kill Fung and instead got killed? Or what if I did kill him but failed to get away? I had no illusion that I'd be shown any mercy by the law. Yet I was resolved: If I was captured, I'd die fulfilled. I had endured being a prostitute only to find my mother and avenge my father. So when I'd achieved these, I would never put my feet inside any turquoise pavilion again. But what would come next?

I started to make small talk to the waiter, anything from the weather to business to comments on the old barbarian customers. I also tipped him four times more than necessary. The result was exactly what I'd wanted – I was treated like royalty.

Besides eating and sleeping, I'd also hire a car to take me along the bustling Nanking Road, where I'd stroll, window-shop, and watch people wearing the latest fashions, greeting each other with lucky sayings, and setting off firecrackers to welcome the Lunar New Year. I wanted to enjoy cheerful things before I'd plunge into ugly, bloody murder.

One day during my stroll, I stopped to appreciate the goods behind the windows of an antique shop. My eyes were examining the delicate vases, black ink stones, carved rhinoceros horns, and other precious objects, when I spotted something that made me gasp. Lying inconspicuously in a corner of the display were a diamond ring and a jade bracelet. In a flash I recognised Pearl's gifts, which had been lost with her *qin*! A wave of dizziness hit me. Some bandits must have found them in the *qin* and sold them – yet I'd lost the *qin* near Peking, not here in Shanghai.

I grasped the handle of the shop's door and steadied myself for a moment, then marched in. A middle-aged man with a receding hairline and a ruddy face hurried up to greet me.

'Miss, anything you have chosen from our shop window?'

I pointed to the two pieces of jewellery.

He invited me to sit, then went to the window and, with the utmost care, took the jewels and placed them on a felt square on the counter. 'Madame, you have excellent eyes, these two pieces are of the finest quality.' He picked up the diamond ring and shifted it under the sunlight slanting in through the window. The solitaire stone scattered many rainbows, as if desperately trying to tell me its adventures on the mountain. Next he took the bracelet and tilted it high to reflect the sun so I could see the jade's flawless translucency. Then he slipped the ring onto my finger and the bracelet onto my wrist. The diamond's sparkles seemed to almost blind my eyes while the jade felt cool on my skin. Caressing the stone's sensuous surface, I could almost feel Pearl's spirit shivering in its fathomless green.

Tears pooled in my eyes and I blinked them back. I looked up at Ruddy Face. 'How much?'

The man clicked his pudgy fingers on the abacus, then turned to me and smiled. 'Madame, since it's still Chinese New Year and you're our first customer today, I'll give you a special discount – thirty gold banknotes.'

'I'll take them.' I knew the price was excessive but I didn't bargain because I wanted this as a gesture of honour to Pearl.

While writing the receipt, Ruddy Face stole me a few appreciative glances.

I took out the money and casually asked, 'Do you happen to know the person who sold these pieces to you?'

He looked up from his reading glasses. 'We acquire most of our fine jewellery from some of Shanghai's best families. However, sometimes we'll also have people who just drop in and sell, such as the owner of these two pieces. But madame, it's our policy not to reveal any sellers' identity. I apologise I cannot tell you who owned them.'

Of course, he must have known perfectly well that he'd bought them from bandits but was certainly not about to admit it. Bandits often sold what they stole in a province far from their crime so they'd be less likely to be caught.

'That's all right.' I smiled. 'Are there other pieces that came with them?'

'No. But madame,' his face glowed, 'if you want more, we have other—'

I waved a dismissive hand. 'I'm very happy with what I've got.'

I paid, thanked him, and was about to leave when my stomach was ambushed by pangs. I turned to ask Ruddy Face, 'Do you mind if I use your washroom?'

'Of course not, madame,' he said, then showed me to the back of the store.

It turned out that it was not nature's emergency call. I was just overwhelmed by emotion. I studied my shocked face in the mirror, then took several deep breaths to calm myself. Soap and towels were set out on a board behind the broad sink. As I reached for the soap, I spotted something unexpected – shiny lacquer. My heart began to pound. I pushed aside the soap, the pile of towels, and a roll of toilet paper, then lifted up the 'washing board.'

Tears streamed down my cheeks.

I was looking at the remains of my *qin*, now miraculously found. It must have come with the two pieces of jewellery.

Ironically Ruddy Face, an antique dealer, was too ignorant to recognise an antique from the Ming dynasty. I caressed the instrument's still smooth surface, lost in memories of Pearl's teaching and of our life together.

Then I heard Ruddy Face's worried voice streaming through the door. 'Miss, are you all right in there?'

I wiped my tears with the back of my hand. 'Yes. I'm fine,' I said, then opened the door and stepped out.

He looked puzzled when he saw the splintered wood cradled in my arm.

I spoke before he had a chance to ask. 'Can you sell me this?'

He let out a hearty laugh. 'But what do you want this junk for?' Seeing that I was upset, he put on a flattering smile. 'Miss, if you like it, it's yours. Our new year's gift.'

'You're very kind.'

'The man who sold us the jewellery left this in the store and he never came back for it. So I decided to put it in the bathroom. See,' he pointed to the *qin*'s resonance box, 'it's perfect to store soap and other odds and ends.' He cast me a curious glance. 'But why do you want it?'

'Oh, I just like to collect old wood.'

* * *

When I was back in my hotel room, I carefully cleaned the instrument, found the strings, which were still deep inside the resonance box where I'd put them for my escape, then stretched them on the soundboard. Since the *qin* had absorbed so much humidity, the sound was muted. Nevertheless, I was eager to play: 'Remembering an Old Friend,' 'Lament Behind the Long Gate,' 'Three Variations on the Plum Blossom' . . .

The jewellery store incident set back my schedule three days during which I did nothing but play the *qin* while wearing Pearl's diamond ring and jade bracelet. Not until the fourth day was I able to bring my attention back to the reason I was in Shanghai. That afternoon, I soaked in the bathtub, then carefully applied make-up, put on a silk dress, and went for high tea at the rooftop restaurant. The young waiter was so delighted to see me again that he picked up my gloved hand and lifted it to his lips!

When I was performing my ritual of sipping tea, shooting flirtatious glances, and planning murder, I spotted a familiar figure hurrying toward the exit. It was Mama's maid Little Red! I asked *my* waiter to bring her to my table.

When Little Red saw me, her mouth dropped open as if she'd just run into a ghost in broad daylight. 'Miss Precious Orchid! Where have you been? What are you doing here?!'

My waiter pulled out a chair for her and helped her sit down. Little Red, having never experienced such imperial treatment, awkwardly dumped her bottom on the chair, then knocked down the small crystal sugar bowl.

As she was about to stoop down to pick up the bowl, I rested a gloved hand on her shoulder. 'Little Red, please let the waiter take care of that.'

But she was still fidgeting, so I cast her a sharp glance. 'Stop that, Little Red.'

After the waiter finished cleaning the floor and the table, I asked for another order of tea and cakes.

Little Red was still panting from excitement, or fear. 'Miss Precious Orchid, I can't stay long. I'm here to deliver a letter to one of Peach Blossom's guests.'

'It's all right. If you're late, just tell Mama that you ran into me.'

Her eyes widened as large as two quail eggs. 'Oh, no, then you'll be in big big trouble! They've been looking for you everywhere! Mama keeps saying that if she finds you, she'll . . .' She stopped in midsentence to study me.

'She will what?'

Instead of replying to my question, she said, 'Miss Precious Orchid, you look so beautiful and rich.'

'Thank you. Now tell me, Mama said she will *what*?'

'She will whip you till your skin comes off!'

Just then the waiter came back to lay down a silver tray. After he arranged the food and drinks on the table and left, I said to Little Red, 'Relax. Now eat and drink your tea.'

She did. Noisily. All the foreign customers riveted their eyes on us.

When finally, like a gust of wind, she had swept away the last morsel of food and gulped down the last drop of tea, I said, 'Little Red, now please listen very carefully to what I say.'

She nodded, a bit of raisin on her lip synchronising with her head's movements. I reached to pluck off the raisin. 'I want you to take a message for me. When you go back to Peach Blossom, tell Mama you saw me and ask her to meet me here at this restaurant tomorrow afternoon at three—'

'But Miss Precious Orchid, they'll put you in the dark room!'

I glared at her to stop her from yelling. 'No, they won't.'

'They will! Miss Precious Orchid, please leave Shanghai as quickly as possible! You've always been nice to me, so please don't make me tell Mama that I saw you.'

'Little Red, believe me; I know what I'm doing and I won't be in trouble.'

'Are you sure?'

'Little Red, don't you remember that I'm a *ming ji* and have many important customers?'

She still looked too upset to respond.

I went on, 'When you go back to Peach Blossom, just tell Mama and De that I have some extremely important documents to show them. And they have to come here, for I don't want to risk losing the papers. Unless they're willing to take responsibility for the loss.'

She nodded. I changed the subject and asked her about Spring Moon and Aunty Ah Ping.

'Ah Ping is the same, only after you disappeared she stopped talking completely. I mean she doesn't even make sounds. But her cooking is better than ever.' She paused to pick up a crumb of bread on the table and pop it into her mouth. 'But Spring Moon . . . it's bad news.'

I felt a jolt inside. 'What happened?'

'She ruined her face by poking it with a burning chopstick.'

'Oh my heaven, why did she do this?'

'Don't you know that she'd always been envious of your dimples? So after both you and Red Jade left, she thought it should be her turn to become a *ming ji.* She especially wanted to be like you, that's how she ruined her face.'

'Is she still in Peach Blossom?'

'No, Mama and De sold her to another prostitution house.'

'Do you know which one?'

She shook her head. 'I only know it's in Qinghe Lane.'

Qinghe Lane was the lowest of all the pleasure districts.

'Anyway, I heard she also caught the willow plague.'

I sighed, how sad for my innocent friend to end up with a disfigured face and a sexual disease. Then I thought of my parrot. 'What happened to Plum Blossom; did anyone adopt her?'

'One time when Red Jade came back to Peach Blossom to visit, Mama gave it to her as a gift.'

I was horrified that my beloved pet had ended up with Pearl's bitterest enemy. Would Red Jade care for the parrot tenderly as I had? Or just let the pet wither away while she basked in the applause of her admirers?

Little Red's voice rescued me from my nightmare. 'Miss Precious Orchid, thank you very much for your kindness, but I really have to leave now.'

'Of course, but one last question, how's business in Peach Blossom?'

She frowned. 'Not very good.'

'How come?'

'Haven't you heard? The government has been trying to wipe out all prostitution houses in the International Settlement!' She plunged on, 'It's only under Police Chief Che and some powerful customers' protection that Peach Blossom, Temple of Supreme Happiness, Sleeping Flower Pavilion, and a few others are still surviving.'

I sighed. I'd have never imagined that someday these elegant pavilions would be on the decline, or even gone. 'Little Red, now you better go. But don't forget my message to Mama and De.'

She nodded, then hurried away, her thick braid jerking like a frightened viper struggling in midair.

I sipped my tea and reflected on the strange workings of Karma. Mine, like everyone's, was a mixture of good and bad. Now, would it allow me to attain my final goal of avenging Baba? And if so, would that be the result of a good deed in a former life – or a bad one? Would there be some good Karma left over for me to escape, and even to have some happiness in the future? But life had taught me how little point there is to trying to anticipate what will come.

The next afternoon, I spent hours preparing myself for the rendezvous with my old oppressors. I decided to wear a Western dress. If I wore a Chinese gown, no matter how elaborately embroidered and seamlessly tailored, it would only remind Fang Rong and Wu Qiang that I had been, or still was, a prostitute. But Western dress, exotic and aristocratic, would confuse them. They would go crazy trying to guess my present status – whether I had accumulated a huge fortune, become the kept woman of an extremely powerful warlord, or even like the legendary *ming ji* Golden Flower, ended up an ambassador's wife and the mistress of a commander-in-chief. The more puzzled Mama and De were about my background, the more intimidated they'd feel.

The first step was to deflate their egos while inflating mine.

I studied my reflection in the mirror. The pink dress was elaborately laced at the neck and cuffs and tailored tightly at the waist to accentuate my slender figure. My breasts, like twin virgins, were pushed up to peek through the lace at the forbidden world outside. On top of the rising swells lay three strands of pearls. Their discreet twinkles echoed those of the two big pearl globes hanging from my ears. I pomaded my hair, then piled it up into a bun. A fresh pink rose pinned above my ear gave me the elegant-yet-wild look. I held up the crystal flask Ouyang had bought me and generously rubbed the perfume onto my armpits, between my breasts, and behind my ears. Of course, I was also wearing Pearl's diamond ring and jade bracelet so that her spirit would hover menacingly around my former bosses.

I waited until fifteen minutes past three before I went to the restaurant. When I stepped inside the hall, I quickly spotted Fang Rong and Wu Qiang sitting by a table with two guards. I wriggled my bottom and made a slow advance toward the small, evil group. My eyes threw glances here and there; my head slightly nodded to a few familiar hotel guests; the corners of my lips stayed suspended in a half-smile. Heated whispers poured from tables, and eyes clung to me like an old man grabbing a young virgin.

Mama's eyes were crackling silent thunder. The coin patterns on Wu Qiang's indigo jacket resembled dead men's eyes staring from their graves. Clad in a purplish red gown, Fang Rong looked like a mass of shredded beef streaked with blood. Though feeling a slight tingling on my scalp, I kept my smile as mysterious as the kickings of life inside a swollen stomach.

Right then, as if on cue to enhance the drama, the handsome waiter dashed to my side. 'Ouyang *furen.*' He addressed me with the most respectful 'Madame' normally reserved for the wife of a high official. 'Would you like to have the same table today?'

I smiled prettily. 'No, today I have guests.' I walked to my former master and mistress. The waiter swiftly pulled a chair for me and helped me sit; I ordered high tea for four. Before he left, I said, 'Oh, don't forget to put the bill on my room.'

Now the gang of four looked extremely puzzled while scrutinising me like detectives trying to solve a difficult case.

Mama ordered the two guards to move to an adjacent table. After that, she gave me a threatening glance. 'So, Xiang Xiang—'

'I'd like to be addressed as Mrs. Ouyang.'

De chimed in, sneering. 'So you're able to get someone to marry you, eh? May I know whether you're this man's seventh or eighth concubine?'

The two let out some chilling laughter.

I aimed a dimpled smile at the two evil faces. 'Whether I am a wife or a concubine is none of your whoring business. But I did marry a *good* husband.'

The two exchanged glances, then Fang Rong said sarcastically, 'All right, Mrs. Ouyang, then what are you seeing us for? Is it because your good husband can't satisfy you so you want to release your lusty fire by whoring again?'

'Exactly.'

Their jaws dropped. Mama studied me suspiciously for moments before a grin spread across her face. 'You're most welcome. Your favoured guest Big Master Fung still asks about you.'

I felt a jolt inside, but I tried my best to look as calm as a statue. 'Oh, do you mean he still visits Peach Blossom?'

'Yes,' the two said simultaneously. Then Mama added, 'But after you left, he's never been happy with any of the other sisters.'

'I miss him a lot. He was really nice to me.' I paused to study the huge diamond on my finger, then looked up to scan the two faces. 'So Mama and De, can you arrange a meeting for us?'

The three of us stared at each other and waited in silence. Finally Mama blurted out, 'Xiang Xiang, what do you want from us?' She cast a quick glance toward the two guards, then lowered her voice. 'Don't play tricks on me. If you do, beware of your skin!'

'But,' De added, baring his neat white teeth, 'if you come back to whore to pay back your debts, you're most welcome.'

I bit my tongue, warning myself not to lose my temper. 'Wait a minute, De, didn't Mama tell me ten years ago that I was not sold, but given to you two as a gift? So how come I'm still in debt?'

'Ha, ha. That's right.' As Mama laughed, even the mole between her brows seemed to be chortling.

I fought an itch to pluck it off that hateful face.

She went on, 'But what about those art lessons that you took, those nourishing meals, your elegant room, and your custom-tailored gowns? If you think they're free, then either you're too naïve or plain stupid. Those bills run up to thousands! And that doesn't even count the interest.'

I stared at the two evil faces contorting in front of me, while suppressing the nauseous sensation rising to my throat. An idea dawned: After I'd blown Big Master Fung's brain out, should I also eliminate these two scum?

'Mama and De,' I tried my best to keep my composure, 'now may I invite you both to my suite upstairs? I want you to appreciate a very nice piece of calligraphy that I've recently acquired for my collection.' I motioned to the guards. 'You can bring them along if you want.'

Once in my room, the gang of four kept casting glances around the elegant, Western-style decor before finally sitting down. I called and asked my waiter to bring up the tea and cakes.

De smiled at me curiously. 'Hmmm, Xiang Xiang, not only have you married a good husband, I bet he's very wealthy, too.'

'I don't really care about his money, only his connections.'

A long, meaningful silence. The bell rang; it was my waiter bringing high tea to the room. I gave him my usual big tip; he bowed and thanked me profusely before he left. Mama and De watched the drama with intense curiosity.

'Please,' I said, and we began to eat.

After the four hungry ghosts had devoured the last morsel of cake and drained the last drop of tea, I said, 'Now let's appreciate my recently acquired art. I'm sure you'll love it as much as you love cheating the sisters.'

Fang Rong and Wu Qiang exchanged suspicious-cum-puzzled glances. I led them to the bedroom where I'd hung up Mr. Ouyang's scroll.

When the two started to read, their expressions had changed from doubt to surprise, then finally fear – as I'd expected. The moment they spotted Ouyang's signature and seal, their jaws dropped. They turned to stare at me, faces pale and pupils darting around like trapped mice.

'Mama and De, don't you think that this calligraphy is more than enough to pay my debt?'

A long, ghostly silence before obsequious grins stretched on the two faces.

Mama said, her voice suddenly turned very weak and tender, 'Oh, Xiang – no, Mrs. – no, Ouyang *furen,* what . . . what can we do to serve you?'

De couldn't even lift his head to look me straight in the eyes; his voice spilled fear. 'Yes. Ouyang *furen*, what can your humble servants do for you?'

I didn't respond right away, but took out a silk handkerchief and began to play with it in a dancer's elegant gestures. It gave me indescribable pleasure to watch the subtle alternating of colours on Mama and De's faces. Not until this moment had I truly understood the pleasure and addiction of power!

I continued to play with the handkerchief for a while, then put it away and thrust my face close to the two pathetic ones. 'Mama and De.' I paused again to create suspense.

'Yes, what can we do for you?' the two yelped in unison.

'I want you to arrange a meeting for me with Big Master Fung at Peach Blossom during the Lantern Festival.'

De blurted out, 'Of course, Ouyang *furen*. No problem.'

Mama looked a bit uneasy. 'But what if Big Master Fung can't make it that day?'

I threw her a sharp glance. 'You mean he won't have time even for *me*?'

'Oh, I'm so sorry, Ouyang *furen*, that's not what I meant—'

'I don't care what you meant, I only want you to clean the welcoming-guests room thoroughly and decorate it with one hundred flowers and scent it with the most expensive perfume. Also, buy a new red bedcover, sheets, and pillowcases. And don't forget to prepare several of Fung's favourite dishes, and bottles of whisky and champagne.'

'You have our word,' the duo yapped again.

'Besides, I want to have a nice little chat with my old favoured guest, so I don't want anybody bothering us. No sisters, maids, *ni-*

angyi, servants, guards – no one – near the room. Have you got all this?'

The two heads bobbed in the air like jumping beans. Mama said, 'No problem. Since that day is the Lantern Festival, most of us will be out to celebrate anyway. I promise that you two will have the whole Peach Blossom to yourselves.'

'Good.'

A long silence. Mama squeezed out a meaningful grin. 'But Ouyang *furen*, I thought you're married . . .'

'Fang Rong.' Instead of addressing her as Mama, now I deliberately called her by her whole name to show the change between us. Not only was I no longer under her control, I had become her superior (since I had the arrogance to call her by her whole name). 'This is just for old times' sake. Anyway,' I threw her a sharp glance, 'this is none of your *whoring* business. Just do what I ask and don't ask too many questions; it'll never do you two any good. You understand?'

'Yes, Ouyang *furen*,' Mama said, her voice powerless as a boneless dog's.

'One last thing. Don't ever tell anyone that you've seen me or the calligraphy.'

They barked like lost dogs at the sight of their master.

I went to make a telephone call to ask my waiter to come up.

When the black-tuxedoed and white-gloved young man escorted the gang of four to the door, I lifted my thumb and forefinger to aim at the four receding backs, then fired four imaginary shots, just for a foretaste of my upcoming spree.

33

Revenge

On the evening of the fifteenth of the first lunar month, I hired a car and headed for Peach Blossom Pavilion. When I spotted the all-too-familiar pink building a hundred yards in front of me, I asked the driver to let me off so I could walk the short distance.

'Miss, you want me to come back and take you home for your *tuanyuan* dinner?'

'No, thanks.' I smiled. 'I think you should stop work early tonight and go home for *your* family reunion.'

I watched the car drive away before I started to walk.

I had chosen this particular day because Fung and I would be left alone, and also because it seemed perfect to kill the destroyer of my family on the day of family reunion.

'Take you home for your *tuanyuan* dinner.' The driver's words kept spinning in my mind as I sauntered toward the home, or prison, that I'd been thrust into when I was thirteen. But instead of going home for dinner, I was now going 'home' to carry out murder! I reached inside my coat's inner pocket and felt the knife. Feeling the sharp steel stirred both fear and determination. The knife was there just in case my main plan didn't work. I intended to get Fung drunk – never hard for me to do – then take the pistol he always carried and turn it on him.

A few pedestrians scurried along the street in front of Peach Blossom, probably on their way home to eat the sweet, round dumplings symbolising *tuanyuan* – reunion. After that, families would go out together to parks or temples to admire lanterns and read riddles.

The popping of firecrackers and hammering of drums punctuated the silence of the evening, welcoming the new year and scaring away evil spirits. I rubbed my cheeks and pulled the shawl around my chest. Suddenly I thought of Teng Xiong and wondered where she might be. I hoped she had not been caught, for if she had, it was certain she'd be tortured, or even killed.

'Teng Xiong!' I said aloud. Hearing her name ring in the cold air reassured me. I hoped she was still alive, even if fleeing for her life to the remotest corner of the world. I continued to walk, humming a Peking opera tune to calm myself. The moon now appeared low on the horizon, looking intimidatingly huge like a spiked iron ball.

I whispered to its enigmatic, mask-like face, 'Justice will be done!'

The two stone lions at the gate appeared to be smiling, as if they were welcoming me home. Did they know that I only came back to eliminate their big protector of sexual Dharma?

Now, a few feet from the turquoise pavilion, Fang Rong suddenly materialised in front of the gate. Dressed in a purple jacket and trousers, she looked like an overripe eggplant. Little Red followed right behind her, holding a lantern in the shape of the moon goddess.

Mama squeezed out a huge grin. When she spoke, her voice oozed honey. 'Ouyang *furen*, welcome back to Peach Blossom!'

Determined not to waste any of my precious breath on nonsense, I came straight to the point. 'Has Big Master Fung arrived?'

'Not yet, he said he has to finish his reunion dinner with his family before he comes. He'll be here in an hour.'

'That's fine. Is the room cleaned and flowered and perfumed as I've instructed?'

'Of course.'

'All right, then you can leave and go celebrate the Lantern Festival.'

'What about Little Red, do you want her to stay behind to serve you?'

'No.'

'But our two guards,' she pointed to the two oafs standing a few feet away, 'they—'

'Tonight Big Master Fung and I do not want to be disturbed.'

'Of course, Ouyang *furen*.'

'But Ah Ping can stay, since I may want her to cook more food.'

'Sure.' Mama smiled mischievously. 'Anyway, she's crazy.'

'All right, then you can leave now. I know my way around here.'

'Yes. Ouyang *furen*.' She threw me a licentious-cum-meaningful glance. 'Have a very wonderful evening.'

'You can be sure I will.'

I waited until a car pulled up to take Mama, Little Red, and the two guards away before I turned to walk inside Peach Blossom.

My heart began to pound; everything looked so familiar, and yet so strange. Memories flooded back – when I'd been a little girl of thirteen entering this beautiful mansion thinking that it was a rich man's residence. In the distance, the pavilion's upturned eaves looked like welcoming hands luring me back to this domain of the pleasurable and decadent. The lovely maidens on the garden walls seemed to wink, their mischievous glances following me as I strode up the winding, cobblestone path beside the bamboo grove. I paused to look at the pond and dropped my gaze to the patches of gold, orange, and white shimmering under the moonlight. Oh, how I wished I were a carp, so detached and carefree. And oblivious to the upcoming murder! I cast a lingering glance at the courtyard, then turned around to walk toward the main building.

Inside, I climbed steps, turned corners, and passed through corridors. Finding myself outside Fang Rong and Wu Qiang's room on the second floor, I halted. In all the years I'd spent in Peach Blossom, except for a few glimpses and peeks, I'd never really had a good look at, let alone entered, this forbidden chamber. Now the opportunity was too good to resist. I turned the knob with all my strength until my hand was sore. But nothing happened. The round lump of copper adamantly remained in the same position. Unwilling to yield to defeat, I took off my hairpin, inserted it in the keyhole, and twisted. There was a soft click. I pushed and the door, to my surprise, glided open.

I found a small table lamp and switched it on, revealing the secret interior – a deep purple *zitan* table, a chest with bronze hinges in the shape of bats, a full-length gilded mirror, a huge *luohan* bed . . . Then my eyes fell on a tall, elaborately carved cupboard inlaid with mother of pearl. I dashed toward it, pulled open its doors, and saw what I'd been looking for – the safe. I began to twist its lock but to no avail. However, when my hand finally let go of the lock, my feet were unwilling to leave the room.

Suddenly I noticed a chest. I tugged at its drawers but with no result. Then I used my hairpin again, but no matter how hard I twisted and turned it in the hole, the drawers refused to budge. Desperate, I used my full force to yank open the top one. It worked. I tried pulling on the other knobs and discovered that now that the master lock had been broken, the rest could be opened. I began to shuffle through the papers, filling the room with sounds like splashing water. Letters, notes, documents, receipts, contracts stared at me, as if begging to be read. At the top of one drawer was the photograph of a very young and pretty girl with a sweet expression.

'Who's this?' I asked, then took out the picture and scrutinised it more. When my eyes alighted on the mole staring like a third eye between the brows, I realised this girl was none other than the teenage Mama! No wonder she was named Fang Rong – Beautiful Countenance. It was hard to believe that the years could be so cruel to a person's face – or was this change the work of her own decaying heart? Though stories tell of ugly ducklings turning into beautiful swans, life usually presents the opposite. Before Fang Rong had been poisoned by the life of the wind and dust, had she once been innocent? Or was she just born wicked? Had she left her Buddha nature (as Mother insisted we all had) in some cobwebbed corner of a past life?

I let out a heavy sigh, then put back the picture.

My hands continued to shift through papers until three characters burned into my eyes – Hu Xiang Xiang.

My heart fluttered like oil sputtering on water.

I picked up the letter and recognised my mother's handwriting. There were more – altogether ten – stained, yellowed letters from Peking. From my mother.

I tore open one and read:

My dear daughter Xiang Xiang:

This is already my seventh letter that I've written you over a period of six weeks. Why don't you answer? I want very much to go to Shanghai to see you but can't because I don't have the money to undertake such a long journey. Besides, the temple is developing very fast and they need me here every day, almost every minute.

However, Aunty Fang wrote to me a few times describing your situation. She said you've grown stronger and prettier and are very much liked by your master and other members of the household. In one letter she told me that two young men – one the master's son and the other his friend – are both infatuated with you. She hopes one day you can be betrothed to one of them. Even though I don't put too much hope on matters like this, I still feel glad to hear about it.

I can't write long. Not only do my eyes hurt, but, as a nun, I am not supposed to be attached to worldly affairs – including my family. Moreover, I simply can't afford to write you very often, for stamps are costly and hard to obtain. But of course I can't help it. I only hope the Mother Abbess won't find out that I've been writing to my daughter. She's a very nice lady, but unfortunately, at eighty-nine, she's growing weaker and more obstinate each day.

Xiang Xiang, I don't mind if you have no time to write. I just want you to have a peaceful life.

Your mother
December 19, 1918

P.S. I hope that by now you've received the top and trousers that I sewed for you. And the pair of cloth shoes that I embroidered with orchids?

Tears streamed down my cheeks. But I had no time for sorrow. Starting to feel nervous about Fung's impending arrival, I stuffed all the letters into my coat pocket and hurried to the welcoming-guests hall. Here I took off my coat and began to preen in front of the mirror – batting my long lashes; flicking my eyes this way and that; wetting my lips; squeezing my breasts together to have deeper cleavage. Now face flushed and lips slightly parted, I looked as if I were longing for passionate love, or a brain-emptying *fuck*. Nobody would have guessed that my heart was now beating frantically, not out of passion, but fear.

I stood up and began to pace. My ears listened to the murderous clicks of my heels synchronising with that of my heartbeats. My gaze fell on the hundred roses I'd ordered Fang Rong to provide, now silent in their vases, about to witness a brutal bloodletting. I closed my eyes and inhaled the decadent aroma. I would be a prostitute one last time, just until I put a knife in Fung's heart or a bullet into his head.

I didn't know how long I'd been pacing until I was startled by frantic knockings on the door. I'd been waiting for this moment for ten long years and now it was finally about to happen! I opened it to reveal Big Master Fung – my favoured guest and my bitterest enemy – who scrutinised me with eyes glowing like lanterns. Behind him towered two giant mountains – his two bodyguards.

I put on my best dimpled smile and spoke through the door, '*Aii-ya*, Big Master Fung,' I tilted my head toward the two moving muscles. 'I don't want them near us. Haven't you forgotten that tonight is our reunion night?'

He reached to pinch my cheek. 'But I need them to keep an eye in case—'

'*Aii-ya*, Big Master Fung, don't worry,' I shifted my feet and wriggled my waist, 'tonight everyone is out to see the lanterns! Besides, you know, I haven't seen you for a century . . .'

'All right, all right, my little pretty. You've persuaded me.'

When he was about to signal the guards away, I placed my hand on his arm. 'This is a special night, Big Master Fung; please give them money to buy wine to celebrate.'

'Ah, Xiang Xiang,' Fung looked at me curiously, 'I haven't seen you for a few years and you've turned into such a sophisticated woman!'

After the two guards had left, I invited Fung in. Then I kicked the door shut and flung myself into my enemy's arms as if he were my sweetest love. Fung kissed me passionately on my lips, his hand reaching inside my dress to squeeze my breast. When we finally disentangled ourselves, I helped him to sit on the sofa, take off his shoes, then served him food – just like before.

While we were eating, drinking, and making small talk, his bony hand, like a little beggar's, kept reaching to grab me. My hands kept his wineglass full, as my eyes kept shooting him soul-sucking glances.

He asked me how and why had I run away and what had I been doing since.

I picked the biggest shrimp and put it on his plate. 'Big Master Fung, please don't listen to all the rumours spread by Mama and De. I didn't run, but walked away. Because I was not sold into Peach Blossom, I didn't owe them any money.'

He lifted one brow. 'Eh? Is that true? Xiang Xiang, you've never told me about your past. Why don't you tell me now?'

I felt a jolt inside. To calm myself, I lifted my cup and took a long sip. '*Aii-ya*, Big Master Fung, tonight is our reunion night, so let's enjoy ourselves. I'll tell you about that later.'

'All right, all right.' He paused to pick up a piece of duck liver the colour of mud soaked with blood, then popped it into his mouth. Chewing noisily for a while, he turned to look me in the eyes. 'Xiang Xiang, why did you come back here?'

My heart skipped a beat. I yanked the handkerchief from my sleeve and flung it at Fung's flushed face. 'Big Master Fung, what a question! I came back because I just can't stop thinking of you!'

Suddenly I thought: Could I use my handkerchief to strangle this heap of moving wrinkles right now?

Eyes glazed over with alcohol, he said, 'Is that true, my little fox spirit?'

I nodded, flicking my eyes to meet his.

'Why didn't Mama punish you?'

I chuckled. 'You think they're so stupid as to punish *your* favourite sister? I'm but a worthless whore; it's you they're afraid of, Big Master Fung.'

Fung first looked pleased, then lost in thoughts. He sipped more wine, and when he looked at me again, his expression turned serious.

My heart almost stopped. Did he sense something wrong?

But he said, 'Xiang Xiang, why don't you marry me?'

I was so surprised to hear this that I didn't know how to respond.

'Xiang Xiang, why hesitate? I'll give you a very good life. I love you.'

Right then Teng Xiong's image flashed across my mind. Had he caught and murdered her? I conjured in my mind pictures of her body – gnawed by wild dogs; hanging limp from a tree; floating on a river turned red from blood spilling from her mutilated torso.

To collect myself I took a sip of my wine, popped a piece of dried bean curd into my mouth, and chewed meditatively. I refilled Fung's cup, then threw him a glance horny enough to melt his heart while hardening his stalk. 'Big Master Fung, how do I know that you really love me?'

'Xiang Xiang,' he pulled out from his pocket a velvet box, 'open it; see what I've brought to prove my love for you.'

When I clicked open the box, my eyes fell on a dragon. Though small, it was exquisitely crafted and animated with *qi*. I could almost see the energy emanating from the sinuous body inlaid with hundreds of pave diamonds. The dragon's eyes were two big rubies, and its gold claws and tail stretched elegantly. I picked up the brooch and moved it this way and that for the diamonds to cast their brilliance on the mirrored wall. A dragon! Fung had remembered I was born in the year of the dragon and so he'd brought me one to celebrate our reunion day.

Tears pooled in my eyes. Fung could not have known why the gift touched my heart. It made me remember how Baba would tell me that any baby born in the year of the dragon was considered extremely lucky. That was why he had always predicted I'd become the first eminent woman *zhuang yuan*, who'd bring prestige and glory to our family and ancestors. '*Feilong zaitian* – dragon soaring in the sky' had been Baba's favourite phrase to predict his daughter's bright future.

Tenderly Fung reached to wipe my eyes with his handkerchief. 'Don't cry, Xiang Xiang, your suffering will soon be over. If you marry me, not only will you have the best clothes and food and jewellery in the whole world,' he paused, then spoke again his voice filled with passion, ' I'll also pamper you like you were my daughter.'

His daughter! I bit my inner lip till I tasted blood. I looked at Fung – a ghost coming back to haunt me from a past life. We stared into each other's eyes for what seemed an entire incarnation before he suddenly pulled me into his arms. 'Oh Xiang Xiang, Xiang Xiang.' He kept cooing as if he were singing a lullaby for his dead daughter.

Then, very gently, he wiped the blood from my lips with his fingers. After that, he began to kiss me passionately. And I let him. In his delirious state, he carried me to the bed, took off his clothes and mine, pressed me down, and thrust his filthy stalk into my precious gate . . .

When I woke up, Fung was sound asleep, or dead drunk, next to me in bed. There was not a single thread on his body, nor on mine. My gaze surveyed the gaping mouth, sagging skin, and tofu stalk as disgust rose inside me. His clothes, lying on the floor in a heap of wrinkles, matched their master's face. Cautiously I got off the bed. When I was tiptoeing toward my coat, where I'd put my knife, I spotted something bulging underneath the crumpled heap.

With my toes, I lifted the clothes and saw what I'd dreamed of – Fung's pistol.

My heartbeat accelerated like the tick tock of a clock gone awry.

I imagined the loud 'bang!' shattering the evening and ending my agony. I could almost see Fung's blood – like crimson serpents returning to their holes – quickly filling all the creaks and cracks in the room. I could also see his eyes, protruding with shock and disbelief, stare at me as if I were his daughter's ghost emerging from the *yin* world to smother her father's soul. I imagined my delirious, victorious laughter startling everyone from their lantern riddle reading . . .

I bent to pick up the gun. It was the first time that I had held one in my hand. I now possessed the power to kill. My hand began to tremble.

The rustling leaves outside the window cried *Sha*! *Sha*! 'Kill! Kill!'

Now the gun suddenly looked small and insignificant.

Can this little pathetic thing take away life?

I held it with both hands and aimed at Fung's head.

A loud bang cracked the evening sky. I let out a sharp cry. The next moment I realised it was only the fireworks. And a startled but alive Fung was staring incredulously at me.

'For heaven's sake don't play around with that! Xiang Xiang, that's not a toy!'

Although my hands continued to tremble, the 'toy' was still held tightly in my grip, aiming at Fung.

'Xiang Xiang, what's the matter with you? I told you to drop that gun. It's loaded. You might shoot me by mistake!'

'Big Master Fung, then it'll serve you right!'

'What are you talking about?'

'I'm going to kill you.'

To my surprise, instead of looking frightened, he burst into laughter.

'Ha! Ha! Ha! Xiang Xiang, what's the matter with you? Are you drunk or out of your mind? Come, let's make love again, you look so lovely with no clothes on, and so much like my daughter.'

I felt queasiness simmering in my stomach. My fingers tightened on the trigger. 'Damn you and damn your daughter!'

Fung stared at me in silence for a moment. Then his expression changed; now he looked scared. 'Wait a minute, Xiang Xiang, what the hell—'

'Big Master Fung, I've been waiting for this moment for ten long years. Once I pull this trigger, all my shame will be behind me.'

'What the hell are you talking about?' Beads of perspiration were forming on his forehead.

'Does the name *Rumbling Thunder* sound familiar to you?'

He didn't respond.

I went on, 'That was my father. Ten years ago you had him executed for a crime *you* committed. That was why I was sent into this prostitution house, because you destroyed my family. Now it's time for you to pay for your evil deeds. It's your Karma that you became my favoured guest so I have the chance to kill you tonight.'

It seemed Fung was still too shocked to say anything. He shifted his body like a snake trapped in a cage.

I tightened my grip on the gun. 'I'm going to kill you. Right now!'

'Xiang Xiang, please don't! I'll give you whatever you want.'

'Can you give me back my parents?'

He was speechless.

I squeezed the trigger. Again. And again. *And* again. Until I realised I just couldn't pull it to release the 'bang!'

My back and armpits were soaking wet and beads of perspiration gathered on my forehead. I felt my throat burning while chills seeped into my marrow. Everything around me seemed to be frozen in time and space.

Seeing that I was not able to shoot, relief washed over Fung's face. He stood up and walked toward me.

'Stop right there, or I'll really shoot!'

To my surprise, he burst into delirious laughter. 'Ha! Ha! Ha! Xiang Xiang, I dare you to go ahead and shoot me! Come on! Shoot!' Then his voice turned fierce and mean. 'You ungrateful bitch! You try to kill me after what I've done for you?!'

Fung dashed forward and snatched the gun from my grip. 'Fuck your mother's smelly cunt! You dead bitch! Next time when you try to kill someone, be prepared. Take some shooting lessons first! Damn you and your whole family!'

He looked at me with disgust. 'You know the saying "Some would rather drink the wine of punishment than that of respect"?'

I didn't respond. He spat, 'That's you! I treated you well, bought you all these expensive gifts, and loved you like my own daughter, but you tried to kill me! You cheap, dog-fucked bitches would rather be punished than respected! That's why you're all whores!' He spat again as loudly as the fireworks, 'Smelly cunt!'

Suddenly I no longer cared if Fung sent me right to the *yin* world. Maybe if I ended this way, I'd unite with Baba, Pearl, and even Guigui, my puppy whom I'd eaten with relish when I was thirteen.

I spat back with full force, 'It's stinking males like you who turned me into a whore! I was supposed to be a female *zhuang yuan!*'

He stared at me incredulously for seconds before bursting into laughter. 'Oh, is that so?! Then Fate surely knows how to play tricks on you, eh? So that's what your father hoped his whore daughter would be! A *zhuang yuan*. Ha!' He paused to think, then, 'Yes, now I remember him; he was a cripple.'

I trembled with anger, yet I couldn't deny the fact that Baba had been a cripple – after he'd broken his leg during the fateful Peking opera performance.

Fung went on thoughtfully, 'I wonder how a cripple could have fathered such a beautiful daughter like you. It must be your mother.' He threw me a licentious glance. 'I'm sure she's a great beauty; where is she—'

My whole body seized by horror, I blurted out, 'No! She's a nun!'

'A nun? That'll be more exciting!'

I lunged at this incarnation of evil. Fung pointed the gun at my head. 'All right, Xiang Xiang, enough of all this nonsense! If you didn't remind me of my daughter, I'd already have put a bullet in your pretty head. Now listen very carefully. You better be out of Shanghai within three days. If I, or any of my men, see you here after that, then you're asking for an interview with the King of Hell.' He tilted my chin with the gun's barrel. 'Xiang Xiang, I don't want to have to shoot my "daughter" a second time.' He paused, his hand jerked the gun to fire an imaginary shot. 'Bang! That's how I put a hole between my fourth concubine's pretty brows. Ha! Ha! Ha! Too bad she didn't look a bit like my daughter, otherwise I would have spared her life as I did yours.'

'You killed Teng Xiong!' I spat hard on Fung's face. He flinched.

Suddenly I remembered my 'melon chopping' night – accidentally I'd kicked him in the face.

I gathered all my strength and drove my foot into his filthy stalk.

'Ahhhhhhh!' he screamed, clutching his private parts. The gun dropped to the floor. I snatched it up and aimed at his heart.

He looked up, sneering despite the pain, 'Go ahead, shoot! Don't be a coward this time!'

I pulled the trigger.

The 'Bang!' was so loud that I thought I had turned deaf.

But Fung's inhuman, explosive cry jolted me right back to the here and now.

Fung didn't crumple to the floor as my father had when the bullet hit his head. Like a ghost struggling to return from hell, Fung now stood in front of me, blood sprouting from the side of his head. As he extended his hand pleading with me not to shoot again, I realised his ear was gone!

I closed my eyes and squeezed the trigger to release another deafening 'Bang!'

When I opened them, I didn't see the incarnation of evil breathing his last agonising breath on earth, nor a dead body shattered like a slaughtered beast. Fung was simply gone! Only a zigzag trail of blood witnessed his malevolent presence in this murderous room. I'd missed his evil heart a second time – maybe because he didn't have one!

As agitated as if a cat were being beaten in my trousers, I dressed hurriedly, then sprinted out of the welcoming-guests room and ran toward the kitchen. I knew I should escape right away. But I had to see Ah Ping one last time – for Pearl.

With not a soul around, the turquoise pavilion had the appearance of an ancient mausoleum. Outside the window, the sudden thunder of firecrackers broke up the ghostly silence.

My mind would not let go of the image of Fung with a missing ear and blood all over his face. Why, Heaven, didn't you direct the bullet right between his eyes – as he'd done to Teng Xiong!?

Then I imagined I saw Teng Xiong with a big hole in her third eye. She looked too stunned to die; her lips stirred as if saying, 'Precious Orchid, please love me in this life. Even for a moment.'

I was running, trembling, and muttering, 'Oh Teng Xiong! Teng Xiong!' Finally I reached the kitchen. With a slight push, the door creaked open to reveal a room bathed in pale moonlight.

I moved cautiously and spoke in a heated whisper, 'Aunty Ah Ping?!'

There was no response, the only sound being the *Sha*! *Sha*! – 'Kill! Kill!' – from the rustling leaves outside the window. I called several more times but still to no avail. As I was about to give up, I noticed in a far corner a figure crouching next to a huge cauldron.

I hurried toward the container and screamed. 'Aunty Ah Ping!'

The figure jolted. She blinked hard, as if to shake away the still lingering dream. She stared at me with startled eyes for long moments, then suddenly said, 'Are you Xiang Xiang? What are you doing here?'

I was shocked beyond myself. Wasn't Ah Ping mute and crazy?

Like two frightened cats, we stared at each other for an entire incarnation. Finally I spoke, 'So Aunty Ah Ping, you're . . .'

'Yes, I'm not mute and I'm not crazy.'

'Good Heavens, Aunty Ah Ping, then why did you—'

She waved a dismissive hand, then went to get a clean towel and a basin of water, and started to clean my face. After that, she asked, 'Xiang Xiang, why have you suddenly turned up here?'

Breathlessly, I told her everything.

'Oh heaven, Xiang Xiang, please leave right away! Big Master Fung is too evil and powerful! He'll have to explain to everyone how he lost his ear. When he catches you, he'll be merciless!' Abruptly she stood up from the chair and pulled me along. 'Come, follow me to where you can hide safely for a while.'

Ah Ping led me all the way to the haunted garden. We entered the deserted temple and knelt down in front of the altar.

She said, 'We'll pray to my two daughters in the *yin* world and ask them to protect you.'

After we finished, I threw myself into her arms and blurted out, 'Ma!' on behalf of Ruby and Pearl.

She caressed my hair with her crooked, arthritic fingers. 'I know that you and Pearl had sworn blood sisterhood.'

'How did you know all this?'

'Pearl told me everything.'

'But I thought—'

'Although she believed that I had lost my mind, she was a nice daughter. So she still came to report things, even though she thought that I wouldn't understand. It was a filial ritual of hers.'

'Aunty Ah Ping, I'm so sorry for everything that's happened to you.'

'Life is suffering. It always has been, and it always will be.'

I studied her leathery face, feeling too pained to respond.

She went on, 'Xiang Xiang, you want to know why I pretend, right?'

I nodded.

'Surely there's always a reason for things to happen, or not happen. It is called Karma. As you must have already known, my Karma is bad. Very bad. Some people stop eating meat to dissipate their bad Karma, but I'm not able to do that, since I'm a chef and can't be a vegetarian. After I'd tried but failed to ruin my voice, I decided to accumulate merit by not talking. That way, words can't contaminate the original purity of my mind. Xiang Xiang, to stop talking is to stop "killing." It's words that killed Pearl.'

I was still stunned that this frail, homely, once deaf and crazy woman was now talking so sensibly, and so eloquently.

She spoke again, her voice now urgent, 'Xiang Xiang, now leave, quickly.'

'Aunty Ah Ping,' I searched her eyes, 'please come with me to Peking.'

'I can't. I have to stay here and watch over my daughters' spirits. Besides, I'm an old woman. I don't give much thought to the future, only the past.'

In the garden under the moonlight, we embraced, then bade each other farewell. Forever.

When I was by the gate, I turned back and stared at her. Her face, an enigmatic mask that was both the witness and embodiment of sufferings, now shone bright and pure under the moon.

'Aunty Ah Ping, please come with me.'

She shook her head.

I knew it was futile to try to persuade her. 'Then take very good care of yourself.'

She cast me a meaningful look and made a gesture as if to say 'you, too.' Then, silent once again, she began to walk and soon disappeared around a corner.

PART FOUR

PARLHOUR

34

Ginseng Tea

Both Jade Treasure's and Leo Stanley's pens scratch noisily on the paper, materialising my sufferings and nightmares into salable dreams.

When Jade finally puts down her pen and clicks off the recorder, she exclaims, 'Wow! Grandmama, that's really wonderful!'

'Wonderful?' I cast her a chiding glance. 'My miseries and sufferings?'

She makes a face like a child's when accused of lying. 'You know what I mean!'

'Of course I do, that my sufferings can be translated into wonderful stories and sold for a wonderful price.'

She imitates my Chinese. '*Aii-ya*! Grandmama!'

Leo immediately comes to his fiancée's rescue. '*Popo,* what Jade means is that you're a wonderful person.'

'All right, all right.' I lift the corners of my lips – as I did seventy-odd years ago – to resemble a blooming lotus. 'I've told you my life is even soapier than a TV soap opera.'

Jade asks, 'Grandmama, how could you miss killing Big Master Fung?'

I throw her an annoyed glance. 'Because I'm not a born murderess, that's why! Do you want a criminal in your family?'

'I think I already have one – your father.'

'But he was not. I told you he was convicted of a crime he'd never committed.'

'Sorry, Grandmama, of course not.' Jade pauses, seemingly thinking very hard, then, 'But you really shouldn't have missed, because killing Warlord Fung was your entire goal in life.'

'Yes, but a lot of goals never get fulfilled in life, right?'

The two exchange a curious glance. Then Jade says, 'I think you were just so scared that you missed his heart.'

'Yes, I was scared, very scared, but I think the real reason was my Karma.'

Jade stares into my eyes. 'So your Karma wouldn't let you kill Fung?'

'Yes. Maybe it was my mother's talk about the Buddha's compassion that my gun was directed not to his heart but instead to his ear.'

Leo asks, '*Popo*, did you ever regret it?'

'At first I did, very much, but not now.'

Jade makes a face. 'But why not? Grandmama, I still think you should have killed him.'

'My big princess, let me ask you a question. Do you want to strangle your little cat?'

'Oh, no, of course not!'

'Then how can you think that I should take away the life of a human being?'

'But that's different, he's your enemy!'

'How do you know your cat was not your enemy in your past life?'

'Grandmama!'

Leo pats his fiancée's hand.

I sigh. '*Hai,* maybe deep down I just didn't have the heart to kill him. Although he didn't have one either. But who knows?' I pause, then, 'However, I did shoot off his ear. To a man like Fung, the loss of face over losing his ear would be almost worse than if I had killed him.'

Another long silence during which my two *yin yang* kids are busy capturing my feelings and reminiscences in words.

Then Jade leans close to me, widening her eyes. 'Grandmama, after you'd escaped from Shanghai, did you go back to . . . to . . .'

Since she feels too intimidated to finish the sentence, I finish it for her. 'To being a prostitute?'

The two heads, one black and the other blonde, bob like a pair of *yin yang* balls.

I chuckle inside. Why are decent, highly educated, American young people so interested in whores? With all this sex education and talk about freedom of sex, why are they still starving for more?

Now Leo says in the Mandarin Chinese he learned so elegantly in Ge-lin-bi-ya. '*Popo,* please tell us how you came all the way here to the States. We want all the details.'

I wave an arthritic hand at both of them. 'Be patient, young people! I've promised you I won't board the immortal's journey to the Western Paradise, nor take the crane's flight, not until you two have my whole story safely in your hands! Not only that, I still have to muster up all my remaining strength to go on the,' I swiftly switch into English, 'book two for publicising this memoir.'

Leo looks puzzled, and even handsomer. 'Book two? *Popo*, do you mean you have enough materials for a second memoir?'

Before I have a chance to answer, Jade casts him a chiding glance. 'Leo! Grandmama means "book tour." Listen more carefully next time!'

Now it's my turn to cast Jade a sharp, chiding glance while leaning to whisper into her ear. 'Jade, stop that! Don't ever make fun of or chide someone you love and who loves you even more. True love happens only once in your entire incarnation; you understand?'

She makes a face, trying to look cute (she does, though). Then she shoots up from the sofa. 'Grandmama, I'm going to fix you another cup of ginseng tea. Leo, you want me to fix you one, too?' Now she turns to shoot her fiancé a soul-sucking glance.

I shake my head. *Hai*, that's how young people lose their minds when their hearts are burning in the illusory flames of passion. Then I almost burst into laughter when I see Jade walk in imitation of the shredded-golden-lotus steps. Leo's eyes follow her bare legs and red-nailed toes like a cat watching the rolling of a spool.

In no time Jade comes back with cups of amber liquid. She

hands one to Leo, then pushes the other one right between my lips. 'Grandmama, please drink. I've put lots of honey in it. It'll give you smooth skin and lots of *qi*.'

At ninety-eight, what do I need smooth skin and abundant *qi* for? To seduce another soon-to-be-corpse-one-hundred-year-old-and-dying? Of course the smooth skin is for my TV appearances (predicted by Jade), and the *qi* for the many hectic book tours!

Suddenly I decide to play child to satisfy Jade's 'motherly' instinct as well as her good intentions. I obediently drain the bittersweet tea as if swallowing my equally bittersweet Karma. Then I go on, 'I made a promise to myself that I'd not go back to "you know what" and I did—'

Leo widens his beautiful, almost feminine eyes. '*Popo*, you mean you did go back to . . .'

I bite my lips hard to prevent myself from exploding into laughter. But alas, I fail miserably and guffaw like a demented woman.

Jade pats my back and massages my arms; Leo sits right opposite me, looking stupefied. Finally I have to will myself to stop. Jade dashes inside the kitchen to prepare me more ginseng tea.

When she runs back and hands me the cup, I take several sips, then say to the two comical faces, 'All right, where was I before you two tried to murder me with my own laughter?' I put on a poker face. 'All right, I was starting to say that I *did* keep my promise and never went back to you know what.'

The two sigh. I don't know whether it's from relief, or disappointment.

35

Back to Peking

After I'd left Peach Blossom Pavilion, I hailed a rickshaw and had it take me straight back to my hotel. I took off my clothes and soaked in the bathtub, hoping the hot water would remove the soiled feeling that was left from my last sex with the still-living Fung and also cleanse the blood still splattering in my mind. Now one thing was certain: I would not go back to prostitution.

That night I didn't close my eyes. My mind was swirling with scenes of the failed murder. Why had I missed Fung's heart? I kept asking myself but no answer came except my own sobbing. Like a wounded animal, I crouched, waiting for dawn to drive away the darkness.

I couldn't stay in Shanghai, and so Peking would be my refuge. At least my mother – or Mother Wonderful Kindness Abbess – was there. I'd either find a small inn or, with her consent, stay in Pure Lotus Temple. Then I'd plan my next move, though I had no idea what it would be.

The next morning I arose while it was still dark and hired a car to North Station. The sky was the colour of diluted ink; a cold and dank mist hung sadly in the air. Even though it was only five-thirty in the morning, a crowd was already milling in front of the imposing facade.

Vendors stood guard next to their baskets and screamed at the top of their voices.

'Fresh doughnut and congee!'

'Pig's feet! Smoked fish heads!'

Children held on to the hems of their mothers' clothes; men hauled luggage with determined expressions. A young woman was combing her daughter's hair. Next to them stood two big brown suitcases – like huge dogs guarding their mistresses. A young couple jumped off from a rickshaw. The man dropped a few copper coins into the coolie's calloused hand, then half-pushed the woman toward the station's entrance. The coolie, after letting out grunts, squatted down on the curb, took out his long pipe, and waited for the next customer. I noticed a big scar – the colour of a dead pig's snout – peeking through the hole of his filthy, padded trousers. His feet were two big barges anchored on the dusty asphalt sea.

Who were these people and where were they heading? I wondered how many of them had a purpose in life. But a goal can turn into a nightmare. Like mine, in which I was now shivering in front of the train station, trying to flee from my bleak Karma. I hurried inside the station and bought a third-class ticket, hoping to merge into the crowd like a drop of water falling into the sea. Trying to look as unlike a *ming ji* as possible, I had not put on make-up and was dressed in a worn coat and the rough clothes Qing Zhen had bought for me with his begged money.

I found the track, boarded the train, and squeezed my way along until I found a seat, luckily, next to the window. The third-class car stank: human sweat; piglets, chickens, and ducks knocking around in small cages; children's urine. I spotted people picking their noses and spitting on the floor and felt a distaste so strong that it took all my willpower to suppress a rising nausea.

Finally the train started forward, the cold breeze from the window helping only slightly to dispel the odours. And then, the sun made its gentle appearance, lighting and warming up the air. I dozed off for a while, and when I awoke, the train had stopped at a small station. Through the window I could see tides of people, flowing as if pulled by irresistible forces.

As the train started to move, from the corner of my eye I saw a pleasant-looking, middle-aged man hopping onto the train. His large eyes and square jaw looked familiar but I couldn't quite place him.

In a few seconds, the man materialised in my car. Since many people had gotten off during the brief stop, there were now a few empty seats. He looked around, then to my surprise, came and sat right across from me. Perhaps he recognised me from a past meeting. Or maybe he was a former one-time customer whom I failed to recognise. Then an ominous thought entered my mind – was he one of Fung's men sent to harm me? As my heart began to pound, the man cast me a few curious glances, then took out a book and started to write.

My heartbeat accelerated. Was he writing a report about me? But I tried to comfort myself that this intelligent-looking man didn't seem to be the kind of person who'd work for Fung. I kept stealing glances at him, thinking maybe he was a writer.

Then, when we finally caught each other's eyes, he smiled apologetically, then returned to his notebook. My palms began to sweat and I decided to move to another car. But when I picked up my luggage and my *qin* and started to stand up, I saw that the man was not writing, but sketching – me.

Suddenly a light went off in my mind and relief washed over me. I put my things down as I sat back onto the seat. 'Are you Mr. Jiang Mou?'

The man looked up, his eyes searching mine. 'Yes I am. But how do you know my name?'

It was such an involved story that I didn't know how to respond.

He went on, 'Have we met somewhere?'

'Yes.'

Now he studied me with great interest. 'You do look familiar, but I can't think of where we might have met.'

'I'm Hu Xiang Xiang. We first met ten years ago at the *yuanxiao* Festival in the White Crane Immortal's Hall.'

I could see he was straining to remember.

'I was with Sister Pearl. She introduced me to you. She also told me that if I was lucky, you might agree to paint me someday and make me very famous. Remember?'

'Yes, now I remember. But you've changed so much—'

'But of course, Mr. Jiang, many years have passed!'

We stared silently at each other, digging up old memories and wounds.

I said, measuring my words, 'In Pearl's last letter, she said that in case I'd run into you someday, she wanted me to tell you . . .' Suddenly I felt so angry at this man's callousness that I wondered if he deserved to be told about Pearl's love.

He leaned forward a little. Now I could see that his eyes were turning red.

'Tell me what?'

'Tell you that you're still . . . the man she loved the most.'

Upon hearing this, Jiang Mou's voice cracked. 'I miss Pearl . . . so much.'

I sneered. 'Then where were you when she needed you the most? Why didn't you at least send her some words of comfort?'

'Was that what Pearl thought, that I'm so heartless?'

I nodded.

'When it happened, I was in Peking, painting on commission for a rich patron. I knew nothing until I got back to Shanghai. Not until a whole month after she . . . died. I felt heartbroken when I learned about this. But then there was really nothing that I could do.' He stopped, then spoke again, now looking happier, 'Thank you for telling me what Pearl said.'

I felt my anger dissipate. Under the morning light streaming in from outside the window, I could see what had attracted Pearl to him: broad forehead, square manly jaw, and an intense, artistic air.

After I finished telling him the details of Pearl's death and burial, he sat silently, melancholy hovering on his face. Then he asked me what I'd been doing during the years since we'd last met. Of course, I left certain things out, particularly the reason I was now leaving Shanghai in a third-class railroad car.

After I finished, Jiang Mou studied me meaningfully. 'Xiang Xiang, I want to do something to atone for Pearl and carry out my promise.'

'What is it?'

'To paint you.'

'In oil?' The words *oil painting* were rarely heard in China. My heart raced. It would be such an adventure to be painted not in ink, but oil!

He nodded. 'I have a rich patron in Peking who has rented a studio for me. I can paint you there.'

Jiang Mou told me he could complete the portrait in only three days if I was willing to pose seven or eight hours each day. Since neither of us had empty time to pass (I had to find Mother and he had to fulfil his commission), the arrangement was agreed upon right away.

The next day as we arrived at the Peking station, I got Jiang Mou's studio address and bade him a quick farewell. Instead of going to look for my mother in Pure Lotus Temple, the first thing I did was to make my way to a cheap but decent inn which I'd found near Wangfu Jing in my earlier wanderings in the city. After I checked in, bathed, and changed, I dined on a large bowl of dan dan noodles, then took a rickshaw to Jiang Mou's studio. The address he had given me turned out to be an old house in Wangfu Jing that had been divided into apartments. I dashed up to the fifth floor and rang the bell. Jiang Mou opened the door and let me into a spacious room nearly empty except for a canvas mounted on a stand and a table covered with painting paraphernalia.

He stared intently at my face. 'Should we start right now?'

I nodded. Though we had not discussed it, we both knew it was to be a nude portrait. So, as soon as I was settled, I began – without consulting him – to peel off my clothes as if I were still in Peach Blossom Pavilion. Fortunately, the room was heated by two braziers. I twisted my body, trying to find the perfect pose. Jiang Mou slightly rearranged my limbs and torso. To my disappointment, he looked at my body without recognition. I didn't mean that he looked as if he hadn't seen me, but rather, as if my body stirred no passion, aroused no desire in him. Was he that professional? But I, too, was a professional – in pleasing, seducing, arousing. Then why, now that we were in his studio, did he succeed in his profession while I failed in mine?

Finally I found the perfect pose – my right hand behind my head, while my other hand rested on my *yin* part, with my pubic hair sprouting from underneath my lacy fingers. My breasts protruded, as if eager to be fondled, caressed, kissed.

Jiang Mou cast long, steady glances at me before he started to sketch on the canvas. He'd lift the charcoal stick to measure, then attack the canvas with sweeping movements, with the charcoal making harsh, scraping sounds. The first day was only for sketching; it was not until the second day that he started to paint. In order to catch the right quality of light streaming in from the window, Jiang Mou worked fast. Paint, as if enamoured of the artist, clung to his robe, fingers, face, hair. I dared not utter any sound, fearing the slightest distraction would cause a wrong move of his brush.

Now and then he'd also stop to jot down notes about what colour to use, places of shadings, positions of my arms and legs, and the like. So after I went back to my inn, he'd continue to work.

On the afternoon of the third day, Jiang Mou added a few details and corrected some minor mistakes. Finally, as it was getting dark, he set down his brushes, then turned the easel around to give me my first look at the finished work.

I was fascinated by what I saw. Jiang Mou had managed to add sparkles of mischief to my eyes. The lifted corners of my lips conjured the image of an uncurling lotus. The contrast of my dark hair against my fair skin seemed to express some profound insight into my personality. And the rich, vibrant colour in oil!

Now that he'd set down his brushes, Jiang Mou's eyes regarded me quite differently – I'd come back to life as a woman.

When I was trying to put my robe back on, he held up a halting hand. 'Xiang Xiang, just leave it, please.'

I stared hard at him, letting the robe slip down onto the floor like leaves falling in an autumn breeze. Now I was standing completely naked in front of a man. It might seem hardly worth mentioning since I'd done that nearly every day for all of my adult life. But this time it was different. A dragon was twisting inside me, struggling to break away from the confines of my body. Now I remembered Pearl's telling me of her infatuation with Jiang Mou. Suddenly I was seized by a strong urge to experience Pearl's feelings. I wanted to recreate the night in the temple of the haunted garden where I'd first witnessed the balance of *yin* and *yang*, the mating of heaven and earth – an artist and a prostitute enacting the ageless act of passion.

I wanted to live through Pearl's emotions.

I wanted to be Pearl – at least for a few moments.

Slowly I walked toward Jiang Mou, Pearl's former lover, and reached for his face. He immediately pressed his mouth against my palm, then I felt his tongue caress it with long, wet strokes. He let out an almost painful moan as his jade stalk hardened against me.

Jiang Mou carried me back to the sofa where a few minutes ago I had been posing and gently pressed me down. Swiftly he stripped off his clothes, then knelt beside me sucking the same nipples and licking the same navel he'd just so subtly rendered. Then, like a panther, he lunged on top of me. I heard myself moan as his hands slid under my hips, lifting me up to better fuse with him. Now too aroused to balance the *yin* and *yang*, instead we toppled that balance. Fumbling frantically, we fell off the sofa and rolled onto the floor, knocking over a small table. Brushes and tubes of paint flew around. A jar leaped off, spilled oil on our bodies, then slunk away to a corner. As Jiang Mou's jade stalk thrust deep and hard inside my golden gate, I let out a long, animal-in-slaughter scream. As he began to thrust harder, I dug my nails deeply into his back, until he suddenly gave out an inhuman cry and went limp on the body he'd just so perfectly commemorated with his brush . . .

I lay beside Jiang Mou, my mind empty in a half-sleep. Then gradually, my sense of where I was returned. I knew, and I was sure he did also, that this losing of our souls was our first and last time. I was pretty sure that when we'd been making love, his mind had been filled with Pearl just as mine had been on my only love, Qing Zhen. Not that Jiang Mou bore any resemblance to my Taoist monk lover; nor did I to Pearl. We had only used each other to once again stir these hopeless passions.

Yet, perhaps this was my most satisfactory affair. A brief afternoon unspoiled by futile wishes for permanence and a beautiful painting that would last forever. I rose up, dressed, took the painting that Jiang Mou had wrapped for me, and left for my simple hotel room.

We never saw each other again.

36

The Nun and the Prostitute

The next day, I lay in bed until late in the afternoon. The euphoria of the three days with my oil portraitist lover was gone, leaving me drained. I'd been about to accomplish my lifelong goal of avenging Baba but, as Lao-tzu said, more things are spoiled in the end than in the beginning. Worse, now my money was nearly gone and I could not live in hotels much longer. Though I thought of visiting Qing Zhen, I was too ashamed to return. Then Mother's image flashed into my mind. But in her years as a nun she'd overcome her attachment to me. True, it had returned briefly when she cared for me after I'd fainted on the mountain. Maybe it was still there somewhere, but I did not know how to bring it back. I couldn't faint whenever I wanted some tenderness from her. Nevertheless, my only choice now was to return to her in Pure Lotus Nunnery. At least I'd have a roof over my head and food – though hardly the delicacies Aunty Ah Ping had spoiled me with. And my gaudy gowns and the make-up skills Pearl had taught me would have no place there.

My stay at the temple was likely to be a long one so I had no inclination to rush my arrival there. I wanted to enjoy Peking for a few more days. On the top of my list of soon-to-be-forbidden pleasures was a luxurious meal that would not be allowed in the nunnery.

The Longevity Restaurant was very famous and I decided to

spend some of my dwindling funds on a last sumptuous dinner there. The eatery was an old one with dark furnishings and dim light. I ordered several of their most renowned dishes and set about eating them with relish. Then I looked across the room and my enjoyment vanished. A group of men were sitting around talking loudly, eating, tossing the bones on the floor and drinking toast after toast to each other. They made an unpleasant intrusion in this elegant setting but that was not what bothered me. Two of the men, I was almost certain, were Fung's bodyguards! They did not seem to have noticed me since my table was in a dimly lit recess. But this gave me scant comfort. Did their presence mean that Fung was also in Peking? Alarmed, I realised I was hardly any safer here than in Shanghai. I had no mood now to finish my abalone in oyster sauce or the spicy fish lips. I did gulp down what was left of my shark's fin soup to strengthen my bones, then paid quickly and left.

Back in my room at the inn, I collapsed, sobbing. It seemed that I could never be free of Fung's evil. If only I had been able to kill him, I'd be safe now and would not hate myself for letting my father's murderer continue to live under the same sky with me. But at least I'd mutilated him by shooting his ear off. I did take some pleasure in imagining him trying to explain his missing ear.

That night, I barely slept, and as soon as the grey dawn entered the window, I jumped from bed, gathered my sack of possessions, and paid the bill. I climbed into a waiting rickshaw, gave my destination, then slumped back and drew my shawl around my face. In my anxious state, the ride seemed to go on and on. Now, Mother's temple would at least be safe, for I didn't think Fung or his men would ever come for me inside the empty gate. But even this did not leave me free of worry. I'd been forced to fit myself to life in a prostitution house and was now forced into the life of a nunnery. The first change had been extremely painful. How would this one be?

Finally the coolie grunted, 'Lotus Temple. Get out. Pay now.'

I dragged my bag through the main gate, stopped the first nun whom I ran into, and asked about Wonderful Kindness.

The round-faced nun smiled. 'The Abbess has been back for a while.'

'Can you show me where her office is?'

The nun pointed to a subtemple under two ancient pine trees. 'Abbess's room is on the third floor to the right.'

I put my hands together and made a deep bow. 'Thank you,' I smiled, then hurried toward the green clusters.

The door was left ajar, so I peeked in. Mother, her face pale and her scalp shining like a light bulb, was shuffling piles of papers spread over a large wooden table.

As I was about to knock, a soft voice rose in the air. 'Venerable Mother Abbess Wonderful Kindness, this miss asks for you.' I turned and saw the same nun whom I'd just talked to in the courtyard.

The young nun pushed open the door and signalled me in. After that, she went straight to stand protectively behind *her* venerable *my* mother abbess.

I set my luggage on the floor. Mother looked up and our eyes met. Pangs stabbed my heart. It had been barely a month since we had last seen each other, but Mother seemed to have aged a lot. Her face was paler and those once luminous eyes now looked like two dried-up wells. Or two dusty windows, reflecting nothing in life but images of continual suffering.

She waved a bony hand. 'Please be seated, Miss Hu.'

Miss Hu? Didn't she recognise me as her daughter?

'Ma—'

'Miss Hu, I would like to be addressed as Wonderful Kindness. Miss Ma was my lay name, which I've abandoned for a long time.'

Wonderful Kindness. I would certainly like her to show a little kindness toward her daughter. And Miss Ma, what a clever lie! But I was almost relieved by her impersonal behaviour. At least I now knew how I was supposed to behave around her. Since she resumed her role as a 'business nun' and preferred our meeting to be businesslike, I'd start with business myself.

'Wonderful Kindness Abbess, I've recently moved from Shanghai to Peking permanently. I'd like to know whether I can stay in your temple for a short period of time . . .'

Mother looked surprised, even pleased. Just as my heart was responding to the happiness blossoming on her face, her expression changed again. Now looking serious and detached, she turned to ask the young nun to bring us tea and snacks.

After the nun was gone, she turned to me. 'Xiang Xiang,' she said, the flicker in her eyes betraying emotion behind her bland expression, 'so you've finally decided to join me and become a nun?'

She sounded so eager that I had to lie. 'Ma, I'll certainly consider it, but for the time being I need time to think and reorganise my life.'

'That's fine. Of course you can stay here as long as you want. But tell me, will you still . . .'

'Ma, don't worry, I'll never again set foot inside a turquoise pavilion.'

To my surprise, Mother reached her scarred hand to pat mine.

I knew my face looked blurred to her eyes as hers did to mine. I also knew that, after all these years, we'd become experts at not letting our tears fall – the most prestigious prostitute couldn't afford to mar her make-up and reveal her true feelings; the most revered nun could not afford to let people know of her worldly affections.

Just then the young nun came back with a tray set with a teapot, two lidded cups, and small plates of dim sum.

Mother said, her tone now dignified, 'Miss Hu, you are most welcome to stay in Pure Lotus to chant sutras and search for your Buddha-nature.'

It was not easy for me to get used to the temple routine of arising at four in the morning and spending much of the day chanting and meditating. There was no maid to bring me beef congee for breakfast or Ah Ping's delicious dishes for lunch and dinner. Indeed, breakfast was not served until we'd been up chanting and meditating for several hours. Then we would all tramp over to the Fragrant Kitchen. The food was vegetarian, not bad, but monotonous.

People were nice enough to me but I made no real friends. I had little in common with the nuns, who were mostly ignorant of any other sort of life. Nor would it have been suitable for me to talk to them about my own life. There were a few other laypeople, who spent their time making offerings to the Buddha to earn merit for their children and ancestors. Their conversations were usually gossip about events in the nunnery though sometimes the outer world would enter in. One elderly woman kept talking about the Japanese and what they would do if they arrived in Peking.

I heard and saw nothing of Fung's henchmen. Nor did I expect to. Anyone – even a bandit or a murderer – once inside a temple, was left in peace. To trouble someone who had taken refuge in the Buddha was to upset the way of heaven. The bad Karma thus generated would last for many generations to come. This also gave me a simple way to be rid of Ouyang. I wrote a letter telling him that I was now practising meditation at Pure Lotus. I told my big protector of sexual Dharma that, devastated by my father's death as well as disillusioned by affairs of the red dust, I was seriously considering becoming a nun. At the end of the letter, I thanked him profusely for his generous patronage as well as for introducing me to Pure Lotus. Finally I asked him not to send any letter of reply to the nunnery.

I never heard from him again.

Though I now felt safe, the unvarying routine and endless chanting made me restless. When I saw Mother, she avoided any reminiscence of our happy family but instead mostly talked about the Dharma and how it would release me from my unhappiness. Mother now called me Miss Hu. After our week together on the mountain and that first meeting in her temple office, she never called me Xiang Xiang again.

When I wouldn't be missed from the temple activities, I'd slip off to my room, take out my poor, battered *qin*, and play 'Remembering an Old Friend' or some of my other favourites. Sometimes I'd imagine what it would be like if Pearl were still alive and we were nuns together.

One day, three months into this monotonous routine, I was sitting in my room, half-heartedly tuning my *qin*, when a novice arrived and told me that Mother wanted to see me in her office. I set down the instrument and walked through the cold air to the main building and up the stairs to her room. Once I'd sat down opposite her and tea had been served, she looked at me intently. I was quite surprised but happy to see a pink glow on her face.

'Miss Hu, I have some very good news for you!' Before I could respond, she was speaking again. 'Our temple has just received a big donation and we have decided to use it to open a school.'

'A school?' How could a school be good news to a prostitute, or ex-prostitute, like me?

She ignored my interjection. 'And I want you to help with the teaching.'

This took me by surprise. 'But Ma, I'm not a teacher, I'm a—'

'This will be a special school for special people – sisters fallen in the midst of the wind and dust.'

'Ma, how—'

'We plan to open a school to rehabilitate ex-sisters.' She paused, then recited something like a poem, 'In Buddhism there are no distinctions. Charitable deeds can only be carried out when many work together.'

I cast Mother a doubtful glance. 'I've never heard of anything like a school for prostitutes.'

'It's something new. The whole temple will be devoted to bringing Dharma to the sisters.'

I almost laughed, remembering Pearl's joking about 'offering one's body to preach the Dharma,' meaning bending forward to show off one's breasts. With effort, I put on a serious expression. 'But Ma, I've never been a teacher.'

'But you were a good student, right? You're very good at the arts and the classics. So you can teach these to the girls, and after they've graduated from our school, instead of prostitution they can make their living either as artists or teachers.'

I wanted to say something, but she already waved a dismissive hand. 'I'm afraid the matter has already been decided. The school will be named New Model School, and you'll be responsible to teach music, painting, and literature, especially to the sisters who can't read. We've found five ex-sisters who'll join you in teaching.'

When she finished, we looked at each other in silence. Then I picked up my tea and took a long sip, hoping the steaming liquid would dissipate the doubts in my mind.

The New Model School was to be opened on April 28, 1929. A month before, on March 28, Mr. Dong – the big protector of the Dharma who'd donated the money for the school – held a grand opening party at a Western restaurant. Among the throngs of people, there were no nuns from Pure Lotus. Their absence was understood – it's one thing for monks and nuns to preach equality among all living creatures, it's another for them to actually mix with prostitutes in public. Of course, the nuns had attained non-discrimination and non-attachment, but they knew the public hadn't.

The next day, the event was reported by a columnist in the most popular newspaper *Sheba*:

... An opening celebration of the New Model School was held at the Grand Fragrance Restaurant, where it was attended by many sisters together with merchants, government officials, scholars, artists – all prostitute rehabilitation enthusiasts.

At five o'clock in the afternoon, black sedans began to pull up to the entrance of the restaurant, disgorging elegantly dressed ex-*ming ji*. Pedestrians gathered around to watch these beautiful women as if they were fairy maidens descending on earth.

Western food and drinks were served – ham, Russian soup, roast beef, Ceylon tea with milk, sherry, champagne, whisky. After plates were put away and the tables cleared, Miss Red Fragrance, a former sister from Jade Gate Pavilion and the newly elected principal of New Model School, stood up to deliver a speech stressing the importance of education for women, their independence, and their role in contributing to the world. Then she went on, announcing the school's goals: To rebuild the sisters' character. To educate and rehabilitate sisters so that they can hold decent jobs. To help sisters to attain financial independence or to get married. 'The new school would be like a beam of light in hell,' she said, concluding her speech.

She announced the names of the staff. One teacher, by the name of Precious Orchid, was a *ming ji* well versed in the Classics and all the arts, especially the ancient seven-stringed *qin*.

After an evening of endless discussions, picture taking, eating, and drinking, the meeting finally ended with all the sisters singing: 'Sisters, let's all stand together!'

> Sisters, let's not waste our life amid the smoke and ashes of
>   the red dust,
> But contribute our youth to reform!
> Success is close at hand, and we'll all be blessed.
> Let's stand up and get together.
> Let's build ourselves a better, happier, and brighter future!
> Let's be the new models for our fellow sisters!

Other major newspapers and magazines also reported the opening of our new school. To my surprise, all of them had a few lines about me – that I was the most prestigious sister from Shanghai and an expert in all the arts – especially the *qin*. I had no idea whether I received this attention because reporters had found out about my relationship with the Venerable Mother Abbess of Pure Lotus Temple or simply because my fame had spread from Shanghai. Anyway, I greatly enjoyed being the object of attention once again.

A month later, we had thirty-seven students – an encouraging number. Mother predicted we'd have more than three hundred in a year. I knew Pure Lotus worked very hard not only to get donations, but also to attract students – whenever a nun saw a sister come into the temple, she'd tell her about the school and try to persuade her to attend.

When I saw my new pupils on the first day of class, I was surprised – though I shouldn't have been. They all dressed in lavish gowns, wore heavy make-up, and threw flirtatious glances. Didn't they realise that they were here to be rehabilitated, to learn, not to flirt?

Despite this unpromising beginning, I worked very hard in preparing lessons, usually staying after class to give extra help and scrupulously attending all the meetings for discussion of school policies. But I quickly realised that teaching these girls to understand the classics was a fond hope. They could write their names and knew a few other characters, but it seemed beyond possibility to teach them even to write a simple letter. These flower girls of the new generation simply had no interest in being educated.

But instead of giving up, I decided to teach something special – the *qin*. Just as Pearl had passed its music on to me, I wanted a student to continue this precious lineage. I picked a girl named Baobao because she dressed the best and seemed to have an artistic air. She showed great interest at the first few lessons but then it waned as quickly as snow melts on a mountaintop. Soon, she stopped practising. Her explanation was that she had become so popular she barely had enough time for all her customers, let alone the *qin*. Then one day I waited for half an hour before she showed up for her lesson – her hair unkempt and her clothes wrinkled.

'Baobao, please wash your hands before you play,' I said, not hiding my annoyance.

Reluctantly she went to the washroom. When she came back, she plopped gracelessly down on the chair and started to play without tuning the *qin*. Before I had a chance to scold her again, she suddenly stopped in the middle of her playing and, to my utmost shock, took out a cigarette and lit it.

'Baobao, show some respect to this sacred instrument!'

'Sorry, Miss Precious Orchid.' She squeezed a flirtatious smile and drew on her cigarette; ashes fluttered onto my silk-stringed pure land.

That was when I decided not to teach the *qin* any more.

When I'd started to teach at the school, I'd imagined I could do for the students what Pearl had done for me. I wanted to transform common girls into elegant, artistic women. But now I had to painfully admit that it was hopeless – they had no interest in being taught the arts. Pearl had predicted, when Red Jade had won the contest, that ours would be the last generation of *ming ji*. Now I realised with sadness that she had been right. The era of the elegant courtesan was receding into history.

These new flower girls were different. All they knew how to do was lie down and spread their legs!

37

An Unexpected Visitor

The growing heat of summer reminded me that I'd been living at the nunnery and teaching at New Model School for almost two years. For a while I pretended that, as a teacher, I could fulfil Baba's idea of being a Number One Scholar. But I had no patience for my slow students and I had no chance of being hired at a respectable girls' school. And even if I were, teaching gave me little enjoyment.

One day, as I was tidying up the table in my office, the school maid came to tell me that someone had asked for me and was waiting in the lobby. Few visitors ever called on me, and I suddenly wondered if Ouyang, or worse, Fung, had after all decided to come for me. But when I asked the maid what he looked like, she said he was a *laofan*. I assumed the visitor was a foreign reporter who wanted to write about our school for the English newspaper *North China Herald*. Or perhaps a Westerner secretly curious about Chinese courtesans but afraid to actually visit a turquoise pavilion.

As I was approaching the lounge, I saw a middle-aged, pale-haired man pacing up and down, the soles of his leather shoes tapping impatiently on the floor. Once he saw me, a warm smile broke out on his face and his blue eyes seemed to glow. I was astonished to see someone I didn't expect ever to see again – Mr. Anderson.

It had been a long time, probably nine years, since he'd mysteriously stopped coming to Peach Blossom. He'd been so kind to me and then never came back. But I'd done no better to Qing Zhen. Though, of course, Anderson had never made love to me – I always wondered why. To my delight, though he had aged quite a bit, he nevertheless looked well. His body seemed to be stouter but his face radiated a healthy glow. His fatigued look had been replaced by a confident one. But the warmth of his eyes, which I so clearly remembered, had not changed.

There was an awkward silence before I said, 'Mr. Anderson, what an unexpected pleasure!'

He came forward to grasp my hand. 'Miss Precious Orchid,' he said excitedly, 'how nice to see you again.'

When he finally let go of my hand, we remained silent, scrutinising each other. As I'd noticed that he had changed, he must also have noticed how I had – my plain indigo cotton dress; my straight hair pulled into a tight bun; my un-made-up face; my proper teacher-like manner. Suddenly I feared he might not find me appealing in my new incarnation as a schoolmistress living in a nunnery. I reached to smooth my unpomaded hair.

'Mr. Anderson.' I searched his face. 'How did you know that I'm here?'

He smiled demurely. 'Miss Precious Orchid, you've become . . . famous all over again. I saw your name in the newspaper; that's how I found you.'

'But how did you know it was me? Since you only knew me as Xiang Xiang but not Precious Orchid.'

'Because not many sisters would come from Shanghai and play the *qin*,' he said, casting me appreciative glances. 'Of course I was not one hundred percent sure, so I had to know if it was you.'

I decided to throw him a soul-sucking glance, just for old times' sake. 'So Mr. Anderson, what kind of wind has blown you here?'

'I've been closing a business deal in Peking.' He stopped to search my face. 'Xiang Xiang, how . . . are you?'

'I'm fine,' I said, feeling so touched at hearing my real name uttered that I had to blink back tears.

He cast me a tender look. 'Do you enjoy teaching here?'

'Hmmm . . . I would say that it's interesting.' He stared at me but said nothing, so I asked, 'Mr. Anderson, it's been such a long time since I last saw you. Has life been nice to you?'

He smiled. 'Indeed it has. My business has been more successful than I expected.'

'So you must be a very happy man now.'

'In a way, yes. But, of course, I don't have everything I want.'

I felt I should not ask more, so I just smiled. Then we continued to talk about odds and ends of years passed. Though overall more confident in his manner, Anderson still seemed a little stiff with me. Happy as I was to have him visit me, I could not quite figure out why he had. And soon the visit was over.

'Xiang Xiang, it's wonderful to see you again.' He looked at me for a long moment, then politely kissed my hand before taking leave.

That night I slept restlessly. Anderson's image kept spinning in my mind. He was much older than me and though I could not call him handsome, he certainly was not ugly. I hadn't thought about him much over the years, yet now I found myself hoping he'd want to see me again. But his goodbye was as reserved as ever and his sudden departure left me anxious. Would he visit again or, like nine years ago, disappear as mysteriously as he had come?

My suspense didn't last long. The next morning, a maid sent by Anderson came to deliver a note – he would come to visit me after class.

At five-thirty in the afternoon, my American friend arrived and, to my surprise, invited me out to an expensive hotel restaurant in the commercial district. It had been a long time since I had had a chance to go to an elegant place like this. Memories of my glorious days back in Peach Blossom and with Ouyang flooded back. I only wished Anderson had told me earlier so I could have put on make-up and changed to a silk dress.

As I entered the imposing Western-style stone building and passed through corridors lined with frescoes and marble pillars, heads turned and eyes riveted on me. I was pleased that, although I'd stopped being a *ming ji*, my prestigious air still seemed to linger around me like expensive perfume. Despite my time among nuns and my resolve never again to be a sister, male attention – something I'd almost forgotten about – still delighted me.

The tuxedoed waiter seated us at a table beside a tall plant in an ornate cachepot. He set down the tea service and a plate of cold appetisers.

After the ritual of making small talk had been fulfilled, Anderson cast me a meaningful look. 'Xiang Xiang, you mind if I ask you a personal question?'

I smiled. 'Please, Mr. Anderson.'

'Are you happy with your new life as a teacher?'

The question caught me off guard. Since I'd fled to Peking, I didn't think much about happiness or unhappiness. I didn't even think much about the future. I just lived or, to be more accurate, worked.

I arranged my fingers to resemble an orchid, then picked up the porcelain cup and took a delicate sip of my tea. 'Mr. Anderson, nowadays I don't think much about transient things, such as happiness.'

'Xiang Xiang, then please start thinking about it.'

I quietly put down my cup and threw him a curious glance. 'Why?'

'Ever since I used to visit you before, I've thought about you often.'

'Is that so?' I cast him a chiding glance. 'Then why did you stop going to see me at Peach Blossom?'

'I'd wanted to,' he said, looking awkward. 'But then my partner Mr. Ho got sick and stopped visiting sisters. Anyway, shortly after that, my business switched mainly to Peking. But Xiang Xiang, I never stopped . . . thinking about you.'

I put on a skeptical look. He went on, struggling for words. 'Xiang Xiang, you're a very talented, artistic woman.'

'Mr. Anderson, overpraise. I'm sure a man like yourself must be around sophisticated women all the time.'

'Maybe, but none like you.'

I raised a questioning brow.

He fidgeted with his teaspoon, then put it down and said softly, 'Xiang Xiang, forgive my bluntness. I . . . hate to see you living a lonely life.'

'But Mr. Anderson,' I felt pressed to hide the truth of his remark, 'every day I'm surrounded by students and nuns. So I don't think my life—'

'Xiang Xiang, I know what it is like to face an empty room each night after work.'

Anderson's words stirred something inside me, but I didn't respond. I was beginning to suspect the purpose of his visit.

He went on, 'Xiang Xiang, I'm a man of few words, so let me be honest with you. After all these years of doing business, I've acquired enough money to make me feel safe. And,' he paused for several moments, blushing, 'I want you to be safe, too – with me.'

Over the years, men had told me all sorts of things that they wanted to do with me, but never this. I was taken completely by surprise. I didn't think I loved this man in front of me, but I didn't dislike him either. In fact, I felt some true affection for him, for his kindness toward me since I'd been thirteen. He did not make me feel as Qing Zhen or Jiang Mou had, but I felt good being with him.

Now Anderson seemed to mean marrying him and most likely going to live in a strange country. Although I'd dreamed of leaving China to see the world, now confronted with the chance, the idea suddenly seemed far-fetched and confusing. Besides, I had my new life as a teacher. Although, of course, I didn't really care about teaching but did it mainly to please Mother – and also because there was nothing else for me to do.

Seeing that I was not able to answer, Anderson went on, carefully choosing his words, 'My years in China have taught me what Karma is. Xiang Xiang, our paths have crossed, more than once, and this must not be purely accidental. Things happen for a purpose.'

I took a delicate bite of a miniature ham sandwich and chewed meditatively without savouring the taste. Finally I said, 'Mr. Anderson, I'm very flattered by your offer, but I . . . have just started my career. And the New Model School needs me—'

'Forgive my bluntness again, the school is a wonderful idea, but do you really believe that it'll last?'

This question took me by surprise, for the idea that the school might close had never entered my mind. 'Mr. Anderson—'

'Xiang Xiang, from now on please call me Richard, that's my first name.'

Richard, I silently repeated the two enigmatic syllables, as if savouring a secret suddenly revealed. '. . . Richard,' I cast him a mock chiding look, 'it's bad luck for you to say something like this about our newly opened school!'

'I didn't mean to offend you. But I'm a businessman, and a businessman must be practical and realistic. We can have dreams and ambitions in life, but we can't afford illusions. They're too expensive.'

I remained silent; he looked down at his tea and stirred it nervously. Moments passed before he looked up at me. 'Xiang Xiang, you probably don't follow politics but things are very dangerous with the Japanese. I fear they may invade any time.'

His statement startled me. I'd heard talk before about the Japanese, but living a secluded life inside the nunnery and occupied by my teaching, I'd never given much thought to the issue. 'Is the situation that bad?'

'Xiang Xiang, the Chinese are not facing up to the threat. And when the Japanese come, they won't be very nice to pretty women.'

My heart began to pound. Yet another event now threatened to send my life off on a different course, one that might be far worse than what I'd already been through.

He took a sip of his tea, then put down the cup and looked at me deeply. 'Xiang Xiang, I want to give you a good life; can you fulfil this wish of mine?' He plunged on, 'I know I'm much older than you, and you might not even love me. But that doesn't really matter, does it? As a Chinese, I'm sure you know well that most couples cultivate their love after marriage. Xiang Xiang, I do think an older man is much more suitable for you. Because we know how to love and take good care of a woman. Xiang Xiang, I love you and I'll give you a very good life.'

I giggled a little to dissipate the tension in the air. 'Mr. Anderson—'

'Please call me Richard.'

'Richard, I am flattered! But . . .' Since I didn't have the heart to say that I didn't love him, I had to think of something else. Finally I came up with, 'Due to my work in the past, I don't think I'm . . . suitable to be your wife.'

His face flushed and his voice tensed. 'Xiang Xiang, this is pure nonsense! I'm very proud of you. You're a distinguished artist and an outstanding *qin* player. Besides, we'll be going to a new country where no one will know you.'

Like a cat chasing its own tail, it seemed Anderson would not give up, and the conversation led to no conclusion.

Finally he said, looking distressed, 'Xiang Xiang, I know I can't force you or even talk you into doing anything you don't want to do. But please think about my offer. I'll be going back to the United States soon and I don't know when I'll come back, maybe never, or at least not for a very long time. Since I've made a lot of money, I am thinking of retirement.' He reached to take my hand and put it to his lips.

And I kept my hand there.

That evening when I went home, Anderson's image and proposal kept spinning in my mind like a merry-go-round. Yes, I was sure he'd be a good husband. And I was also sure with the money he had, he'd provide security to me for the rest of my life.

But I didn't love him.

I chuckled at this thought. When did my former profession afford me to think about love? In my decadent years, I'd served many older men. So, what difference did it make to serve one more? But there would be a difference – I'd be Anderson's proper, lawful, first – and only – wife.

Then I remembered Pearl's saying years ago:

If this Anderson ever comes back and offers to pay your debt or even proposes marriage, accept right away even if you feel no love for him. This kind of chance only happens here once in a lifetime.

I flipped and tossed in my solitary bed, agonising over whether I should take the plunge and say yes. But if I did, then there would no longer be a chance for true love. There would be no man like Qing Zhen with magic over my heart, body, and soul.

Then I imagined Anderson's compassionate face looming above me and his lips muttering, 'Xiang Xiang, give both yourself and me a chance. I love you.'

This was followed by images of Japanese soldiers marching inside the nunnery . . .

* * *

Anderson continued to visit. The more I saw what the passage of time had done to his kind face – and what it would inevitably do to mine – the more I thought I should accept his proposal. Three weeks later, I went to Mother's office to break the news. Before bringing up the subject, I asked her what was she going to do with the temple if the Japanese came.

To my surprise, she said, 'I'm not going anywhere.'

'But Ma—'

'I'm a nun. Everywhere is the same – both nirvana and samsara.'

At that moment I honestly thought Mother was out of her mind. What if the Japanese soldiers knocked down the temple, smashed all the Buddhist statues, then raped and killed her? Maybe she'd become so detached that she didn't even care about that? But doesn't Buddhism, besides teaching us to detach, also teach us to protect our bodies?

'Ma, then do you also want me to stay?'

She looked surprised. 'No. My daughter, you're not a nun.'

It had been a long time since she'd called me daughter. Tears brimmed over my eyes. 'Ma . . .'

'Yes?'

'I think I'm . . . getting married.'

To my surprise, Mother's pale face glowed. Moments passed before she said, her voice slightly raised in excitement, 'May I know who's the groom?'

'Richard Anderson, an American merchant.'

Her eyes widened, and she asked eagerly, 'Does that mean you're going to America?'

I nodded.

Her answer surprised me. 'Good.' She went on, 'There's too much misery and suffering here in our country. My daughter, marry this Richard Anderson and leave China as quickly as possible.'

'Ma, don't you want me to become a nun?'

She cast me a meaningful look. 'But things are different now. They have changed; they always do.'

'But Ma, I want you to come with us. I want—'

Before I could say more, she dismissed me with a frantic wave of her bony hand.

* * *

A month later the New Model School, after all the fuss and publicity, closed, less than two years after its opening. Then another month later, on September 18, a small bomb exploded on the tracks of the Japanese-owned South Manchurian Railway. The Japanese army used this as a pretext to occupy the Chinese province – although we Chinese were certain that the bomb was, in fact, planted by the Japanese soldiers.

After the takeover of Manchuria, the whole capital was thrown into panic overnight. Some newspapers predicted that the Japanese would soon be pushed out. Others warned that the *wokou* – Japanese bandits – were unstoppable and would soon be invading all the major cities in China – Nanking, Chungking, Peking, Shanghai. Alarm spread quickly. The black societies – the famous green gang and the *hong* gang – took advantage of the situation to seize control of prostitution in the International Concession, abusing the poor girls and extorting nearly all of their income as protection fees.

China was heading into chaos.

I thought that before I decided whether to marry Anderson and leave China, I should visit Shanghai one last time. I wanted to say goodbye to Aunty Ah Ping, as well as pay my last respects to the ghosts of my two sworn blood sisters, Pearl and Ruby.

I only planned to stay a day. So right after I arrived at the North Station, I hired a rickshaw and asked the coolie to go directly to the International Concession. When the rickshaw neared the elegant pink building from across the wide boulevard, I asked the puller to stop. There was Peach Blossom Pavilion. I was eager to run into Auntie Ah Ping, and maybe some other old acquaintances, and also glimpse – for the last time – my former home, or prison. One or two pedestrians scurried on the street, faces tensed and heads lowered. I saw a few expensive cars parked outside the pavilion. It made me think of an old prostitute whose once glorified fame and beauty were as remote as the setting sun. However, despite the forlorn appearance, light and faint sound poured from the windows. Peach Blossom was still in business! Were Fang Rong and Wu Qiang now entertaining Japanese soldiers? I felt a mixture of emotions. In a way, I wished this gold-powdered hell would vanish forever, but it had been, after all, a roof over my head for many years.

Suddenly I saw the door swing open, and out walked a lean figure in a blue jacket printed with huge gold coins. Was it Wu Qiang? My 'De'? Or one of my former guests? Because the boulevard was very wide, I had to crane my neck . . .

'BBBBOOOOOOOMMM!!!'

My rickshaw flew up then crashed onto the ground. Smoke stung my eyes, choking me. My ears temporarily turned deaf. I could almost hear my bones shattering inside. I opened my mouth, but no sound came out, only gasps.

The coolie's panicked voice made another explosion in my ears. 'Bomb! The Japanese have invaded!' Frantically, he lifted up the rickshaw and pulled, knocking me off with the sudden motion.

After I struggled to get up, I looked and couldn't believe what I saw – or didn't see.

Peach Blossom Pavilion was gone!

Guests were starting to pour out. A few rats, too, scurrying in different directions, followed by something round rolling on the ground. Were these human heads!? It took me a few seconds to realise that they were the two heads of the protective stone lions!

I felt a jolt inside, remembering Pearl's words ten years ago during our last day together.

The day will come when Peach Blossom Pavilion will be torn down.

Just then I spotted another rickshaw puller trying to flee. I screamed at him to stop but to no avail. Then, by dashing in front of him and holding up a fistful of bills, I was able to force him to halt so I could jump on. I kept turning my head to see whether Peach Blossom Pavilion was still there. But all I could see was heavy smoke, as I was carried away from the Concession forever.

In December 1931, at twenty-six, I finally closed one chapter of my life and started another. I married Richard Anderson, boarded the ocean liner *President Cleveland*, and left my mother's cold mountain for America's Gold Mountain.

Epilogue

'That's it, Grandmama! You just left your mother behind and married that old man?' Jade Treasure asks me with eyes widened.

'Jade, that "old man" was your great-grandfather.'

She makes a face. 'Sorry, Grandmama. Then what happened to Great-great-grandmama?'

I smile. 'After I settled in San Francisco, my mother wrote and this time I did receive her letters. Unlike those written to me over a decade ago, these were short, only a line or two telling me about her work in the temple, or asking me about my new life. She survived the Japanese occupation but died a few years later in 1948, just before Mao Tse-tung's victory and the closing of the nunneries by the Communists.' I pause for a brief moment, then go on, 'I hope she had finally attained the enlightenment she had strived for so hard.'

Jade asks, 'Then what about you and Grandpapa, were you happily married ever after?'

I think for a while. 'Boringly ever after, if you want me to be honest for the memoir.'

'Boringly – ever – after,' Jade mouths while scribbling this precious piece of information on her notepad.

I peek at Leo. I'm sure now he wants very much to pull his fiancée into his arms and kiss her on those pink, sensuously pouted lips.

Jade looks up at me with her – or my – big, dark eyes. 'Grand-mama, why did you choose to marry an old barbarian?'

This time I scold her for not showing proper respect for my late husband, her great-grandfather.

'Grandmama, but that's exactly what *you* call Americans!'

I pick up my tea and take a sip, while appreciating the lovely lines of my great-granddaughter's lips, resembling a temple's curved crim-son eaves. 'All right,' I put down my cup, 'the reason I married a barbarian is because your great-grandfather was a most honourable man. He always treated me as an equal. During our years of marriage, he worshipped me like a queen, so I bowed to him as if he were a king.'

'But did you . . . love him?'

'Not in the beginning, but later, yes. We came to understand each other very well.'

I take a long sip of my longevity brew. 'Your great-grandpapa lived to ninety-five, forty-odd years after we'd gotten married. Since he had a lot of money, he helped me open the Elegant Orchid Art Gallery, where I taught arts – painting, calligraphy, the *qin*.'

Leo leans forward and asks, 'What kind of people came?'

'Mostly rich *tai tai*. Also a few whom I suspect somehow heard about my mysteriously prestigious past.'

Jade and Leo's pens press and scratch on the notepads as if they were unbearably itchy, dying to be relieved. When they finish, my eyes are lingering on my oil portrait – painted seventy-five years ago in the final days of my career as the last eminent poet-musician-courtesan in Shanghai, China.

Jade points to my immortalised self. 'Grandmama, do you like this painting?'

'I like what it is and what it reminds me of.'

Now Leo's eyes caress the twenty-three-year-old me. Then he turns to the ninety-eight-year-old me and smiles sunnily. '*Popo*, you were such a great beauty.'

It's always pleasurable to tease this naïve American boy, so I ask, '*Were*? So you're telling me that now I'm but an ugly old hag?'

He looks so stunned that I burst into laughter.

Jade smacks him hard on the shoulder. 'Leo, watch what you say to Grandmama!'

I wave Leo a dismissive hand. 'All right, all right, my big prince, don't panic. Of course now Jade is the most beautiful woman.' I wink. 'How can she not be? Since she's inherited *my* beauty.'

The young faces break into two blossoming lotuses. Then Jade asks, 'Grandmama, how do you feel about having been a . . .'

My spoiled American princess actually looks embarrassed. I've already guessed her question. 'My darling, you want to know whether I feel ashamed or proud to be a *ming ji*, right?'

The two heads eagerly nod, like two balls buoying on a sea of happiness – enjoying the tales of my suffering.

I let out a long sigh. '*Hai,* that's the question! All right. I was lucky. Though I was given to a prostitution house, it was of the highest level. And there I met Pearl without whom I'd never have learned the *pipa* – or the *qin*. As for the stinking males, sometimes it *was* pretty hard to be with them. But now it hardly matters, for they've all gone to the Yellow Springs. But my four-hundred, now turned five-hundred-year-old *qin* with its three-thousand-year-old melodies is still with me.' I pause; my eyes land on the slender instrument hanging on the wall. My pure land. Always.

I pause to search the two young faces. 'You know what it is that I feel most proud of in my whole life?'

Jade leans forward, thrusting out her chest. 'Your talent in the arts?'

I shake my head.

'Your *qin* playing?'

I shake my head again, then search their eyes while remaining silent.

'What then? Grandmama, please don't tease us all the time!'

'Ah,' I chuckle, 'but unfortunately, "teasing" is the main part of my training as a *ming ji*. Although it might get a little rusty after seventy-odd years, I don't think I can get rid of it completely.'

'Grandmama!' Jade protests again.

Leo puts a loving hand on her thigh while addressing me, 'Please tell us, *Popo.*'

'All right, all right.' I pause for yet another moment before I say, carefully choosing my words, 'The one thing I feel most proud of myself is not what I did do, but what I didn't . . .'

Jade widens her eyes. 'Grandmama, what is there that you didn't do?'

'I didn't . . .' This time I pause to change my breath. 'Put a bullet into Big Master Fung's heart.'

She makes a face, reading from her notes. 'Oh yes, of course, it's because of your mother's talk about Buddhist compassion that your bullet was directed to Fung's ear instead of his heart.'

I continue, 'Anyway, Fung died of a stroke shortly after the incident. And I believe this was because I'd shot him.'

'But you missed!'

'He was killed by his own bad Karma.'

'Wow!' Jade exclaims. 'Perfect!'

Leo asks, 'Were you happy when you heard that he died?'

I think for a while before I answer, 'Not happy, but sad.'

Both Jade and Leo make a face. 'Sad?'

'I didn't feel sad about him, but about human life. The strange workings of fate.'

Another long silence during which my two *yin yang* kids are busy capturing my feelings and reminiscences in words.

When they finish, Jade throws me an unexpected question. 'Grandmama, how come after you'd eaten all the infertility soup in Peach Blossom you were still able to have my grandma?'

'Because I also ate all Qing Zhen's longevity soup on the mountain!' I laugh. 'The real reason was because your great-grandfather was very rich, so he was able to send me to the most expensive hospitals and best doctors for treatment. Or because I also saw the most famous herbalist in Chinatown, who treated me with expensive herbs like *hong hua* to warm my blood, *dong gui,* bird's nest, and special wild ginseng from Tianshan.'

'*Dong gui* and bird's nest, yuck!' Jade exclaims, while earnestly writing down these expensive herbs on her cheap paper. When she finishes, she looks up to search my face. 'Grandmama, after Grandpapa died, you must still have been very attractive. Why didn't you marry again?'

'Jade, are you kidding? After all these men in my life, weren't they enough? Besides . . .' I pause; my thoughts fly back to my pure love – the young, handsome, mountain-dwelling, concoction-brewing, alms-receiving (or street-begging), *qin*-playing Taoist monk. 'I had, albeit very briefly, my true love in life – Qing Zhen.'

The impossibly young and beautiful couple exchange smiles. Their youthful passion makes me feel sweetly sad. Now scenes of me and Qing Zhen, like excerpts from a silent movie, flash across my mind. I still remember clearly how his long, glossy hair fell over his face under the moonlight; how he touched me with his mystical hands, transforming me from an unfeeling prostitute to an eager lover; how he moaned and screamed and squirmed when he reached sexual nirvana . . . All these seem so fresh in my mind though seventy-six years have passed!

The ancient sage was right – one day spent in the mountain is a thousand years passed in the world.

I wonder, as I have for so many years, if Qing Zhen is still alive. If he is, he should be one hundred and six! Then he would truly have succeeded in becoming an immortal. If he hasn't lost his mind from drinking that concoction with the dead bird floating in it, does he still think of me from time to time?

'Grandmama, are you all right?'

'Yes, I'm fine, why?'

'Because you're crying!' Jade says; then she plucks a couple of tissues to wipe my face. I imagine her gentle hand is that of my one-hundred-and-six-year-old lover.

With my tears dried, the three of us sit in silence, busy sipping tea and nibbling the dim sum Jade and Leo brought from my favourite restaurant, the Emperor's Wok. Like an empress, I feel great content surrounded by the familiar sounds of laughter, bickering, rattling plates, clicking chopsticks, smacking lips, and noisy sipping of the longevity brew.

My family reunion. At last.

If only Pearl were here.

'Jade,' I point to the chest next to the TV, 'in the bottom drawer, there's a manila envelope, can you get it for me?'

She dashes away then back and, putting on the air of a filial, submissive Chinese daughter, hands me the envelope with both hands.

'Thank you, Jade,' I say, pulling out a picture from the envelope.

The photograph shows a youth standing in a daring pose, wearing a white Western suit, a hat, a pair of gold-rimmed glasses (although the gold doesn't show in the black-and-white picture), and shiny, black-and-white leather shoes. The legs are apart, one in front of the other; one hand is on the hip while the other touches the brim of the hat. A cigar and a mischievous smile dangle from the sensuous lips to complete the decadent dandy look.

Jade pipes up, her voice thrilled, 'Wow, cool! Who's he? Is he . . . Qing Zhen?'

'No, Qing Zhen's a monk and he never cared about pictures. All my fond memories of him are stored in my head,' I say, then caress the handsome youth in the picture. 'This is Teng Xiong.'

Jade exclaims, 'Shoot, I should have guessed!'

Leo chimes in, 'She really looks like a man!'

I think of the woman who loved me so well but whom I could never completely love back. She had escaped to live in her own eccentric way, only to be captured by her ruthless husband, my father's murderer, Fung. She'd wished she could have died cuddling with me in the bell under the moonlight, but had ended up being shot by the husband she hated. I remember how, as we parted, she told me that she hoped we'd meet again in a future life. Perhaps we would after I finally board the immortal's journey, not too long from now, and perhaps then I'd desire her kind of love.

I sigh inside, then pull out another picture. The two *yin yang* heads lean forward to look.

'Awesome!' Jade exclaims. 'Who is she, so beautiful like a movie star!'

'Pearl, my blood sister,' I say proudly, tears brimming in my eyes.

Pearl is now staring back at me with her lips in the perfect shape of a crescent moon and her eyes smiling – as if she's envious of my longevity and my beautiful Jade Treasure and handsome soon-to-be great-grandson-in-law Leo Stanley. Yes, maybe I'm lucky to be still eating, sleeping, laughing, crying – and fortunately or unfortunately – not coupling, in the *yang* world. However, there won't be much time left before I'll join her in the *yin* sphere. Ironically, the thought doesn't make me sad.

After all, waiting for almost a century, I'll finally be able to join my beautiful, talented, *ming ji* blood sister.

PEACH BLOSSOM PAVILION

MINGMEI YIP

ABOUT THIS GUIDE

The questions and discussion topics that follow are
intended to enhance your group's reading of
this book.

Discussion Questions

1. How do you feel about Precious Orchid's mother giving away her own child?

2. When Precious Orchid is put into cruel circumstances, what means does she use to cope?

3. What do you think about the bond between Precious Orchid and Pearl? Given that they are very different, what qualities do they appreciate in each other?

4. In the early part of the story Pearl is stronger than Precious Orchid, while ultimately Precious Orchid survives the harsh life and Pearl does not. Is Precious Orchid simply luckier or does she have inner resources that Pearl lacks?

5. Do you think Pearl's suicide is an heroic act or an act of cowardice?

6. What does the existence of official contests for prostitutes tell you about attitudes toward women in pre-modern China?

7. How would you characterise Precious Orchid's relationship with men: the monk Qing Zhen, Big Master Fung, the Military Chief Ouyang, the oil portraitist Jiang Mou, and Richard Anderson, her eventual husband? And with women: Pearl, Teng Xiong, Spring Moon, and her mother, Aunty Ah Ping?

8. Why does Precious Orchid decide to sneak away from the monk Qing Zhen?

9. Why doesn't Precious Orchid's mother acknowledge her daughter when they reunite in the nunnery?

10. Why at the last moment does Precious Orchid fail to kill her father's murderer?

11. Why does Precious Orchid decide to marry Richard Anderson? Does she feel real love or does she have another motive?

12. What role does playing the *qin* occupy in the novel?

13. How does the calligraphy that Precious Orchid shows to Mama and De change the balance of power between them?

14. What does the yellow butterfly symbolise?

15. Can you identify Buddhist themes in the novel such as non-attachment, non-distinction, compassion, and non-killing?

16. Why do you think Precious Orchid, at the end of her life, is ambivalent about the disappearance of the artistic courtesan culture?

17. Compare the fates of the different women in the novel: Precious Orchid, Pearl, Teng Xiong, Red Jade, Spring Moon, Aunty Ah Ping, Mama, and Wonderful Kindness Abbess (Precious Orchid's mother)? To what extent was each able to exert some degree of control over her life?